To liz,
What a happy
accident, meeting a
poet!.

[signature]

Sea Changes

Sea Changes

Gail Graham

For information about this title or to order other books and/or electronic media, contact the publisher:

Jade Phoenix Publishing
www.jadephoenixpublishing.com

Library of Congress Control Number: 2009920650

ISBN: 978-0-692-00100-4

Printed in the United States of America

Book and Cover design by: 1106 Design

Author photograph by Russell Recchion

This is a work of fiction. Names, characters, incidents, locales, organizations and places of business are either the products of the author's imagination or are being used fictitiously. Any resemblance to actual organizations, events or persons, living or dead, is unintentional and entirely coincidental.

Dedication

In loving memory of my mother

Helene Tepperman Kellert

1917–2003

Chapter One

It's different in Australia. People don't drive. They walk, or catch the bus or train. Just as easy to use public transport, they'll tell you. When Charles's mother came to visit and they all took the train from Cronulla to Sydney, she said it was like being in Disneyland. She practically shouted it; everyone in the carriage heard.

Charles's mother blames Sarah for his death and hasn't called or written or acknowledged either of her letters. Sarah suspects she'll never hear from her, or from any member of Charles's family, ever again. It goes without saying that none of them attended the funeral.

"It's your own fault, Mum," Felicity admonished. You have to look at it from Grandma's point of view. She lost her son. Of course she's upset. How do you expect her to feel?"

This was at a time when Sarah was still numbly sheltering in a silent and oddly merciful place where nothing hurt. Nonetheless, Felicity's words shocked her. She felt as if she'd been slapped.

"Her son, yes. But Charles was my husband. That's different. I've lost my husband, Felicity. Don't you understand that?"

"And I've lost my father. You're the one who doesn't understand! Why do you always have to act as if you're the only person in the world who has feelings?"

A daughter is supposed to be a comfort at times like this. But Felicity is not a comfort, has never been a comfort.

"You have to stop dwelling on things. You and Dad had wonderful years together, but Dad's gone now. I mean, other women lose their husbands, but they get on with it. They get on with their lives. Max says it's time you moved on."

Max would.

"Are you still seeing that shrink?" Felicity asks.

"He's not a shrink. He's a psychologist." Sarah doesn't want to get into this. "And yes, I still see him twice a week."

"Now, that's what I mean. It's been nearly two years since Dad died, Mum. You know what Max thinks? Max thinks the shrink—sorry, the psychologist—might actually be holding you back."

Holding me back from what?

"What do you talk about with him, anyhow? What's he been telling you?"

"He doesn't actually tell me anything. That's not how it works. Mostly, he just listens."

"But he gives you advice."

"Only if I ask for it."

"He's the one who told you what to do with Dad's super-annuation, though. Isn't he?"

Sarah had been told she must choose between a lump sum payment and an annuity. "No matter what you decide to do," Charles's accountant said, "you won't be looking at a great deal of money. My advice is to take the lump sum, make down payments on as many flats as you can afford, live in one, let the others out, and use the rent to cover the mortgage payments. You'll have to borrow, of course. And you'll have to manage tenants. But you'd be keeping up with the market, growing your money. If you were my mother, that's what I'd be telling you to do."

It sounded sensible enough, but it also sounded complicated. Flats, tenants, mortgages. "And if I take the annuity?" The accountant frowned and again punched at the tiny keys of his calculator. "You'll receive monthly payments, about double what you'd get on the widows' pension, for the rest of your life. And it's indexed, which means it'll keep its value. You'd live comfortably enough, but not the way you're accustomed to living. As I say, it's not a great deal of money."

"Mum, there's no point in pretending I don't have feelings about this because I do. I think you should have taken the lump sum, and Max agrees with me. As things stand now, when you die there won't be anything left for us, for Sean and me. The annuity only lasts for as long as you live. Max looked it up. Maybe you didn't realize that."

"Actually, I did. I'm not stupid, Felicity."

"I didn't say you were stupid. But do you really think this is what Dad would have wanted? He worked hard. He wouldn't want you to just throw it all away."

"I'm not throwing it away. I'm living on it."

"But you don't need to live on it, that's the whole point. You could invest it in real estate or stocks or something. And get a job."

Sarah feels her lips tremble. "It's all been settled, Felicity. I've taken the annuity. And it was my decision," she adds, even though it's none of Felicity's business one way or the other. "Kahn had nothing to do with it." What on earth would make Felicity think psychologists hand out advice on such matters?

"So what happens when you die? What do we get besides that dinky little house?" Sarah remains silent. "Don't you think you should have at least discussed it with us?"

"No, I don't."

Eight months after she bought the house in Bondi Junction, Sarah learned she was within walking distance of the beach. A neighbor told her. He said it was a longish walk and not worth the bother, not as far as he was concerned. But then, he added, he wasn't all that keen on beaches.

It is a long walk, but Sarah doesn't mind. She likes walking. Above her head, the morning sky is as bright and blue as the inside of a Faberge egg. It's been like this for weeks. There's been no rain since before Christmas.

She passes an old cemetery slumbering behind a low stone wall. The cemetery originally belonged to a church, St. Margaret's, but the church building was demolished after the war. There was a shortage of building materials, and people needed the bricks and blocks of sandstone. A wisp of cloud passes across the sun, reflecting gold and amber off shards of broken beer bottles discarded by the homeless men who congregate here at dusk in the weeds that grow between the graves.

Closer to the beach, tidy rows of Federation brick terraces flank the sidewalks on both sides of the street, similar to New York City brownstones although not so well-proportioned. Like most Australian buildings, they're made entirely of dark red brick, the color of dried blood.

The shop at the intersection is boarded shut, the sheets of newspaper taped across its front window faded to the color of sugar cookies, and curled at the edges where the tape is pulling away from the glass.

From here you catch your first glimpse of the sea, a shimmering blue line beyond the red tile roofs. The land, the houses, everything is more expensive here, enhanced by the possibility of a water view. The sidewalks are wider and the houses, or cottages as Australians call them, are bigger too, set back from the street on allotments large enough to accommodate garages and well-tended walled gardens.

It's hot and humid, even this early in the day. Sarah wishes she'd worn a hat.

The wail of a siren splinters the silence. Reverberating off the glass windows of the houses, gathering volume. It rises and falls and rises again as it bears down upon her, an avalanche of sound, enveloping her, immobilizing her. Her heart pounds. She closes her eyes.

TWO MEN CROUCH IN FRONT of an ambulance parked inside a carport, their faces in shadow, their shoulders silhouetted against the glare of the summer sky. Sarah watches them cover Charles with a dun-colored blanket, carefully tucking its edges around him. Their tenderness reassures her.

She stands quietly off to one side, neither speaking nor crying. She does not interfere. She doesn't want to get in the way.

The men confer, then lift Charles onto a wheeled stretcher, carefully levering it into the back of the ambulance. Sarah remains silent and motionless, and the men climb into the ambulance. One of them leans forward across the other to shut the door.

The ambulance begins to move, backing slowly out of the driveway into the road. It turns right at the corner and disappears behind the houses on the next street, its siren wailing.

Alone, Sarah walks unsteadily through the empty carport and down the driveway to the sidewalk. The late afternoon sunshine is slanting down upon the parked cars. Where have they taken Charles? To a hospital, yes. But which one?

I should have said something. I should have asked them where they were going. I should have gone with them. She is appalled, overwhelmed by the things she should have done. How could she have let them take Charles away from her?

A patrol car eases its way slowly down the silent street, stopping at the curb. Two uniformed policemen come toward her. "Mrs. Charles Andrews?" She nods. "You'll want to come with us. Get in, then. And mind your head."

Just like on television.

(((©

"DEATH WAS INSTANTANEOUS," the doctor says.

He seems very young. The collar of his jacket is turned in, and he's wearing round rimless glasses, probably hoping they'll make him look older. "I'm sorry, but there really wasn't anything we could do. He was already dead. I suspect he was dead when you found him." Sarah stares. "It was his heart, I'd say. But we'll know more after the autopsy."

This isn't happening. It can't be happening. The doctor is gazing expectantly at her. They all are; the doctor and the nurses and another man wearing a baggy green tunic over baggy green trousers who has just come through the swinging doors. They're becoming impatient. There is obviously something she is supposed to say, or do, but Sarah doesn't know what it is.

"Can I see Charles?" They stare, blankly. One of the nurses sighs and turns away, scribbling something. "I want to see Charles." The doctor looks at her and shakes his head.

Sarah says she doesn't want an autopsy, doesn't want them to cut Charles open.

"It's not up to you," the nurse says. "It's the law."

And the doctor was right. Charles suffered a massive cardiac infarction, they told her. A heart attack.

"TELL ME WHAT YOU REMEMBER," Kahn says.

Sarah remembers the doctor's rimless glasses. She remembers the ambulance and the vast, echoing silence in its wake. She remembers how hot it was, that the parked cars in the street looked as if they were melting. She remembers the smell of gas. Gas? Kahn looks puzzled.

"Petrol," Sarah explains, because of course, that's what they call gas in Australia. "It's not that I don't remember. The problem is that I've suddenly got this . . . this compulsion to talk about it."

"But that's normal."

"No, it's not." She doesn't want to say the wrong thing. But if he is to help her, he must understand. "I'm sorry, I didn't mean to contradict you. What I was trying to say is, I don't think what I'm doing—what I keep finding myself doing—is normal. That's all I meant."

He settles back.

"For instance, I can be standing in the middle of a shop, and all of a sudden I'm explaining to everybody that my husband died two months ago. Or I start talking to people on the train. Or people in a queue at the bank, telling them my husband is dead. And once I've started, I can't stop. I go on and on, telling them about it." Sarah drew a shaky breath. "Talking to strangers like that isn't normal."

He's Australian rather than English, she can tell by his accent. So he knows what she means. Australians don't talk to strangers, not even at social functions, and certainly not in the street.

"I can't seem to stop myself. It's embarrassing. It's . . . perverse."

Sarah watches as he shifts in his chair, purses his lips, steeples his fingers, nods. Unable to think of anything to add to what she's already told him, she folds her hands in her lap and waits.

"As a matter of fact," Kahn says at last, "it's quite natural for you to want to talk about what happened. It's normal, it's healthy. Charles's death was completely unexpected. You had no time to prepare yourself. You came home, and you found him. It was a terrible, traumatic experience. It was . . . it was a catastrophe."

Kahn is not what Sarah expected. She agreed to these sessions reluctantly, resigned to enduring an hour of plati-tudes, the things people say to someone whose husband has died. That she should be glad Charles didn't suffer. That she should cherish her memories of their good years together. That life must go on. That things will get better.

"A catastrophe. And you know, I'm thinking it might be helpful for you to think of yourself in those terms. I mean, as someone who has survived a terrible, meaningless, and utterly devastating catastrophe." He pauses, waiting for her to respond.

Charles is dead. What more is there to say?

"You're sad, you're devastated. You've sustained a terrible loss. But you're angry, too. And that's natural, Mrs. Andrews. Anger is a completely normal reaction under the circumstances."

Anger?

"You've every right to feel angry." He pauses again, but only for a moment. "And guilty, too. You feel as if somehow all of this is your fault. You think if only you'd done this, or hadn't done that, Charles would still be alive. It's natural. It's normal. Survivors often feel guilt."

He's wrong, though. She doesn't feel angry, or guilty. Maybe she ought to feel these things, but she doesn't. She feels numb. She doesn't tell him that.

"We both know you're not to blame for what happened to Charles. It wasn't your fault." Kahn's tone is firm, as if he expects her to disagree.

Of course it wasn't her fault. But she's on her guard now. Why would he think she blames herself for Charles's death? What sort of things do they teach psychologists in Australia?

He leans forward.

"Things will get better," he says. But she must be patient, she must take things a day at a time. She needs to be kind to herself. She needs to give herself time to heal. And he's sorry, but he has to stop now. He'll see her again on Friday.

(((◦

BIRDS SING OUTSIDE SARAH'S WINDOW each morning; shadows form and shift and lengthen as the sun moves across the sky. At night she can sometimes see the stars, but these southern constellations are not the ones she knows and recognizes.

She calls Felicity every morning, but Felicity rarely returns her calls. Felicity hasn't got time for her.

Weeks pass. At least she's stopped bursting into tears, and talking to strangers.

But the pain is still there. The pain is like a predator, biding its time and then striking when you least expect it. The pain is like certain people Sarah has known: a teacher, a supervisor. You learn to live with them; you put up with them and make the best of it, because you don't have a choice.

She is occasionally overwhelmed by paroxysms of unreasoning panic, and when these engulf her she must get away from people, she must hide. Episodes, Kahn calls them. She must get hold of herself, he tells her gravely, especially when she's in public places.

"People are edgy these days, worried about terrorists, remembering what happened in Bali. It only takes one person to ring the police and say there's someone acting crazy. And once they've got you, once they've put a label on you, it can be difficult to sort things out."

Sarah understands. This is Australia. If they think you're crazy—a danger to yourself and others is how they phrase it—they lock you up. You're detained at the pleasure of the queen, which means forever. Kahn is right. She needs to stop behaving inappropriately in public places.

She remembers when the weather turned cold, too cold for the long, aimless walks that filled those first unbearable days of widowhood. Gusty winds bring rain, and Sarah huddles next to the electric fire. Most Australian houses don't have central heating, or air conditioning.

Winter passes.

"What do you do with yourself all day?" Kahn asks.

"I read. I look out the window. I wait for it to be night, so I can go to sleep."

"You're coping. But that's all you're doing, and it's not enough. You need to make more of an effort. You need to start living again. You need to go out and meet people. You need to do the things you used to do."

Sarah comes to realize that although grief is private, bereavement is public, a kind of performance art. There's a whole catechism of bereavement, and people expect you to know it, to learn it the way once you learned the times tables, or the Gettysburg Address.

How are you?

I'm well, thank you.

It was very sudden.

Yes, it was.

It'll be hard at first, but it gets easier as time goes on.

Yes.

You will let us know if you need anything.

Yes, of course. And thank you so much.

Evenings, Sarah falls into the habit of watching the news, sipping scotch, and listening to Brian and Geraldine, looking forward to their ongoing, undemanding dialogue. They're like friends, better than friends. They ask nothing of her, unlike Felicity, who wants to borrow money for new furniture.

"I haven't got any money," Sarah tells her.

"What about Dad's superannuation?"

"That's for me. It was in the will. You were there when they read the will, Felicity."

"I'm sure Dad didn't mean for you to keep everything for yourself."

Kahn wants to know about Charles's funeral.

It was a memorial service rather than a funeral. Non-denominational, as she supposed Charles would have wished. Sarah remembers a crush of people, many of whom she didn't know, all of whom knew Charles. Solemn faces, somber clothes, respectful murmuring voices. Women embracing her, kissing the air above her right cheek.

What will you do now, Sarah?

What are your plans?

Where will you live?

The vice chancellor's rangy, raddled wife finally stomps across the room and stands directly in front of Sarah, settling things once and for all.

"You have a daughter in Sydney. If I were you, I'd go there, to Sydney. If I were you, I'd want to be with my daughter."

Felicity comes down for the funeral, of course. She doesn't want to stay at the house, so Sarah puts her up at a motel. After the memorial service, they stand side by side in the funeral parlor and watch Charles's coffin disappear through silent sliding doors. Charles is gone. It's over. It doesn't seem possible.

"What are you going to do?" Felicity asks.

Sarah doesn't know.

Days pass.

"I can't say here forever," Felicity says. "You've got to decide what you're going to do."

The vice chancellor's wife is right, that's what everyone keeps telling her. Sarah is alone now, and she must move back to the city, to Sydney. She's never actually lived in Sydney, but this seems petty, a point not worth making. If she doesn't stay here, she must go someplace else. And she doesn't want to stay here, never wanted to come to this dreadful country town in the first place.

The wives rouse themselves to do what's necessary — Felicity has already left—and all Sarah has to do is stay out of the way. Tears seep steadily from her eyes, rolling down her cheeks and onto the loose fabric of her jumper, but nobody notices. Or maybe they notice, but don't think anything of it; this is what women do when their husbands die. The wives take Charles's books off the shelves and empty the cupboards. They wrap the dishes and glasses in newspaper and pack everything into cardboard cartons. Men in shorts and work boots load the boxes into a truck to be taken away and put into storage until Sarah finds a place to live. Men in suits draw up papers for her to sign. The house she and Charles were building must be sold, accounts must be settled, but she needn't worry. The men will take care of everything.

It might not be so bad, living in the same city as Felicity. Now that Charles is gone, things might be different. They're mother and daughter, after all. Sarah imagines them having lunch, someplace close to Felicity's work, someplace convenient. Or shopping together. But Felicity isn't interested.

"Just because Dad's gone, it doesn't change anything," Felicity says. "I'm busy. I've got a lot on my plate. You need to find friends of your own, Mum."

THE WAIL OF THE SIREN CEASES, so abruptly that the sudden silence is jarring. They've turned it off, just like that.

Sarah is standing in the middle of the sidewalk with her eyes tightly shut. She opens them and blinks. She isn't disoriented. She knows she's on Beach Street, but just for a moment, she doesn't know why she's here or where she's going.

An episode, after all this time.

Breathe. Take deep breaths. Try to act as if everything is all right. This is Kahn's advice. Try not to attract attention.

But there's nobody here. The windows in the houses on either side of the street are blank and silent. Even so, somebody might be watching her. Sarah envisions a pair of suspicious eyes, squinted against the sun, peering out at her from behind drawn curtains.

D'you see that woman out there?

Where?

Just there, on the footpath.

What about her, then?

I think she's got something wrong with her.

How long has she been standing there like that?

I don't know.

D'you reckon we should call 000?

Quite deliberately, Sarah lifts her chin and stares at the curtained bay window of the nearest house. Then she frowns, shakes her head, and lets her gaze move slowly to the next house, and then to the next, as if she's searching for a particular address. Let them see there's nothing amiss. She's just a woman looking for a house number and realizing it's a bit further along.

She's going away.

I still think we should call someone.

What's the point? She'll be gone by the time they get here.

Sarah continues on toward the beach. Above her head, pale, fern-like acacias quiver, responding to the intermittent salty breeze blowing off the sea.

The ocean appears as a green band sandwiched between the red tile rooftops and the blue sky. In another five minutes, she'll be there. Then the tip of her sandal catches on an uneven bit of pavement and she stumbles, arms flailing, only just managing not to fall.

The sidewalk here has fractured into broken shards of concrete. It's dangerous, and you'd think someone would have fixed it by now—it's been left long enough to allow straw-colored moss that looks like pubic hair to grow through the gaps. Sarah steps down hard on the moss, but it immediately springs back when she lifts her foot.

Step on a crack, break your mother's back.

Funny, the things you remember. Sarah can almost hear the rhythmic slap of skipping ropes on asphalt, hear it, see it, and even smell the tang of burning leaves wafting over a school playground on the other side of the world, five decades ago.

Do little girls still skip rope? Felicity didn't. But Felicity didn't play with dolls, or go to ballet, or Brownie Scouts, or do any of the things other people's daughters did. You can't judge by Felicity.

Sarah closes her eyes again, allowing the sun to warm her eyelids just as it did on a morning in that long-ago childhood world. She remembers how nice it was, just standing there in the warm sunshine, listening to the steady, predictable slap of the skipping rope.

Step on a crack. Break your mother's back.

When Papa first told her about television, Sarah laughed and reminded him that she was eight years old— too big to believe such stories. So he took her downtown, to a shop that sold television sets. There. You see? Astounded, Sarah gaped at the flickering screens. Anything was possible.

Step on a crack. Break your mother's back.

Why not? It was no different than television. But is that all you had to do? Just step on a crack? Sarah longed to ask but was afraid the big girls would laugh at her.

That afternoon she stepped on all the cracks, all the way home. But there was Mama, waiting for her on the porch just like always, tapping the slender honey-colored cane. Worse than always, because Sarah was late, and that meant consequences.

Maybe you weren't supposed to step on all the cracks. Or maybe there were words you were supposed to say, a magic spell. Sarah decides to ask Miss Henry.

"But how could you even think of doing such a terrible thing?" The little pleats of skin beneath Miss Henry's chin quivered, and Sarah fell silent. "Surely, you didn't really want to break your mama's back."

Sarah dropped her eyes, scuffed her feet.

"Of course you didn't. I'd be surprised, a quiet little thing like you. All the same, still waters."

Miss Henry had big yellow teeth and a mole beneath her left eye. Through the window, Sarah could hear the other children on the playground. It probably wasn't even true. It was probably just a jumping rope song.

Miss Henry sighed again, opened a little drawer in her desk and took out a chocolate kiss from Hershey, Pennsylvania. The whole class went to the Hershey Chocolate factory last month, everyone except Sarah, because Mama wouldn't sign the permission note. Miss Henry handed the chocolate kiss to Sarah and told her to go on out and play. As she left the room, she heard Miss Henry quietly ask the dear Lord to give her strength.

Sarah has reached the crest of the hill and pauses to gaze at the sea, its surface like beaten silver in the intense Sydney light. Whatever became of Miss Henry? She must be dead by now, or terribly old. But not that old, not really. Miss Henry may still be alive, tending her garden and feeding her cat. Yet Charles is dead.

It isn't fair. Charles can not, should not, be dead. Sarah begins to walk again, slowly, watching her step, thinking she should have brought the ashes.

Charles's ashes are in a box wrapped in brown paper, sealed with brown tape. She'd planned to bring them, but it struck her that it was the sort of thing people might notice, a woman carrying a box into the sea. So the ashes are still at home, on a shelf in the closet next to a box full of photographs she never got around to sorting and pasting into albums.

She doesn't know what to do with the ashes, never thought about what happens after the cremation. But weeks later she received a registered letter advising her that the deceased Charles Gerald Andrews's ashes were available for collection during regular business hours. "Like something I ordered from a catalogue," she tells Kahn.

The office is on the ground floor of an unprepossessing brick building in Randwick, just far enough away so that she has to drive. Felicity can't come with her. "We're having a farewell lunch for one of the interns. It won't look good if I don't show up."

"Can I help you?" says the girl on the far side of the long counter.

Sarah pushes her letter across the counter, but the girl is already handing her several printed forms. One of them looks like a job application form.

"I'll leave you to it, then." The girl settles herself in front of a computer terminal, holding her hands gracefully before her and tilting them this way and that so that tiny points of light glint off her long crimson fingernails. Sarah looks too, marveling. How can she possibly type with nails like that?

The girl glances up at her with the beginnings of a smile that suddenly changes its mind and quivers uncertainly upon her mauve lips. Sarah understands, having seen this look on other faces. She's having another episode; she's begun to cry, can feel her tears hot on her cheeks. So embarrassing. The two tiny creases that have appeared at either side of the girl's mouth make her look suddenly older.

"Are you all right? D'you want a glass of water?"

"No, I'm fine." Sarah dabs quickly at her face with the backs of her fingers. But she doesn't apologize, because Australians never apologize, for anything. Here, apologizing is considered a sign of weakness.

"D'you want a tissue, then?"

"No. Really, it's all right."

With an air of having exhausted all other options, the girl crosses the room, selects a box wrapped in brown paper from a shelf with similar boxes, and places it on the counter in front of Sarah.

"There you go, then. But you still have to finish the paperwork. I can't release them if you don't sign for them."

Sarah looks at the box, then back at the girl. "Release them?"

"You know, give them to you."

"But you sent me this letter. That's why I'm here, because I got this letter."

"Yeah, well . . ." The girl licks her lips with a little pink tongue. "The computer writes the letters, it's all automated. And it's no big deal, you just sign your name there at the bottom of the form."

Sarah remembers pressing the tips of her fingers very hard against the surface of the counter, trying to concentrate, trying not to cry.

The girl says, "It's for your own protection."

A cell phone starts playing "Advance Australia Fair" and the girl races back to her black patent leather knapsack from which she extracts a cell phone the size of a deck of cards, and then disappears into an office, kicking the door shut behind her.

Sarah uses the ballpoint pen chained to the counter to sign the forms, picks up the box, and walks out into the street. You wouldn't think of ashes as being heavy, yet the box, small as it is, weighs as much as a house brick.

She unlocks the car, puts the box on the passenger seat, then touches it lightly with the tips of her fingers. What if these aren't Charles's ashes after all? What if they've made a mistake?

"They couldn't get Charles's wedding band off his finger," she tells Kahn. "The gold wouldn't have burned. I should have opened the box, I should have looked at the ashes. If they really were Charles's ashes, there would have been a little lump of gold in the box."

"Then why didn't you?"

"I couldn't."

"What *did* you do?"

"I asked myself, 'What would Charles do?' And I know. He would have said it doesn't matter. He would have said, dead is dead. He'd have picked up the box and got into the car and gone home."

Because the ashes weren't Charles, aren't Charles. Because Charles no longer exists. The ashes are just ashes. She drives home with the box on the seat beside her, remembering how much Charles hated being a passenger, no matter who was driving. Even on holidays, he always insisted on renting a car at the airport so they could drive to the hotel themselves rather than take a taxi.

For some reason, Kahn continues to take an interest in Charles's ashes. "What did you finally do with them?"

"I didn't know what do with them," Sarah says. "I still don't. They're in the house, but that's no good—Charles would have hated that house."

Kahn asks what she thinks Charles would want, where he'd want to be.

Sarah has no idea. They never talked about things like that. It never occurred to them to discuss it, what they wanted done with their remains. People their age didn't expect to die. Although once, Charles had said he'd like his ashes to be scattered from the cliffs at Eze, a little village in the south of France. They were there on holiday. It was May and the gardens were just coming into bloom. She remembers they practically had the place to themselves.

They'd walked side by side along the gravel paths where Nietzsche had walked. Charles wondered whether it was before or after he went mad, but the guidebook didn't say. Later they sat on a tiny terrace sipping cold white wine at one of the cafes clustered at the foot of the hill. They were the only customers and the proprietor asked where they were from. When Charles told him, the proprietor beamed and said his cousin Jacques lived in Australia. In Adelaide. Had they ever met Jacques?

Charles loved Eze. The sky, the sea, everything about it was magnificent to him. That's when he said it, about his ashes. But he wasn't being serious. Certainly he didn't think he was going to die.

KAHN IS LOOKING INTENTLY at her as if she were a puzzle he is determined to solve. He's always asking her about her childhood, but Sarah can tell that little of it makes sense to him.

"Growing up in the United States is different," Sarah told him once. "Americans admire people who are intelligent and ambitious. In the United States, everyone wants to be the first, the best, the smartest." Tall poppies, Australians call such people, and immediately set about cutting them down. "It's just the way it is."

Charles tried to instill American values in Sean and Felicity, but the other kids were Australian, and in the end, so were they. Excellence sucks, Sean said once. It was the closest Charles ever came to hitting him.

What might Sean have done if they'd stayed in the United States? Sean was bright but he hated school, dropped out. Lots of Australians drop out. Sarah and Charles feared he'd end up in jail, or on drugs, or dead in a ditch. But he landed a job on an oil rig somewhere in the North Sea, and now he earns more money in a month, Charles liked to tell people with mock chagrin, than I earn in a year. It always annoyed Sarah when Charles said that, because it wasn't true. But Sean had turned out better than they'd dared to hope.

It took three days to get word to him that Charles had died. He telephoned the day after the funeral, his voice deeper than Sarah remembered, breaking up with distance and sorrow. He'll forfeit his contract. He'll get the next flight out. Felicity talked him out of it. "No matter what you do, it won't bring Dad back. Come at Christmas instead. It'll be an awful Christmas for Mum without Dad."

It was.

You never appreciate what you have until you lose it, one of Charles's colleagues said at the funeral.

"I thought it was such a peculiar thing to say," Sarah tells Kahn. "Not appreciate Charles! I practically worshipped him. I thought I was just so incredibly lucky to have found him."

"I think you were both lucky." Kahn seems slightly embarrassed. "You obviously had a very happy marriage, I'm not denying that. But it's a two-way street. I think you made each other very happy."

"But it was such a fluke! Pure coincidence, a quirk of fate." Sarah shakes her head, still wondering at the sheer fortuitousness of it. "In the normal course of things, I'd have never even met Charles. He was a scientist. We lived in different worlds. But one night I was filling in for a friend at a fund-raiser, sitting at the desk taking names and addresses, when this guy walks in and asks if this is the Wainwright Building. Well, it wasn't. I said I'd draw him a map, but then my friend came back, so I said I'd show him a shortcut. Then we got to talking, and he asked if I had time for a coffee, and three months later we were married."

"It's a lovely story. But you know, it wasn't exactly divine intervention. You were ready for a relationship, and if you hadn't met Charles, you'd have met someone else. That's how life is."

It isn't, though. You don't necessarily get what you deserve. You can live your whole life trying to be good and have nothing but bad luck. Or you can be selfish and cruel, and have it all. Look at Mama.

Mama disliked Charles even before she met him. "So what's wrong with him? Has he got a disease? Is he paying alimony? Has he been in prison? What's the catch?"

"There isn't any catch."

But Mama was unconvinced, her voice as clear as if she was standing there in the room instead of three thousand miles away. "You think I was born yesterday? What does a man like this Charles want with you? What have you got to offer him? You're not even pretty." Mama said she wouldn't be able to come to the wedding anyway. "I'd have to fly, and you know how much I hate flying."

"You fly to Europe every summer."

"That's different. That's over water."

Sarah pretended to be sorry, but wasn't. She invited Mama, of course, even pleaded with her to come. How could her own mother not come to her wedding? Charles didn't understand and even offered to pay Mama's airfare, but Mama remained adamant.

It was a beautiful wedding. "Although," said Sarah's maid of honor Sally O'Loan, "it's absolutely the last thing in the world anyone expected, you and Charles Andrews getting married."

It's apparently the last thing Charles's friends expected too. In the ladies room, Sarah overheard someone saying that Charles's new wife seemed to be a sweet little thing.

Charles was unperturbed. You *are* a sweet little thing, he told her.

For the next few years, Sarah had a recurring nightmare; Charles had left her. It was never clear why he left, but he was gone, irrevocably. In the dream, she wandered bereft through the bare, empty rooms of their house. The dream stopped after Sean was born, but the fear of losing Charles remained. People die. People get killed. Or he might fall in love with someone else. There were so many women in Charles's world, clever, intelligent, unattached women.

"How can I compete? I can't help him with his work. I can't even type up his papers for him," Sarah told Sally. "Everyone says he's a genius. I'm married to the man, and I don't even understand what he does!"

"Charles could have had anyone he wanted, and he wanted you. So stop beating yourself up. Sure, he's surrounded by smart women. He always has been. But you're the one he married."

"You're special," Charles told her. "Most of the women I meet are scientists and mathematicians and physicists and they all want my job. There's always the competition thing,

I'm always watching my back. But it's different with you. I'm different, when I'm with you. I'm a different person. You read books, you go to art museums, you sing songs from Broadway musicals. You're fun. And being with you is fun, more fun than I've ever had in my whole life."

The first year of their marriage was like dating. They were still getting to know one another. Sarah learned about Charles's life: his family's farm, his years at MIT, a Merit Scholarship Oklahoma boy in Boston, the time his roommate Phil invited him home for the weekend. *His dad offered me a glass of sherry. Sarah, I didn't even know it was alcohol. Then we sat down and when their maid brought in the first course, it was snails. Six snails on a big white plate. I didn't know what to do so I watched Phil and did what he did. I couldn't believe I was going to eat a snail. And then I couldn't believe how good it tasted.*

Charles's collection of books included volumes by Brillat-Savarin, Escoffier, Pellaprat, and Careme. Two years after they married, he published an article about the wines of Alsace Lorraine. He loved good food, fine wine, even the paraphernalia of dining: English bone china, sterling silver, cut-glass goblets, fresh linen napery, flowers, candles in silver candlesticks.

"I bought cookbooks," Sarah tells Kahn. "I took courses. I learned how to make puff pastry, from scratch. And pasta, on a machine imported from Italy. I even learned how to bone a duck. I wanted to please him. He came first, he always came first. Even after the children were born."

This seems to surprise him.

"I suppose it sounds crazy. But it isn't, it wasn't. It was wonderful. I enjoyed it. I enjoyed pleasing him. I wanted to please him. I loved him."

Kahn looks away, as if embarrassed for her. He probably is; it's different here. Even the language is different. It's still the English language, but the words have different meanings. That's something you don't realize at first, because people don't tell you when you get it wrong. They let you just keep making a fool of yourself until you figure it out.

Sarah falls silent, unable to bridge the gap. Kahn will never understand, and neither will she. So why does she keep coming here? It's not grief counseling anymore. It's not anything.

Kahn clears his throat and looks up. "When I was growing up, we used to get all these films from the States, Doris Day and Rock Hudson, *Pillow Talk, The Tunnel of Love.* We could never understand what all the fuss was about."

"Australians aren't romantic."

"Not like Americans, no. We're more like the English. We keep our feelings to ourselves."

Sarah says nothing. Kahn continues to stare at her, making a steeple with his fingertips and contemplating it thoughtfully.

"I wonder what made you come to Australia in the first place."

Wondering is part of Kahn's therapeutic technique. He'll say, I wonder what you were thinking when that happened. Or, I wonder how that felt. But he doesn't wonder, not really. It's just a prompt, a way of moving from one topic to the next.

Was Kahn ever in love? It wouldn't be the same. Australians don't seem to fall in love, not the way Americans do. There aren't any heterosexual Australian love stories that end happily. That tells you something, doesn't it? Kahn believes the self must always keep its boundaries intact. Otherwise you end up like Sarah, sitting in the black vinyl chair.

Silence envelops them again, heavy and itchy as humidity. He sits there opposite her, waiting unobtrusively and occasionally glancing at the clock that's been tactfully positioned behind a box of tissues. Kahn ends sessions precisely on time, jumping in as soon as she pauses to think or draw a breath and saying, I have to stop now.

I have to stop. As if it's something beyond his control.

"It's not as though you're mentally ill," Kahn told her. "There's nothing wrong with your mind. You're grieving, that's all. And it'll end. In time, you'll feel better. I can promise you that."

"I don't see why you have to see a psychologist," Felicity says, more than once. "It's not doing you any good, it's not making you feel any better. So why bother?"

"Because it gives me someplace to go. It gives me a reason to get out of bed, and get dressed, and wash my face and brush my teeth and do the laundry so I'll have something clean to wear."

"But you'd do those things anyway."

"Would I?"

"Of course you would, Mum! You're sad, that's all. But you're not crazy."

And it's true, being counseled—talking to someone they call it here—is out of character, not the kind of thing Sarah has ever done. She always thought counseling was for people who couldn't function, couldn't manage their lives. It would be different if she were seeing a proper psychiatrist, undergoing analysis. A friend of hers in Melbourne used to do that, is probably still doing it, three times a week.

DRIVING THROUGH THE LIGHT TRAFFIC, Sarah glances at the box there on the passenger seat next to her. She reaches out and touches it with her left hand, patting it as if it were a puppy. What will I do with you? What do you want me to do with you?

She parks her car at the curb and sits there for awhile, glancing at the box and wondering what ashes look like. Perhaps she ought to mail them back to Oklahoma. But Charles hated Oklahoma.

You don't want me to send you to Oklahoma, Sarah tells the ashes. But what do you want me to do with you? Where do you want to be?

She'd hoped Charles would come to her in a dream and tell her. But he didn't, and Sarah found herself moving the box of ashes uneasily from room to room, trying—she knows how this sounds—to make it comfortable. The ashes seem heavier each time she moves them. They aren't happy here. Charles wouldn't have been happy here either. He disliked old houses, said they were too much work, couldn't understand what people saw in them.

THE SUN IS HIGH, almost directly overhead, although it'll be cooler down on the beach. Sarah walks on, past a final series of detached cottages. Suddenly, nothing seems real. It's too still, too bright.

Suppose it isn't real? What if she's dreaming? In a moment she'll wake up, and she'll be home, in her own house, in their bed, and she'll turn over, and Charles will be there beside her.

No, she's here, it's now. This is it, *this is all there is.* And she's sick of it, weary of the sun and the heat and the harshness of the place and the people, sick and tired, fed up. She doesn't want to hurt any more. It's time to end it. If she were a dog, Felicity would have put her down months ago.

Beach Road runs out where it intersects with Beach Esplanade. One last asphalt road to cross, black and slightly sticky beneath the sun. Last week there were men working here. Sarah tries to remember how many men, what they looked like, whether they were young or old. How much did they earn in a week? Probably more than I ever earned.

She had work, in that other life that ended when Charles died. It didn't pay much, but Sarah considered it work worth doing. And Charles was proud of her. He thought finding volunteer visitors for the aged and infirm was a meaningful contribution to society, and often said so. That's why she really did it, so Charles would be proud of her. Although she liked the work, she felt good about being able to brighten the lives of people who seemed to have so little.

But she can't cope with it now. She doesn't seem able to cope with anything. They gave her time off, of course. And when that ran out, Sarah took what they called compassionate leave. Compassionate meant without pay. She offered to resign but everyone said no, she ought to keep her options open.

Kahn thinks she should go back to work. "Not necessarily at your old job, but at something. You need a project, a focus. You need to set goals and start rebuilding your life."

No more Kahn. No more little clock hidden behind the box of tissues. It annoys her, that little clock. Everyone who sits in Kahn's black vinyl chair knows the rules. You get your fifty minutes, no more and no less.

She crosses the road, skirting the bus shelter, and makes her way slowly down the flight of concrete steps that leads to the sand.

It's much cooler, here by the sea. A salt breeze ruffles softly through the wispy hairs at her temple and at the nape of her neck. Sarah slips her feet out of her sandals and carrying them in her left hand, steps down onto the hot coarse sand.

Bare bodies lie everywhere, motionless and glistening with oil. Occasionally one stirs, to roll over or to sit up and light a cigarette. Unclothed, they're much the same. Golden tanned backs, buttocks, firm bare breasts, perfect nipples pointing at the sky.

Following the ellipse of paving, Sarah walks to the far side of the beach, past the closed café and the cliffs to where the sea slaps peevishly at rows of unperturbed, fastidious gulls. The tide is out. Just beneath the water, the beach shelves off sharply, and even though you can't see it, there's usually a rip. It's a treacherous beach, as Sydney beaches go. People tend not to bring small children here. Sarah puts her things down in the lee of an overhanging rock.

She's left this morning's newspaper open on the kitchen table and her unwashed dishes from last night in the sink. People will think she intended to do the housework later, after her swim. What she *does*, most days, is sit by herself in the house, sipping red wine from one of Charles's goblets, as one by one the minutes drip away like water from a leaky faucet until the sun goes down and the street lights come on, and she can go to bed.

But she was such a good swimmer, such a strong swimmer.

Something must have happened.

It must have been a cramp.

Or a shark.

You'd think someone would have seen something, if it was a shark.

Felicity and Sean will share what's left. Not a fortune but a tidy sum, with the insurance and what they'll get for the house. Felicity can buy her new furniture, and then some. Better than nothing, as Australians say. Better than a poke in the eye with a burnt stick.

She has not left a note. No insurance payout if you commit suicide. It's rather a shame, really. Writing the note,

Sarah has always believed, is the best part. Sometimes, you don't even have to kill yourself. Sometimes, just writing the note is enough to make you feel better. Sarah knew a girl like that at college, who not only wrote the notes but even read them out loud to the other girls in the dormitory, claiming they were too good to waste.

The sand is warm and soft beneath her bare feet. And there's still a breeze. This is nice. She'll miss the beach.

She folds her glasses (the frames Charles chose for her in Hong Kong, big white frames) and places them carefully upon her towel, next to her sandals. Then she walks the last few yards down the slope of the beach into the sea. The sand beneath her feet is soft and the waves cover her ankles, her shins, her knees. The sandy shelf falls away just beyond the place where the waves are breaking, and now she's up to her shoulders in water. It's cold, but not as cold as she expected. She eases herself all the way into the water, turns her back to the beach, and begins to swim.

She'll swim out far enough so they'll never actually find her body. They'll find her things, of course. But that's part of the plan. She wants to be dead, not simply missing. At least, nobody will have to worry about what to do with her ashes.

She hears something, a voice.

Startled, Sarah swallows a mouthful of sea water and splutters. A pair of gulls swoops low, but what she heard wasn't a gull, she knows what a gull sounds like. Treading water, she scans the heaving, sparkling surface of the sea. She's quite alone. But she heard a voice. She did.

Wait. There *is* someone, off to the right and barely an arm's length away. It's a young girl. Maybe she's a surf life-saver. When they first came to Australia, women weren't allowed to be surf lifesavers or even drink in pubs. The girl's hair falls in abundant wet waves, curling into soft ringlets upon her bare shoulders. "You can't do it, you know," the girl says.

"Can't do what?"

"Drown yourself. That's what you think you're going to do, isn't it? Well, you can't."

It's a hallucination. Or maybe not; the girl may be real, and high on something. Or neurotic, doing her own thing. There are a lot of peculiar people in Sydney, pushing shopping carts filled with bulging plastic bags, screaming abuse at departing trains in underground railway stations, sleeping on benches in doorways and bus shelters. Nobody takes any notice of them.

Although both the girl's arms are visible beneath the surface of the water, they don't seem to be moving. That's strange. Sarah's own arms are tiring. Treading water in the swell is a lot harder than swimming.

"Come on. It'll be easier if you just follow me." The girl tosses her dark, wet curls, dives like an otter and vanishes.

Seconds pass. Nothing happens.

It must have been a hallucination. Sarah looks hard at the spot where the girl disappeared, but there's nothing, just ocean. If the girl was real, she's drowning. And I should be trying to save her, shouldn't I? But that's ridiculous. There wasn't any girl, there couldn't have been.

Sarah begins to swim again, away from the beach and toward the horizon. It's not too late. She can still change her mind. But what's the point? She'll die someday, anyhow. It might as well be today.

Her arms rise and fall rhythmically, in a purposeful crawl that carries her easily through the undulating swell. Struck by a sudden determination to do this one, last thing perfectly, Sarah concentrates on her form, meticulously executing each separate stroke. It doesn't matter that nobody can see, or will ever know.

The girl was imaginary, like the people in her dreams. She's always dreamed vividly, in cinematic detail. Sometimes she flies in her dreams, arms out wide, swooping and dipping above the green tops of trees, skimming turquoise tropical oceans. She hasn't flown since Charles died. Her dreams have been earthbound, peopled with strangers, dozens of people she's never known, never met. Yet their faces are so individual and distinct that she could describe them, even sketch them.

There's no hard and fast difference between a dream and a hallucination. One happens when you're asleep, the other when you're awake, but the states aren't absolutes. Sleeping becomes waking by degrees, the way water boils into steam or freezes into ice.

The girl's head suddenly reappears, bobbing above the water to Sarah's right.

"Are you ready?"

"You're not real," Sarah says.

"Of course I'm real."

"No, you're not. You're a figment of my imagination."

"You don't think I'm real? Then touch me!" The girl moves closer, reaching out to Sarah. "Go on, touch me! Take hold of my hand."

Sarah doesn't want to touch her. "It wouldn't prove anything, anyway. If I'm imagining that I see you and hear you, I'll probably think I feel you too. It still doesn't make you real."

"Oh, come on. You're not afraid, are you?"

"Of course not."

"Then take my hand. Just for a second. I won't hurt you, I promise."

The girl's hand is floating, palm upward. It's a small pink hand, the tips of the fingers plump and seemingly unaffected by the water. She waggles them playfully at Sarah.

Sarah reaches out and grasps the hand, mildly surprised to feel fingers and fingernails and the warmth of circulating blood.

The girl's head disappears beneath the swell, and Sarah feels herself being drawn after her, down beneath the surface. She inhales a last breath of air before she goes under, but she's not unwilling, or frightened. She can free herself simply by letting go, but she chooses not to and keeps holding the girl's hand.

This isn't exactly what she had in mind, but it will do. She feels a strong sense of something finally coming to pass. There's a tightness in her chest, but that's all. No pain. This is going to be easier than she thought.

She opens her eyes but there's nothing to see, only a dark, fluctuating pressure pulsing against her face like a heartbeat. Her lips part slightly, releasing a row of tiny bubbles. It's true what they say about drowning. It doesn't hurt a bit.

Her last thought is of Kahn.

He'd wonder how it feels.

Chapter Two

Everybody, everything dies. The rest is a distraction, something to keep your mind off the worms. That's what Charles used to say.

Sarah is dead. It's the only logical explanation. So this is what it's like to die. And this must be the tunnel they always talk about, where you're guided forward into the light. Everyone knows about the tunnel and the light—a brilliant, dazzling, welcoming light.

She has just entered the tunnel, and she can't see the light yet. She'll have to keep going until she finds it. But what if only good people can see it, people who believe in God? No, that wouldn't be fair. Besides, Sarah has been good, as good as anyone else she knows. She's done a few bad things, everyone does, but nothing awful.

And she's probably not even dead yet. People get this far and then turn back, or get sent back, because it isn't their time to die. They're the ones you see on televison shows, explaining how it is.

What happened to the girl? Sarah doesn't recall letting go of her hand, but she must have. She frowns. Was there really a girl there at all? She peers into the opacity that surrounds her, narrowing her eyes. What is this stuff? It's not water, but it's not air either. It can't be air.

There are colored lights, or clouds, or something. They flicker, fading in and out, becoming darker as she stares at them. The colors are soft, pinks shading into coral, blue topaz, pearl, and they seem to be accompanying her. She waves her arm, and the colors wave back, like pennants of silk.

Sarah closes her eyes, forcing herself to use her other senses, to smell and touch and listen. One of Charles's theories was that there are more than five senses, but modern man has forgotten how to make use of them. "They're still there, though, deep in the cerebral cortex. For all we know," Charles said, "the ancient Egyptians built their pyramids using electromagnetic telepathy." It's possible, Sarah supposes. Anything is possible.

The colors seem to be growing darker. Mostly it's shades of red, opaque yet translucent, a gentle, rhythmic pulsation of color, like the inside of a womb. Is that where I am? In a womb, waiting to be reborn?

No, that can't be right. You'd have to believe in reincarnation, and Sarah doesn't. Besides, this isn't how reincarnation is supposed to work. You're meant to forget your former life, to go through it again and again until you get it right. It's a learning process, that's the point.

She ought to be frightened. Most normal people would be frightened, finding themselves God knows where. But normal people don't drown themselves. Besides, there's nothing frightening about the lights, or the changing colors. They're interesting.

She's still moving forward, putting one foot ahead of the other but going faster than that, the way you do on moving pedestrian ramps in airports. She tries slowing down and then speeding up again, but all that happens is that the colors grow lighter, streaming out around her head and shoulders in ragged wisps. If this is what happens when you die, this is what must have happened to Charles. Poor Charles! He wouldn't have liked it, not one bit. Charles was never much good at just going along with things. Charles would have dug in his heels and refused to take another step until he'd spoken to whoever was in charge.

Charles wouldn't have automatically assumed he was dead. She shouldn't either. How can you be dead when you're conscious, and cognizant?

On the other hand, it's possible that dead people don't know they're dead. At least not at first. Or perhaps they aren't dead at all, not in the sense that the living use the word. Perhaps they're just someplace else. If that's the case, then Charles might be somewhere up ahead, and she might eventually catch up with him. Does he know, somehow? Will he stop to wait for her?

There *is* someone waiting for her, silhouetted against the changing colors. It's the girl, the dark-haired girl from the sea. With a hesitant smile, she falls into step alongside Sarah and they continue on together, their shoulders almost touching, down what might be a sort of corridor.

"What are all the colored lights for?"

"They're not lights. They're you. They're your feelings, reflecting. Yours and mine."

Sarah frowns, and the pinks darken to purple.

"Think of something nice," the girl says. "Something you really, really like."

Hot fudge sundaes. The purple dissolves into a shimmer of pink and coral, orange at the edges.

"Did I do that?"

The girl grins. "It's fun, isn't it? Xaxanader used to bring me here when I was little, to teach me how to think happy thoughts."

"But what is it?"

"I told you, it's reflections. It only happens here, in the Outer Perimeter. It was once supposed to be some kind of warning system, Xaxanader says. But the only people who ever came this way were vestigants, and there are no more of them."

A turquoise swirl wafts so close to Sarah's face that she snatches at it—and is immediately distracted by her fingers, which are definitely her fingers but have become long and tapered and elegant, tipped with opalescent nails. What magic is this? Sarah knows quite well what her hands look like, small and strong and capable. "The hands of a potato farmer," Mama used to say. "If it was your nose, we could fix it. But we can't do anything about those hands."

Now, I've got hands to die for. And that's funny. Because that's what I did. I died.

"No, you didn't." The girl's tone is matter-of-fact. "You didn't die, you see. You're not dead."

"But I am. I drowned."

"No, you didn't. You're a vestigant, and vestigants can't drown."

Vestigant, that word again. It isn't a word Sarah can remember ever having heard. She considers it, picturing the letters in her mind, deciding how it might be spelled.

They continue along, side by side, almost companionably.

"Do you mind? That you're not dead, I mean." The girl's tone is serious, concerned. "It wasn't my fault, you know. It's because you're a vestigant. Otherwise, you'd have drowned."

Charles's death wasn't anyone's fault, either. Nothing ever seems to be anyone's fault any more.

This is a dream, one of those quirky dreams that you have when you fall asleep in the afternoon. It was hot on the beach, and she was tired, and the glare of the sun on the water and the sand hurt her eyes. So she closed them, just for a moment, and she fell asleep. In that case, it all makes sense, because otherwise, none of this can be happening. For a start, people can't talk underwater. Although, Sarah muses, they might be able to communicate telepathically, by reading one another's minds—there's some impressive, if controversial, research about that. It doesn't matter, though. It doesn't have to make sense. You can do anything you like in your dreams.

This girl, does she have a name?

"Of course I do. It's Bantryd. And you know," Bantryd adds, "there's a difference between telepathy and reading peoples' minds. Telepathy is cooperative. But when you listen to what someone is thinking without their permission, that's snooping. We don't do that, ever. It's considered rude."

Sarah once read a book by a Jungian psychoanalyst who devoted a whole chapter to dreams like this. Life-transforming dreams, he called them; dreams in which an archetype from the collective unconsciousness appears to the dreamer and offers guidance. But this isn't the Divine Child or the Great Mother or even The Trickster. This is just a girl, like the ones who hang out at the mall on Saturday mornings, talking into cell phones and checking out boys.

"What's a mall?"

Sarah is mildly taken aback. "I thought you said you didn't read minds."

"We don't. But you were thinking out loud."

"A mall is a place where people go to shop." Bantryd is staring at her. "To buy things," Sarah says.

Bantryd looks unconvinced. She must be the only kid on the face of the planet who's never been to a mall. But we're not on the face of the planet anymore. We're at the bottom of the sea. What an extraordinary dream.

"It's not a dream," Bantryd says. "But I'm glad I found you. I mean, I'm glad it was you. I thought you'd be a man, because vestigants almost always are. It's much more fun that you're a woman. It's like having a friend—we can be friends, can't we?"

She seems like a nice enough kid, maybe a little young for her age, but sweet. Pretty, too.

"Me, pretty? Do you really think I'm pretty?" Bantryd beams and blushes and gives a happy little skip. It ought to be annoying, someone reading your thoughts like this. But Bantryd's exuberance is contagious. It would be absurd to be angry. "As pretty as the girls in the mall?"

"Much prettier, actually."

Certainly prettier than Australian girls, who tend to be sturdy, with big breasts and thick ankles. Totally unlike Bantryd, whose bones are small and delicate. And Australian girls don't glow. Bantryd glows.

"Nobody ever said I was pretty."

"Not even your mother?"

"I don't have a mother."

"Oh." Sarah doesn't know what to say. "I didn't know. I'm sorry."

The glow has vanished. Why did I have to bring up her mother? Why do I always say the wrong thing?

"You didn't say the wrong thing. I never knew my mother, that's what makes me sad. She went away when I was a baby. She went to find my father, because she loved him, and nobody else could go. His name was Evans, and he was a vestigant, like you. Mirjk says they're both probably dead, but I don't know. I'd feel it if they were dead, wouldn't I? Maybe I'll find them someday. It's possible. Xaxanader says anything is possible."

"Who's Xaxanader?"

"My uncle."

The people in your dreams are supposed to be part of your psyche, incorporeal progeny of your imagination. So where did Bantryd spring from? She's nothing like Sarah, nothing like Felicity, either. Absolutely the opposite of Felicity, and Felicity is Sarah's flesh and blood. Felicity never wanted to take her hand, not even when she was little. Felicity never skipped, either.

It crosses Sarah's mind that if she has fallen asleep on the beach, she'd better wake up soon. The Australian sun is unforgiving and this is the worst time of day to be out in it, unless you're covered up or under a beach umbrella. She needs to wake up, right now.

But she's not sure she wants to wake up, not yet. It's an interesting dream, not like any other dream she can recall. She wonders how it will end.

Bantryd is tugging gently at her hand. "Even if you were dreaming, wouldn't you take it seriously? There's a reason for dreams, you know. You're meant to pay attention to them. Maybe this dream is telling you something."

"It's telling me if I don't get out of the sun, I'll end up in the hospital."

Mama always said, If you're pretty, the world is your oyster. Sarah gazes at Bantryd's wonderful mane of curls, their darkness setting off the fine planes of the face, neck, and shoulders. Most girls who blossom early lose their looks by the time they're twenty, as Felicity did. Still, you never know.

Bantryd is still holding her hand. "We're almost there. Xaxanader will know what to do. But you have to tell him everything."

Everything about what? She feels as if she's getting the hang of it, though. Not just the telepathy but the rest of it too. Being here is emotional as well as physical. It's something you feel, the way you feel music, or love. Living totally in the moment, that's how the Buddhist monk who tried to teach her to meditate would describe it. Meditation was Kahn's idea. It sounded easy enough, but Sarah never quite managed it and after several attempts quietly gave up. Perhaps this is what they meant, this feeling. Whatever it is, she cannot recall ever having been anywhere so completely, except in her own mind. But that's where she is, of course. In her own mind, dreaming.

"Tell me about Xaxanader."

"He was very handsome when he was young, and all the girls were in love with him. Then he had this dream, about a vestigant. And that changed everything. I think secretly he's been waiting for her, all his life. The vestigant in his dream."

"So he has no wife, no family?"

"He has me. He's the one who took care of me after my mother left."

But it's not the same, caring for a child, or a niece. It isn't the same as being in love. Of course, Bantryd's still too young to understand such things.

Sarah looks about, realizing that the lights have vanished. "What happened to all the colors?"

"We're in the Inner Perimeter now."

Dream or no dream, it has a certain logic of its own. It's not impossible to believe in this world. You don't necessarily have to understand everything, to accept that this or that is so. Like the law of gravity. The earth spinning beneath everyone's feet, does anyone really understand how that works? But there it is, and you don't argue, but nobody actually expects you to understand it, either. Sarah remembers a picture she drew in school of the world as a round green ball studded with little stick figures, some of them upside down, all being held in place by the law of gravity. Mama said it was the stupidest picture she'd ever seen, and for once, Sarah agreed with her.

"You're not scared, are you? Evans was scared, at first. He thought he was in hell, damned to burn for all eternity." Bantryd says this with a certain gravity, as if she's casting a spell. "What does that mean, exactly?"

"It's an idea about what happens to bad people, after they die. They think God punishes them by sending them to hell. But that only happens to bad people, to sinners. If you've been good, you go to heaven."

"What's that like?"

"It's nice. It's pretty. It's full of clouds, and angels playing harps. The point is, you're with God." Bantryd looks confused. "It's complicated. It has to do with religion."

"It sounds like a story."

"It *is* a story. It's a whole book of stories, called the Bible."

"But stories aren't real."

"Some people think they are. If you believe in God, you believe the stories. It's called faith."

"We'd call it superstition."

So does Kahn. He doesn't believe that anything happens, once you're dead. Dead is dead, Kahn said when she asked him what he thought, and the bright light is an illusion. Or if it does exist, it's the product of neural synapses, the final flicker of dying brain cells. Kahn says people who think they've had near-death experiences are perpetrators of innocent hoaxes, fooling only themselves. "If you're dead, you don't come back. If you come back, you weren't really dead."

They've reached something like a wall, although it's the color and consistency of its surroundings and presents no windows, doors, or obvious edges. As Bantryd reaches out to touch it, her fingertips blur and dissolve, and then she moves forward and gradually disappears, the way someone might vanish in a mist. Sarah moves impulsively toward her and immediately finds herself standing alongside Bantryd in a different, sheltered space.

The space is knowledge—Sarah perceives this at once—and it baffles her. She has never experienced knowledge as a place. All her life, she realizes, she has been outside knowledge; now she's inside, she and Bantryd and someone else as well.

All she can see is the silhouette of his face, limned against the otherwise featureless background. He is as yet unaware of their presence, totally engrossed in the task at hand. He's standing quite still, arms extended, palms downward, fingers slightly flexed as if poised over the keys of an invisible piano. He's not nearly as tall as she thought he'd be, but his back and shoulders are broad and his profile is strong, even determined.

"Xaxanader, it's us."

He glances up with the courteous half-smile of someone interrupted in the midst of absorbing work and turns with some reluctance to face them. He's not all that old, not really, although his face is finely lined and set in an expression that suggests a sort of weary acceptance of whatever may be coming. It's not sadness, though. It's certainly not resignation. Whatever has happened, he hasn't given up, he still believes in himself. Sarah smiles tentatively and their eyes meet, but only for an instant. He has amazing eyes, blue and as vivid as the autumn sky. If he stared at you, you'd melt; you'd simply disappear. Xaxanader turns away, toward Bantryd.

"Who in the name of Commons is this?"

"She's the vestigant, the one I saw on the beach. She was in the water. She was going to drown, so I helped her."

His face is grave. "You interfered? We discussed this. You could have killed her."

"But she's a vestigant."

"But you didn't know that at the time. You had no way of knowing. Bantryd, I've gone along with this idea of yours, but there are limits, things you simply cannot do. We agreed, didn't we?" Very slowly, Bantryd nods. "No risks. Not to you nor to anyone else. What if you had killed her?" Bantryd's lower lip quivers, and she suddenly looks very young.

"But she didn't," Sarah says. Xaxanader stares at her. They both stare at her. "And it wouldn't have mattered if she had. I wanted to die. That was the whole idea. I was trying to drown myself. So what does it matter?"

He takes this in, obviously unconvinced. But he no longer looks quite so dismayed. Sarah tries to get a sense of what's going through his mind and feels it shut as palpably as a slamming door. Now, she's offended him.

"I'm sorry," Sarah says quickly. "But it's a bit tricky, and I'm only just getting the hang of it."

"Even so, we don't intrude upon one another like that. It's considered extremely impolite."

"I know. Bantryd told me. I didn't mean to intrude."

He continues to gaze at her for several seconds longer with a puzzled expression. "I still don't understand. You say you were trying to drown yourself. Trying to drown yourself?"

"Yes. I wanted to die. So you mustn't blame Bantryd. She dived, and I followed her. That's all." She wishes he'd say something. "I was going to swim until I got tired, until I drowned. So it doesn't matter."

"You keep saying that it doesn't matter. But it does. Everything matters."

"In the real world, maybe. But this is just a dream. Things don't matter in dreams, because dreams aren't real. You aren't real. None of this is real. It's a dream, that's all. And you're part of it, part of my dream."

Xaxanader looks at Bantryd, who shrugs.

"A dream. Is that what you really think?" He raises his hand but Sarah doesn't flinch, not even when his fingertips touch her cheek and trace the contour of her jaw. "I don't know," Xaxanader says. "You seem quite real to me."

"Of course I'm real. I'm the one who's having the dream."

"Are you sure? After all, it might not be your dream at all. It might be my dream. I had a dream something like this, once." Is he making fun of her? He's smiling. "Or it might even be a communal dream, you and I both dreaming the same thing at the same time."

"I've never heard of that."

"Nor have I. But that's not to say it couldn't happen. Anything is possible." His smile opens out, transforming his face. "We got off to a bad beginning, I think. So let's start over. I'm Xaxanader. Who are you?"

"Sarah."

"Sarah." He says her name as if he's tasting it. Beneath the thinly arched brows, his eyes darken to a deeper blue. "Do you often have dreams like this?"

"No, never. Nothing even remotely like this." It's not the answer he wants, but it's the truth. He continues to gaze intently at her, and she resists the urge to try to read his thoughts. "Besides, vestigants don't exist."

"You're wrong. You certainly exist." His eyes blaze like twin blue suns. "How many of you are left?"

"I'm sorry," Sarah says. "I don't know what you're talking about."

This is what happens in dreams. One thing doesn't necessarily lead to the next, there's no cause and effect. All of a sudden, everything changes. Dreams aren't meant to make sense, and they don't. I'll try to wake up.

"Don't be frightened."

"I'm not frightened." She is, though. Why can't I wake up? You're supposed to be able to wake up. If you can't, that means you're dead. Well, that was the original plan, wasn't it? "Why can't I wake up?"

"You can't wake up because you're not asleep. But you can go back, whenever you like."

"No, wait!" Bantryd cries, startling them both. "Xaxanader, she's a vestigant! You can't just let her go!"

"What am I supposed to do? We can't keep her here if she doesn't want to be here. You know the rules."

Bantryd turns back to Sarah. Her expression is pitiful. "I thought we were going to be friends."

"We are friends. But this is just a dream. And now it's time for me to wake up. That's how it is with dreams. Look, I'm sorry. I really am."

"There's no need for you to apologize." Xaxanader takes a step closer to Sarah. "Bantryd gets carried away sometimes. I'll take you back now. Come on."

Sarah hesitates. She's not sure she wants to leave, not like this. She feels like a child who's being sent off to bed. Which is absurd. Now that she's made such a fuss about waking up, she can't very well say she's changed her mind.

"I'll need to hold your hand." Nobody has held her hand since Charles died. Nobody has touched her at all, except Bantryd. And now, Xaxanader. His fingers close around hers, and she grips them firmly. "What you must do now," Xaxanader says, "is focus on the place where you entered the sea. If you do that, you'll return to the same spot. That's where you want to go, isn't it?"

It isn't where she wants to go, not really. But that's not the point. He's still holding her hand. This is ridiculous. It isn't a question of what she wants. Xaxanader doesn't exist. He's a figment of her imagination.

"That's all?"

"That's all. Yes, like that. Visualize. That's right, that's it." Gently, he releases her hand. "Now imagine yourself there. Goodbye, Sarah."

EVERYTHING IS HERE ON THE TOWEL, just as she left it, except her sunglasses, which have vanished. They were prescription glasses, and she's hung onto them for years, even after they went out of fashion, because they fit so well and looked so good. Sarah knows she should have tucked them under the towel, out of sight. She would have, if she'd thought she was coming back.

Frowning, she rubs the ball of her right thumb against her forefinger. Her fingertips are still unwrinkled, so she couldn't have been in the water for more than a few minutes. Yet the sun is low, and the beach is all but empty. She must have been asleep for hours.

She walks home cautiously, watching her step and peering into the shadows. She misses her glasses. She'll never find a pair like that again. Charles bought them for her, in Hong Kong. They were unique.

Her house is cool and dark and silent, its sandstone bricks and unpolished floorboards indifferent as always to her comings and goings. It's all she could afford, after Charles's death. It isn't what she wanted. But none of this is what she wanted.

She sits quietly, watching the walls of the small front room soften in the deepening twilight. Nothing actually happened. And even if something did happen, nobody knows. Nobody need ever know. She fell asleep on the beach and she had a fantastic dream. She was probably still half asleep when she waded into the water to cool off. It's the sort of thing that could happen to anyone.

God knows, it was a strange dream all the same. That man, Xaxanader, he was amazing. He seemed so real, not at all like someone in a dream. She can still feel his fingertips touching her face, the firmness of his hand clasping hers. She squeezes her fingers, trying to recreate the feeling, just as she used to lie in bed in the dark hugging her pillow, pretending it was Charles, knowing it wasn't.

You'd think if she was going to dream about someone, it would be Charles. After all, she loved Charles. She still does. Xaxanader is nothing like Charles. Xaxanader isn't like anyone she knows, anyone she's ever known. So how was it possible for her to make him up?

But what if she didn't make him up? Suppose he's real? It didn't feel anything at all like a dream. It still doesn't. Suppose it really happened?

That's insane. She gazes idly about the room. Everything here is normal; everything is as it should be. Ordinary, normal, dull. Maybe she'll paint the walls a different color, aquamarine, or yellow, or even red. People will think she's gone mad. Maybe she has.

It would be wonderful if Xaxanader was real, but he isn't. Yet she can still feel the warmth of his flesh. She can still see his smile, his eyes. She frowns, telling herself that it wouldn't matter if Xaxanader existed or not, because she's still in love with Charles.

It's not healthy to sit alone in the dark like this. Sarah switches on the lights, blinking in the sudden brightness. The blinds need dusting. And the dirty dishes she left in the sink will have to be washed, left to dry in the rack and then put away. She sighs. It's such a small kitchen, there's no room for a dishwasher. And no point in having one, not for just one person.

There's sand on the floor. She'll have to vacuum tomorrow and spray for sand fleas, which have been bad this summer. Her hair is still damp and sticky with salt. She needs to shower. Instead, she goes into the kitchen and pours herself a scotch.

Just for the sake of argument, then. Suppose it did happen? In that case, Bantryd and Xaxander are real people, inhabiting a separate, parallel world at the bottom of the sea. And Sarah herself is a vestigant, able to come and go between these worlds. Is that any more preposterous than feathered dinosaurs?

Life began in the sea, you learn that in school. The chemical composition of human blood is similar to sea water, except sea water is saltier. William Beebe thought you could calculate back to when the sea was less salty, and thus identify the moment when man became amphibious. She'd read that somewhere, and even though Charles told her it was nonsense, she still thought it was interesting.

And parallel worlds do exist. Cyberspace is a parallel world. Charles said so. Holograms are parallel worlds. Particles of matter so tiny they can only be seen in a computer simulation exist as well. And what about the world of a housefly? It doesn't look anything like this world, but it exists.

Sarah sips her scotch, thinking that the world is as full of wonders as it ever was. Just because people no longer gaze in awe at seashells and sunsets doesn't make them any less awesome.

Reality, Charles maintained, is simply an idea. Sarah smiles, remembering. She can almost hear his voice, explaining that reality is a social construct, a working hypothesis made up of probability and consensus. For the sake of convention and convenience, human beings agree to accept certain things as given. We used to think the earth was flat, says Charles. Now we think it's round. So long as we agree, reality can be anything we say it is.

This conversation took place over dinner, shortly after they were married. They sat facing one another across a white damask tablecloth, the table lit by flickering yellow candles set in a chunky pair of pewter candle holders, a wedding gift.

Charles was saying that facts only exist after the fact. Sarah was surprised, because Charles is a scientist, and scientists believe in facts. Charles picked up a dessert spoon.

"What do you think will happen if I drop this spoon?" he asked.

"It'll fall in the soup."

Charles waved the spoon slowly back and forth, like a maestro wielding a baton. "Based upon your past experiences with spoons and soup, you think that if I drop this particular spoon at this particular point in time, there's an extremely high probability that it will fall into the soup. That's what you're saying, isn't it?"

"Well, it certainly won't fly into the kitchen and wash itself." She remembers how clever she felt, definitely a match for him. "Okay, yes. If you drop it, it'll fall."

"Are you sure?"

"Absolutely."

Charles dropped the spoon, and Sarah applauded.

"You were right this time. But next time, the spoon might fly away, or disintegrate, or even turn into a watering can. I'm not saying it will. In fact, it probably won't. But it's possible. All those outcomes are possibilities. Remote possibilities, but possible nonetheless. Do you see what I'm getting at, sweetheart?"

She did. And it was interesting. "But if anything like that did happen, nobody would believe it. They'd think it was a trick. They'd demand a scientific explanation. And there would have to be one, wouldn't there?"

Charles shook his head. "Explanations are the same as facts. We used to say everything that happened was the will of God, and we got along that way for thousands of years. Now we say everything that happens is governed by the laws of physics. Science is just another idea, like God. No better and no worse."

Closing her eyes, Sarah can see Charles's face, his gray eyes, and the flickering candlelight. The meal, she recalls, had been planned to complement a white wine grown and bottled at a tiny Alsace vineyard and presented to Charles by one of his students. It was a special wine and deserved a meal worthy of its virtues.

How had it tasted, that rare, delicate wine? She can't remember. What she recalls is the epiphany of suddenly seeing the world in a new way, in which hitherto inviolate certainties acquired limitless possibilities.

Anything is possible.

She sold the dining room suite after Charles died, for a fraction of what it was worth. You'll get more for it in Sydney, people said, but Sarah didn't care. She could neither bring herself to sit in Charles's chair nor bear to see it empty.

It didn't really happen, though. It couldn't have. There can't be a world at the bottom of the sea. It was a dream, the kind of dream you have when you fall asleep on the beach, in the sun.

Or else she's crazy.

Yet even sanity is only an idea, like reality and God and science. Charles once told her that the idea of insanity was invented by European burghers who were trying to justify the continued existence of lazarettos. Charles knew so much, about so many things.

The scotch helps. She finishes it, wondering if she should have another. She feels better, although she's read that drinking alone is a sign of depression and that alcohol actually depresses the central nervous system.

Returning to the kitchen, Sarah pours more scotch into the glass, adds water and the last of the ice cubes. When Charles was alive, they had a refrigerator that made and dispensed ice cubes automatically.

I'm a widow, alone. My husband is dead. Of course I'm depressed.

The vestigant thing intrigues her. It's a fascinating idea— how did she ever manage to come up with it? But if it was her dream, it was her idea. A crazy idea.

Vestigants aren't crazy, though. Vestigants actually make a certain kind of sense. Might there be others? Sarah imagines meeting these other vestigants, comparing notes with them over a coffee in a café. How would she find them, though? Where would she even begin to look? Do they even know they're vestigants?

She begins to compose an imaginary ad she'll place in *The London Review of Books.* Can you breathe under water? Do you know Bantryd and Xaxanader? It would be fun, and safe enough. The ads are always outlandish, that's the point. But what if someone replied?

Five hundred years ago, nobody would have batted an eye. Vestigants, mermaids, werewolves, ghosts, vampires, no problem. They'd have believed her, back then. Although they might have also thought she was a witch and burned her at the stake.

Sarah sits quietly, drinking scotch on an empty stomach, knowing nothing has been settled.

If she kept a journal, she could at least write it down. Writing things down helps sometimes. Charles used to create what he called decision trees, branches of possibilities and alternatives. Seeing it all set out on paper made him think more clearly, he said.

Sarah puts down her glass and looks around for pen and paper but can't find any. Paper is no good, anyhow. Something like this requires a proper journal, a bound book of some sort, and she doesn't have anything like that.

She doesn't even like writing, in the sense of holding a pencil or a pen and pushing it across paper. It's too slow. When Sarah writes letters—and she rarely does, because most of the letters she used to write were to Charles—she prefers to compose them on a computer, even though it's supposed to be bad manners to send printed letters.

What would Charles say? He'd be fascinated. He'd want her to go back again tomorrow, with a camera and a tape recorder. But of course if Charles were still alive, she wouldn't have wanted to die and none of it would have happened.

She certainly can't tell Felicity. Are you crazy? Felicity would say. So would Kahn, although probably not in those words. But it would help to talk to someone. What about Sean? He believes in SETI and extra-terrestrial communication. But he's so far away. Besides, he'd probably end up calling Felicity and saying, Mum's going a bit strange in the head.

She could tell her best friend, if she had one. But Charles wasn't big on friends, and besides, Sarah found it difficult to make friends in Australia, where everyone seemed to have known everyone else since grade school.

It didn't matter. We were all we needed. That's probably why we stayed in Australia, because being isolated suited us. We could live the way we wanted to live, without making excuses.

Outside, the streetlights have come on. Backyard barbecues are belching smoke and ash, and the smell of burnt meat hangs pungent in the air. Televisions blare, and children on skateboards zoom back and forth. Sarah sits on the couch, legs curled beneath her, sipping an unwonted third scotch.

Xaxanader wanted her to stay. Sarah wanted to stay, too. So why did she come back? What would Charles have done? He wouldn't have stayed, because he wouldn't have left her.

But he did leave me. That's exactly what he did. She feels a flash of anger and thinks Kahn would be pleased; it seems to disappoint him that she feels no anger. She doesn't, though. Charles didn't want to die. It isn't his fault. It isn't anybody's fault.

Her glass is empty, but she doesn't want any more to drink. She wants to go back, into the swirling, changing colors. It wasn't a bad thing, having people know what you're thinking, knowing what they were thinking. And at least Bantryd and Xaxanader liked her. Nobody here likes her. Nobody here cares, one way or the other.

Sarah sits for a while longer, her thoughts vague and unfocused. She's tired, she feels old. Slowly she climbs the steep narrow stairs to the tiny bedroom, even though it's much too early to go to bed.

((◎

THE SKY IS A DUSKY YELLOW when Sarah awakens, the sun is about to rise. Lingering beneath the cozy quilt, she watches the incoming tide of light upon the ceiling, listens to the ebb and flow of street sounds beyond the open window.

She's here, not there. This is real. The other was a dream. Sometimes you can go back to sleep, though, back into the dream. Closing her eyes, she summons up images of Xaxanader and Bantryd, her imagination painting in a background of swirling color. For a moment it seems to be working, but then there's the thud of metal upon metal in the street outside, car horns, angry male voices. It's no good. Wearily, Sarah opens her eyes.

Never mind, it was an amazing dream. She makes her way carefully down the stairs (her ankles are always stiff in the morning) and brews coffee, watching it dribble into the glass carafe, thinking stiff ankles are a sign of old age. The windows are open, and she can still hear the men arguing on the footpath.

She doesn't make toast. She's not hungry. When the coffee is ready, she carries the mug upstairs and climbs back into bed.

She doesn't have to get up if she doesn't want to. She doesn't have to do anything. Propped against the pillows, she watches the changing patterns of light filter through the branches of the tree outside her window. She could lie here until Friday and nobody would know or care. But that would be giving up. You're not supposed to give up. You're supposed to keep trying, whether you feel like it or not. If you keep going through the motions, sooner or later, something will kick in.

So she gets up and dresses, even though she's not going anywhere. She puts on clean underwear and clean, pressed clothes. Her appointment with Kahn isn't until Friday, but that's not the point. You can't spend the day in your nightgown.

There's nothing much in the newspaper. There rarely is. It's Australia, only eighteen million people in the whole country. Sitting at the kitchen table with a second mug of coffee, Sarah tackles the crossword puzzle. It was years before she mastered Australian crossword puzzles, which contain fewer words than their American counterparts and are shaped differently, more like skeletons than grids. The spellings are different too.

She hasn't eaten since yesterday and she should be hungry, but isn't. French women don't get fat because they don't eat unless they're hungry. Sarah looks in the refrigerator, but nothing tempts her. She needs to go shopping. Later, perhaps, when it's not so hot. She wishes she had a ceiling fan, or better still, central air conditioning. Nobody in Sydney has air conditioning. They don't think it's necessary, not with the beach so close. Nobody has central heating, either. They say it doesn't get cold enough, but it does.

Sarah picks up a novel from the library and tries to concentrate. It's not a very good novel, although it's supposed to be a bestseller. That doesn't mean anything these days. Everything's a bestseller. The protagonist has left his wife, is having an affair, has just learned he has cancer. He'll probably die at the end. Sarah thinks he deserves to die and dozes off on the couch. When she opens her eyes, damp and sticky with the perspiration of an afternoon nap, it's already getting dark.

The telephone rings. Nobody calls her, except telemarketers and sometimes Kahn, when he needs to cancel a session. If it rings five times, the machine will answer it. Five, six, seven. Maybe she's forgotten to turn the machine on.

"Yes? Hello?"

"Mum? It's me, Felicity. I wanted to make sure you didn't forget about tonight."

Last week, Sarah agreed to have dinner at Felicity's place. But that was last week, when there wasn't supposed to be a tonight.

"You did forget, didn't you?"

She can say she has a headache. Or that she's been sneezing all day and thinks she might be coming down with something. But Felicity will have already bought food and perhaps even begun to cook it.

"I didn't forget. I was having a nap, that's all."

Felicity rents a flat in an old house on a shabby street in what she insists is—technically—the suburb of Watson's Bay. The flat is smaller than the previous one, with no off-street parking and significantly higher rents.

"You're paying for the post code," Felicity says. "When you tell people you live in Watson's Bay, they assume you're successful and open up. Nobody wants to spill their guts to a loser. Believe me, Mum. I know about these things."

Felicity is a journalist, so she probably does know about these things. Besides, she has Max to help her with the rent. The parking doesn't matter because Felicity doesn't own a car.

"Mum!" Felicity says as she opens the door. "You're looking well." Felicity puckers her lips, leans forward and carefully kisses the air above Sarah's left ear. "Just like your old self. Actually, better than your old self. Have you lost weight?"

Felicity is trying to be nice, trying to be a good daughter. And I love her, Sarah tells herself. Of course I love her. We just don't get along.

Felicity was born angry and no matter what you did for her, it was never enough. Felicity always wanted more: more toys, more spending money, more love. Maybe it was my fault, Sarah told Kahn. I loved Charles best, so Felicity and Sean had to make do with what was left. Sean coped, but it was never enough for Felicity. Still, she's a grown woman now, an adult. And it's not as though she's alone in the world. She has Max.

Max is Australian. So is Felicity, even though she was born in the United States. Australia has been Felicity's home since she was three, and she's grown up Australian, unromantic and unsentimental. Felicity has always fit in, it's important to her. And, she hated it that Sarah wasn't like the other mothers. Why can't you wear jeans? Why do you always have to use big words? Why can't you sew? Why won't you let us watch television while we're having tea?

"So," Felicity says, "tell me your news."

"What news?"

"Oh, I don't know. Whatever's happening in your life. Like, have you started to look for another job?"

Felicity is bustling about in her tiny well-organized kitchen, peering into a bubbling pot, fiddling with plates. White steam rises into a whirring fan above the stove, but Sarah can't smell anything.

She looks around. "Where's Max?"

Felicity's lips compress. "Max has things to do. He says to give you his regards."

Max is rarely present at these dinners. "I sometimes get the feeling that Max doesn't like me very much."

Felicity sighs, and rolls her eyes. "It's not you, personally. It's the situation. Max doesn't like drama. He hates it when you cry. And when you're not crying, you're always talking about Dad, and how much you loved him, and how perfect your marriage was, and how happy you were. I mean, I know it's all true. But that's not the point. People just don't want to hear about it, all this stuff about love and feelings. It makes them uncomfortable. It makes Max uncomfortable. It's like you're criticizing him, like you're saying he can never be as good as Dad."

Felicity and Max began their relationship shortly before Charles's death. (But what does it mean? Charles said. What kind of relationship? Are they engaged? Are they going to get married? Sarah had to explain—all it meant was that they were living together.) The four of them met for dinner. Sarah remembers that Max didn't offer to pay for the excellent wine he'd ordered in advance because, as he explained to Felicity, he knew Charles appreciated a good bottle of wine. Not that Charles would have let him pay, even if he'd offered.

"Besides," Felicity says, "Max knows perfectly well that you don't like him. Or should I say that you don't approve of him. You don't think he's good enough for me."

"But that's not true."

Max is quite good enough for Felicity, who is past thirty and thanks to long hours in the sun, losing her looks. I warned her about the sun, what it would do to her skin. But she wouldn't listen to me. She's never listened to me.

"Oh, Mum. Stop pretending."

With an angry flourish, Felicity places a bowl of pasta in the center of the table. There's salad in another bowl, torn green leaves, but no salad dressing. The table has been set with smaller bowls, spoons, and serviettes. Felicity prefers to eat and drink from bowls. It's so French, she says.

Wine is French, too. But there are no wine glasses on the table, and no wine. There are, however, two plastic bottles of imported mineral water. Everyone seems to be carrying these bottles now, carrying them and sucking at them at frequent intervals, lest they become dehydrated. When Sarah was Felicity's age, people drank water with meals, and that was the end of it.

"Have some water, Mum." Sarah shakes her head. "You really ought to drink more water, you know. At least two liters a day. It's cleansing."

Sarah does not reply. To say what she thinks will precipitate a quarrel, and she doesn't want to quarrel with Felicity. Better to simply let it go. One of the gentler skills of bereavement is that you learn how to let things go.

"You could have brought a bottle of wine, if you wanted wine." Felicity sounds slightly defensive. "I mean, you know I don't drink wine. But I don't mind other people drinking it, if that's what they want to do."

Felicity heaps pasta into Sarah's bowl. She's prepared a prodigious amount of food, enough to serve an entire dinner party. The pasta steams and glistens with minute speckles of some sort of herb. Sarah sniffs hopefully, but still can't detect a recognizable aroma. Maybe she really is coming down with something.

"It all looks very nice," she says carefully.

At least, Felicity is eating normally. During adolescence, her eating habits veered from idiosyncratic to alarming, lettuce leaves, cucumber, and carrots washed down with endless glasses of tap water, and nothing else. You couldn't tempt her, and you certainly couldn't argue with her. She'd go into her room and slam the door. While watching a documentary about anorexia, Felicity said, "Those girls look fine. They aren't skinny at all. They look like models. I'd kill to look like that."

A friend advised Sarah to keep calm and act normal. Under no circumstances, she warned, should you urge Felicity to eat. And don't make disparaging comments about her weight, either. Don't say anything. She'll get over it. Charles had worried terribly, though.

Felicity did get over it. And here she is, alive and healthy. It's Charles who's dead. Tears sting Sarah's eyelids, and she quickly knuckles them away. Not that Felicity would notice.

Felicity eats her pasta with a fork and spoon, but when Sarah tries to emulate her, the strands slither and slip and slide back into the bowl or onto the table, and Sarah goes back to winding the pasta in skeins around the tines of her fork, as she's always done. There's no grated cheese on the table, and no salt.

I'm too critical. I expect too much. Besides, it might have been different if I'd devoted myself to my children instead of Charles, sewn little stuffed animals for school fetes, baked fairy cakes.

She wishes she'd brought wine. "Is there any salt?"

"Too much salt is bad for you," Felicity says. "Especially at your age. And that reminds me. I've been meaning to ask you, and I keep forgetting. Have you been keeping track of your cholesterol?"

Sarah shakes her head. She doesn't have Pap smears either, and nobody examines her breasts, or her moles. Australian doctors are only half as well educated as their American counterparts, and Sarah doesn't trust them. Socialized medicine is all very well in theory, but in practice, where there's no competition, there's no accountability.

Sarah chews and swallows. Even now, she isn't particularly hungry, although she'd love a glass of white wine.

"This is good," she tells Felicity, trying to sound as if she means it.

"It's pesto but it's my own recipe, without all the garbage in it." Sarah nods, wondering if this is how Kahn feels when he's trying to keep her talking. Felicity says she grows her own basil and pounds the leaves in an organic stone mortar with an organic stone pestle. "Nothing added.

Unadulterated. And not cut with a knife, or chopped. Pounded."

That's what the little green specks are, then. Organically grown basil, organically pounded. Politically correct. She wonders what Xaxanader would say if he could see her now, imagines his amused smile.

Felicity finishes and takes her plate to the sink, running water over it. Sarah knows the plates will be washed and dried and put away before Felicity goes to bed tonight.

"So what's new and exciting in your life, Mum? Any new men?"

"Men? God, no."

Felicity smiles again. She's smiling a lot tonight. She's up to something. Kahn wonders if Sarah doesn't think she's sometimes too hard on Felicity, if she mightn't have unrealistically high expectations where Felicity is concerned. Sarah doesn't think so.

"It's your birthday next week." Felicity produces a long white envelope she places ceremoniously upon the table in front of Sarah. "So, happy birthday. Go on, Mum. Open it."

It can't be a birthday card. Felicity hasn't given her a birthday card in years. This is a matter of principle with Felicity; she refuses to acknowledge any occasion that requires a gift or a card. Not just birthdays, but Mother's Day,

Valentine's Day, Easter, Christmas. All crass, commercial American imports, according to Felicity.

Turning the envelope over in her hands, Sarah tries to guess. It can't be a card, it's much too thick. Using a table knife, she carefully cuts it open, feeling uncomfortable, as if she's killing something.

Inside, there's a sheaf of papers, folded and stapled at the upper left-hand corner. Nothing else. A contract? A manuscript? Sarah unfolds the papers, looks at the letterhead at the top of the first page. Partnerships Pty Ltd.

"Felicity, what **is** this?"

"It's a service. They introduce single people like you to other single people. You've seen it advertised on television. It's very reputable." Sarah is speechless. "It's the best introduction agency in Sydney. They've been in business for over twenty years, just doing this, just introducing people to one another. You know, Mum, you're not the only person in the world who's lost someone. It happens all the time. People die. They get divorced."

Sarah says nothing.

"Look, it would be different if you were old, because you'd be dead too, in a couple of years, and it wouldn't matter so much. But you're not that old. You'll probably live another thirty years, and you don't want to spend all those years alone, do you?"

It isn't something she's thought about, spending the rest of her life alone. Without Charles, yes, but that's different. She'd like to say there's nothing so terrible about being alone, but Felicity wouldn't understand.

"You do have to try, Mum. You do have to make an effort."

Sarah feels her throat tighten. Felicity sounds like Kahn. It's none of her business, none of anybody's business what she does.

"You don't have to feel embarrassed. Being a widow isn't anything to be ashamed of. There are thousands and thousands of women in the same boat. Look, it's all completely confidential. All you have to do is fill out the questionnaire and post it back to them. See? There's the envelope, and I've even put a stamp on it for you."

"And then what?"

"They introduce you to someone. Actually, I've signed you up for a guaranteed minimum of four introductions." Felicity smiles—a bright, determined smile. "It's been almost two years since Dad died, Mum. And you know what I think? I think you should celebrate your birthday by getting on with your life."

She has to say something. She has to at least pretend to be grateful. Sarah lowers her head and goes through the papers page by page, not so much reading them as stalling for time.

"You'll enjoy it, Mum. You will. You used to love going out. I was talking to Sean last week and he said the first thing he can remember is you and Dad were going out for dinner and leaving us with a babysitter. You went out all the time, just the two of you. Remember? Well, I said to Sean, She doesn't go out at all any more. She never does anything. She just sits there in that house."

"And then Sean said, What about one of those singles clubs? And I said, Mum would hate a singles club, she's not the type. And Sean said, Well, she needs to get out and meet people. And we sort of tossed it back and forth, and I said I'd look into it, and I did. So happy birthday, from both of us. Who knows?" Felicity smiles archly. "You might meet someone you really like. You might even end up getting married again."

(((©

ON FRIDAY, Sarah tells Kahn.

"It seems to have upset you."

"No, but it took me by surprise. It's the last thing in the world I'd have expected from Felicity. I don't know what to make of it." She glances up at him. "Why? Do you think I ought to be upset?"

"On the contrary. I think it was a lovely, thoughtful gesture."

But Felicity isn't thoughtful, has never been thoughtful. And don't tell me I'm being critical, because I'm not. It's the way she is. You can love your children without being blind to their faults. Felicity has done this because she wants something, she has an agenda. Felicity always wants something. She was born wanting, screaming with rage and frustration, inconsolable.

Kahn repositions himself in the black vinyl chair. "I wonder what you're thinking."

Kahn has no format. If she wants to talk, he'll listen. If she remains silent, he waits, or wonders. His features are composed, revealing nothing. But there's nothing left to say to Kahn about Charles, about Felicity, about anything. He's heard it all. He knows more about her than anyone in the world. Yet she doesn't know anything about him. She doesn't even know his first name. For some reason, this strikes her as funny.

"Something made you smile." His tone is studiously neutral, like a stranger pulled up alongside you at a stop-light, telling you that your dress is caught in the car door. "I wonder what it was."

Sarah stares at the floor.

Very gently, and after what seems to be an inordinately long time, Kahn says, "I wonder if you're still having those dreams."

"What dreams?"

"Dreams full of strangers. You said you never dream about Charles, you dream about strangers."

He's always curious about her dreams. Possibly, he believes they reveal things she doesn't want him to know, although she has no secrets other than the pathetic little secrets everyone has.

"Actually, I did have a sort of weird dream, a couple of nights ago."

Kahn relaxes, settles back into his black vinyl chair. "Tell me about it."

"I dreamed I was someplace else."

Kahn is gazing steadily at her, smiling slightly, nodding encouragement. It's so still you can almost hear the ticking of the little clock behind the box of tissues. Maybe this wasn't such a good idea.

"Someplace else?"

"I mean, totally someplace else. I dreamed I was in a different world, a sort of parallel universe at the bottom of the ocean."

Kahn's face remains inscrutable, professional. Sarah thinks it's like talking to a machine attached to an automatic timer set to run for fifty minutes, no more and no less.

"There were people there. There was a whole society, a whole civilization, men and women just like us." She pauses. How much should she tell him?

"How did it feel?"

"It didn't feel like a dream. It felt real. It felt the way it feels to be somewhere, the way it feels to be here. But I knew that was impossible. I can't really be here, I kept telling myself. This can't be happening."

"So you were dreaming, but in your dream you were thinking, This isn't real. Perhaps you were having a lucid dream. Have you ever had a lucid dream?"

"I don't know. I don't think so. I've certainly never had a dream like this one. I knew I couldn't be there at the bottom of the sea unless I was dead. And I wasn't dead. But I was definitely there."

"Why would you think you were dead?"

There's another long silence. Kahn steeples his fingers and moves on. "These people you saw, these men and women. What were they like?"

"There was a girl called Bantryd and a man, Xaxanader. He's her uncle, and he was really extraordinary. We could sort of read each other's minds, but that was okay. He had blue eyes," Sarah adds, as if it matters. Maybe it does. Kahn, she realizes, has blue eyes too. She's never noticed that.

Kahn nods, his pale, unblinking eyes fixed on her face.

"I'm a vestigant. That's what they told me. It's a sort of mutation. Vestigants can breathe under water—like amphibians, I suppose. They can live on land or on the bottom of the sea." Sarah pauses. It sounds like bad science fiction.

"Vestigants," Kahn says.

"Half the time, I didn't even know what they were talking about. But then Xaxanader said it was all right, it wasn't my fault."

What if she'd stayed? Would she still be here, sitting in the black vinyl chair? Impossible. Even vestigants can't be in two places at once. But what if she had stayed? Xaxanader wanted her to stay.

"And then I woke up."

Kahn nods and nods. "How did it feel?"

"I already told you, it felt real. It felt as real as sitting here in this chair."

"No, I meant, how did it feel emotionally. Were you angry? Were you frightened?"

"At first, I didn't know where I was. So I was confused, but I wasn't afraid. It wasn't bad, it wasn't threatening." She remembers the colors, the lights. "Just the opposite, actually. But I thought I must have died. You know, drowned."

Kahn gives her a strange look. "That's the second time you've said that. Why would you think you'd drowned?"

"Because I was there, in the ocean." Oh, God. "In my dream, I mean."

"But you knew it was a dream."

"I didn't, actually. Not until I woke up. In the dream, it felt real. That's what I'm trying to tell you. It was so real. And it felt good, too. It felt right. It was almost as if I belonged there." He's staring. "Well, you asked me how it felt. I'm trying to tell you." He doesn't understand, can't possibly understand. "It's almost as if it really happened." But it couldn't have happened. "It wasn't a bad dream. It wasn't a nightmare."

Sarah watches a new, deep crease form between Kahn's eyes as he nods to himself. Placing his left hand over his mouth, he gazes at her for what feels like rather a long time. The vinyl is making the backs of her legs perspire, and she moves uncomfortably.

"I feel as if I'm missing something," Kahn says at last. "This man, this Sandor. Was he angry when you couldn't answer his questions?"

"Xaxanader. No, it wasn't like that."

"What was it like?"

"He was . . . gentle. There was something about him, I can't explain it. And he liked me, I could tell. He was attracted to me, he didn't want me to go. And I wanted to stay too. I wanted to stay there, with him. With both of them. I could actually imagine it." Sarah stops and puts a hand to her lips. "I can't believe I just said that."

"Why?" Kahn's voice is unmodulated, neutral. "He was attracted to you, and you were obviously attracted to him. What's wrong with that?"

"I still love Charles. How could I even think about being with another man?"

"An imaginary man, in a dream."

"It was my dream, though. They were my thoughts."

Slowly Kahn shifts position, uncrossing and recrossing his legs and wrapping his arms around himself, mirroring her own posture. His eyes are still fixed upon her. He begins to nod his head, up and down, up and down. His right hand moves to his mouth, over his mouth, covering it.

"But it was a dream. It wasn't real."

"Yes, it was. I mean, it was real to me."

And if she tells him the truth? What can he do? He's only a psychologist. He can't certify me, or schedule me. That's why they say, in Australia, They don't commit you, they schedule you.

"What did he look like?" Kahn is asking. "The man, Xanader? Whatever his name was."

"Average height, I think. Brown hair shot with gray. And he had the most wonderful eyes, like the people you sometimes see in crowds, in Renaissance paintings. You know, the onlookers, in the background. But you always notice their eyes." Sarah is taken with the elegance of her comparison, but Kahn breezes right past it.

"Did he remind you of anyone?"

"I don't think so."

"He didn't remind you of Charles?"

"Not at all."

Sarah sees him glance toward the little hidden clock. "I have to stop now."

Slowly, he gets to his feet. Sarah stands up too, retrieving her handbag from where she placed it on the floor alongside the chair while Kahn walks unhurriedly across the room to the closed door.

"Wait," Sarah says. "There's something else. It's important."

His hand is on the knob of the door. "I have another client."

"It'll only take a minute." She needs to tell him now, while she can. "I've got to tell you something."

He opens the door. "It's a very interesting dream, Mrs. Andrews. We'll talk about it more, next time. But I do have to stop now."

Chapter Three

What possessed her? Sarah makes her way along the shabby corridor that leads from Kahn's room to the outer door, wondering what she'll do if Kahn changes his mind and calls her back. Will she go through with it, tell him there really is a parallel world at the bottom of the sea?

He doesn't call her back. Relieved, she leaves the building, stepping gratefully back out into the humid Sydney morning. She feels an odd little surge of exhilaration, the heady high of a close brush with disaster. It's not unpleasant. It's what makes people climb Everest, or run with the bulls at Pamplona.

It doesn't last. And taking risks isn't exciting, just risky. There are enough catastrophes in life without looking for more. On their honeymoon, Charles wanted to ride mules down into the Grand Canyon, and although she managed to talk him out of it, the issue surfaced again several years later, in Giza. You can't come all the way to Egypt and not ride a camel, Charles said. At least Giza was flat. The camels were called Hercules and Sunny Boy. Charles gleefully kicked Hercules's flanks to make him gallop, while Sarah clung to Sunny Boy's pommel and waited for the ordeal to be over.

Charles loved Egypt, especially Aswan. Next time, he said, we'll stay at the Old Cataract for a few days. We'll sit on the veranda in deck chairs, drinking champagne and reading Agatha Christie. They traveled every year. They were planning a trip to Venice when Charles died.

You can still go, Kahn told her. There's nothing to stop you, no reason why you shouldn't.

It wouldn't be the same.

But that's not to say you can't enjoy things. Charles may be dead, but you're still living.

He's wrong. This isn't living. She's alive, but that's all. Spiders are alive. Worms are alive. The crud growing underneath the sink is alive. She was supposed to drown. She wanted to drown. She'd had it all planned.

It's quiet here, even though she's only a block east of Oxford Street. Sarah walks slowly, scuffing her feet in the drifted leaves, sending the shiny black beetles beneath them scuttling for cover. There's a park farther along, a tiny triangle of grass and trees tucked into a space too small for anything else.

Therapy is supposed to make you feel better, but it doesn't. After sessions with Kahn, Sarah feels numb, and exhausted. It's probably not much fun for him either, although Kahn would never admit to such feelings or to any feelings at all where she's concerned. He's probably writing a paper. She imagines herself sitting in someone else's waiting room, picking up a journal and suddenly realizing that she's reading about herself. *The subject, a middle-aged woman who has recently lost her husband, presents with the typical symptoms of insomnia, loss of appetite, and depression . . .*

The park is a miniature oasis of grass and gum trees cantilevered over the top of a ravine that tumbles away to streets and back gardens below. There's a bench, and Sarah sits on it, gazing up through the branches at the sun-gilded leaves.

It did happen. She wasn't dreaming. It couldn't have happened, but it did, and she can't pretend, she won't pretend it didn't happen. That settled, Sarah closes her eyes for a moment. The sun is warm on her face, and she can hear the distant hum of a lawnmower.

There's an explanation for all this. There has to be. She's not crazy, she's not losing her mind. Meanwhile, there's no harm done. Nobody knows about it, not even Kahn, not really. If he asks about the dream, she'll say she forgot. People do forget dreams.

A magpie swoops, and Sarah ducks, shielding her head and face with her hand. It's mating season, and there are probably chicks in a nest nearby. Magpies can be mean. This one veers away but perches upon a nearby branch, continuing to keep an eye on her.

If she *was* crazy, she wouldn't give a damn what Kahn thinks. Crazy people never do, because they don't know they're crazy. It's not as if she's seeing visions or hearing voices. What happened was more like an elaborate fantasy, or a daydream.

Daydreams are normal, Kahn said so. So are fantasies. "Children often believe the characters in stories their parents read to them are real. Some children even have imaginary friends. Did you ever have an imaginary friend?"

This was during their second or third session, when Sarah was still unsure what was expected of her. It wasn't the sort of thing she felt comfortable about discussing.

Probably in an attempt to encourage her, Kahn told her a story about a pregnant woman whose fantasy was that she'd marry her baby's father, even though she knew it was impossible. Kahn said this woman even went shopping for a wedding dress and when she found one she liked, she put down a deposit. "Does that make her crazy?"

Sarah thinks so, yes.

Kahn doesn't. "The woman is fantasizing, certainly. But she knows she's fantasizing. She knows she's pregnant, she knows the man isn't going to marry her. The fantasy makes her feel good, that's all." Sarah gave him a doubtful look. "It would be different if she denied the pregnancy, the reality. Or if she thought it was all right because she was the Virgin Mary. Oh, yes, women who can't accept what they consider the shame of an out-of-wedlock pregnancy sometimes do believe they're the Virgin Mary. And it assuages their guilt. The problem is, someone like that isn't just fantasizing. Someone like that has lost touch with reality."

Sarah has the uneasy feeling that he was talking about a real person, someone who sits in the vinyl chair. "What happens to people like that?"

"The point I was trying to make is that nearly everyone daydreams, everyone has fantasies. It's part of the human condition."

He was wanting her to make a connection, but she'd lost the thread. Childhood, imaginary friends. That's it, he was asking if she ever had an imaginary friend.

"I didn't, actually. But at one point, I had imaginary parents. My imaginary father was a famous photojournalist, and his wife was a concert pianist who died giving birth to me. So I lived with my aunt and uncle, and we all pretended they were my real parents, but deep down, I knew they weren't."

Kahn nods, then sits there quietly, expectantly. Sarah doesn't like to talk about her childhood. She might have had the best childhood in the world, and it wouldn't have made any difference. Charles would still be dead. Her childhood has nothing to do with anything, and in any case, it's none of Kahn's business.

They sit stubbornly facing one another for the rest of the hour, not speaking, while the clock behind the box of tissues ticks silently toward the moment when Kahn can stand up and say he has to stop.

((◦

THE WOODEN SLATS OF the park bench are cutting into the backs of her thighs. Above Sarah's head, birds flutter from branch to branch, emitting tuneless cries. She hears them although she can't see them, just their flickering silhouettes in the silvery sunlight, barely distinguishable from the shimmer of foliage.

She always knew they were imaginary, her imaginary parents. Even as a very young child, she knew what was real and what wasn't. So did the Virgin Mary, Sarah suspects. She lived on a farm, she knew where babies came from. One night she dreamed an angel came to her and said she was going to give birth to the Son of God. That was extraordinary, impossible. But it happened. Jesus Christ was a real person.

Nobody would believe a story like that today. It was a different world, two thousand years ago. Modern science hadn't been invented yet. Sarah wonders what the next thing will be, the thing after science.

Another black bird swoops past her and perches at the edge of the footpath, its bright eye glistening against the sleek helmet of feathers. The eye seems sightless, synthetic. Does it know she's looking at it? Does it care?

Sarah suddenly wishes she'd thought to bring something back with her, some object from Xaxanader's world that would prove it wasn't a dream, it really did exist, does exist. A shell, or even a pebble. If it was something that could only come from the bottom of the sea, that would settle it. She'd have proof she was there, proof it was real. Not for anyone else, just for herself.

She stands up abruptly, alarming the clutch of sparrows. She'll go back. There's nothing to stop her. She'll go back, for proof. It's impossible, of course, there's no such thing as a parallel world at the bottom of the sea. So, what harm can it do to try? At least she'll know.

Leaving the park, Sarah makes her way in the dappled sunlight, absorbed in the audacity of her plan. Charles, she feels certain, would approve. Replicate, that's what he always told his graduate students. Repeat the experiment, do it again, exactly the way you did it the first time. If you get the same results the second time, they're probably valid. Replicate was one of Charles's favorite words.

But does it matter? Sarah smiles. It matters. Xaxanader is right. Everything matters.

She stops at the intersection of Spring and Oxford, waiting for the light to change but only peripherally aware of the traffic. Suddenly, a hand slams hard into her left shoulder, pushing her backward an instant before a careening bus jumps the curb.

Sarah staggers, staring with stunned disbelief as the bus jolts off the footpath and onto the road again, mesmerized by the parallel black marks its huge wheels have left on the concrete. The light changes. The man who pushed her out of the way gives her a jaunty wave, crosses Oxford Street, and disappears into Grace Brothers before Sarah has time to thank him.

She steadies herself against a metal rubbish bin. The lights have changed again, and the ill-tempered river of impatient late-morning traffic resumes its flow along the narrow thoroughfare. If that bus had hit her, she'd be dead. And she'd never know, one way or the other. That would be awful, to die like that, without knowing.

By the time she gets home, she's not so sure. It's all very well to say, I'll go back. But what does that mean? How will she go back? Walk into the ocean, just as she did last time. Swim. Dive. Either it will work, or it won't.

The morning newspaper is still lying on the kitchen table, and Sarah reads her horoscope. Four stars. Mars is in Venus, and this is propitious. However, she must guard against mistaking procrastination for caution.

Well, fine. She'll be careful. She won't drown. She can't drown. She's a vestigant.

BY EARLY AFTERNOON she's back at the beach, barefoot on the wet sand, the ebbing tide sucking gently at her toes. Replication means doing everything exactly as she did it last Tuesday. She's wearing the same sandals, the same bathing suit. She's brought the same towel. (She doesn't have the sunglasses, but there's no help for that.) It's as close as she can get, and it'll have to do.

Wade into the water. Swim out. But it was different, last week. She was different—last week, she wanted to die. All she's trying to do now is prove something. Sarah hesitates, letting a wave wash across her ankles. Isn't this what scientists are always trying to do? Isn't proving things the whole point of science?

It's just past noon, and the sun is blazing down on her bare head. At the horizon, the pewter-colored sea merges seamlessly with the haze and the bleached white sky. The tide is about to turn, sending fretful little waves across the sand.

Sarah wades in, moving confidently through the shallows, feeling with her toes for the sudden dropping away of the shoreline, the abrupt plunge into deeper water. There's no surf, and she begins to swim, just as she did last time, unhurriedly.

After a while she flips over, floating on her back, eyes closed, allowing the gentle swell to wash across her breasts, to lap at her face. It feels as if time has stopped. Licking the salt from her lips, Sarah opens her eyes and gazes up at the sky. There's a single white cloud directly above her head.

What now? Dive, the way she did last time. But she'll need Bantryd.

Closing her eyes again, Sarah attempts to summon Bantryd. I'm here, I'm waiting for you. Come to me, Bantryd. I need you to help me.

When nothing happens, Sarah sighs and opens her eyes. She's not surprised or even dismayed, she didn't really expect Bantryd to materialize at her side. Bantryd doesn't exist. It was a dream, after all, or a fantasy. Her thoughts drift to Xaxanader, to the timbre of his voice, to his improbably blue eyes.

But it seemed so real. Her arms are starting to tire, so Sarah stops swimming and hangs vertical in the water, treading water while she catches her breath. When she turns back, she's mildly alarmed to discover that she can barely see the beach. She can hardly see anything anyway, without her glasses; even so, she'd better not go much farther, or she won't be able to make it in.

Did she really think she could go back to a place that doesn't exist? A wave slaps her mouth with salt—the tide has turned. Beneath the surface of the water, the surge of invisible currents pluck at her legs, evoking the distant sway of plants on the ocean floor, the movement of fish.

Follow me, Bantryd said.

And dived.

Sarah inhales deeply and thrusts herself down, head first, stroking and kicking vigorously, impelling herself into the colder, darker depths. She knows she should have at least a minute's worth of air in her lungs, but seemingly within seconds the need for oxygen, the need to breathe, is overwhelming.

Pressing her lips shut, she clenches the muscles of her jaw while her arms continue to pump and flail. The water has somehow thickened, as if the sea itself is rejecting her. Her hair streams out behind her, combed by the current, and her aching lungs and chest feel as if they're about to burst. She releases a little bit of air through her lips, and this helps, but only for a second or two.

Her legs are leaden, her arms weary. Flashes of white light burst like stars upon the lids of her closed eyes, and she is suddenly bitterly sorry.

Mama's voice in her head is asking, "Can't you do anything right?"

Think about something else. She's drowning, this is the end, she doesn't want her final thought to be about Mama. Think about Charles. Think about Xaxanader.

Sarah is floating away from herself—and suddenly nothing hurts, there's no pain, no pressure. According to old wives' tales, drowning is an easy death. Would I be considered an old wife? She's pondering this when she realizes that she's looking at Xaxanader, staring into his face. Beyond him there are other faces, a veritable sea of faces, a semi-circle of strangers obviously in the midst of something.

My God, I did it. I'm here.

Xaxanader is taller than she remembers, more imposing. And he's important. You can tell by the way the others are looking at him. She's close enough to reach out and touch him but she doesn't dare, is suddenly reluctant even to meet his eyes. The presence of all these other people is unsettling. Simply being here is unsettling. A minute ago, she was in the water. She's still in the water, but it doesn't feel like water.

Nobody speaks or moves. It feels like getting in trouble at school and being sent to the principal's office, waiting to see what they'll do to you. Sarah shifts her weight from one foot to the other, feeling suddenly ungainly, not knowing where to look. This isn't how she thought it would be.

"How *did* you think it would be?" Xaxanader asks.

"I don't know."

She remembers last time, the strange elision between thought and speech that constitutes communication. She must have been thinking out loud. He isn't, though. Xaxanader's mind is closed to her. All their minds are closed. But it doesn't matter what he thinks, what any of them are thinking. She's obviously dreaming again, or hallucinating.

Behind her and to either side, Sarah is aware of murmuring and shuffling. The crowd, she realizes, is retreating, moving quietly and tactfully away.

She continues to look at Xaxanader. His eyes are as vertiginously blue as she remembers them, and his manner is gradually becoming less solemn. It's quite incredible, really.

"Why have you come?"

"I thought if I could come back, it would prove it really happened. But it doesn't. It's not enough." He is silent, waiting. "If I could take something back with me, something from here, that would prove it. But it would have to be something that could only come from here. A pebble, maybe. Or something you've made."

"We don't make things," Xaxanader says slowly. "Ours is a cerebral existence. Artifacts are merely distractions. We have what we need. As for the rest, we try to live intellectually, in our minds. We find it satisfying, even exciting."

That's the way we lived, Charles and I. Xaxanader makes it sound normal, rather than exceptional. Maybe it is normal, here. A cerebral existence. Living intellectually, in your mind.

"It would be wonderful, if it was true."

"It is true."

No, it isn't. It can't be, although Sarah takes pains not to think this thought out loud. She wishes Charles was here. Charles would have been able to explain it to Xaxanader, why none of this can even be happening. Charles had a knack for exegesis. Even when you disagreed with him you had to admire his logic, the way he marshaled his evidence, leaving out the bits that didn't suit him, making his conclusions seem inevitable. Charles could say just about anything and get away with it.

"What is this place?" Sarah asks.

"It's a place for learning. We call it a House, because it houses our Tellings. We gather in Houses to make ourselves aware of things we might not know, or have forgotten. This Telling belonged to my grandfather. Now it's mine."

Sarah looks more closely but sees nothing except sinuous, winding tendrils that remind her of sculpture. Following her gaze, Xaxander smiles. He lays a hand on one of the rising, rope-like tendrils.

"This is old learning." He moves his hand along the surface of the thing, to where a bud seems to swell outward from the main branch. " Go ahead. Touch it." Sarah reaches out, places the tip of her forefinger upon the thing and instantly recoils.

"It's alive."

"All knowledge lives," Xaxanader says. "Here, give me your hand."

Hesitantly, Sarah extends her hand, palm upward. "Open your mind. It can't hurt you. Try again."

She feels his palm warm against the backs of her fingers. She allows him to take her hand in his, to raise it until her fingertips brush the curving, looping branch that seems to have imperceptibly lowered itself so she can more easily reach it. It throbs, beating like a tiny heart against her fingers. Sarah gradually becomes aware of an answering pulse beginning at her fingertips, gathering strength, and radiating through her hand and down her arm. She seems to see large dark angled things, not exactly before her eyes but more like a film playing behind her eyelids. Flames licking toward a shrouded black sky, anguished wails and desperate prayers in a language she doesn't recognize. What she's seeing is an old ship, a wooden ship with sails, sinking in a terrifying sea.

This all happened, Sarah understands. A ship was lost at sea and one of the men on that foundering ship was a vestigant, Xaxanader's grandfather. Sarah is somehow inside his mind, seeing the things he saw and feeling what he felt. But how can that be? Xaxanader's grandfather is dead. Slowly she withdraws her hand.

"That's amazing."

Xaxanader looks pleased.

"But I still don't understand. Are you … some kind of mutation?"

"No, it's the other way around. It was you who left the sea. We stayed. Over many lifetimes, you developed the organs that enable you to survive out of water. But you began here. All life began here."

It's no more incredible than being here in the first place, being able to come and go as she pleases. And Sarah likes the feeling of connectedness and the effortlessness of this world, being able to comprehend rather than apprehend. There's a rhythm to existence, after all, and being attuned to it is like dancing, when you know all the steps. It would be wonderful if it was real—this world, and this way of being in the world. But it isn't real. Of course it isn't.

Sarah frowns. "I'm dreaming. I must be. And when I wake up, I'll be back the real world. My world. And you'll be gone, because you don't exist in the real world."

"The real world? There are as many worlds as there are conscious minds to perceive them. And all of them, and all who inhabit them, are real. Including this world. Including me."

Xaxanader places his hand lightly upon her shoulder, and Sarah doesn't resist, not even when he draws her close to him. It feels good to be held, even in a dream. Nobody has held her since Charles died.

"I wish it was true. I wish I didn't have to wake up."

"You don't."

Reluctant to meet his gaze, she takes a step backward and gazes distractedly past him into the dreamy swirl of tendrils, the insubstantiality. "It was such a waste," she says softly. "We thought we had it all worked out, you know. We thought we were the luckiest people in the world. The children were grown up, Charles was going to put in for early retirement, and we were going to sell our house in Australia and buy one in the Dordogne. And then he died. Charles died. So it was all for nothing, wasn't it?"

"Of course it wasn't. You loved one another, you had time together. Charles was fortunate, but you're even more fortunate because you have the past and your memories, and the future as well."

The future.

"There'll be someone else."

She hesitates but doesn't argue. "Someone else?" Does that happen here, too? Do people in this world fall in love? "You mean you feel the same things we feel?"

"Why not? It all started with us. Love, marriage, babies." He grins mischievously. "Same organs. Same processes."

Before Sarah can think how to respond, Bantryd bursts upon them.

"You came back! Xaxanader said you would!" Bantryd is hugging her now, her long black hair swinging and swirling everywhere, tickling Sarah's nose. Sarah hugs back warmly, meaning it. It's been so long since she felt truly welcome, anywhere. Releasing Sarah, Bantryd whirls around to face Xaxanader. "Is she going to help?"

Sarah glances at Xaxanader. "Help?"

"Bantryd thinks Thasqia—her mother—is still alive and somewhere in your world."

"But what's that got to do with me?"

"I need to go and look for her," Bantryd says. "If she's alive, I'll be able to find her. But I can't go alone. They won't let me." Bantryd is gazing earnestly at Sarah. "Don't you see? That's why I needed to find a vestigant. That's why I needed to find you. Because someone has to help me."

"Why can't Xaxanader help you?"

"Because I'm not a vestigant. Bantryd is the only one left. If we lose her, we lose our ability to interact with your world."

Sarah turns back to him. "You want me to take Bantryd back with me? You can't be serious."

"But why not? It's your world," says Bantryd. "You already live there, you know all about it. And you wouldn't have to do anything, just tell me about things. Like malls, for instance."

Oh, no. It's impossible.

"This is crazy," Sarah tells them. "You're talking about the world as if it's some sort of little village, and it isn't. It's huge. You can't just go looking for people somewhere in the world."

"We're more advanced than you," Xaxanader says. "We have abilities that allow us to do such things."

"No, you don't. Listen to me. The world is enormous. There are continents, there are oceans, there are hundreds of different countries and billions of people. Where would you start?"

"At the beach where I found you." Bantryd's confidence is so unnerving that Sarah waits for Xaxanader to contradict her. He doesn't, and that's even more unnerving. "She was there, I know it. I can feel it, even after all this time. She'll have to return to that beach, to make the transition."

"So why don't you just wait there for her? Why do you need me?"

"Because if she could come back, she would have by now. Maybe she needs help."

"Maybe she's dead," Sarah says.

"I've got to find out."

Sarah understands. And she sympathizes, she does. Uncertainty and hope leave you dangling. And she likes Bantryd and she wants to please Xaxanader, but even so. "It won't work. If I thought it would work, I'd help you. But it won't. You can't just wish your way around the world."

Xaxanader's expression is unreadable.

Bantryd stands looking at her and biting down on her lower lip, wide eyes brimming with tears. Sarah feels guilty— and angry. This is unfair. She can't possibly do what they want her to do. For all their so-called advanced civilization, they haven't a clue, they have no concept of what the world is like, not so much as a conceptual framework into which such an idea might fit. Bantryd probably thinks the world is a beach.

"Besides," Sarah says slowly, "this is only a dream."

"And that's the beauty of it, don't you see? If it's a dream, everything's all right. You can do anything you like in a dream." Xaxanader is smiling, hugely pleased with himself. "Isn't that so?"

He's made an interesting point. And he's right. She can say anything, she can agree to anything, and it won't make a shred of difference because none of this is real. And she wants him to like her, even if it is only a dream.

"All right, then."

With a little shriek of joy, Bantryd flings herself into Xaxanader's arms, jumping and wriggling while he gazes over her head at Sarah, his eyes eloquent. Sarah grins happily back at him. She's made everybody happy. It won't work, of course. But if it's a dream, what does it matter?

"This is for you." Xaxanader opens his hand and looks down at it and Sarah looks too. He's holding a pebble. "I don't know if it's special or not." He places it in the palm of her hand, and she closes her fingers around it. The pebble is small and smooth and hard.

"Okay," Sarah says. "I'll do it. I'll do my best. But what if something goes wrong?"

He ponders this for a moment. "You'll know what's necessary, you'll know what's right. I trust you, Sarah. I trust your instincts. You'll be fine. You'll both be fine. "And as you say, it's only a dream."

Xaxanader moves toward her and for a moment Sarah thinks he's going to take her in his arms again. That's what he wants to do—he's drawn to her, she can feel it. She's drawn to him, too. She hasn't felt like this in years and years. It's wonderful. It's awful. How can she think such things? She loves Charles.

It's a dream, she reminds herself. It doesn't matter, it doesn't count. When she wakes up, she'll be alone. Xaxanader and Bantryd are figments of her imagination, characters she's invented. Charles is real, though. But Charles is dead. She smiles helplessly at Xaxanader.

"It's crazy. You know that, don't you? It's completely crazy."

"Don't worry. It'll be all right. It might be better than all right. In any case, it's only a dream."

And if it isn't?

Chapter Four

The water is warmer than the air, but it's dark, pitch black. That's not right. It shouldn't be dark yet. Disoriented, Sarah treads water, blinking through wet lashes, searching for something familiar—a contour, even a building. She can hear waves breaking, but the darkness is impenetrable. Swimming toward the sound of the waves, she finds herself in shallow water, her knees scraping the sand. She scrambles to her feet, wading through knee-deep water, already shivering.

Behind her the sea heaves and sighs beneath a blank, black sky. Small waves wash across her feet as she makes her way through the soft, cold sand. Is she still asleep? Still dreaming?

Above her head the sky is overcast, with streamers of cloud blocking the moon and stars. Toward the west, city lights cast a dull, reddish glow. She's standing directly in front of the massed contour of the cliff, which rises pitch black against the sootier blackness of the sky. This is no dream. She's awake. She's here, on the beach.

She's never been here at night, not even during the summer months. Nobody comes here at night, except fishermen, because there's no reason to come here after dark. It's not that kind of beach; there are no barbecues, no shelters, not even any lights. Occasionally, there's a party at the Surf Lifesaving Club at the top of the cliff, but not tonight.

A brisk wind gusts intermittently off the water, and Sarah hugs herself, hands and arms still wet, the fabric of her bathing suit clammy against her skin. She needs to find her towel and her glasses, and the keys to the house. Cautiously, she moves toward the rocks.

But something happened. Something must have happened. I'm here on the beach, in the middle of the night. And there's a pebble in my hand. I'm holding a pebble. Obviously, something happened.

The wind picks up. Sarah turns her back to it and hunches her shoulders together, which doesn't help. She needs to find her towel and the rest of her stuff.

It worries her that she can't see where she's going in the dark. People leave all kinds of rubbish lying around in the sand and if she steps on a piece of broken glass, it'll be nasty. But she can't stay out here in the cold, either. She makes her way a cautious step at a time, guided by the phosphorescence of the breaking waves and the murmur of water against rock.

She begins to relax—and stubs her toe. It's her big toe, the one she broke ice skating when she was twelve, and the stab of pain is disproportionate, leaving her breathless. You wouldn't think a toe could hurt so much.

The cliffs loom above her head, black on black. And then icy fingers catch hold of her hand in the darkness.

"Where did you go? Why did you leave me? Oh, I'm cold, I'm so cold. Is it always as cold as this in your world?"

It can't be. Not here, not now, not when everything else is normal.

"This isn't what's supposed to happen," Sarah says. But she doesn't pull away. She allows Bantryd's cold fingers to close around hers, even gives them a reassuring squeeze.

"What do you mean?" Bantryd's voice is reedy, uncertain. "What's not supposed to happen?"

"Nothing. Everything's fine. And I didn't leave you. I've been right here, waiting for you. Come on, now. I've got to find my stuff, my keys. Otherwise, we won't be able to get into the house."

"I'm too cold. And it's dark. I can't see anything. I didn't know it was going to be like this. I didn't know it would be dark."

"It's night, that's all. It's always dark at night. And this was your idea, you know. So, come on!"

"I don't want to. I can't see."

"Wait here, then." Sarah disengages herself. "I'll just be a couple of minutes. Stay right here. Don't move. I'll be right back."

It's only a few more steps to the base of the cliff. More confident now, Sarah drops to her knees and gropes in the sand, feeling through the rock niche for her bundled towel. It's not here. Take your time. Don't panic. It's here, it has to be here. Searching systematically, Sarah feels her way through all the rocks down to the water's edge, and then back again.

"Where are you? I can't see you!"

"I'm right over here. And stop shouting. I told you, I have to find my keys."

Bantryd seems to have settled down upon the sand, a motionless lump in the darkness. Of course, the lump might not be Bantryd at all. It could be a rubbish bin; it could be anything.

Feeling around in the dark like this is futile. Better to leave it be. She'll come back tomorrow, when it's light. She can manage without the keys. They'll be able to get in through the unlocked bathroom window at the back of the house.

It does annoy her to leave without her glasses. That's two pair she's lost in less than a week. Now the only ones left are the awful tortoise shells the Dior guy talked her into buying, insisting that they made her look interesting.

"All right. We're going." Bantryd's fingers are like icicles. "Come on. It'll be warmer once we get off the beach."

They trudge along silently, the sea a diminishing grumble behind them. Halfway up the beach, the streetlights from the road become visible, welcoming bursts of yellow in the darkness. It's already perceptibly warmer, even though they haven't even reached the esplanade.

"Hold onto the railing," Sarah says. "These are steps. You have to climb them. Pick up your feet."

Bantryd is panting slightly, and trembling with fear or cold. "Is it much farther?"

"We've still got a bit of a walk, maybe twenty minutes. But it won't be so cold once we've gone a few blocks inland. Come on."

The brick cottages that line the far side of the street are dark and still, but there are no parked cars along the curb, and there's no traffic. Sarah and Bantryd move like ghosts through the sleeping suburb, their bare feet soundless upon the cold concrete pavement. Maybe she is still dreaming, after all.

"Look! What's that?"

Ahead of them, a car has rounded the corner and is coming slowly down the street, its headlights two bright circles of light that grow slowly larger and brighter.

Bantryd clutches at Sarah's hand.

"What is it? What is that thing?"

"It's nothing. It's just a car."

Twin shafts of blinding light suddenly envelop them, and Bantryd moans. Blinking in the glare, Sarah sees more lights, red and blue. A patrol car, making its rounds. And Bantryd is terrified.

"Bantryd, it's all right. Just calm down. It's only a police car."

The car moves unhurriedly to the side of the road and stops at the curb, a few steps ahead of them. Sarah approaches it, unperturbed. They're probably wondering what she's doing out in the middle of the night. Well, so what? There's no law against being out in the middle of the night.

"Everything all right, ladies?"

"Everything's fine."

"Been for a swim, have you?"

"Yes, we have. It was lovely, in the water. It's been such a hot day." She pauses, but he doesn't say anything further. "We were just on our way home."

"On your way home. Bit late in the night to be swimming. No law against it, though." He's looking past her, at Bantryd. "Just you and the young lady here?"

Sarah turns toward Bantryd and tries not to stare, or to react in any way to the fact that Bantryd is stark naked.

"Yes, just the two of us."

"Wouldn't happen to have a bit of identification on you?" He can see that neither of them is carrying anything. Sarah feels suddenly conscious of her body, her bare arms and legs.

The officer waits, his back to the headlights and his face in shadow, one hand resting lightly on his holstered gun.

"No, I left my bag and things at home. It was hot, and I couldn't sleep. So I thought, I'll just go for a swim and cool off. You know, on the spur of the moment. I didn't think I'd need identification."

She's talking too much, she's babbling like someone who's done something wrong.

"At home, you say. Where's home, then? Anywhere near here?"

"Patrick Street. Number twenty."

"And your name?"

"Sarah Andrews."

"Hang on a tick." He turns away from them and leans back into the car, says something to his partner, who's still sitting behind the wheel. Sarah hears the crackle of a radio, disembodied voices. The policeman looks back at them. "Won't take a minute," he says, then slides back into the car, leaving the door ajar.

"Do we have to stay here?" Bantryd asks.

"Yes. We do."

"Why?"

"Because they told us to, and they're the police."

"What will they do to us?"

"Nothing."

"Then why can't we run away?"

"Because you don't run away from the police unless you're a criminal. Just be quiet, Bantryd. It'll be all right."

Inside the patrol car, a conversation is concluding. The second policeman nods, opens the door, and heaves himself onto the pavement, walking ponderously around the front of the car to come to a stop directly in front of Sarah, too close.

"Sarah Andrews. That's your name, right? Sarah Andrews."

She nods, somewhat bewildered by his apparent incredulity. She isn't a film star or a fugitive or a politician's mistress. There's nothing exceptional about being Sarah Andrews.

"Look, I don't understand. What's this all about?"

"What it's about is that Sarah Andrews's daughter reported her missing a few days ago."

"My daughter? But that's ridiculous. And I'm not missing. I'm right here."

"In that case, I'm sure your daughter will be pleased to see you. If you're really Sarah Andrews, that is." He turns back to the car, opening one of the back doors. The little light mounted on the ceiling inside the car comes on, illuminating the gray upholstery. "Right now, we're going to need you to come with us, Sarah."

She hates it when strangers use her first name, implicitly suggesting equality and friendship. Mateship, Australians call it. In fact, it's a kind of intimidation.

"Why? Am I under arrest?"

"Under arrest? Why would we want to arrest you, Sarah? You haven't murdered anyone, have you? Or robbed a bank?" The headlights are blinding her, so she can't see his face, can't tell if he's joking.

"Then why do you want me to come with you?" But she knows why. It's Bantryd.

"Just get in the vehicle, Sarah. We'll drop you off home, so you can call your daughter and tell her you're all right."

"Look, that's very kind of you. But it's not far, only a few blocks. I think I'd rather walk."

"We need for you to get into the vehicle."

Sarah and Bantryd sit side by side in the back seat of the patrol car, closer to one another than necessary, their hips and shoulders touching. Bantryd is still trembling. Sarah realizes that she's still clutching the pebble.

How could she have not noticed that Bantryd wasn't wearing anything? It was dark, but even so. How had she missed something like that? Sarah frowns, thinking back. Has she ever seen Bantryd wearing clothes? Not clothes, not exactly. But she wasn't naked. None of them were naked— not Xaxanader, none of them. Not naked, but not clothed, either. How can that be? How can any of this be? She looks down at the pebble. It's there in her hand, it's real. *All of it is real.*

The car slows, turns right, and Sarah forces herself to pay attention. "Excuse me, but you're going the wrong way. Patrick Street is down there, to the left."

"We're stopping at the station for a tick. Nothing for you to worry about." Sarah gazes at the backs of their heads, uncertain as to which one of them is speaking. "We need to ask you a few questions, and there are a couple of things you need to sign. Makes more sense to get it all cleared up now, don't you think? Saves you a trip back in the morning."

"I don't mind. I'd rather come back in the morning."

Neither of them replies.

The area in front of the police station is bathed in yellow light. Newly planted saplings in the nature strips on either side of the footpath cast mauve shadows across Bantryd's bare back and shoulders as she walks slowly along the path, guided by one of the officers. The other officer remains with Sarah, slowing his pace so they fall several steps behind, his hand light on her forearm. Two policewomen suddenly emerge from the shadows and take hold of Bantryd's arms, one on each side.

"Wait a minute!" The officer's grip upon her arm tightens, holding Sarah back. "But what are they doing? Where are they taking her?"

Bantryd is already being marched through the swinging glass doors. "Don't worry." Still holding her arm, he moves in front of her, blocking her view. "Nobody's going to hurt her. She'll be fine."

She can't stop them. They're the police. They can do whatever they like. This isn't the United States. People don't have rights here. The police officer steps to one side and releases her arm, but Bantryd is already gone. The officer takes a step toward the door.

"Come on, then." The inside of the police station is brightly lit, and now Sarah can see both their faces. They're very young, not much older than Sean. There's no sign of the policewomen or of Bantryd. "We just need you to come this way."

She's ushered into a large, rather bare room bisected by a high counter. There are chairs set along a wall and a door at the far end of the counter. The policemen walk her past the chairs and through the door into a longish corridor lined with smaller doors, most of which are closed. At the far end of the corridor they enter a windowless room furnished with a desk, chairs, and a cheap wooden bookcase. There's a computer on the desk, and the round clock on the wall shows 4 a.m.

"If you'd just like to take a seat." Sarah sits down, and the younger of the two policemen closes the door behind them. "Now we just have to wait for Constable Wysincky. Won't be a tick."

The door opens again, and a policewoman enters. She looks like one of the pair that took Bantryd, but Sarah can't be sure. "I'm Constable Wysincky." She sits down at the desk opposite Sarah, crossing her legs. She has thick ankles and is wearing flesh-colored cotton hose and sensible black lace-up shoes.

The two male officers ask questions, taking turns. Name. Address. Place of business. "I'm not working at the moment," Sarah tells them.

It isn't so bad, and she begins to relax. She can't blame them, not under the circumstances. They're only doing their job, after all. But she doesn't understand why they keep asking the same questions.

"I told you. It was hot, and I couldn't sleep, so I went to the beach for a swim."

"And where were you before that?"

"I was at home. I just told you."

"You were at home. You're sure about that."

"Of course I'm sure."

"Then why does your daughter reckon you've been missing since Tuesday?"

Since Tuesday? But it *is* Tuesday, or rather, it's Wednesday, Wednesday morning. Even so. She opens her mouth, then closes it again. "I honestly don't know."

"You know where you are now, don't you?"

"Of course I know where I am. I'm in a police station."

He riffles through some papers in a cardboard folder, frowning. "According to your daughter's statement, you haven't answered your phone since Tuesday. And yesterday, you apparently didn't show up for a doctor's appointment. You'd never do a thing like that, your daughter said. You're very reliable. If you're going to miss an appointment, you always telephone. So she went round to your place to make sure you were all right, and you weren't there. Your handbag was there, and your car. Your daughter said it was all very strange, out of character."

Sarah frowns, trying to make sense of it. They must be referring to her regular session with Kahn, but that can't be right. She's not due to see Kahn until Friday.

"We can give her a call, if you like." Sarah looks blankly up at him. "Your daughter, I mean. We can ring her up right now and you can talk to her and tell her you're all right."

Sarah shakes her head. "No, don't do that. I think there must have been some kind of mix-up. I haven't been missing. But you know, now that I think of it, I haven't been home a lot, either. I go for walks. I lost my husband, you know. And it helps. Walking, I mean."

He nods sympathetically at this, glancing down at the folder for confirmation. "That's what it says here. That's why your daughter was upset. She was worried about your state of mind." All three of them are staring at her, their eyes wide and young. "She said you took your husband's death pretty hard. She was afraid something had happened to you. I'll tell you what, she'll be that relieved, knowing you're safe and sound." He lifts the receiver of the telephone and holds it out to Sarah. "Tell her yourself."

"No," Sarah says quickly. "It's too late. She's a journalist, she works until midnight. She'll have just gone to bed. I'll ring her later in the morning." They can't keep her here. She hasn't done anything wrong. Felicity has reported her missing, but being missing isn't a crime. "I'm tired, I'm really tired. I'd like to go home now." Nobody objects. Nobody says anything. "I'm sorry for all this trouble. It's probably my fault.

But honestly, it was just a breakdown in communication. It didn't occur to me that Felicity would worry. It should have, I suppose. But I haven't really been myself lately." They're looking at her, frowning, trying to make up their minds. "We weren't doing anything wrong, you know. I mean, it isn't a crime to go skinny dipping, is it?"

They look at one another. Sarah waits. "Not a crime, no. Who is she, anyway? How did the two of you happen to be together?"

"I don't know her name. I only just met her."

Bantryd needs a cover story, but Sarah can't think of anything to say that mightn't make things worse. Besides, she's never been much good at lying. Better to stick to the truth, as much as possible.

"Any idea what she's been taking?"

"Taking? You mean drugs? I don't know, I don't think she's taking drugs." Carefully, now. Bantryd has no clothes, no I.D., and no idea of this world. You don't know what she might have told them. "I mean, she didn't act high, or anything like that. She seemed perfectly normal to me."

"So you don't actually know her."

"She was just there, on the beach." Sarah tries to think of something that will sound plausible. "We sort of struck up a conversation. I mean, there we were—the two of us, alone on a beach in the middle of the night. It seemed like a natural thing to do. Talking to one another, I mean. I said I couldn't sleep, and she said she couldn't sleep, either. She'd just had a row with her boyfriend, walked out on him. She didn't have any place to go, so she was going to stay on the beach all night. She said she had friends nearby but didn't want to wake them up in the middle of the night. I felt sorry for her, so I said she could stay at my place." Sarah pauses again, trying to get a sense of how all this is sounding. "Just for the night, just until morning. And you know, the offer still stands. I'm quite happy to take her home with me, let her spend the night. So it's not as if she hasn't got someplace to go."

"What happened to her clothes?"

"I don't know. It was dark. I couldn't really see, but I just assumed she was wearing a bikini or something. I didn't realize she was . . . "

"So you don't know her name and you don't know where she lives. She's just a kid you met on the beach."

The three of them look at one another, then back at Sarah. Some sort of signal has clearly passed among them, a decision has been made. Sarah continues to sit quietly, hands folded in her lap, giving them no reason to suspect anything amiss.

Constable Wysincky speaks for the first time since introducing herself. There's nothing wrong with taking a midnight dip, she tells Sarah. Nothing at all. "I've done it myself. But you've got to try and see things from our point of view. We're just doing our job here. We don't want a repeat of what happened last Christmas."

There were riots last Christmas. Gangs from the western suburbs surged unchecked through the streets of Bondi Beach and Waverley, throwing bricks and smashing windscreens. Nothing like that had ever happened in Sydney before. Sarah frowns slightly, unable to see the connection.

Constable Wysincky says she's sure Sarah appreciates the situation. Now that everything's been cleared up, of course she's free to go. "But promise me something. Promise me you'll give your daughter a ring later this morning. My mum lives by herself too. And I know how I'd feel if I thought she'd gone missing."

Sarah promises, thinking that Constable Wysincky's mother is fortunate to have a daughter who cares about her. They stand up like actors at the end of a scene, and all three of them accompany her back to the entrance of the police station. Through the glass doors, Sarah notices that the sky has grown perceptibly lighter.

"I was just wondering, what's going to happen to the girl?" The officers remain silent, watchful. "Look, I'm sure she wasn't taking drugs. I've got children of my own, I know how it is. She was upset, that's all. She'd just broken up with her boyfriend. Why not let her come home with me? I've got plenty of room. And besides, it's almost morning. In a couple of hours I'll get her to call her parents, and we can sort things out."

They seem to be considering this.

Then Constable Wysincky says she's sorry, but it's out of the question. "We can't just let her go, not in the circumstances. And as you say, you're a parent yourself. So you can understand our concern."

"Can I at least talk to her? Just for a minute?"

"I really don't think that would be wise. Don't worry, she's in good hands. She'll be fine."

Sarah gazes at the floor. Police custody isn't what she'd describe as being in good hands, but she knows better than to say so.

One of the male officers says, "Most likely, it's not true— all that about breaking up with her boyfriend. I reckon she's a runaway. Probably heading for the Cross and got lost. We see a lot of them, especially at this time of year. Christmas, you know. They want to stick it to their parents." He compresses his lips, thrusts out his chin. "And if you don't mind me saying so, I don't think it's very bright, inviting a total stranger into your house. Look, I know you mean well. People like you always do. But you don't stop to think." Sarah tries to look respectful. "You don't know what this kid has done, you don't know what she's been taking, you don't know shit, if you'll pardon the expression. She might be working with someone, did you ever think of that? You take her into your home, she waits until your back is turned and then bashes your head in. It happens."

"But there wasn't anyone with her on the beach. And she didn't act like someone on drugs, either. She was just upset."

He shrugs. "The thing is, you don't know, do you? So why not play it safe? Let Community Services sort it out. That's what they're there for, all those shrinks and social workers. They're professionals. They know how to handle situations like this."

"I really would like to see her," Sarah says.

"I'm sorry. It's not possible."

"Why? Where is she? You didn't arrest her, did you?"

"She's in protective custody, that's all. It'll only be for a couple of hours, until Community Services sends someone over here to fetch her."

"And then what?"

He looks across at Constable Wysincky, who nods and says that really, it depends. "Once we hand them over to Community Services, we don't usually see them again. And that's generally a good thing, because it means that whatever the problem was, it's sorted. If she's a runaway, I expect they'll get her some clothes and give her a feed and a bus ticket back to wherever she came from."

They won't do that, they can't. There aren't any busses back to where Bantryd came from. But Sarah can't say that, can't say anything. It would be insane to argue with them when they're so close to letting her go. She hates leaving Bantryd behind, but she needs to think. She needs a plan.

"Will you at least do me a favor?" They look at her, non-committal. "If there's a problem, if there's anything I can do, will you call me? You already have the number, don't you?" The male officer looks at Constable Wysincky, who nods. "And give her my number too. That girl. Tell her that if she needs anything to just call. Will you do that? Please?"

(((◎

OUTSIDE, IT'S PLEASANTLY COOL. The sky is luminous, opalescent, like the choker of seed pearls Charles bought her for their twentieth anniversary; its clasp fashioned to look like the head of a Chinese dragon, gold with ruby eyes.

Constable Wysincky accompanies them to the patrol car and opens the door so Sarah can climb in, solicitously warning her to mind her head. One of the young policemen slides in beneath the steering wheel, buckles his seat belt and turns the key in the ignition. The pebble nestles in Sarah's closed left hand like a talisman.

Sarah wonders what the neighbors will think, seeing her brought home at dawn in a patrol car. She doesn't really care what they think, she hardly knows them. In any case, they're probably asleep. The patrol car turns onto Patrick Street behind the newspaper delivery boy, who weaves precariously down the center of the narrow street on his motorbike, tossing paper batons over brick walls and through gates.

They stop in front of her house and Sarah climbs out. She thanks the young policeman, unlatches her front gate, and even manages a cheerful wave as the car finally moves slowly away down the street.

To her bemusement, there are four newspapers lying in front of the door, each sheathed in green plastic. Sarah gathers them up, holding them awkwardly in her arms, like kindling. She can read the dates through the plastic wrapping—Wednesday, Thursday, Friday, Saturday. Four newspapers, four days. It wasn't a dream. It may have been a hallucination. But whatever it was, it lasted four days. Whatever it was.

The door is locked. There's a wrought iron grille over the front window, but it's always locked and bolted too, for good measure. Sarah puts the newspapers down on the doormat and opens the gate again, peering out to make certain the patrol car has gone. It wouldn't do for the police to see her climbing into a back window of her house.

The sun still isn't up, but you can already tell it's going to be another hot day. Sarah makes her way around to the back alley and the rear entrance to her property, a splintering wooden gate set into the brick wall and secured by a bolt latch. Reaching over the top of the gate, she slides the bolt, and the gate opens. It's ridiculous, all these locks and bolts. Anybody could get in if they really wanted to.

If the bathroom window is locked, she'll break it. But it isn't, she hardly ever locks it. Hoisting herself up onto the window ledge, bare legs scraping against the bricks, she pushes the window as wide as it will go and wriggles through.

She's still holding the pebble. She looks at it for a moment before placing it thoughtfully on the glass shelf above the sink, next to her toothbrush. It's just an ordinary pebble. It could have come from anywhere.

Four days?

The house is dim and still, and an unpleasant odor emanates from the bin beneath the sink. Walking briskly through the two small rooms, Sarah opens the front door and picks up the newspapers. Back in the kitchen, she fills a coffee maker with water, fits a filter into the carriage, and spoons in coffee. As soon as she throws the switch, the water begins to hiss. Charles used to call it the Instant Gratification Coffee Pot.

She supposes she should be hungry, but she's not. Even so, she opens the refrigerator. There's some bread and butter, some jam. She could make toast. Coffee, toast, and jam is what she usually has for breakfast. But she doesn't want anything.

The coffee is trickling into the glass carafe and there's already enough to fill a mug. Returning to the front room, Sarah sits down on the sofa and tears the plastic covering off the fattest of the newspapers. It's the Saturday paper, bloated with five sections of classified advertising.

Today's paper. How can that be? How can any of this be happening?

Sarah sits quietly, looking at the newspaper. Some of the ink has come off on her hands. She smoothes the first section flat and looks more closely at the date on the masthead. Then she opens the other three, already knowing what she'll find. Wednesday, Thursday, Friday. In the kitchen, the coffee maker heaves a final sigh and goes quiet. Moving carefully, as if she's recovering from an injury, Sarah returns to the kitchen and pours herself a second cup of coffee.

Four days.

Clasping the coffee mug in both hands, taking comfort from its warmth, she stands still, thinking. All of this is happening, all of this is real. It isn't a dream. She raises the mug to her lips but the newly-poured coffee is too hot to drink. She looks back at the newspapers scattered across the floor.

The telephone rings, but Sarah doesn't move. Six rings, seven, eight. Who could it possibly be at this hour of the morning? It must be the police, calling about Bantryd. Or perhaps it is Bantryd. Oh, my God. Spilling coffee across her legs and bare feet, Sarah lunges for the phone and snatches the receiver from its cradle.

"Mum? It's me, Felicity. Mum, where have you been? The police just called me. How could you do this? How could you just disappear?"

The spilled coffee is spreading in a widening amber pool across the floorboards. Damn the police. Why can't they just mind their own business?

"I was half out of my mind, Mum. I mean, what was I supposed to do if you didn't come back? Who'd pay your bills?" Anger crackles like static electricity at the edges of Felicity's words. "What if you were dead?"

"Well, I'm not."

"But where were you?"

"I needed a break."

"From what? You don't do anything. You just sit around in that house all day." Sarah remains silent. "Fine. You needed a break. You might have at least told me where you were going."

The pool of spilled coffee has lengthened into an oblong liquid amoeba slanting along the floorboards toward the fireplace. None of the surfaces are completely level in these old houses, none of the walls are square.

"Since when do I tell you everything I do? And calling the police, what was that about?"

"Well, what did you expect me to do? You could have been lying dead somewhere, for all I knew. Where were you, Mum? It's been *four days*."

Sarah hates to lie, not because it's bad, but because it requires effort and concentration, and she's not good at it.

"Where have I been? But I told you, Felicity. Yes, I did. I'm sure of it. I left a message on your machine."

"On what machine?"

"At work, I think."

"I haven't got a machine at work."

"Well, maybe it wasn't a machine. Maybe it was a person I spoke to, a secretary or something. But I did leave a message for you. Didn't you get it?"

"No."

"They must have forgotten."

"Mum, it's a newspaper and I'm a reporter. They don't forget to give us our messages."

"Maybe they didn't think it was important. I did say I was your mother. So they knew it wasn't about a story. I just said to tell you that I was going away for a few days and that I'd be back on Saturday. And it's Saturday, and I'm back."

"But where did you go?"

"Just down the coast."

"How did you get there? You didn't take your car. You didn't take your handbag, either."

"I'm tired, Felicity. I've been up all night. We'll talk about it later."

"I don't want to talk about it later!" Felicity sounds teary, but that doesn't mean she's hurt, or even sad. Felicity only cries when she's angry. "I already know what happened, anyhow." Sarah sips at her coffee, silent. "They just told me. They said they found you wandering around in your bathing suit, barefoot. You told them you'd been swimming. And you were with some freaked-out naked street kid. Mum, what's going on?"

"She wasn't a street kid. And she wasn't freaked out, either."

"So who was she?"

"Just someone I met."

"Met where?"

"On the beach."

Sarah holds the receiver at arm's length. Now she can hear the crackle and hiss of Felicity's voice, but the words themselves are inaudible. Bantryd has probably never seen a telephone. Or clothes, for that matter. Sarah shouldn't have abandoned her, even if it meant getting arrested.

"Felicity, I'm tired. I'm going to bed."

Sarah hangs up, then reaches over and pulls out the cord. The deep, cold silence of early morning envelops her. Everyone is still asleep, even the birds are sleeping. The boy who delivers the newspapers must get up very early, but he's probably used to it. You can get used to anything.

UPSTAIRS, HER UNMADE BED is cold in the gray morning light. Sarah crawls between the sheets, shivering and pulling the comforter up around her shoulders, burrowing beneath it, cupping her hands and breathing into them for warmth. None of it could have happened, and it did. Maybe it was some kind of psychotic break, maybe she's going mad. But she doesn't feel mad. The police didn't think she was mad. This must be what it's like for people who are kidnapped by aliens. Nobody believes you. You don't even believe yourself.

How do such people cope? How is she supposed to cope? And what about Bantryd? Sarah rolls over on her back, staring wretchedly at the shadowed ceiling. What in God's name am I going to do about Bantryd?

THE ROOM IS FULL OF LIGHT, and she's perspiring beneath the bedclothes. Sarah kicks off the comforter and squints at the clock on her bedside table. It's already nearly eleven, but there's nothing she has to do on Saturday mornings, so it doesn't matter.

Downstairs, newspapers are scattered across the floor like area rugs: Wednesday, Thursday, Friday, and Saturday. It wasn't a dream.

(((©_

THE COFFEE SHE MADE EARLIER is still hot in the carafe. Sarah pours some of it into a clean mug and sips it at the little table. She's still in her bathing suit. She needs to get dressed so she can go find Bantryd. She drains her mug and goes back upstairs, where she rummages half-heartedly through the rumpled clothes on the floor of her closet, extracting a pair of jeans and a shirt. She must remember to do the laundry before her next appointment with Kahn.

The jeans are tight, and she has to suck in her breath to do up the zip. That's how she found out she was pregnant with Felicity. All of a sudden, none of her clothes fit. But she's not pregnant, she can't be. All of that's finished.

In the bathroom, Sarah peers at her reflection in the mirror over the sink, thinking that her face looks rounder. This is extraordinary, because if it's really Saturday, she hasn't eaten since Tuesday. The pebble is still where she left it, on the glass shelf next to her toothbrush. Sarah touches it. It's just a pebble. No, it's not.

As soon as she plugs the telephone back in, the green light on the answering machine begins to blink furiously. Was it blinking last night? She can't remember, doesn't care.

They won't harm Bantryd, they wouldn't dare. They'll give her clothes, they'll give her something to eat, they'll lock her in a cell. She'll be frightened. Anyone would be frightened. But she's not in any danger. There won't be anyone from Community Services around, not on a Saturday. So it's all right, there's still time.

Bantryd was naked, but what of it? Being naked isn't any kind of crime. It's not like robbing a bank, or stabbing someone. What if she were to go back there, right now? What if she simply offered to take Bantryd home? A jail is no place for a young girl. She'll even offer to post bail, if they insist. Just until Monday, just until someone from Community Services can take over. Yes, and that's what she'll say. Surely, they'll agree that what she's proposing is a better idea than keeping a frightened young girl behind bars all weekend.

She shouldn't have just walked away like that last night. She should have known the police wouldn't call her back. It's just that everything happened so fast. Never mind. There's still time to fix it.

The police station is only a few blocks away and police stations are always open, the way churches used to be. There's nothing to fear, not in broad daylight. And it feels good to be walking, to be out of the house. Sarah doesn't recognize the young man sitting behind the counter, the shift must have changed.

"I was here a few hours ago, there was a young girl with me. They took us into different rooms, and they asked me a few questions, and then they took me home. But I don't know what happened to the girl." The young man gives her a blank look. "I was just wondering. Is she all right?" The young man is Constable Ames. It's on his badge. He still looks blank. "I don't think she has any place to go. To stay, I mean. But she's welcome to stay with me, and I was thinking, maybe you could tell her that."

His Adam's apple goes up and down, and Sarah tries not to stare at it. Finally, he places both of his hands flat on the counter in front of him and pushes himself to a standing position. He asks her to wait and goes out through the door that leads to the warren of corridors and offices.

They've probably got cameras. Someone is probably watching her every move, so Sarah concentrates on looking unconcerned, even nonchalant. She's an ordinary, middle-aged woman trying to do the right thing. For all they know, she's somebody's grandmother, somebody's nana. That's what they call grandmothers here—Nana. Like the dog in Peter Pan. Where have they hidden the camera? In the ceiling, probably. Disguised as a light fitting.

There's a big round clock on the far wall with black hands that move convulsively, a minute at a time. She gazes at it. There's nothing unusual about looking at a clock, especially when you're waiting. Finally Constable Ames returns and gives Sarah a bright, satisfied look.

"They've taken her to hospital," he says.

"But why? There was nothing wrong with her. Where did they take her? Which hospital?"

"Northside Community, I reckon. That's where they usually take them." He offers a tentative smile. "I don't really know much about it. I just came on duty a few minutes ago. But I'll tell you what. Why don't you ring the hospital and ask them?"

Sarah thanks him for his help.

Walking home, she feels disembodied, not quite inside her skin. The colors seem too bright, the sounds too loud. She would like to press a button on a remote, turn down the volume.

Schoolboys on skateboards surge toward her, dividing, clattering past, and then coming effortlessly together again like a school of fish. Sarah stops at a bakery, buys a fruit scone and bites into it, but finds she's still not hungry. It seems a shame to throw it away, a waste of good food, so she puts it back into its brown paper sack.

The green light on her answering machine is still blinking, will go on blinking forever. Sarah is sorry she ever bought the thing. It was Felicity's idea. "If you won't get a cell phone," Felicity said, "the least you can do is have an answering machine. People have to be able to reach you."

Surely there must be a way to erase the messages without having to actually listen to them. A book of instructions came with the machine, in five languages, but Sarah can't remember where she put it.

How difficult can it be? Sarah thinks for a moment, and selects Delete. Nothing happens. She presses Delete again, holding it down for several seconds. The green light continues to blink. Sarah looks balefully at the machine, reminding herself that it's only a mechanical device, it doesn't have feelings. Turn it off, destroy its memory. But when she turns it back on, the light starts blinking again.

She selects Play. You have seven new messages, the machine says.

The first three messages are from Felicity. Delete, delete, delete.

"Hi, Sarah." It's not Felicity. It's a man. Sarah stares at the machine in mild astonishment. She doesn't know any men, except Kahn. "It's me, Brian Masters. You've had my profile for a few days now, so I thought I'd give you a call and set up a time for us to meet. I'm thinking dinner, maybe this Saturday night. There's a decent Thai place on Oxford Street, probably not far from where you live. It's called the Bangkok Wok. Do you know it?" Sarah has walked past it, but she's never been inside. She hasn't had a meal in a restaurant since Charles died. "Let's say seven. At the Bangkok Wok. If that doesn't work for you, give me a bell. Otherwise, see you Saturday. Looking forward to it."

Delete.

The fifth message is from Felicity. If she hasn't heard from Sarah by six o'clock, she's going to call the police. Delete. Then a message from Kahn, wondering if she forgot their appointment. Delete.

Felicity, again. "All right, Mum. I've just been to the police. I filed a Missing Persons report. Just so you know, all right? Everybody's really worried." Felicity doesn't sound worried, she sounds furious. "I don't know what you think you're doing, Mum. I really don't." Delete.

Sarah sits motionless, listening to the whirr as the tiny tape inside the mechanism rewinds itself.

Brian Masters. She'll have to call him back and cancel. Presumably, his profile includes his telephone number. She remembers the large envelope, although she didn't bother to open it.

Life was simpler before they invented all these machines. People rang you up and if you weren't home, they rang back later. They didn't just make appointments and expect you to keep them. Although maybe she should go. Sarah paces restlessly through the two little rooms and back into the kitchen, trying to work out what to say to this Brian Masters person. She doesn't want to have dinner with him tonight. She doesn't want to have dinner with anyone. She wants to find out what happened to Bantryd.

Her eye falls on the magnetized card from Local Council on the front of her refrigerator. Emergency Telephone Numbers. Police. Fire. Ambulance. Northside Community Hospital.

Taking the card with her, Sarah returns to the living room and dials. A mechanized voice says, "You have reached Northside Community Hospital, a modern health care facility dedicated to the welfare and well-being of the community it is proud to serve. Please listen carefully, as our menu has recently changed. This call may be monitored for educational or training purposes."

A different voice. "For an emergency, press one. For billing inquiries, press two. For admissions, press three. For the main nursing station, press four. For Intensive Care, press five."

Five.

"I'm looking for someone who was admitted last night," she says. "Well, this morning, actually. A young girl. I don't know her name."

"One moment." Sarah waits. "Sorry. We didn't have any admissions last night. But you know, your friend might still be down in Emergency. Hold on, and I'll transfer you."

"Emergency."

Sarah repeats her request.

"Are you a relative?"

"No, I'm a friend."

"Sorry. We can't give out patient information to anyone except relatives."

"But I just want to know if she's there!"

"Sorry."

Wandering back out to the kitchen, Sarah opens the refrigerator and pours a glass of white wine. It's five o'clock somewhere, that's what Charles would have said. At the far end of the house, she can still see the newspapers strewn across the floor—four days' worth.

If Bantryd hadn't been naked, the police would probably have let them alone. Has Bantryd ever worn clothes? Sarah frowns, trying to remember. She rememers Bantryd's face, her shining eyes, her long hair. But not clothes. What about

Xaxanader? She feels her face getting warm. No clothes. But not naked, either. How can that be? How can any of it be?

Sarah puts her empty glass in the sink with the rest of the dirty dishes. Telephoning is useless. She'll go there in person, to Northside Community.

But she can't find her car keys. They're not on the table, and they're not hanging on the hook where they belong—of course. Her keys are still wrapped in a towel, on the beach. Her glasses, too. Never mind. She can walk to Northside, it's only at the south end of Randwick Road, just past the Catholic school.

It's hot now, and humid as well. The Saturday morning traffic, heaving and belching exhaust fumes, makes it worse. Sarah has never walked through this part of town and is surprised to find so many little shops so close to Bondi Junction. It's a longish walk, farther than she thought, and her shirt is damp by the time she reaches the hospital grounds.

Emergency is located at the end of a long driveway that loops beneath an avenue of eucalyptus at the rear of the main hospital building. Finally pushing open the heavy, double glass doors, Sarah enters a large, empty room. At least it's air conditioned in here. But the place appears to be deserted. It's Emergency. Surely there must be some kind of bell, or buzzer.

"You looking for somebody?" A man in a white uniform and white rubber-soled shoes has come up behind her, silent as a cat.

"A girl. The police brought her in, a few hours ago." Sarah pauses. "Her name might be Bantryd."

"Yeah, that'd be right. Never heard a name like that before, but she's not here."

"Where is she, then?"

"Who wants to know?"

"Please. I really need to find her." Sarah smiles hopefully. "Please," she says again. "I am just in so much trouble. I promised her mother I'd keep an eye on her, but she's a real handful. When she didn't come down for breakfast this morning, I thought she was still in bed, but when I went up to wake her, she was gone. Well, I don't know what to do. Her mother will be back in a few hours and what am I going to tell her? When I finally called the police, they said she was here."

"Yeah, she was. And I'll tell you what, lady, whatever that kid was on, it fried her brain. Took the three of us just to get the restraints on her, and then . . . are you all right?"

Before Sarah can reply, a stout middle-aged nursing sister wearing an upside-down watch on her bosom confronts them, arms akimbo.

"You, there! You have no business talking about the patients! Get back to your job or I'll report you." She turns to Sarah. "He's just an orderly. He doesn't know anything. I'm in charge here."

"It's my fault. I'm sorry," Sarah says. "Maybe you can help me. I'm looking for the young girl. The police told me she was here."

Sister's small eyes grow even smaller behind her spectacles, and she purses her lips. "Now, hold on. You don't mean the little mermaid, do you?"

Of course they'd have questioned her. What's your name? Bantryd. Where do you live? At the bottom of the ocean. What happened to your clothes? I don't have any.

"There was a girl brought in, right before dawn." Sister's expression has softened. "Long dark hair, and naked as a jay-bird. Is that who you mean?" Sarah nods. "She thought she was some kind of fish. Take me back to the ocean, she kept begging the coppers. That's where she thought she lived, in the ocean. Nothing we could do for her here. We transferred her to West Sydney, to the adolescent psych unit. They've got staff to handle that kind of thing. Are you a relative?"

"A friend, actually. I was supposed to be looking after her." Sarah moves slowly away from the desk, feeling suddenly nauseous, sorry she drank wine on an empty stomach.

"It's a shame, but what can you do with these kids? They've got minds of their own. Some of the things I see, you wouldn't credit it," Sister says. "And she could have been real pretty, too. You do wonder why they do it to themselves." Sarah stumbles, regains her balance, steadies herself against the wall. "You all right, dearie?"

"Just tired."

SLOWLY, SARAH MAKES HER WAY through the hospital grounds and back out onto the street, where she collapses upon the first bench she sees, her knees shaky. She'll go home, she'll drive to West Sydney. But she can't, not until she's found her car keys. So she'll have to go to the beach first. Walk to the beach, find her keys, and walk home again. That will take hours. And then drive out to West Sydney. That'll take another hour, more if there's a football game. It's too late. She's left it all too late. She can't do anything about Bantryd until tomorrow.

There's a bitter taste in her throat, and she suddenly feels sick. The wine, probably. She closes her eyes, feels as if she's falling and opens them again. She mustn't faint. The sun is high in the sky and hot on her bare head, reminding her she should have worn a hat. It's shadier on the other side of the street. She needs to cross the street, get out of the sun.

Usually, she does wear a hat. Australians have the highest rate of skin cancer in the world.

The sidewalks and shops are crowded. It's Saturday and everything is moving, everyone's in a hurry. Sarah watches a blue bus nose its way to the curb, discharge passengers, and move back into the traffic, stopping and starting. A woman carrying plastic shopping bags full of groceries sits down heavily, her buttocks nudging Sarah's hips. Sarah automatically moves, making room.

"It's not the heat, it's the humidity," the woman says, settling herself. "That's Sydney, but. Hot and humid." One of the bags sags, and oranges roll out onto the pavement and into the gutter. Sarah helps the woman retrieve them and then another bus comes, wheezing and belching fumes, and the woman leaps to her feet and drags herself and her plastic bags aboard.

Sarah can't just stay here. She crosses the street and starts to walk home, passing a chemist, a green grocer, a hardware store, a veterinary clinic, and a Salvation Army thrift shop, all of which are still open. She can remember when Australian shops closed at noon on Saturday and didn't open again until Monday morning, but that was decades ago. Now most shops stay open seven days a week, and you can buy necessities like pet food and toilet paper whenever you like. Nevertheless, many people still prefer to do their weekly shopping on Saturday mornings, queueing and jostling and squinting at lists scrawled on bits of paper the way they've always done.

She pauses in the shade and watches them, women dragging shopping carts, women pushing prams, flushed children crying, punching one another, chasing each other down the sidewalk. It's very hot. She wishes she was home.

It crosses her mind that she has money, she doesn't have to walk. She can go to a pay phone and call a cab, or catch a bus. There are plenty of busses. One just passed, lumbering toward the next stop a couple of blocks away. This cheers her up, but by the time she reaches the bus stop, she decides that she might as well walk after all. Busses only run every twenty minutes on Saturday, and in another twenty minutes she'll be home.

Sarah needs to think about Bantryd. But not here, not now. It's too hot in the street, too bright, too noisy.

Her house is deliciously cool and dark. They knew what they were doing, back then. They built unfashionably but to suit the climate, with thick walls and small windows. Sarah pours herself another glass of wine and takes it and the fruit scone up to the bedroom. She's still not hungry but doesn't want to drink on an empty stomach. She finishes the wine, places the glass on the bedside table, and stretches out on top of the quilt, closing her eyes. Saturday sounds waft up from the street. The whine of a power drill. A car door slamming. Someone's telephone ringing again and again until an answering machine picks up.

She needs to sort it all out in her mind, to understand. Certainly, there was a girl with her on the beach. That was real, that happened. It constitutes, as Charles would say, a definite data point. The girl was Bantryd. She lost four days. It wasn't a dream. It happened, whatever it was.

She dozes off, dreaming that she's asleep. When she wakes up, she's hungry, so she goes back down to the kitchen and makes toast, buttering it and scraping the last bit of Petit Maman jam from the jar. Charles loved Petit Maman. Sarah got rid of most of Charles's special foods, throwing perfectly good jars of sambal olek and capers and Major Grey's chutney into the rubbish because she couldn't bear the sight of them. But this jar had been in the cupboard and unopened, so it got packed and moved. It was as if Charles left it there for her, a farewell gift.

The telephone is ringing. Sarah hesitates, not feeling up to another conversation with Felicity. What will Felicity do if she doesn't answer? Leave a message? Call the police again? Let her leave a message. But she can't leave a message, because Sarah's turned off the damned machine. She plucks the receiver from its cradle.

"Sarah? It's Brian here. Brian Masters. Just thought I'd ring up and confirm tonight, seeing as I haven't heard back from you. Seven-thirty at the Bangkok Wok. That's all right, then?"

He's Australian, but he went to private school. Sarah can tell by his accent. Australians boast that theirs is a classless society, but Sarah and Charles soon learned that you had only to listen to the way people spoke to know how many years they'd gone to school, and where, and how much it cost.

"Brian, yes. I'm sorry I didn't return your call. I've been away, in Victoria. I did get your message, though. It was on my machine. Actually, I'm glad you called, because I was about to call you."

She pauses, trying to think of a plausible excuse.

"No worries. We're all set, then. Oops, sorry, got another call coming in. See you later, Sarah."

She needs to be alone, she needs to think things through. She'll have to call him back—there's no help for it. She'll have to find his telephone number and call him back.

The usual papers and envelopes are scattered across the coffee table, mostly bills and Charles's magazines, which she never opens. It's here, somewhere. She remembers the large envelope and finally finds it. Brian Masters. Middle-aged, middle management, divorced. Enjoys dining out, water sports, and travel. And—thank God—a telephone number.

There's also a letter from Partnerships Pty Ltd, explaining that due to the shortage of eligible single men in Sydney, the men get to choose the women rather than the other way around. "We have forwarded your Personal Profile to the men in our data base who want to meet women of your age, background, and interests. We are pleased to enclose a photograph and profile of Brian Masters. Whether or not you chose to meet Mr. Masters is, of course, up to you. But we advise you to be flexible and open-minded. Remember, you can't always judge a book by its cover."

Brian Masters looks all right. He's not particularly hand-some, but he's not bad-looking, either. He could be anybody. But what is Brian Masters expecting? Which photograph of me did Felicity send to these people?

She could ask Felicity. But then Felicity will know the agency has arranged a date for her. An introduction, as they call it. And she'll be furious if I don't go. But maybe I ought to go. He's in middle management, so he's not some unemployed loser. And he likes water sports. Maybe he has a boat. That could be fun, spending a day sailing on Sydney Harbour, lying back against the bulkhead, sipping a drink.

She runs a bath and sinks into it, resting her head against the tiled wall and closing her eyes. After she's washed her hair she blows it dry, standing barefoot on the wet floor, wrapped in the last of the clean towels and reminding herself that she really must do the laundry. The pebble is still there on the shelf. She touches it with her fingertip. It's just a pebble. She looks at herself in the mirror, leaning so close that her breath fogs the glass. It's too bad she's lost her nice glasses. She hasn't been out on a date since she married Charles. Well, of course not.

And Bantryd?

Bantryd is all right. A hospital is no fun, but it's better than a prison. Nobody will understand her but nobody will harm her, either. Sarah feels guilty about going out to dinner, but what difference does it really make? There's nothing she can do about Bantryd until tomorrow.

She dresses thoughtfully, choosing a yellow blouse she hasn't worn since Charles died and a long skirt patterned with bursts of yellow, ochre, and brown. She feels vaguely guilty, dressing up to go out as if Charles was still alive, as if nothing had happened.

Back in the bathroom she puts on makeup, something else she hasn't done since Charles died. Foundation, eye shadow, mascara, blush. Her hand shakes slightly. Kahn often tells her that she should get out more, that she needs to be with people. Kahn will be pleased. So will Felicity. Everybody will be pleased. She applies lipstick but blots most of it off. Had she really worn such bright lipstick?

The Bangkok Wok is on Oxford Street, a block past the pubs, practically around the corner. It's still early for a Saturday night. Sarah says she's meeting someone and is ushered to a small table near the windows where she peruses the drinks menu, finally deciding on a glass of white wine—not because she wants it, but because she's suddenly nervous, and it will give her something to do with her hands. There don't seem to be any waitresses around. Someone else arrives, a man who sits down at the bar and orders a beer. He's obviously not Brian Masters.

She gazes out at the people walking along the street, keenly aware of her status as a lone woman sitting at a table in a restaurant and wishing a waitress would come and take her order. Too bad she didn't think to bring along something to read.

A couple arrives, laughing. We don't need a menu, the woman says loudly. We'll just have the usual. For some reason they all burst into laughter, including the waitress who has bustled out to greet them. She seats them and immediately brings their drinks on a little tray, along with lacquer bowls of crisps and salted nuts.

It's getting busy. A party of four hovers uncertainly, an older couple with two adolescent girls, probably their grandkids. The waitress seats them at the back of the restaurant, and in a few minutes another couple joins them. Sarah watches as the waitress brings them a frosted jug of beer and soft drinks for the girls.

A queue is forming at the door.

Sarah tries in vain to catch the waitress' eye. Suddenly Brian (who else could it be?) is standing before her, carrying a bottle of wine wrapped in a brown paper sack. He's quite a bit heavier than his picture, and older. The waitress appears at his elbow, all smiles, offering menus and taking away the bottle of wine to be opened.

Mercifully, the menu provides an immediate topic of conversation. Spring rolls to start. A green curry for Brian, pad thai for Sarah. Boiled rice. Brian proves alarmingly well informed with regard to coriander. Does Sarah know the term comes from the Greek word for bedbug? And that the Romans used coriander to stimulate the jaded appetites of invalids?

Sarah dislikes coriander, which has become inexplicably popular. They agree that the weather is getting warmer, noticeably so. The waitress returns with two wine glasses and the open bottle of wine. She pours a little of the wine into Brian's glass and he tastes it and after a long hesitation, finally nods approval. It isn't an expensive wine. The waitress fills their glasses, takes their order, and leaves them alone.

"Am I your first?"

It takes a moment for Sarah to grasp his meaning. "You're the first person the agency has introduced me to, yes."

"I thought so. They want the ladies to have a positive experience the first time. So they use people like me, people they know they can count on." Sarah remains silent, not knowing what to make of this. She thought he'd chosen her, wanted to meet her. "Also, I'm not choosy. A lot of men are very particular, you know. Too particular, if you ask me. They don't want to meet anyone over thirty. And of course, they want someone who turns heads. Well, don't we all? But you know what? Looks aren't everything. You expect a woman to be neat and reasonably attractive, that goes without saying. But we can't all marry a film star, can we?"

Sarah supposes not.

"I've never refused to meet anyone," Brian says. "In a way, I feel it's my duty. After all, I'm a man. I'm good-looking, I've got my health. And I've done well, you know what I'm saying? I'm at the stage of life where I feel I should give something back. And there are so many lonely women out there, it just breaks my heart. Some of them are quite nice-looking, too. You'd be amazed. Do you know how many women I meet every month?" Sarah has no idea. "At least a dozen. And you know what else? Every single one of those poor lonely women has something to offer."

At a loss, Sarah sips her wine.

"I try to limit myself to three nights out a week," Brian says. "Sometimes four. But I could be out with a different woman every night, if that's what I wanted."

"Is it?"

He scowls. "What's that supposed to mean?"

"You said, if that's what you wanted. Well, is it?" Sarah smiles, trying to make a joke out of it. "To be out with a different woman every night?"

"I was speaking metaphorically."

The spring rolls arrive three to a plate, with a separate bowl of dipping sauce. At least Thai food keeps you busy. Sarah moves all the coriander on her plate off to one side. The spring roll is so hot it burns her mouth.

"Actually," Brian says through a mouthful of food, "I happen to enjoy the company of women. And I don't think I'm flattering myself if I say that women enjoy my company too. Most women, that is."

Sarah makes a fluttering gesture, meant to indicate that she doesn't want to talk with her mouth full.

"Obviously, I enjoy the company of some women more than others. But I try to conduct myself like a gentleman. I treat women with respect. I do. I can honestly say to you, I've never hit a woman in my life."

"Never?"

"Well, not with a closed fist."

"Of course not. You're a gentleman."

"My point exactly."

Sarah swallows the last of the spring roll, which tastes mostly of bean sprouts and is disappointingly watery.

The curry and the pad thai arrive, each in a lidded ceramic bowl decorated with orange dragons. There's boiled rice in what looks like a chased silver basin but is really a thin aluminium bowl, cleverly worked. The restaurant is almost full. It must be considered good, by Australian standards.

They eat, taking it in turns to comment on the food. Charles wouldn't have liked it. He was fond of Asian food, but preferred it much hotter and much more highly spiced than any of this. Brian proves to be a fast and efficient eater, so much so that Sarah wonders if he has another date. But that's unfair. Maybe he's just hungry. At any rate, he's finished. Settling back into his chair, he begins a discourse on Thai cuisine. Food, he informs Sarah, is an extremely important part of Thai culture. Thai kings write cookbooks. And even ordinary people prepare collections of their favourite recipes which are printed and distributed to the mourners at their funerals. All of this is news to Sarah, who knows little about Thailand except that it's where Chang and Eng came from.

"Who?"

"Chang and Eng," Sarah says. "The original Siamese twins."

"Never heard of them."

"They were very famous. Someone even wrote a book about them."

"You don't say. You almost finished?"

Sarah nods, wondering if he's referring to the meal or Chang and Eng. Less than an hour has passed, although it feels longer. Brian orders a coffee and drinks it in silence while Sarah sips wine. The waitress brings the check, a folded bit of white paper on a plastic tray, and places it at Brian's elbow. He picks it up, glances at it, and passes it across the table.

"You'll have to get this. Sorry, but I was running late. And I couldn't find an ATM."

Sarah simply looks at him.

"Like I said, I'm a gentleman. I couldn't stand the thought of you sitting here alone, waiting for me. It must be awful being a woman, sitting by yourself in a place like this."

"I can think of worse things, actually. And there's an ATM outside, just across the street." Grinning, Brian makes an empty-handed gesture. He's planned this, the son of a bitch.

"You expect me to pay for your meal?" Sarah remains silent. "Tell you what. Fix it up, and I'll send you a check for my half. I mean, what's the alternative? We don't want to make a scene right in your backyard, do we?"

If they'd gone someplace in the city, it would be different. But he's right. She doesn't want to make a scene, not here in a restaurant that's around the corner from where she lives.

Wordlessly, Sarah extracts two twenty-dollar notes and places them on the plastic tray. Slow minutes pass. There isn't anything else to say and neither of them is up to making the effort. When the waitress returns with the change, Brian reaches across the table and removes five dollars from the tray, pocketing it. "Your share of the wine. You drank most of it."

Sarah doesn't argue. She wants to go home. In a few minutes, it'll be over.

On the sidewalk Brian turns toward her and for a terrible moment, Sarah thinks he's going to try to kiss her. Instead, he shakes her hand. "I think you're probably a very nice woman, deep down. But you've got an attitude problem, you know what I'm saying? I'm only trying to be helpful. But I have to be honest here. I don't think we've made any kind of connection, so I don't think there's much point in pursuing this. And that being the case, I won't be calling you again."

"I guess I'll just have to live with that."

He nods, sympathetic. "Look, it's just one of those things. It doesn't mean you won't find somebody, someday. There's somebody for everybody."

"But I need to work on my attitude."

"That's the spirit! The attitude thing is a real turn-off, you know what I'm saying? So what else can I say? All the best, and thanks for dinner."

"Don't hit any women," she says. Seeing his expression, she smiles. "It's a joke."

"Yeah, but you see? That's what I mean. A person could easily take a comment like that the wrong way. A person could get really upset."

"Yes, I do see. Goodbye, Brian."

They part, heading off in different directions, although Sarah looks back in time to see him hailing a cab in front of the train station. Stiffed, and at her age. Pathetic. But that's how these agencies stay in business, she supposes. Guaranteed introductions, to an endless supply of Brians.

She mustn't blame Felicity, because this is not Felicity's fault. Felicity meant well and besides, it's the thought that counts. That's what Charles would say if he was here.

She had to leave the front door unlocked, but took the precaution of turning on all the lights and the television, too. Anyhow, it's too early for burglars, even if she had anything worth stealing, which she doesn't. Lots of books, and Charles's collection of prints, and a very old television set. Burglars don't want stuff like that. They want jewelry and electronics, things they can sell. But when they go to all the bother of breaking in and don't find anything worth stealing, they sometimes get mad and trash the place, just for the hell of it. Sarah locks the door, from the inside. Tomorrow she'll go back to the beach and retrieve her keys, or if she can't find them, call a locksmith and have a new set cut.

Meanwhile it's nice just to be back home. Sarah lies in bed, the light from the street shining through the quivering leaves and making patterns on the walls and ceilings that continually change. The contours of the quilt and mattress are comfortable, familiar against her body. This is real, this room and this bed. This is the only world that exists.

But four days. What really happened?

IN HER DREAM, XAXANADER presents her with a gift of five bamboo shoots growing in a shallow golden bowl filled with pebbles. As he places the bowl in her hands, the tips of their fingers touch. It's like sunshine, or electricity. Somewhere, music is playing. The music continues, even after Sarah opens her eyes and recognizes the sound of her neighbor's bamboo wind-chimes outside the window.

Another dream. And Sarah is in no doubt as to the difference between dreaming and wakefulness. She was asleep and now she's awake, in her own house, in her own bedroom. But when she sits up and swings her bare feet over the side of the bed, she frowns at the sight of her skirt, lying in a heap on the floor. Brian Masters really happened. There are a lot worse things than sitting by yourself in a restaurant.

She's hungry. She's slept really late, but she'd like a real breakfast for a change, eggs and bacon and hash brown potatoes, and toast with jam. This is unusual. In the past, she only craved big breakfasts when she was pregnant.

Sarah slips on her robe, belts it, and partially shuts the bedroom door so she can examine her reflection in the oblong mirror nailed to the back of it. Her waist does seem to have thickened. Or maybe she's imagining it, or getting old. She hasn't really looked at herself in a mirror since Charles died.

It's Sunday. Yesterday was Saturday, and Sarah remembers yesterday. She also remembers Wednesday, Thursday, and Friday, despite the fact that what she remembers could not have occurred. She goes downstairs to start the coffee.

Sunlight dazzles through the mesh of the curtains. She certainly isn't pregnant, she didn't do anything. And even if she had, it would be too soon to know one way or the other, much less for anything to show. It's probably just bloat.

THE PROBLEM ISN'T THAT SHE'S PREGNANT. The problem is that she's spent nearly four days at the bottom of the sea, in a world that doesn't exist, but does. The problem is that she remembers everything about that world as clearly as she remembers dinner with Brian Masters.

She needs to find out what happened to Bantryd. Western Sydney, the nurse said. She could telephone. Although it would probably be better to drive out there and see for herself. But she can't do that unless she finds her keys. Better get dressed and go back to the beach to search for them before it gets crowded.

She's just putting on her sandals when Felicity rings to ask if she has time for a quick cup of coffee. Sarah understands that this constitutes an apology, is as close as Felicity will ever come to saying sorry. It's so late she'd rather go straight to the beach, but she doesn't want to remain on bad terms with Felicity, so they agree to meet at Indigo Café, one of Felicity's favorites.

Attached to a bookshop, Indigo Café is a colorful muddle of plastic tables and market umbrellas spilling out of a leafy Woollahra courtyard and surrounded by trendy antique shops and boutiques that won't open until noon. Everybody comes here, God knows why. The coffee is expensive and not particularly good. Of course, the coffee isn't the point.

Felicity has already arrived and has even managed to secure an outside table, something of a coup on a Sunday morning. Sitting down in the shade of the umbrella, Sarah suddenly remembers she gave Felicity a spare set of keys. But if she asks for them, she'll have to explain. And Sarah doesn't want to explain anything. Not yet, not until she understands, herself.

Felicity orders iced green tea, without the ice. Sarah order a long black.

"You'll never guess what I did last night." Felicity looks up. "I had a date. It was one of those men, from that agency. His name was Brian."

It was almost worth it, just to have something amusing to relate, to be able to talk to Felicity and not have it end with the two of them arguing. By the time Sarah gets to the part where Brian is explaining he's too much of a gentleman to pay for his dinner, they're both laughing. This is pleasant. This is how it should always be.

"So what do you think happened to that girl?" Felicity says suddenly. "You know, the one at the beach who wasn't wearing any clothes."

"I don't know yet. Why?"

"I was just thinking, I'd really like to interview her. You don't know her name or anything, do you?"

"No, I don't. But why on earth would you want to interview her?"

"Well, here's the thing. They want me do a series of articles, six of them, about street kids. Where they come from, what happens to them, that kind of thing. It's going to be, like, ten thousand words. It's an important issue, Mum. Do you know how many girls go missing every year, just in New South Wales?" Sarah doesn't know, doesn't want to know. "And how many unidentified female corpses there are in the morgue? That's how that girl might have ended up, dead. And that's why I want to interview her. I mean, how do you end up naked on a beach?"

"I don't know. But I don't think she was a street kid."

"Mum, you don't know anything about it."

Sarah decides to change the subject. "That's wonderful news, Felicity! Your first series. Congratulations."

Felicity shrugs. "I don't know, it's going to be a lot of work." Australians shrug off compliments, shrug off people who take pride in their accomplishments. Even so, Felicity must be pleased. "They usually give things like this to Jilly, but she's on holiday. And Ben is off sick. I'm the only one who's around. So there you go."

Sarah tries to remember who Jilly and Ben are. Mostly, Felicity talks about someone named Carby, who rides around in police cars and occasionally takes Felicity to a club called Catshit. And Mr. Ballsworth, Ballsy. The city editor, her boss.

"I'm thinking I'll take a different tack." Felicity is frowning slightly. "They've given me a file full of photos and police reports, but I don't want to go the usual shock horror route. I want to do something more personal. The first piece has to be an overview and the final piece has to be a wrap, but I can do what I like with the other four. I'm thinking a cop, a social worker, a parent, and a street kid. But all connected, you see what I'm getting at? And that girl would be perfect, if she'd talk to me." Felicity rests her chin on her palms and stares at Sarah. "Do you think she would?"

"I don't know." Sarah feels a pulse beating in her throat. "You'd have to find her first."

"I've already requested the police report." The waitress brings the check and Felicity picks it up and gets to her feet. "My treat," she says, and heads off to join the queue in front of the cashier.

The beach is going be crowded. Sarah wishes she'd set the alarm and got up early. Maybe it would be best to ask Felicity for the duplicate set of keys, after all. Then she could just get in the car and drive straight to Western Sydney. But she doesn't want to drag Felicity into it, especially not now. And she knows exactly where everything is, tucked under a shelf of rock in a deep crevice just beyond the place where the sand beach ends. It'll all be there, of course it will.

Who'd bother to steal a towel, an old pair of glasses, and a bunch of keys?

Half a dozen people at a large round table near the curb push back their chairs and stand up. Behind them, Sarah catches a glimpse of a couple sitting at a tiny table for two, practically in the street, and gasps. It's her, it's Bantryd. That mass of black hair falling in wavy cascades of curls down her back is unmistakeable. It's her.

"Mum! What's wrong?"

Sarah is staring. The girl turns abruptly and stares back at her, and Sarah looks away. She was wrong. It's not Bantryd. They're the same height, the same build, and they've both got strong cheekbones and dark eyes. But this girl's face is slightly more rounded, and her lips are thinner, although there *is* a resemblance. It's the hair, that glorious mane of tumbling hair. That's what fooled her.

"Mum, why are you staring at that girl?"

"I'm not. I mean, I thought she was somebody I knew, that's all."

"You've gone all funny. You're not having a heart attack or something, are you?"

"A heart attack?"

"My friend Maree was out with her aunt last week, having coffee just like this. They were talking about the sales and then all of a sudden, she was dead. The aunt, I mean. She just keeled over, right there at the table."

"That's horrible."

"But are you all right?" Sarah nods, tries to smile. Felicity is gazing at the dark-haired girl.

"You thought it was her, didn't you?"

"Who?"

"That girl you were looking at just now. You thought she was the girl from the beach."

Felicity's acuity astonishes her. Despite the fact that they're mother and daughter, there is nobody Sarah feels is less attuned to her than Felicity.

"I know why you thought you recognized her," Felicity is saying. "I sort of recognize her too. I've seen that face somewhere. I know that face."

"All sorts of people come here. Maybe she's a model, or someone you once interviewed."

Felicity shakes her head impatiently. "She's not a model, she's not tall enough. And if I'd interviewed her, I'd remember her. I don't think I've ever met her. But I do know that face."

Chapter Five

Kahn rarely asks direct questions, but he might say something like, I wonder what happened to you on Friday. She'll tell him she went away for a few days. Or that she overslept, or forgot.

After leaving Felicity on Sunday, Sarah did go to the beach, and to her relief, found her things where she'd left them. But then she had to walk all the way home again and by the time she got there, it was too late to drive out to Western Sydney.

She telephoned first thing Monday morning, and after spending ten minutes listening to a loop of symphonic music, was put through to the adolescent psychiatric unit. "Everybody not here. Doctors all go seminar, all day. In-service seminar, yes. Maybe you try tomorrow, okay?"

They wouldn't have told her much, anyway. She must drive out there, that's the only way to find out what's going on. But it will take at least an hour to get to Western Sydney, through awful traffic. And what's the point, if none of the doctors are around?

Meanwhile, she's here in Kahn's office, not saying anything.

Kahn crosses his legs and rests his hands lightly upon his thighs. He can sit staring benignly at her for whole minutes at a time. It's part of his technique. Sarah stares back at him. If he wants to know where she was Friday, he's going to have to ask.

But he doesn't. And Sarah doesn't know quite where to begin, isn't even sure she should begin. It's been a whole week since she's seen him. She might tell him about Bantryd, or about dinner with Brian Masters.

"I'm wondering," Kahn says, "if you've had any more dreams like the one we were talking about last week. You remember, the world at the bottom of the sea."

He shifts position and resettles himself, crossing one leg over the other and letting his hands hang loosely in his lap.

"It was more than a dream." His forehead furrows, but he doesn't comment. "It wasn't like any other dream I've ever had. It seemed real." Kahn covers his mouth with his left hand. "Even now, sitting here and thinking about it, it still seems real. I know it isn't, I know I was just dreaming." She pauses. "I don't understand it, though. I don't understand why all of a sudden, I'm having these weird dreams."

"You've had another one, then." Sarah nods. "The same dream? About the same place?" Again she nods. He considers this, gravely. "What does it feel like, when you're having the dream?"

"It feels real."

"And when you wake up and realize it was just a dream, how does that feel?"

"Sometimes, I don't wake up. I want to wake up, I'm trying to wake up, but I can't."

"You dreamed a whole world into existence. But you're awake now."

"If it really was a dream," Sarah murmurs.

"Of course it was a dream. You say it seemed real. But all this seems real too, doesn't it?"

"It depends on what you mean by real." Kahn doesn't respond. "Your desk isn't really a desk, it's a lot of molecules, moving. That's not what it looks like, but that's what it is. That's what everything is. So isn't a dream as real as anything in this room?"

"Dreams aren't made of molecules," Kahn says. "And although molecules are too tiny to see with the naked eye, they're still matter. They're real, they're tangible. Whereas dreams aren't."

"But dreams exist."

"Only in our minds." Absently, his hand strokes the sparse hairs of his beard. Psychologists in films always have goatee beards and wear tweed jackets with leather patches on the elbows. Kahn's tweed jacket is hanging on a rack in the corner, out of Sarah's line of vision.

Sarah knows nothing about Kahn. She understands she's not meant to know, because psychotherapists aren't supposed to be real people, not to their clients. Yet there's a real Kahn who exists outside this room, a Kahn who goes to pubs and parties and laughs at jokes, a Kahn who loves someone. It occurs to her that she knows much more about Xaxanader than she does about Kahn, even if Kahn is real and Xaxanader isn't.

"I wonder what you're thinking."

He's not Xaxanader, he can't read her thoughts. "I was thinking about you, actually."

He doesn't pursue this. Personal remarks aren't allowed, not even innocuous ones. Otherwise, anything goes. You can say anything, you can cry, you can rage, you can even laugh. But you can't get up and leave before your hour is up. Sarah tried that once, but Kahn stopped her. Not physically; he's never touched her, not even to shake hands. But he did ask her please not to go, to please sit down. As a special favor to me, he said.

He doesn't really want to know what she's thinking, anyway. He just wants her to say something, anything at all, so he can respond to it.

She wriggles uncomfortably, crossing and uncrossing her legs. Opposite her, Kahn settles into a quiet, glazed watchfulness.

"I sometimes think there really are worlds besides this one," Sarah says. "Parallel worlds. Millions of them, maybe billions, each one almost identical to the one next to it, but also just a little bit different." His eyes widen slightly to show her that he's paying attention to what she's saying, no matter how inane it sounds. "For instance, in the world next door to this one, we're still sitting here in this room, you and I. But it's a minute sooner or a minute later. Or maybe those geraniums aren't dead. Or maybe there isn't a window box. Do you see what I mean?"

Kahn opens his mouth as if to speak, but then closes it again. Sarah waits. His lips seem to tremble slightly.

"Parallel worlds," he says at last.

"It's possible. Anything is possible."

Kahn's expression is wary, but he doesn't say anything. Sarah watches him swallow and lick his lips. It would be interesting to know what he's really thinking.

He purses his lips slightly and rubs the bridge of his nose.

"I think these dreams you've been experiencing have triggered some very disturbing feelings and emotions. But that's all right. It simply means they're important dreams, they're significant. And you need to pay attention to them. You need to listen to what they're telling you. Dream language is symbolic language. Think about the sea. What does the sea mean to you? What feelings does it evoke? What do you think about when you envision the sea? What's the first image that comes into your mind?"

"A mermaid, I suppose. Poseidon. The Birth of Venus." He's got it wrong, he's totally misunderstood. "The Little Mermaid," she adds, thinking of Bantryd.

"What about Nereus?"

"Who?"

"Nereus, the Old Man of the Sea." There's the slightest trace of a smile upon his lips. "His hair and beard were made of seaweed, and he ruled the kingdoms at the bottom of the ocean. He was very kind, they say. His wife was Doris and they had fifty daughters in all, the sea nymphs."

"I thought that was Poseidon."

"Poseidon was Nereus's son-in-law. He married Amphititre, one of the daughters." Sarah is gaping, can't help it. "I minored in Greek mythology," Kahn says.

Is he going to recite the names of the other forty-nine? Sarah knows a bit about Greek mythology too, although she's never heard of Nereus. "I don't know. I don't think this is about mythology, though."

"What do you think it's about?"

"Feelings."

He leans forward. "Tell me."

"It isn't how it looks, or what it's like. Its how it feels. It feels real, as if it's actually happening. And that's how I remember it. Not the way you remember a dream, but the way you remember something that really happened."

"But what did happen? What did it look like at the bottom of the ocean?"

He's asking the wrong questions. Never mind that they're the same questions Sarah asked herself, at first. They're still the wrong questions.

"It doesn't look *like* anything. It doesn't work that way."

"How does it work?"

"Seeing and hearing aren't important. Feeling is important. It's the way it feels. You sort of open yourself up to it, and it's so enormous, so vast. Being there feels like being a note in a beautiful symphony. You're just one note among thousands and thousands of other notes, but you're not competing with them and they're not competing with you. You're all important. You're all part of the rhythm. You are the rhythm." How to make him understand? "It flows," Sarah says. "Everything flows. Everything is the way it's meant to be. You feel as if you could just go on and on forever, do anything. You feel safe."

"And now?" Sarah blinks, and stares at him. "Do you feel safe here?"

Here, in this room? Or here in Australia? Sarah folds her hands in her lap and looks at them. "No, not really. I haven't felt safe since Charles died."

"But you did feel safe in your dream, in the world you created. And that feeling of safety, that feeling of belonging, it was wonderful, wasn't it?" He pauses. "Do you remember the last time you felt that way? It was a long time ago, when you were a little baby, safe and warm in your mother's arms. That memory of being held and safe and loved stays with us all our lives. We may not consciously remember it, but we search for it all our lives. That feeling of being held, and loved, and safe."

Did Mama ever hold her? Someone must have held her when she was a baby. Held her, fed her, changed her diapers. Sarah remembers an old photograph of her as a baby, wearing a pink bonnet edged with lace. Somebody had to have bought that bonnet and tied it onto her head, somebody who loved her.

"You dreamed a wonderful dream," Kahn says, with something like approval.

"But that's just it. It wasn't a dream, I wasn't dreaming." This is how she felt forty years ago, when Billy Hanks dared her to jump off the high diving board, when she was halfway up the ladder and knew she couldn't climb back down, that she had to do it. "It really happened. I was there. I didn't just imagine it, and I didn't imagine Bantryd and Xaxanader, either. They're real. They're as real as you are."

Kahn continues to look at her, his expression revealing nothing.

"So what do you think?" Sarah suddenly wants to laugh and knows she mustn't. "Am I crazy? Should we call in a proper shrink?"

"Is that what you'd like?" He seems concerned, but in a distant, professional way. "Would you be more comfortable talking to someone else?"

Whatever she says will be wrong, so she doesn't say anything.

"Because that's what all this is about, isn't it?" There's an unwonted edge in Kahn's voice. "You're angry at me. You've been angry from the moment you walked through that door. I've obviously said something, or done something, that's upset you." He pauses, but Sarah only shakes her head, baffled. "That's why you didn't come on Friday, isn't it? You didn't keep our appointment because you were angry at me and you wanted to punish me."

"But I don't, I didn't. And I'm not angry."

"I think you are."

"I'm not. It isn't about you. It's about me, it's about something that happened to me. Something that really did happen. And I don't understand it. That doesn't make me crazy, though."

"I didn't say you were crazy."

"It wasn't a dream." Sarah can hear herself speaking, one word following the next like footsteps. But going where? "It happened. It's real, all of it. There's another world, there's another universe. And I've been there."

"What do you want me to say?"

"I don't want you to say anything. I want you to listen."

"But I am listening. That's my job, to listen. And do you know what I hear?" Kahn leans forward. "I hear someone who is very, very angry at me."

She *is* angry, now. He won't listen to her, he doesn't want to hear what she needs to tell him. And if he won't listen, who will?

"We need to talk about your anger."

Sarah is too furious to do more than glare at him. She sits back, folding her arms across her body. She will sit here, like this, until he responds to what she has just told him. Not to what he thinks she means, but what she actually said. He owes her that much.

"You're not crazy," Kahn says at last. "You know the difference between dreams and real life."

"Yes, I do. That's what I'm trying to tell you. It wasn't a dream. I know it wasn't a dream."

"How do you know?"

What will happen if she tells him about Bantryd? Probably nothing. But she decides not to risk it, not just yet.

"There were consequences. Things happened. Here, in what you call the real world."

"What sort of things?"

What can she possibly say? They gaze helplessly at each other, like strangers in a train wreck.

"You're not crazy, Mrs. Andrews." Kahn proceeds slowly, with care. "And you're not delusional, either. If you were, there would be no point in our continuing these sessions. That's why I'm thinking perhaps that's what you want." He leans forward slightly, the way he does when he's telling her something he thinks she needs to know. "It's all right, you know. You won't be hurting my feelings. If you want me to refer you to someone else, all you have to do is ask."

"God damn it!" He's shocked. Sarah is shocked too. She rarely swears. Charles didn't like it. "I don't want you to refer me to anyone else! I just want you to believe me."

"But I do believe you."

It's not what she expects, and she's instantly on her guard. She doesn't trust Kahn, she's never trusted him. Maybe that's been the problem all along. But why should she trust Kahn? He doesn't care about her. She's a client, nothing more.

"I also believe you're quite sane," Kahn says. "You're not delusional, and you're not untruthful. What you're saying is that you've found an alternative universe, a world at the bottom of the sea. And it's a wonderful world, much better than this one. You seem to like it there."

"I do."

She shouldn't have started this. She should have known better.

"A wonderful world," Kahn says again. "A safe world, filled with people who seem real to you. You haven't said much about them, but I suspect they're kind and gentle and intelligent. And why shouldn't they be? It sounds lovely. A perfect world, filled with perfect people."

"It's not perfect, I never said that. It's just more advanced. At least, that's what they think."

"And what do you think?"

"I think you're making fun of me."

"I'm not, not at all." Kahn smiles, and this further unsettles her. "Don't you see what's happening here? Don't you see what you've done? You've created exactly what you need. You've found someplace where you can be happy, even without Charles. You've found a place where everything doesn't remind you of something Charles said or did, a place where Charles never even existed. It's perfect. It's wonderful. And you're right, it's not a dream. But it's not a delusion, either. It's more like a daydream, a waking fantasy."

She's told him the truth, and he still doesn't think she's crazy. He thinks she's done something wonderful. That's the word he keeps using, wonderful. He doesn't get it. But at least he listened.

"And I'll tell you something else," Kahn says. He's still smiling. "It wouldn't surprise me if you didn't always experience this phenomenon as a dream. I suspect that sometimes you find yourself drifting off, even when you're awake. In your mind, in your thoughts. Like a reverie."

"I don't know. It all seems so real."

"Of course it does. If it didn't seem real, what would be the point?" His smile is warm and complicit. "If it didn't seem real, it wouldn't distract you. It wouldn't hold you. But it does distract you, and more importantly, it allows you to escape for a little while. In fact, I suspect that's what you were doing on Friday. And then when you realized you'd missed our session, it was too late. And you were embarrassed, weren't you? You didn't know how to explain what had happened. And then you got scared, because you thought you were losing your mind. And that's why you were angry. Because you were frightened."

Sarah sighs but doesn't disagree. She's glad to be off the hook. He's got it wrong, but that's not her fault. She told him the truth.

"In America," Kahn says, "I suppose you'd say you made lemonade."

"Lemonade?"

"If you get lemons, make lemonade. Americans say that, don't they? I have a friend who collects American sayings." Kahn thinks for a moment. "Don't vote, it only encourages them. When the going gets tough, the tough go shopping. What color is your parachute?"

"I think that's the title of a book."

"If you get lemons, make lemonade. It's very American."

"I suppose it is."

They gaze at each other for a moment. Kahn leans forward, hands on his knees, suddenly intense. "You really were angry, weren't you? But it's all right. Anger is good. It's a normal response, a sign of healing. But you have to be patient, you have to give it a chance. The grief process is different for everyone."

Sarah mentally reviews the stages of the grief process: Shock, and denial, and then anger, sometimes all at once. Bargaining. Finally, acceptance. Bargaining is the part she's never understood. Bargaining for what? And with whom?

"You'll never forget Charles. But the time will come when your thoughts of him will be happy thoughts, happy memories of everything you shared. You've already come a long way. Do you remember how much pain you were in that first morning you came to see me?"

She does remember, but the way she remembers child-birth, as an abstract recollection, recalled and reconstructed rather than felt. She still misses Charles, still thinks about him. But the pain is no worse than a cut finger, no longer excruciating. It has to be that way. Otherwise life couldn't go on, and it does.

Sarah looks up in time to see Kahn glance swiftly at the little clock behind the box of tissues. Pretending to need a tissue, she nudges the box out of position so that he can no longer see the clock.

"There's something else." She knows Kahn doesn't want to start anything new, not this late in the session. "It's something that happened Friday night. It was hot, and I couldn't sleep, so I went for a swim. There was a girl there on the beach when I came out of the water. We started to walk home but the police stopped us." Kahn tries to say something, but Sarah keeps talking. "It wasn't anything, really. And they were very nice about it, very polite. They even drove me home afterward. But you see, it was dark on the beach. So I didn't notice that she wasn't wearing anything. I mean, she wasn't wearing a bathing suit. She was naked."

Kahn's expression doesn't change.

"I don't know what she told them at the police station because they had us in different rooms. But I was concerned, I sort of felt responsible for her. They said she was a runaway and they were going to send her back home. But they didn't. They sent her to some hospital in Western Sydney."

"Brothwick, probably. I know of it." Kahn fidgets, unable to see the clock and not wanting to look at his watch. "It's an adolescent psychiatric unit, and they're very good there. Very caring, very professional. If that's all that happened, I wouldn't worry about it."

"But I am worried. She doesn't belong in a mental hospital. There isn't anything wrong with her."

"You don't know that."

"Yes, I do." She forces herself to look him straight in the eye. "It was Bantryd."

He meets her gaze but doesn't say anything for a moment. Then he stands up, unfolding himself carefully from the black vinyl chair. You'd think he'd have a more comfortable chair for himself.

"As I say, I know people at Brothwick. It's a specialist unit, one of the best." Sarah sits there, stubborn, unwilling to be ignored. "I suppose you could call them," Kahn says at last. "Ask them how she's getting along."

"I tried. They weren't there, the doctors were at a meeting or something. Besides, they probably wouldn't tell me anything over the phone. Hospitals usually don't."

He sighs and looks at his watch. He hates doing that in front of a client. "Then go out there. It's not a prison. Tell them what happened. If she's still there, they'll probably let you see her."

"What do you mean, if she's still there?" He doesn't reply. He doesn't believe her, or else he's trying to call her bluff. "Of course she's there," Sarah says, too loudly. "Where else would she be?"

Kahn's watch has slipped around to the underside of his wrist, and he has to turn it around in order to see the time.

"I am sorry, Mrs. Andrews. But I really do have to stop now."

SARAH MAKES A TUNA SANDWICH for lunch, using the last of the bread, and pours herself a glass of wine to go with it. As soon as she sits down, the telephone rings. She lets the answering machine get it. "Mum? It's me, Felicity. Mum, listen. I need you to call me as soon as you get home. It's really, really important. Okay?"

Felicity sounds excited, almost happy. What would make Felicity happy? It's hard to say. Whatever it is, it'll keep. Felicity is easily aroused, but nothing ever lasts very long.

The most direct route to Western Sydney Hospital is along Parramatta Road, an ugly thoroughfare festooned with power lines, telephone lines and neon signs and hemmed in by old brick buildings and used car lots. Parramatta Road was built for carts and horses. In the United States, they'd have torn it up decades ago and put in parking garages and shopping malls.

The car radio is set to a station that plays songs from the sixties, when songs still had words. Sarah drives, singing along with Patti Page. Even without much traffic, the drive takes over an hour.

The hospital campus is unprepossessing, the buildings so architecturally anonymous they might have come prefabricated, in a kit: pre-cut, shrink-wrapped concrete blocks, reinforced glass, and assembly directions in English, French, German, Spanish, and Chinese.

There's an automated parking garage, but the bays on the lower levels are either reserved for hospital staff or full. Sarah spirals slowly upward and finally finds a place on the roof. A covered breezeway leads from the garage to the main complex, passing above expanses of lawn and flower beds.

Sliding glass doors open onto what might just as easily be a motel lobby. There are framed prints on the pastel walls and clusters of chairs and couches separated by artificial palms in terra cotta pots. A sign says, No Smoking. Another warns, No Cell Phones Past This Point. There's a gift shop and a bank of vending machines. Elevator doors slide soundlessly open and shut. Brothwick's adolescent psychiatric unit is on the fourth floor.

When Sarah steps out of the elevator, it's as if she's in a much older building. There are no windows, no chairs. A high wooden counter runs the length of the area, and a typewritten notice taped to it says, Press Buzzer.

Before she can do so, swinging doors on her right open soundlessly, and a bearded man wearing a business shirt tucked into jeans marches silently past her and vanishes through the doors on her left.

Ignoring the buzzer, Sarah peers through the plastic window set into one of the swinging doors. It's thick and slightly discolored, like the window in an airplane. On the other side of the door, people are sitting in chairs, some of them facing a television set, others not. Sarah pushes it open and goes through.

Other than the chairs, the television set, and an empty bookcase, the large room is quite bare; no rugs, no lamps, no pictures. The walls and ceiling are painted green. The room's inhabitants take no notice of her, but staff in these places no longer wear uniforms, so they probably think she's a nurse. Sarah moves warily around the perimeter of the room, prepared to be challenged. A slender, bowed young man listening to a Walkman glances at her, then looks away. Nobody else moves.

It's not how she thought it would be. Nobody's wearing a hospital gown. Nobody is screaming or pacing. Nobody is doing anything. Cartoon images flicker silently across the television screen, but there's no audio.

The seven girls in the room all have blond or light brown hair. And they're big girls, their bellies and thighs bulging against their jeans. Bantryd isn't here. Maybe they let her go. Maybe she found her way back home, back where she belongs.

Sarah sees a second door, slightly ajar, set into the wall just ahead. She knows she shouldn't, but she passes through it into a windowless corridor flanked by eight more doors, each opening into an empty cubicle containing an iron-framed cot, metal night-stand, and molded plastic chair.

There's someone in the last cubicle on the right, huddled motionless on the bed beneath a gray chenille bedspread. Sarah hesitates in the doorway for a moment and then goes in and leans over the still form.

"Are you awake?"

No movement.

She glances uneasily back over her shoulder, but the corridor is deserted. She leans down again, reaching for the corner of the bedspread. She's only going to peek. She just wants to make sure.

Suddenly, the girl in the bed sits bolt upright, flinging the bedspread onto the floor. It's Bantryd. Her eyes are wide and unfocused, and she holds one arm up in front of her face, as if to ward off an attacker.

"It's all right. Don't be frightened. It's just me, Sarah." She moves toward Bantryd, who flinches. "Bantryd, don't." She sits on the edge of the bed and puts her arms around the girl's quaking shoulders. "You remember me, don't you? I'm Sarah, I'm your friend. Oh, god. What's happened to you?"

Bantryd whimpers, then turns to look at Sarah. Her eyes are huge, the pupils black and dilated. Unintelligible syllables bubble from her lips, but they aren't words, they don't make sense. Sarah holds her as she'd hold a child.

"What have they done to you?"

The black eyes become even wider and slowly fill with tears.

"No, stop it. Don't cry. It's all right, it's going to be all right."

Sarah sees a tiny fluted white paper cup on the night-stand. Medication. She suddenly understands why there are no straitjackets, no nurses.

Now Bantryd is trying to stand up but she staggers, sways, then pitches forward so precipitously that Sarah only just manages to catch her. They rock to and fro, Bantryd sagging and Sarah struggling to hold her up, like exhausted dancers waiting for the music to stop.

"What did they give you? Do you know?" Bantryd shudders, her whole body trembling. "It's all right," Sarah says again. But it isn't, not at all. She eases Bantryd to a sitting position on the edge of the little bed. "I'm going to help you, but you've got to listen, okay? You're to do exactly what I say." They've dressed Bantryd in a pair of old jeans and a faded T-shirt. She's wearing a plastic hospital ID bracelet on her left wrist, but her feet are bare. "You need shoes. You've got to look normal, or we'll never get out of here. They must have given you some shoes. Where are they?" Bantryd stares, expressionless, her eyes bottomless pools. "Where are your shoes?"

Wordlessly, Bantryd pulls up the front of her shirt as a child might, revealing a faded cotton brassiere.

"Okay, fine. But if they gave you underwear, they must have given you shoes."

In the nightstand drawer, Sarah finds a plastic comb, a toothbrush, and a pair of blue sneakers.

"Okay. Just sit there." She kneels down, slips the sneakers onto Bantryd's feet and ties the laces. "There. That's better." Sarah gets to her feet and gently coaxes Bantryd back up into a standing position. "Now, all you've got to do is hold onto my arm. That's right, just like that. Lean on me if you need to. Its okay, I've got you. Now, let's take a step. Good. Now another. Okay. Just follow me, do what I do. Here we go."

The motionless figures in the common room pose no threat. Nobody even looks up. But what if there's someone outside, behind the counter?

There isn't.

Anyone could walk in here, any maniac. By the same token, anyone could walk out. They could all walk out, they could all be kidnapped, and nobody would be the wiser. If that happened, it would be Felicity's kind of story. Patients disappear. Staff suspended pending investigation. Minister demands explanation.

Sarah presses a button and the elevator doors slide open. This is too easy. Inside the elevator she looks up at the ceiling, searching for the video camera that must certainly be mounted there. In the hospital basement, uniformed security guards are probably sitting in front of a closed circuit television monitor and watching everything. Sarah is perspiring. This isn't what was supposed to happen. This isn't what she thought she was going to do.

They'll be there in the lobby, waiting for her. And what will she tell them?

The elevator stops, the doors slide open, and Sarah braces herself, but the foyer is deserted save for an elderly black man pushing a vacuum cleaner across the carpet. Visiting hours are over. The glass door to the gift shop displays a cardboard sign: CLOSED. Sarah and Bantryd pass through the automatic glass doors unchallenged, then make their way along the concrete breezeway, above silent lawns and flower beds. So far, so good. But as they enter the penumbra of the parking garage, Bantryd pulls away.

"Why did you let them take me?"

"I didn't," Sarah says. "I didn't let them, I couldn't stop them. They're the police. They'd have locked me up too. And if that happened, I couldn't help you."

"But where have you been?"

"Trying to find you."

"This is a terrible place."

"I know. It's awful. And I'm going to take you away from here. But we've got to hurry. We don't want them to stop us."

"Is it all like this?"

"Of course not. There are good places too. That's where we're going, to a good place. To my house. You'll like my house." Sarah reaches for Bantryd's hand, tugs gently at it. "Now, come on. We've got to get out of here before someone comes."

They make their way past rows of parked cars, Bantryd glancing around apprehensively and clutching Sarah's hand. At last, Sarah sees her car. A woman wearing tight red leather pants and carrying a doctor's bag is standing next to a black SUV and staring. What does she thinks she sees? Sarah unlocks the door on the driver's side and reaches through to open the other one.

"Get in the car, quick!" Bantryd creeps warily into the passenger seat, and Sarah slides under the steering wheel. The woman is still standing there holding her bag, watching them. Sarah reaches across Bantryd, shuts the door and locks it. "Now you have to fasten your seat belt. Watch me. Like this, see?" Through the rear view mirror, Sarah observes that the woman has finally begun to walk away, but then she pauses, sets down her bag and seems to be writing something, scribbling with a pen onto the palm of her hand.

Sarah turns the key in the ignition. If this is what she was going to do, she should have smeared mud on the number plates and worn a scarf and dark glasses. But this isn't what she was going to do. The whoosh of the air conditioning startles Bantryd, who flattens herself against the seat, so Sarah switches it off.

The parking attendant charges her an extra dollar and she pays without protest, not wanting to be remembered. Back on Parramatta Road, the traffic is building up, but it's no more than you'd expect at this hour of the afternoon and most of it is westbound.

This isn't happening. It can't be happening. Bantryd spoke to her, back there. But Bantryd lives at the bottom of the sea, and she probably doesn't have vocal chords. Sarah glances at Bantryd, who stares back at her. It might not matter, that Bantryd doesn't have vocal cords. Other species communicate vocally, without vocal chords. Whales, for instance. Whales sing, and whales don't have vocal cords.

"No they don't. It's the dolphins who sing." Bantryd's tone is conversational. "All whales do is argue. Whales never agree about anything." Bantryd wriggles in her seat. "What makes you think whales sing?"

"I've heard them," Sarah says. This is ridiculous. But Bantryd seems calmer, and that's something. "I have a whole CD of whale song, recorded by scientists. That's what they call it, whale song. I suppose it could be anything, though." Sarah falls silent, recollecting the ethereal wails and whistles. "Besides, what would whales argue about?"

Bantryd has turned away and is looking out through the side window. "Oh, they argue about whether they ought to go north or south. They argue about whether it's cold or not. They argue about what they did yesterday. They'll argue about anything. They're whales."

Sarah is driving carefully, keeping to the left and slowing down at intersections, letting other vehicles pass her. She wouldn't mind turning the radio on but she doesn't want to do anything that might alarm Bantryd. But as the traffic slows to a crawl between Ashfield and Haberfield, she does turn on the radio. Bantryd stiffens and lets out a startled little yelp of terror.

"It's all right. It's only a radio. I just want to get a traffic update."

Ahead, an eighteen-wheeler attempting a left turn across two lanes of traffic has jack-knifed and is blocking the intersection. It must have just happened. Now the driver is trying to work his way out, edging forward and then backing up again, making progress an inch at a time. The light changes, and changes again. In her rear-view mirror, Sarah watches the traffic pile up behind them, automobiles and trucks, miles of hot metal growing hotter beneath the afternoon sun.

"It's strange," Bantryd says, "the way you keep moving from place to place. You're never still. You never rest. And everyone is so angry. At first I thought you were all angry at me, but you aren't. You're just angry."

"I'm not angry. I'm driving, that's all. In traffic like this, you have to be careful. You have to pay attention."

"You *are* angry, though. I can feel it. I can feel your anger." Sarah glances at her, thinking she sounds like Kahn. Bantryd is peering out the window. "And all those people. Look at them. Look how angry they are!"

Most of them are children, just released from school and wearing their school uniforms and carrying knapsacks. They swarm across the footpaths and into the street like tadpoles, definitely in the majority, although there are other people moving warily among them, mostly older women pushing their shopping carts and clutching bags of groceries.

"They're impatient, that's all. They want to get home, or wherever they're going. But they're not angry." A fight breaks out between a couple of schoolboys and other children form a circle around them, chanting and shouting. "It doesn't mean anything," Sarah says. "Kids fight all the time."

"You all fight, all the time."

"We do not."

"You want to, though. Everyone wants to hit someone. I can feel it." Bantryd twists around in her seat, looking out through the rear window. "That man, just in back of us. He wants to hit you."

"He probably does. It's Parramatta Road."

"I think it's awful," Bantryd says. "I think your life is awful."

"You don't know anything about my life."

"I know you live in a world where everybody is angry."

"That's not true."

"It *is* true. You're all angry at one another, all the time."

"Bantryd, I'm not angry. I'm tired, that's all. I had to drive practically to Parramatta to find you. When people are tired, they're sometimes irritable."

"It feels the same as anger to me."

Bantryd is accustomed to a different psychic atmosphere, a different way of being in which emotion and intuition take precedence over physical perception. It's hard to imagine and even harder to explain. A cerebral world, that's how Xaxanader described it. A world in which there's no rush hour, no traffic. No Parramatta Road.

"It's so ugly," Bantryd says.

"It's a city, Bantryd. Some of it is ugly, but some of it's really beautiful. There's the Harbor Bridge, the Sydney Opera House. People come from all around the world, just to see the Opera House." Sarah has never actually been inside the Opera House. But that's the way it always is, when you live in a place.

The eighteen-wheeler reverses one last time and finally drags itself around the corner. The light changes and they inch along, stopping and starting. Vehicles are already backed up for miles in both directions, rush hour is starting. As the traffic light in front of her blinks from green to amber Sarah accelerates, making it through the intersection but startling a pedestrian, who promptly gives her the finger. Sarah returns the gesture and glances at Bantryd, wondering how much she understands.

"I understand that you hate that man," Bantryd says. "And he hates you, too."

"I don't hate him. I don't even know him."

"Then why did you do that?"

Because it's what Australians do, in the middle of Parramatta Road. "It's a custom."

"It's not very nice."

"No, it's not."

They've been driving for over an hour, and the narrow downtown streets are swarming with commuters. Everyone is in a hurry. Busses block entire intersections. Pedestrians dart recklessly between vehicles, ignoring the lights. Sarah gasps and brakes hard to avoid a boy on a skateboard.

"You almost hit him!"

"I know. He came out of nowhere."

"Isn't it dangerous?" Bantryd is watching the boy pilot his skateboard between two cars.

"Of course it's dangerous. He'll probably end up killing himself."

"You can't blame him." Bantryd sighs. "I'd want to die too, if I lived here."

"He doesn't want to die."

The boy cuts suddenly across three lanes of oncoming traffic, and Bantryd gives a little cry. "Then why did he do that?"

"Because he's stupid."

"You don't care if he dies or not."

"He obviously doesn't care, so why should I? I just don't want to be the person who kills him, that's all."

It would be awful to kill someone, even if it wasn't your fault. It would be even more awful to kill an animal, a cat or a dog. The van in front of her stops suddenly and Sarah brakes hard, sounding her horn.

"All *right*," she says. "I'm angry. And I'm tired. I hate doing this. I hate driving at this time of day, in this kind of traffic."

"I'm sorry. It's my fault."

"It's nobody's fault. We'll be home soon."

Bantryd lapses into silence. Sarah turns onto Oxford Street, watching for busses, watching for pedestrians. Thank God it's not dark yet. Oxford Street is a nightmare in the dark.

"Can I ask you something?"

"Go ahead."

"Are they all dead?"

Sarah is waiting for a break in the oncoming traffic and only half listening. "Dead? Who's dead? What are you talking about?"

"This." Bantryd's fingers tap the dashboard. "These things. This one we're in is dead. But what about the others?"

"It's not dead, Bantryd. It's a car, it's a machine. It can't be dead because it was never alive."

Behind them and off to the left a siren wails, and Sarah's heart sinks. Did she really expect to get away with this? That woman in the parking lot must have called the police. They're hemmed in, with cars in front of them, behind them, and on either side. She can't even change lanes, much less get off the road onto a side street. Maybe it would be best to open the door and tell Bantryd to run for it.

The siren grows louder and traffic on both sides of the road comes to a halt. A police car hurtles past, weaving from lane to lane. Traffic begins to move again. Sarah almost weeps with relief.

When she finally pulls to the curb in front of her house, she feels as if she's come through a war. Sarah unbuckles her seat belt, reaches across, and opens the door for Bantryd.

"Okay, we're here. This is it." Bantryd remains motionless while Sarah gets out and walks around the car. "Come on, get out. This is where I live."

Bantryd climbs out and then falls to her knees on the nature strip, stroking the grass and murmuring.

"Bantryd, what in God's name are you doing?"

"It's alive!" Bantryd smiles, stroking the grass as if it's a kitten.

Oh, no. Sarah looks around. The old woman across the road is practically blind and dotty in the bargain, but who knows who else might be watching?

"It's only grass, Bantryd. Get up, before someone sees you."

"I'm talking to it."

"Talk to me instead. Okay?" She hauls Bantryd to her feet, pulls her into the courtyard, and latches the gate behind them. "We don't talk to grass."

"Why not?"

LEAVING BANTRYD IN THE FRONT ROOM, Sarah goes into the kitchen, fills a tumbler with ice cubes, and pours scotch over them. She sips it standing by the sink. It tastes good.

Bantryd is groping the furniture in the front room as if she's gone blind. Sarah watches her for a moment. Bantryd touches the wall, the laminated coffee table. She moves across the room to touch the blank television screen and the plastic casing of the telephone, her expression intent. Suddenly, she looks up at Sarah.

"Everything in here is dead."

"Stop saying that!" Bantryd's lower lip quivers, and Sarah says, "I'm sorry, I didn't mean to snap at you. All this talk about things being dead is upsetting me, Bantryd. It's not dead. Nothing is dead. It's just furniture."

"What do you do with it?"

"You use it. You sit on it. Like this." Sarah sits down on the couch.

It's beginning to sink in, the enormity of what she's done. She walked into a psychiatric unit and abducted a patient.

Bantryd grimaces. "I think something's wrong." She presses her hand beneath her breasts. "It hurts. And it's getting worse."

"You're probably just hungry. What did you have for lunch?"

Bantryd looks confused.

"I'll get you something to eat." Sarah returns to the kitchen, pours herself some more scotch, and finds a box of chocolate cookies in the cupboard. Of course they don't call them cookies here. They call them biscuits. And they call biscuits, scones. Bantryd is lying on the couch, her knees drawn up almost to her chin. Sarah hands her a cookie. "Go on, eat it. It'll take the edge off."

Bantryd looks curiously down at the cookie, then back up at Sarah. Bantryd has probably never seen a cookie and may not realize that it's something to eat.

"Here," Sarah says. "Watch me." She takes a second cookie out of the packet and bites into it. Bantryd watches, amazed. Sarah chews, never taking her eyes from Bantryd, whose amazement seems to be turning to alarm. "Why are you looking at me like that? What's the matter?"

Bantryd shakes her head, beyond words.

This is what happens, when you meet someone in a parallel world and bring her home with you. This is what you get.

"Bantryd, please tell me what's wrong."

"I thought you were human."

"I am human."

"Then why are you doing that? It's what animals do. It's disgusting."

Even the people in Bantryd's world have to eat, don't they? Sarah frowns. She doesn't recall having eaten while she was there, or having seen anyone else eat. There wasn't any food, not that she remembers, or any mention of food or eating. Sarah picks up Bantryd's untouched cookie.

"This is food. It's nourishment. It may look different from what you're used to, I don't know. But I do know you've got to eat, Bantryd. Everybody has to eat. Otherwise, you die."

"Lower forms of life have to spend their lives searching for food, but we don't. We absorb our nourishment naturally. That's what makes us human."

"Absorb it?"

"From the water, yes. Why do you look so surprised, Sarah? You were there, you know. You were doing it too."

"Well, it doesn't work that way here. We eat. And don't give me that look. It's not so terrible. Have you even tried it yet?" Bantryd shakes her head. "You haven't eaten anything since Saturday." It's a miracle she hasn't simply collapsed. "Then it's no wonder you feel hungry. You have to take nourishment. Everyone does. Do you understand what I'm saying?" Bantryd gives a reluctant nod. "And since you're here, you're going to have to do it the way we do it. Otherwise, you'll starve."

"Isn't there any other way?"

"Not unless you want to be fed intravenously. And you don't, believe me. Here." Sarah holds the cookie out to Bantryd. "Go on, put it in your mouth."

Bantryd stares at the cookie with a sort of transfixed horror, but then she obeys.

"Good. Now bite it, with your teeth. Let it go all the way inside your mouth, and then you've got to chew it. Watch me. See? It's easy."

Bantryd reluctantly bites. Chews. Amused, Sarah watches as a somewhat confounded look appears on her face. She swallows, convulsively. But Sarah can tell—she likes it, she likes the taste. Lips trembling slightly, Bantryd gazes dubiously at the biscuit and then at Sarah, who nods and smiles.

"It's good, isn't it?"

Bantryd takes another, larger bite. This time she chews with her mouth closed, aping Sarah, and seems to swallow less effortfully.

"How many times do I have to do this?"

"It depends on how hungry you are. We usually eat three meals every day." Bantryd puts the rest of the biscuit into her mouth. Sarah thinks she's enjoying it despite her initial misgivings.

"You know," Sarah says, "I think you did eat, even in your world. You must have. Otherwise, why would you have teeth?"

"You're wrong, Sarah. Human beings don't feed. Everybody knows that."

"Maybe not now. But I'm talking about a long time ago, way back in the beginning. Who created your world, anyway?"

"Nobody created it. The world has been the world ever since time began."

"What about before time began?"

"There was nothing."

"How did the world come out of nothing?"

"I don't know."

"But surely you must have stories about how your world was created."

"We have Tellings, but Tellings aren't stories." Bantryd thinks for a moment. "Do you have stories like that?"

"Lots of them. One of the stories is that God made the world. According to the story, it took him seven days."

"Who's God?"

"God isn't a person," Sarah says. "God is an idea."

"That's silly, ideas come from people," Bantryd says. "You can't have ideas if you don't have people. And if there are people, there's already a world. You've got it backward!" She shakes her head and laughs.

"It's not polite to laugh at other peoples' beliefs."

"I'm not. You said it was only a story." Bantryd presses her hand against her stomach again. "It's starting to hurt more. Worse than ever."

"You need some real food. A cookie is nothing, it's just a snack. Come on into the kitchen and I'll fix something for you."

It needs to be something bland, something easy to digest. Porridge would be good, but Sarah loathes porridge and doesn't have any. Soup, then. Although if she hasn't eaten in days, Bantryd should have something more substantial. Sarah takes eggs, butter, and the last of the milk from the refrigerator, breaks the eggs into a bowl, and starts beating them with a fork.

Bantryd watches, clearly fascinated. Charles used to like to watch while Sarah cooked too; he especially liked watching her make strudel, rolling the dough thinner and thinner until it hung in translucent sheets over the sides of the marble slab.

Sarah puts a pat of butter into the frying pan and turns on the burner. The butter begins to sizzle and Bantryd's happy little gasp of astonishment makes her feel like a magician entertaining children at a birthday party. Sarah tips the eggs into the frying pan, draws them toward the center with the fork until they're cooked, then turns them out onto a couple of plates.

"Scrambled eggs," she says, setting one of the plates in front of Bantryd.

Although the scotch has dulled her appetite, Sarah goes through the motions of eating to encourage Bantryd, who proves to be surprisingly adept with her fork. She also seems to be enjoying the eggs and finishes the last bite.

"It doesn't hurt any more."

"You were hungry, that's all."

"It was interesting, what you did. I've never seen anyone do that." Bantryd glances over at the stove. "Is it very hard?"

"It isn't hard at all. Anyone can scramble eggs."

"Could I do it?"

"I don't see why not." But there's only one egg left in the carton and no more milk at all. "Maybe tomorrow. I'll have to get more eggs first. And milk." Sarah stacks the dirty plates in the sink. "Come on, I'll show you the rest of the house. You need to know where things are."

Bantryd follows her without comment through the two downstairs rooms, up the stairs to peer into the bedroom, and back down again. The house seems much smaller with two people in it. Dust motes dance in a beam of late afternoon sunshine. Outside, someone's car radio blares, then falls silent. Back in the sitting room, they sit side by side on the couch. On an impulse, Sarah shuts her eyes and silently counts to ten, half expecting Bantryd to have vanished when she opens her eyes again.

"What are you thinking about?" she asks Bantryd

"They kept asking me, What's your name? Bantryd, I told them. But they wanted to know my second name. I told them, I don't have a second name. They didn't believe me. They said everyone has a second name."

"Everyone does, here."

"Why?"

"I don't know. To help keep us from getting mixed up, I guess. So we know who we are, where we belong." Sarah thinks about what Bantryd has just said. "What else did they ask you?"

"Lots of things. But I didn't know what they were talking about, so how could I answer their questions? I kept saying, I don't know. Well, I didn't know. It was the truth, but it just made them mad. Finally I asked them about my mother. Is she here? I asked. They asked me what my mother's name was, and when I told them Thasqia, they asked, What's her second name? And then we were back where we started."

"It's all right," Sarah says. "It doesn't matter. Your mother wasn't there."

"Then where is she? She's must be here somewhere, in this world."

"You said you'd be able to feel her."

"I can't feel anything at all. Maybe it's because of the anger, and all the dead things getting in the way. I didn't think it would be as bad as this." Bantryd gazes around the room, as if the answers she seeks lie somehow hidden inside the walls. "I don't know what to do. What do you think I should do?"

"I think maybe you should go home." Sarah doesn't want Bantryd to go, not yet. But it isn't a question of what she wants. Bantryd isn't safe here. "Really, that's what I think."

"But I can't just give up."

"Being sensible isn't giving up. It's being realistic. Nobody truly expected you to find your mother, that's not why Xaxanader wanted you to come. I mean, it would have been wonderful if you did find her. But that's not what he thought was going to happen. Or me, either."

"What did you think would happen?"

"This, I guess. That you'd see for yourself how difficult it was. That you'd understand. That you'd accept it—your mother and Evans are gone and you may never find out what actually happened to them. That's what it's like to be grown up. There isn't always a reason, or a happy ending."

"You think it's hopeless."

"Bantryd, listen to me. Time passes more quickly here than it does in your world. Do you know what that means?" Obviously, she doesn't. "It means that if nothing else, your mother would have almost certainly died of old age, years ago. Evans, too. If they're not dead, they must be incredibly old and very fragile. Even if you found them, they wouldn't be able to go back with you. They might not even want to. They might not even recognize you."

Bantryd slumps against the cushions. Sarah puts an arm around her shoulders.

"You tried," she says softly. "You see what it's like here. You can't feel your mother, can you?" Bantryd doesn't speak. "What more can you do? Besides, it could be dangerous. Your mother wouldn't want you to risk your freedom for nothing. If she were here in this room with us, she'd tell you to go home. That's what I'd want you to do, if I was your mother."

It's almost dark enough to turn on the lights.

"Xaxanader said it would be fun. Can't we at least do something that's fun, before I go back?"

"Like what?"

"I don't know. But I haven't really seen very much of this world, have I? Just that awful place. I haven't even seen a mall. You said some of your world was beautiful. Can we go and see something beautiful?"

"Not now. It's too late."

"What about tomorrow?"

"Bantryd, you said you'd listen to me. You promised you'd do what I told you to do. I'm telling you, it's not safe. They'll come looking for you. They're probably already looking for you. They could come in here and take you away, and I wouldn't be able to stop them."

The telephone rings, startling them both. Sarah starts to get up, then stops. There are two more rings and then the machine picks up. "I'm not able to come to the phone," says the machine. "Please wait for the tone and then leave a message." It beeps three times as Bantryd gapes at it, astounded.

"Hi, Mum. It's me, again. Felicity. Mum, you know the Blanchards? The Queensland Blanchards? As in Blanchards Department store?" Everyone in Australia knows who the Blanchards are. "Okay, listen. It's their daughter, Jennyfer. That girl, the one you saw on the beach? That's who it was. They've been trying to keep it quiet, but now she's disappeared again. It's a big story, Mum. It's going to make the front page. Mum? If you're there, Mum, please pick up. I really need to talk to you." Sarah stares at the machine, motionless. "Okay, listen. As soon as you get this message, call me. Even if it's late. Okay? So I'll talk to you later."

Bantryd looks from the machine to Sarah and then back at the machine. "Was that your daughter?" Sarah nods. "But where is she?"

"At work, I suppose. She's a journalist. She works for a newspaper."

Bantryd is still looking at the answering machine, whose green light has begun to blink. "It sounded like she was inside that box."

"Well, she isn't. That was just her voice, a recording. It's an answering machine. It takes messages."

Sarah does not want to talk about Felicity with Bantryd and casts about for something to distract her. Television? She picks up the remote, clicks on an old movie. Clint Eastwood and someone else are beating the hell out of one another, and Bantryd shrinks back against the cushions as the actors' grunts of pain fill the room.

"We call it television," Sarah says, turning down the volume. "It's another kind of machine."

Clint Eastwood is abruptly replaced by a grinning plastic bottle of household disinfectant chatting to an astonished housewife. Bantryd's expression looks so much like the housewife's that Sarah can't help smiling. More commercials follow, one chasing the next, and Bantryd watches each one with avid interest, frowning when Clint Eastwood reappears.

"It's all right. It's not really happening," Sarah says. "It's only a story."

They watch for several minutes and then Bantryd stands up and slowly approaches the television set, not taking her eyes off the screen.

"They're not really in there, are they?"

"No, it's just a picture."

Bantryd touches the screen with the tips of her fingers. Clint Eastwood is having coffee with a woman. He puts down the cup, throws a handful of change on the table, and leaves. The woman stares after him. Stroking the screen with her fingertips, Bantryd shakes her head and returns to the couch.

"Is it a Telling?"

"No, it's a story. It's entertainment. Do you want to watch? Or shall I turn it off?"

"I want to see a Telling."

"There aren't any." Sarah clicks the remote and the screen goes dark. "We don't have Tellings."

"But you must. How do you remember things? How do you learn? You have to have Tellings."

"We don't need Tellings. We have other ways. Better ones."

"Nothing is better than Tellings."

"Writing is better. It's more convenient and it lasts longer." Sarah takes a book from the stack on the coffee table and opens it. "See this? It's writing. And once you write something down, it lasts forever. Hundreds of years after you're dead, people can still read what you wrote and know what you thought." She's picked up a paperback, Tacitus. "This book was written over a thousand years ago."

"It doesn't look very old."

"It isn't the book that's old. It's what's inside it, the writing."

Bantryd takes the book from Sarah, holding it gingerly, as if she's afraid it might break.

"Go on," Sarah says. "Open it." But it's obvious that Bantryd has never seen a book and doesn't know what to do with it. "Like this." Sarah places the open book back on Bantryd's upturned palms, like a platter of cakes. "Look at it. Read it." But of course she can't read.

Bantryd lays the book carefully on her knees and runs the tips of her fingers back and forth across the pages, frowning slightly. "I don't feel anything."

"You're not supposed to feel anything. You're not supposed to touch it, you're supposed to read it. See all those marks? They're words." Bantryd continues to look up at Sarah rather than at the pages of the book. "You can't read it unless you're looking at it," Sarah says, and obediently, Bantryd looks down. "That's right. See, this is a word. And this is another word. All these words together, they make a sentence. They mean something." How do you explain reading to someone who can't read?

"Show me how to do it."

Sarah takes the book, chooses a passage, and begins to read aloud. "This the emperor knew, and he therefore hesitated about bequeathing the empire, first, between his grandsons. Of these, the son of Drusus was nearest in

222 — *Sea Changes*

blood and natural affection, but he was still in his child-hood. Germanicus's son was in the vigor of youth, and enjoyed the people's favor, a reason for having his grand-father's hatred." Sarah looks up. "It's history, Roman history. It's telling us about things that happened in ancient Rome, thousands of years ago. So it's like a Telling, but it's better than a Telling because you don't have to wait for it to happen. You can read whenever and whatever you like."

Bantryd seems dubious and somewhat deflated rather than impressed. Sarah puts the book back on the table. She's not accustomed to having someone else in the house, to having to make conversation. Not to mention all the rest of it. She needs time alone, time to think.

"I don't know about you, but I'm exhausted. I'm ready to go to bed. You can sleep down here, on the couch. It's quite comfortable, really. I'll get you some blankets and a pillow, and you'll be fine."

"What if they find me?"

"They won't find you tonight. And tomorrow, you're going home. So don't worry. You'll be fine."

Bantryd remains silent for several minutes, watching as Sarah fetches bedding from upstairs and makes up the couch for her.

"But I don't want to," she says at last.

"You said you'd listen to me and do what I told you to do. Well, I'm telling you. It's too dangerous. You can't survive here, not on your own."

"But I'm not on my own. I'm with you. You're helping me, you'll take care of me. You promised Xaxanader."

"I wasn't much help when the police decided to arrest you, was I?"

"But you came and rescued me. So it was all right in the end."

It wasn't a rescue, no matter what Bantryd thinks. It wasn't planned, really. And it so easily might have ended badly. It still might.

"Please don't say I have to go back. At least, give me a chance."

"To do what?"

"To find my mother, and Evans. At least, to find out what happened to them."

"But how can you do that? You can't even find your way to the train station!"

Why did Xaxanader agree to this mad scheme in the first place? Bantryd is brave enough, but what she's attempting is totally quixotic. Talk about tilting at windmills!

"What's a windmill?" Bantryd asks.

"It's a machine, with blades. It's driven by the wind. It grinds grain."

"How do you tilt at them?"

"You don't. That's the point. Tilting at windmills is pointless. It's futile. And so is this. And I wish you'd stop doing that, reading my thoughts."

"I'm sorry, but you were thinking out loud. You do that a lot. Sometimes it's hard for me to tell the difference."

If she tried, could she read Bantryd's thoughts? She doesn't have to. She already knows what Bantryd is thinking. But what about Xaxanader? If he was here, what would he want her to do? Sarah glances hastily at Bantryd, wondering if she's thinking out loud again. Bantryd smiles and gives a little shrug. Sarah smiles too. It's hard to stay angry at Bantryd.

It's late, and she's tired. Nothing really needs to be decided now. They can talk about it again in the morning. Sometimes things look different in the morning.

"You mean I can stay?"

"I mean," Sarah says, "we'll discuss it tomorrow. I'm going to bed but you don't have to, if you'd rather not. I'll leave the light on. You can watch more television if you like."

"No, I'll sleep. I couldn't sleep in that place. But it'll be better, here."

Bantryd lies down on the couch on her back and stares up at the ceiling, her hands folded solemnly across her chest. She looks like an effigy, like one of the marble statues carved onto coffin lids that she and Charles saw in France.

"I'll be upstairs," Sarah says. She'll leave the light in the kitchen on. Just in case. "If you need anything, call me."

In her own room, Sarah closes the door. She'll open it before she goes to bed in case Bantryd calls out, but for now she craves privacy. It's odd how quickly you become accustomed to living alone. She should return Felicity's call, even though she doesn't feel like talking to Felicity and isn't particularly interested in Jennyfer Blanchard. But Felicity will call back, Felicity will keep calling until she gets through. Better to simply be done with it. Sarah reaches wearily for the handset.

"Mum! Oh, thank God. Where were you?" Felicity doesn't wait for a reply. "Mum, I have to talk to you."

Felicity must be at her station. Reporters these days don't sit at desks, they work from tiny cubicles made of moveable partitions attached one to the next, each furnished with a computer terminal, a telephone, and a swivel chair. Sarah visited once. But isn't it hard to concentrate, she asked, with telephones ringing and everyone shouting? It is what it is, Mum.

"You got my message?" Again, Felicity doesn't wait for a reply. "Mum, this is really big. Jennyfer Blanchard went missing on Friday, never came home from school. We're talking about *the* Jennyfer Blanchard, Mum. The heiress." Felicity pauses, as if expecting Sarah to say something. "Mum, are you there?"

"I'm here, Felicity."

"Okay. Now for some reason the Blanchards didn't report Jennyfer missing until Sunday afternoon. They're saying they thought she was staying with friends." Felicity's tone is dismissive, she obviously doesn't believe this. "Anyhow, she wasn't missing for very long. The police picked her up early Sunday morning near a Sydney beach, stark naked and severely disoriented. That's what it says in the police report. I've got it right here, in front of me." Felicity pauses again. Sarah can hear her breathing but says nothing, because she can't think of anything useful to say.

"And there's more. The police didn't know who she was, of course. But they sent her to hospital for observation, and the hospital sent her to a psych unit out in Parramatta. This afternoon the Blanchards flew down from Brisbane in their private jet to collect Jennyfer and take her back home. But she wasn't there. She wasn't anywhere to be found. She's gone. She's vanished again. Poof! And nobody's got a clue." Another pause, a longish one. "Mum, say something!"

"I don't quite understand what has any of this has got to do with me, Felicity."

"Mum, your name's right here in the police report. Of course it's got to do with you! You were there, for God's sake! That girl you met on the beach was Jennyfer Blanchard.

Maybe you didn't know it at the time, but that's definitely who it was."

"That's impossible."

"I'm telling you. I've got a photo of her, I'm looking at it. And you know who she looks like? She looks like that girl we saw on Sunday. The one you were staring at, at the café. Remember how I said I knew that face from someplace? Of course I'd seen her before! It was Jennyfer bloody Blanchard."

"But Felicity, it couldn't have been. You just said they took her to hospital, to Parramatta. How could she have been in two places at once?"

"Who knows? Maybe the cops are lying, or the hospital. Maybe she'd already got away from them and now they're covering their asses. The point is, you recognized her and so did I. And even if it was someone who only looked like Jennyfer Blanchard, so what? The real Jennyfer Blanchard is out there somewhere. This is a humongous story. And it's my story, Mum! You've got to tell me the truth, what really happened, everything you can remember. But wait, just a second. Let me turn on my recorder. Okay. Let's start at the beginning. You saw her on the beach, right? What was the first thing you said to her?"

Sarah hears the rasp of the recorder and waits for the obligatory beep. It's supposed to beep every few seconds, letting you know that what you're saying is being recorded by someone. Felicity thinks this is a stupid rule because people don't like being recorded, but rules are rules. The newspaper insists that journalists use recorders on the grounds that it discourages embellishment. Sarah still hasn't heard the beep. Perhaps there's something wrong with Felicity's recorder. Felicity has never been much good with mechanical devices.

"Mum?"

"I don't want to be interviewed, Felicity. I don't want to be recorded, either." Sarah speaks slowly and carefully, so that there can be no doubt in anyone's mind. "Besides, I don't know anything that you don't already know. And I definitely don't want to be involved."

"You're already involved, Mum. I told you, your name is in the police report."

"Then print what's in the police report. Do whatever you have to do. Although," she says, "I'd really rather you didn't mention my name. I was only there with her for a couple of minutes. And I am your mother. And I don't think it was Jennyfer Blanchard, anyhow."

"I can't make an exception just because you're my mother. It wouldn't be ethical. And besides, it *was* Jennyfer Blanchard. I mean, who else could it have been?" Sarah says nothing. Since when does Felicity care about ethics? "Mum, all I'm asking you to do is tell me what happened. Why do you always have to make such a big deal out of everything?"

"I don't want to talk about it. If you want to know what happened, ask the police."

"I've already asked them!"

"Then you probably know a lot more than I do." Sarah can hear Felicity's angry breathing. "And that having been said, it's late. I've had a long day and I'm tired, and I'm going to bed. Goodnight, Felicity."

She *is* tired, but she doesn't go to bed. She simply sits there, contemplating the changing patterns the acacia and eucalyptus leaves make as they rustle in the breeze against the luminous night sky. It's never completely dark here in the inner suburbs. It's never completely quiet, either. Sydney never sleeps.

The Blanchards are an old Australian family. They're important and they're wealthy and Felicity is probably right. Anything that happens to a Blanchard is going to be news. Sarah undresses, climbs into the unmade bed, and picks up the novel she's been reading. But she can't concentrate, can no longer even remember who the various characters are or why she cares about them. They don't exist, they're figments of someone's imagination. Like Bantryd. No, not like Bantryd. Bantryd is real and downstairs sleeping on Sarah's couch.

Sarah turns off the lamp and lies still, staring up at the ceiling, listening to the cars passing in the street, to the sound of car radios and the occasional squeal of brakes.

Suppose Felicity is right? Suppose it really is Jennyfer Blanchard, asleep on the couch downstairs? Now, that would be interesting. That would mean that what I did was walk into a public hospital and abduct the only child of one of the richest men in Australia. As if I'd ever do such a thing. As if I could.

But the thought of it makes her smile.

Chapter Six

As always upon awakening, Sarah reaches across the bed to touch Charles. Nobody is there. Charles is dead and she's alone. Beyond the fan-light above the French doors, street lights glow wanly through a morning mist that obscures the tops of the trees.

Sarah lies in bed for a long time.

Beyond the rooftops, the sun rises over the sea, burning off the mist, extinguishing the sensor-controlled street lights. Magpies squawk. A sudden southwesterly gust of wind spatters rain across the steel roof like a handful of flung pebbles, but a moment later shafts of sunshine strike through the clouds and the magpies resume their quarrel outside the window.

Sarah finally gets out of bed and slips on the silk robe Charles bought for her the last time they were in Paris, after she'd admired it at Galleries Lafayette. Pale blue silk splashed with Monet water lilies; it was the most beautiful thing she'd ever seen. She didn't look at the price—I didn't dare, she told Charles—still doesn't know how much it cost. Charles wouldn't tell her.

She's smiling at the memory, just as Kahn said she would, treasuring one of the many good things she and Charles shared. The years she was married to Charles were the best, the happiest years of her life. Her smile fades. Charles is gone and will never surprise her again.

Making her way slowly down the steps, Sarah enjoys the purely tactile pleasures of the silk, cool upon her skin, of its whisper against the polished wood of the steps. Another tiny fierce squall sweeps past the windows.

She does not go into the sitting room, although she hesitates just for a moment, at the foot of the stairs.

In the kitchen, she runs water into the carafe, fits the paper filter, adds coffee, and flips the switch. The rhythm of these first minutes of the day and the performance of the simple, familiar tasks Sarah has performed every morning since she left Mama's house are comforting.

She's not hungry. That's just as well, since there's hardly anything in the house. She needs to go shopping. Dropping the last slice of bread into the toaster, Sarah thinks about what Kahn said yesterday, about lemons and lemonade. It sounded strange coming from him, as if he were translating words from another language. If you get lemons, make lemonade.

American aspirational, not the sort of thing an Australian would say. They don't even call it lemonade here. They call it lemon squash.

An amber strand of coffee dribbles slowly into the carafe. America might as well be in outer space. She'll never go back, she knows that. What would be the point? There's nobody she cares for in America, and nobody who cares for her. The coffee isn't quite ready, so Sarah walks back through to the front of the house to get her newspaper and sees Bantryd asleep on the couch, as she knew she would. Walking on past Bantryd, who hasn't stirred, she opens the front door and picks up the paper, taking care to make as little noise as possible.

She sometimes takes toast and coffee upstairs on a tray, the way she did when the children were babies and Charles had to teach an early class. But it's probably best to be here when Bantryd wakes up. They'll have breakfast, they'll talk. They'll decide what to do. Although Sarah has already decided. Nothing has really changed. Bantryd must go home.

Sitting at the kitchen table, Sarah sips her coffee and pages hurriedly through the paper. There isn't anything about Jennyfer Blanchard, but you wouldn't expect there to be, not in this newspaper. It may not even be news anymore. Jennyfer Blanchard may have already turned up somewhere. She pours herself a second cup of coffee, then turns to the crossword puzzle and is mildly annoyed to find that she can't finish it.

She reads through the newspaper again. There's nothing much, although one headline does catch her eye: What did the rat brain say to the robot? It sounds like the beginning of one of Sean's jokes, but it's a story about Australian scientists who've built a robot that's being controlled by a rat brain in a petri dish in Saudi Arabia.

There's still not a sound from the sitting room. Bantryd will probably be hungry when she wakes up. Kids her age are always hungry. She'll want breakfast, and there's nothing much in the house except coffee. Suppose Bantryd doesn't like coffee? Felicity doesn't.

Sarah abandons the newspaper for the refrigerator, where she takes inventory. Strawberry jam and marmalade, olives, capers, gherkin relish, mayonnaise, maple syrup and three kinds of mustard, but no bread and no butter. No milk, either. And no juice or eggs. None of the things you'd expect to find in a refrigerator.

She'll go to the corner shop, and while she's there she'll buy a copy of the other morning newspaper, Felicity's newspaper.

(((©_

"HEIRESS VANISHES!" THE HEADLINE SCREAMS. Beneath an enormous photograph of Jennyfer Blanchard that almost covers the tabloid's first page are the words, By Felicity Andrews. Sarah supposes she should be proud.

She buys bread, butter, milk, and eggs and walks home reading Felicity's story. Bantryd is awake, sitting on the couch with the sheet draped around her shoulders. But my God! They do look alike, Bantryd and Jennyfer Blanchard. Sarah looks at the photograph, then at Bantryd. Mostly it's the hair, almost identical, dark manes of cascading curls. But if you look closely it's obvious that Bantryd's cheekbones are more finely drawn, and her face is fuller, healthier-looking. Jennyfer Blanchard diets and purges, Sarah can tell. Even so, the resemblance between the two of them is quite remarkable. It's easy to see how Felicity got muddled.

Bantryd rubs her eyes. "Why are you looking at me like that?"

"A girl has gone missing, a girl called Jennyfer Blanchard. And it's amazing, but she actually looks a lot like you."

"Why is that amazing?"

"It just seems strange. People don't usually look so much like other people unless they're related. But don't look so worried. It doesn't mean anything. It's just a coincidence."

Toward the end of Felicity's story, there's a description of a butterfly-shaped tattoo on the back of Jennyfer Blanchard's left shoulder. Sarah puts the groceries down.

"I need to look at your shoulder," she tells Bantryd. But there's no tattoo beneath the sheet, no mark of any kind. Well, of course there isn't. Even so, Sarah is relieved. She picks up the sack of groceries and carries it into the kitchen. Bantryd follows her, her hands pressed to her heart.

"I can feel it, beating," she says.

"I should hope so. It's your heart. If it wasn't beating, you'd be dead."

Sarah unpacks the milk, butter, and eggs, leaving them on the counter. She puts a couple of slices of bread into the toaster.

"Why are you here by yourself?" Bantryd asks. "Is it a punishment?"

"It's my house. It's not a punishment to live alone, it's a privilege. I'm lucky I can afford my own place."

A bank of clouds blocks the sun, making it almost dark enough to turn on the lights. But this kitchen is always dark. There's only one window, and it looks out onto a brick wall. Sarah once tried putting pots of herbs on the window sill, but they died. It looks like it might rain again.

Bantryd sits at the kitchen table, contemplating the carton of milk. "Are we going to feed?"

"We don't say that. We say, we're going to eat. And yes, we are. I was thinking I'd make pancakes. We had eggs last night."

Sarah hasn't made pancakes since the last Sunday morning of Charles's life. She and Charles always had brunch on Sunday mornings. And it was always something special, sweet rolls or Eggs Benedict or an omelette filled with goat cheese and garnished with mint fresh from the garden. That Sunday she made crepes, Sarah remembers. She sighs. It all seems so long ago.

"I'm sorry," Bantryd says. "I don't mean to upset you. I just forget."

"It's all right, it wasn't anything you said. I was thinking about Charles, my husband."

"What happened to him?"

"I told you, he died."

"But why?"

Sarah stares. "I don't know," she says at last. They don't do autopsies in Australia automatically. Because it's socialized medicine, everyone is theoretically under a doctor's care even if they've never seen a doctor, and so when someone dies, unless it's something like a gunshot or car accident or cancer, the doctor at the hospital they've been taken to just writes *natural causes*. "We don't always know why."

"Usually, people die when they're old."

"Charles wasn't old."

Sarah measures out a precise cupful of milk and pours it into a plastic mixing bowl. She adds a cupful of flour and eggs, cracking them deftly against the edge of the counter, enjoying Bantryd's attention. It's like being Emeril cooking on camera. Instead of mixing the batter with a wooden spoon as usual, she gets out the electric mixer, further astonishing Bantryd.

"Can I try?"

Sarah switches off the mixer, gives it to Bantryd, and shows her how to hold it.

"Okay, now all you have to do is push that button forward to turn it on." As soon as she does, Sarah places her own hand on top of Bantryd's, steadying it. "Hang on, don't let go. Hold it straight so the beaters don't hit the side of the bowl. That's it. You've got it."

Bantryd looks up, eyes shining. "I'm doing it! I'm doing it!"

Sarah had looked forward to teaching Felicity to cook, but Felicity insisted she'd already learned in school. Besides, Sarah did it all wrong. "That isn't how they taught us," Felicity kept saying. "That isn't how you're supposed to do it."

This, now, this is fun. Sarah looks at the pancake batter, which is the consistency of cream. It doesn't matter. You can't mess pancakes up unless you burn them.

"It's done. First, let's turn off the mixer." She helps Bantryd press the button. "Now we have to cook them."

Sarah melts butter and shows Bantryd how to pour the batter into the pan. As the pancakes sizzle, Bantryd wrinkles her nose.

"It smells funny."

"You'll like it. Trust me."

"I do trust you. Everyone trusts you. They wouldn't have let me come if they didn't."

The unexpected change of subject is unnerving. Sarah shows Bantryd how to turn the pancakes, and after another minute, she proudly flips each one over. In no time, they're stacked on plates.

"You like doing this, don't you?" Bantryd says.

"I like to cook, yes. I always did, even when I was a little girl."

Kahn thinks this is a reaction to Mama, who liked to boast that she couldn't even boil water. Sarah always had to make her own breakfast and lunch, or go without. Papa, too. Evenings they ate heated frozen dinners or canned food warmed in the microwave oven, except on Tuesday nights, when Mama played canasta and Sarah cooked a real dinner for herself and Papa. Most kids looked forward to weekends, Sarah told Kahn. I looked forward to Tuesday nights.

She tops the stacks of pancakes with butter and syrup. "Come on, sit down. It's no good letting them get cold."

The table is so small that the edges of their plates touch. Sarah cuts Bantryd's pancakes into bite-sized wedges, as she would for a visiting grandchild. She'll probably never have a grandchild. Felicity doesn't intend to have children, and Sarah can't imagine Sean married, much less a father. He's too young. He'll always be too young.

She watches as Bantryd chews and swallows. "So what do you think? Do you like it?"

"Like it?"

She could as easily have offered Bantryd a bowl of corn-flakes, or baked beans on toast, or dog food. Bantryd wouldn't know the difference, has no grounds for comparison. All she's ever tasted is scrambled eggs and a chocolate cookie.

"Am I supposed to like it?"

"Actually, most people do like pancakes. They're a special treat."

It's unreasonable to feel hurt or unappreciated. Bantryd can't help it, she doesn't know any better.

"I always say the wrong thing, don't I? But we don't do this, we don't feed. I'm only doing it to please you." Bantryd ingests another mouthful, thoughtfully. "I can tell this isn't like last night, though."

That's interesting. She has taste buds. "No, it isn't. Last night we had eggs. These are pancakes. Which do you like better?"

Bantryd needs to think about this. Sarah waits, sipping her coffee.

"I don't know what you want me to say. And I don't want to hurt your feelings. I want us to always be friends."

"You won't hurt my feelings. You can be friends with someone and not agree with them about every little thing. People are different. Some people like sweet things, some people like savory things. There's no right or wrong about it."

"But which is which?"

So the problem isn't Bantryd's concept of taste, it's her lack of vocabulary. Never having experienced the sensation of taste, it makes sense that she can't describe it.

"Pancakes are sweet," Sarah says. "Sweet is the opposite of sour."

There's lemon juice in the refrigerator, in a little yellow plastic container shaped to look like a lemon. Sarah brings it to the table and squeezes a few drops into a teaspoon.

"Go on. Taste it."

Bantryd swallows, then makes a face. "Yuk!"

"It's sour. But the pancakes were sweet. Can you taste the difference?"

Bantryd pokes at the plastic lemon. "What is it?"

"Lemon juice."

Sarah wipes the spoon clean and shakes a little salt into it. "Now try this. It's salt. It's a completely different taste."

"How many more are there?"

"Endless variations but only one more basic taste. Basically, there's sweet and sour, salt and hot."

Cautiously, Bantryd touches the tip of her tongue to the salt. "It's like the sea."

"Salt comes from the sea."

"But it isn't nourishment."

"No, it's what we call a condiment. When you add it to things, it makes them taste better. I put salt on your scrambled eggs last night."

"Sweet and sour," Bantryd says. "Salt, and what was the other one?"

Sarah selects a jar of English mustard from the refrigerator, opens it, and takes a bit onto the tip of the spoon. "Hot. This is mustard. It's a condiment, like salt. Some people like hot things. Charles did." But lots of people don't. "Instead of tasting it," Sarah says, "just smell it."

Bantryd sniffs, and recoils as if she's been stung.

"That's worse than sour! You don't feed on that, do you?"

"Not by itself. It's a condiment, like the salt and lemon juice. It makes other things taste good. Mustard is wonderful on hot dogs. I'll tell you what. We'll have hot dogs for lunch, and you'll see for yourself."

"What's lunch?"

"It's the meal we eat in the middle of the day. Breakfast in the morning, then lunch, and then dinner, at night."

"You feed three times a day? When do you have time to do anything else?"

"We don't call it feeding. We call it eating. And we enjoy it." Absorbing nourishment through your skin may be convenient, but it isn't the same as sitting down to a steak. But how can she make Bantryd understand? "Food is sensual. It's not just nourishment. We eat in order to live, but we live to eat, too. Food is part of human culture."

"But you have to feed. I mean, you have to eat. Didn't you tell me if you don't eat, you'll die?" Sarah nods. "So if you have to do it, how can it be culture? You might as well say breathing is culture."

"We don't see it that way. Eating, actually experiencing the different tastes with your taste buds, is one of the pleasures of life. My life, anyhow. And I'm not the only one. Most people feel the same way. Besides, I like cooking. I think it's fun. I used to love cooking for Charles. Charles enjoyed food more than anyone I know. He was always trying new things. I remember once he found a recipe for boned quail stuffed with an almond forcemeat in some magazine he read on an airplane. You were supposed to wrap the quail in pancetta and serve it on little rounds of polenta." Sarah had never boned a quail before, and it took hours. "It was wonderful, absolutely delicious." She falls silent, self-conscious. Australians don't say food is delicious. When something pleases them, they say it's nice.

"You miss him."

"Yes, I do."

"But you don't want anyone else."

"No."

You could spend your whole life searching for someone like Charles and never find him. Sarah was lucky. It ended much too soon, but even so.

"Are you lonely?" Bantryd asks.

"Sometimes."

"Xaxanader is lonely."

Sarah shivers, the way people say you do when someone walks over your grave. "I suppose it's his choice, though. Isn't it?"

"Not really. It's that stupid dream he had. He believed it, though. He still believes it. Mirjk thinks it's just an excuse, but I don't think so. Xaxanader wants to love someone, of course he does. He told me so. But it's got to be the right person, that's what Xaxanader says. Mirjk says it's all right to feel that way when you're young, but not when you're Xaxanader's age."

"Mirjk is wrong," Sarah says. "Love is important. It's the most important thing there is."

"Even when you're old?"

"Especially when you're old."

"I wonder what its like," Bantryd says. "To be old."

"It's not as different from being young as you might think. You don't feel any different."

"That's what Xaxanader says. And anyway, he's not really alone. He's got me, and my family, when I have one. So there'll always be someone to tend his Telling."

"Is that so important?"

"Oh, yes. Our Tellings are as important to us as feeding is to you."

Sarah stacks the plates and flatware, carries them across to the sink, turns the hot water tap, and squirts detergent over everything.

"What are you doing?"

"Washing the dishes."

"Why?"

"Because they're dirty."

And after she washes them, she'll dry them and put them away. And she'll have to wash them again after lunch and after dinner. Leaving the clean dishes to drain, Sarah sighs.

"I'll go upstairs and get dressed, and then we'll go out."

"Where will we go?"

"Down the street. Maybe to the shops. You need to know where you live, how to find your way home. While you're here, that is."

Bantryd sinks back down on the couch, curling her legs beneath her. Her face is shiny with perspiration. Sarah is perspiring too.

"It's so hot. Is it always like this?"

"Not always. But it's summer now. Summers are hot here."

Especially this morning. The humidity is awful, even worse than usual. It feels as if you could reach up and snatch down whole handfuls of the sky.

"I thought you'd have Tellings, the way we do." Bantryd is looking absently off into space. "If you had Tellings, I'd be able to use them to find my mother."

"You would? How?"

"One Telling leads to the next, and everything's connected, so you just keep following it until you find what you're looking for. But there's nothing to follow here. There's no place to begin."

Sarah thinks what Bantryd is describing sounds a lot like cyberspace or the internet.

"You know what? Maybe there is a place to begin, after all." Bantryd looks up. "It's not a Telling, and it might not work. But it's certainly worth a try. Come on, come upstairs with me."

Bantryd follows obediently, although Sarah is mildy surprised to see that she's clinging to the banister and breathing hard. She's young, she should be to be able to climb a flight of stairs without effort.

Charles's computer stands in a corner of the bedroom. Unable to bring herself to get rid of it, Sarah simply left it in its box until a few weeks ago, when she was offered three months' of free internet access. It was fun for a while, keying in different peoples' names and seeing what came up. But when she typed in her own name, all she got was Charles's obituary notice.

Bantryd stands behind Sarah, looking over her shoulder as she logs on and enters "vestigant" into the search engine. To her surprise, there are six hits. Vestigant is a Latin word, and the six hits are variations of the same sentence; *Ac dum repetunt ictus, dum armorum aditus vestigant.*

"What does it mean?"

"I don't know. Something in Latin. I'm sorry, it's nothing to do with your mother. But we had nothing to lose by trying."

It's starting to rain, a misty drizzle that gives the trees and buildings a sepia blur. Back downstairs, she and Bantryd sit facing one another across the coffee table. In the dreary light Bantryd looks pale, even unwell. It's stuffy in here with all the windows closed. But Sarah can't open them until the rain stops.

Bantryd is looking at the palms of her hands. "I think maybe something is wrong with me."

"Did you hurt yourself?"

"No, it's inside. Look! Do you see how strange my hands look?" Sarah examines Bantryd's palms, which are slightly rosy but otherwise unremarkable.

"Maybe it's some kind of allergy." Half the people in Sydney are allergic to something: pollen, dust mites, monosodium glutamate, dogs, cats, asbestos. And every second child has asthma. "People get allergies all the time. It's nothing to worry about." Bantryd is breathing normally, she's not gasping or wheezing. "Or it might just be the humidity. It'll be better, once the storm passes."

Perhaps she should go upstairs and bring down the electric fan she keeps in the bedroom. She wishes she had air conditioning. None of the houses in Sydney have air conditioning or central heating, not even the big, expensive ones. People will tell you it doesn't get hot enough or cold enough, but it does. You sweat and swelter all summer and then spend the winter huddled next to an electric heater. Electric fires, they call them. The only comfortable months are April and September.

"It's not what I expected. I thought it would be interesting, like an adventure. And I thought I'd find them, Thasqia and Evans. Or at least I'd find out what happened to them."

"And you'd be a hero, and you'd all live happily ever after. The world's not like that, unfortunately."

"I don't care about being a hero, I just want to find them. I want to find my mother."

The naked simplicity of this brings tears to Sarah's eyes, and she turns away. She wishes she could do something, she wishes there was some way to help. But there isn't. There never was.

"There has to be more to your world than this!" Bantryd gazes around the little room, frowning. "What do you do when you're not feeding?"

"Most people go to work."

"Why?"

"To earn a living. To be able to buy food and clothes and whatever else they need."

"Do you work?"

"I did once. I'm retired, now."

"Who buys your food? Your daughter, I guess."

"I buy my own food. I have my own money." God forbid she should ever have to depend on Felicity. She'd rather pick rags. "Charles earned enough money to take care of me, before he died."

Bantryd nods. "So if you don't work, what do you do?"

"All kinds of things. I read. I listen to music. I go to the shops."

"But you don't have a Telling."

"No. I don't."

"Maybe I could teach you how to start one."

"I don't want a Telling."

Bantryd looks shocked. "I'd give anything in the whole world to have my own Telling," she says in a quiet little voice.

"Then why don't you?"

"I haven't got anything to tell."

"Yes, you do. You've been in jail. You've been in a car. You've watched television. You've eaten scrambled eggs, you've made pancakes. Nobody else in your world has done any of those things."

"Nobody would want to. Besides, they wouldn't believe me. And I don't think I'd even want tell them about feeding. People would think it's disgusting."

"Why? I should think if anything, they'd be curious. You have taste buds, Bantryd, the same as we do. And you have teeth, you all have teeth. You wouldn't have teeth if you weren't meant to chew things and you wouldn't have taste buds if you weren't meant to taste things. It's like I said last night, I think your ancestors used to feed. Don't you at least think that's interesting?"

"What are taste buds?"

"Tiny bumps on your tongue."

Bantryd sticks out her tongue and touches it with her index finger. "I don't feel any bumps."

"They're too small for you to be able to feel them. But you've got them, because if you didn't, you wouldn't know the difference between lemon juice and salt. And you do. You probably didn't always live in the sea."

"Of course we did! We've lived in the sea since time began."

"The sea hasn't been there since time began. During the Ice Ages, the oceans dried up and turned into desert. And when the ice melted, the deserts turned back into oceans but they weren't the same oceans." Bantryd startles as hailstones clatter against the window ahead of a gusting, southerly wind. "It's only hail," Sarah says. "It'll stop in a minute."

The squall sweeps majestically in from the south, driving a mixture of hail and pelting rain before it. The rain intensifies, cascading noisily down onto the steel roof, streaming from down-spouts and overflowing gutters to flood the footpaths. The nature strip looks like a lake.

It seems to ease a little, and then a deafening clap of thunder startles even Sarah. Bantryd whimpers with terror as lightening forks down, so close that it fills the room with an eldritch light that's worse than darkness. It struck one of the trees on the other side of the street, and the acrid smell of burning seeps into the room. Bantryd moans and cowers on the couch. Sarah sits down next to her and Bantryd burrows into her arms, forehead pressed against Sarah's shoulder. She's trembling. Sarah holds her tightly.

"It's only lightning. See? It's practically all over now. It's outside, it can't hurt you." She feels awkward, half afraid that Bantryd will pull away from her, tell her to stop being ridiculous. That's what Felicity would do. Bantryd simply nestles closer. It feels good to be able to comfort someone, to seem strong. "There, now. I told you, it's all right. It's all right."

THE TREE OUTSIDE HAS split asunder, wisps of smoke rising above it into the flooded gray sky. Sarah has to get up, to pull the curtains shut. "Bantryd, try to calm down. It'll be over soon."

Bantryd is still frightened, but at least she's stopped shaking. The storm is moving fast, and the rumble of thunder has already abated. The rain is easing too, although it shows no sign of stopping. It could go on like this for hours.

Even so, it's only a storm. And look at Bantryd! She was terrified, is still scared. She can't cope, she can't cope with any of it. Bantryd needs to go home, back where she belongs, whether she wants to or not. But not while it's raining.

Sarah switches on a lamp. In the wan light, Bantryd's face looks oddly thinner, her brow and chin sharply defined against the masses of dark curls.

"You have such beautiful hair."

"That's what one of them said too. The one who brought me nourishment. She brought it on a tray, with a cover over it. But I didn't know what it was, so I didn't know what to do with it. And then after a while, someone else came and took it away."

They wouldn't have cared whether she ate or not, probably wouldn't have even noticed. Just as well, because if they thought Bantryd was trying to starve herself, they might force-feed her, shove a plastic tube into her nose and down her throat into her stomach.

Sarah picks up a magazine and leafs distractedly through it. Charles subscribed to all sorts of magazines: current affairs, book reviews, and professional journals, stacks of which are still in a closet. She can't bring herself to cancel the subscriptions, just as she can't bring herself to get rid of Charles's computer. It doesn't matter. One by one, the subscriptions are lapsing.

It's so dark that the street lights have come on. But now that the rain has almost stopped, traffic is moving again. Headlight beams cut yellow swaths through the curtain of water, reflecting off the streaming asphalt. A few pedestrians venture out, stepping gingerly around the puddles on the footpath. Mostly women, holding umbrellas and dragging shopping carts. The light softens their features, incorporating them into the landscape. They could be French or Italian or Russian, in any city in the world.

Sarah goes upstairs to get dressed, leaving Bantryd on the couch. Self-consciously, she closes the bedroom door behind her. The house is too small for two people, which was why nobody bought it until Sarah came along. It's small and old but it wasn't cheap; you could buy three quite decent houses in an American city for what this one cost. They say Sydney is one of the most expensive cities in the world.

In a few hours, it'll be over. They'll drive to the beach and she and Bantryd will wade out into the surf and hug one another, and say good bye. And it'll be over, as if it never happened.

Bantryd is still sitting where Sarah left her, hugging herself and rocking back and forth the way Sean used to when he was little. Sarah goes to the window and looks out.

"It's just a drizzle now. We don't have to sit here, you know. I need groceries. We can walk up to the shops."

"I don't know. I still don't feel well."

It's likely just a trick of the light, but it seems to Sarah that Bantryd has somehow faded, like Tinkerbell when her light was going out. Clap if you believe in fairies. And everyone except Sarah did. I would have felt awful if Tinkerbell had died, she told Kahn. But I didn't clap because I didn't believe in fairies.

"Does anything hurt?" she asks Bantryd.

Bantryd shakes her head.

It's depressing, being cooped up like this. That's probably all that's wrong. Bantryd needs to get out of the house, to breathe some fresh air. "It's no good sitting in here," Sarah says. "Come on. I'll show you what a mall looks like."

They share an umbrella. The air is mild and warm, although rain continues to patter straight down from the windless sky. It's a relief just to get out of the house.

All the pavements are flooded, and in some places the pooled water is ankle-deep. As usual, the storm drains at both ends of the street are full to overflowing, turning the gutters into angry little rivers. Two barefoot boys in shorts race past them, shrieking as a delivery truck sends a sheet of water over the footpath, drenching a man in a black suit.

Sarah's sandals are soaked through before they reach the corner. They stop, waiting for the light to change.

"Where are we going?" Bantryd asks.

"To the supermarket. There's not much food in the house and we haven't got anything for lunch, unless you want eggs or pancakes again."

They walk another block and cross a second, wider street. Shopping carts are lined up outside the entrance to the supermarket. Sarah disengages one and maneuvers it ahead of her through the automatic sliding doors. A blast of frigid air hits them, and Sarah tucks Bantryd's hand firmly under her arm.

"Stay close to me. You don't want to get lost."

Pushing the empty cart, Sarah steers Bantryd through the produce department, past the bright pyramids of apples, oranges, lemons, and plums from Victoria. Bantryd stares, wide-eyed. The avocados look good. Sarah chooses one and puts it in the cart. Tahitian limes are on special. When Charles was alive, they waited all year for limes to come into season so she could make Key Lime pie. Sarah puts six limes into a plastic bag and places it in the cart next to the avocado.

Next to her, Bantryd is gazing fixedly at something, looking horrified. "Bantryd, don't stare. It isn't polite."

"Some of them are still alive. Can't you hear them?" She's looking at a pile of lettuce. "It's awful. We've got to help them."

Help the lettuce? "I don't hear anything. Come on." They do look fresh, they still bear traces of dirt. But produce is supposed to be fresh. "You're imagining things. Lettuce doesn't cry. Now, come on."

"They're crying," Bantryd says as Sarah pulls her away. "We have to help them."

"We can't help them. It's too late. Besides, it's not allowed."

A woman who grew the best roses in Melbourne claimed she talked to all of them. There may have been something to it, because she won blue ribbons every year. But roses aren't lettuce. People don't grow roses so they can eat them.

They move up and down the aisles, past paper sacks of flour and sugar, past rows of spices, past shelves stacked with loaves of bread. Sarah puts a packet of hot dog rolls into the cart. In the next aisle she selects several tins of soup, creamed corn, and baked beans, wishing she'd taken the time to make a list. Bantryd dawdles, looking back toward the produce. Can she still hear the lettuce? Sarah glances down at the avocado and the limes. Why haven't they said anything? Maybe they're asleep.

"You really don't hear them, do you?" Bantryd says.

"No, I don't. Lettuce doesn't talk, not in this world. Or if it does, we can't hear it."

"Somebody must be able to hear them!" Before Sarah can stop her, Bantryd has approached the woman wearing lace-up brogues who's pushing a cart just ahead of them.

"Can you hear them? Can you hear their voices?"

The old woman blinks rheumy eyes. "Beg your pardon, luv?"

"Do you hear voices crying for help?"

"I'm sorry," Sarah says quickly. "She can't help it. It's best if you just ignore her."

She should have known better than to bring Bantryd into a public space. Bantryd is an alien, a creature from another world.

Sarah glances into the cart. She has everything she needs except the hot dogs, and they're just around the corner in the refrigerated counters next to the meat.

The supermarket brand is on special, and Sarah hesitates. Hot dogs are hot dogs, that's what Charles would say. Bantryd has moved a step or two ahead and is standing in front of the chickens. Oh, God. She's got that look on her face. Sarah moves quickly to her side.

The chickens have been plucked, split, and wrapped in plastic. Bantryd stares fixedly at them, swaying slightly, lips parted in disbelief. Several other shoppers stop to look, afraid they might be missing something, and a woman in a pink velour tracksuit moves closer, prepared to snap up the bargain, whatever it may be. Sarah steps in front of her with an apologetic smile, shielding Bantryd.

"I'm sorry. She can't help it, you know." She turns to Bantryd. "Behave yourself, or I'll have to take you home."

Eyes averted, the woman in pink moves off. Bantryd remains motionless. Sarah pokes her. "It's no good standing here like this. Come on."

"You eat one another."

"We do not. We eat animals."

"But they were alive once." Bantryd's lips are barely moving. "Animals are sentient beings, too."

The hot dogs were a mistake. The avocado and the limes were a mistake. This whole thing was a mistake.

"Come on, let's get out of here."

The market is crowded. People who don't necessarily need groceries still want to get away from the heat and humidity, and the supermarket is air-conditioned.

Sarah pulls Bantryd along toward the front of the store. There are plastic receptacles dispensing newspapers for sale in front of the cash registers. Felicity's newspaper. Jennyfer Blanchard's photograph is staring them in the face. Suppose someone mistakes Bantryd for Jennyfer Blanchard? The sooner Bantryd goes back where she belongs, the better, rain or no rain.

As Sarah places the avocado on the moving surface of the counter, the woman in brogues approaches Sarah and smiles at them. "It's hard, having one like that at home," she whispers. "But it's not as if you have a choice. A child is a child, isn't that so? And one day, you'll be glad of the time you had together." They both gaze at Bantryd, awkwardly clinging to the cart like a gigantic toddler. "God bless." The woman gives Sarah's shoulder a little squeeze and moves on.

The woman ahead of them is buying tins of cat food, different flavors, all in sauce. Her face is deeply lined, pinched and mean-looking, not like the face of a woman who has a cat or any sort of pet. She counts the money out of a small purse, fingering each coin for a moment before she hands it over. Sarah read a story about pensioners eating cat food in Felicity's newspaper. They heat it and pour it over rice.

Bantryd watches the avocado being scanned and placed in a plastic bag. Outside, it's still raining. Squinting up at the sky, Sarah tries to persuade herself that it's grown a bit lighter. It doesn't matter. Rain or no rain, Bantryd has to go. They walk back the way they came, shoulders touching beneath the open umbrella, silent.

It's a shame, really. Bantryd has the wrong idea about this world. "Those chickens would never have been alive in the first place if they hadn't been bred for food."

Bantryd glances up. "That's even worse."

Not everyone eats meat, but what's the point? Vegetarians eat vegetables. Sarah is grateful the avocado hasn't said anything.

Bantryd stops walking so suddenly that Sarah bumps into her. "Now what?"

But before Bantryd can reply Sarah sees for herself. It's a patrol car, double-parked in the street directly in front of her house. There's no siren and no flashing lights, but it's definitely the police, a white sedan with blue markings.

It's bound to be about the girl on the beach they all seem to think was Jennyfer Blanchard. But it wasn't, it was Bantryd. So they mustn't see her.

"We'll go around the other way," Sarah says, "down the lane. We can get in through the back gate." Bantryd hesitates. "Hurry! They haven't seen us yet. Come on!"

They cross the street in the middle of the block and duck into the narrow lane that runs parallel to Patrick Street, behind the houses. Honey wagons once used these lanes, plying back and forth, emptying the septic tanks in the out-houses. And not all that long ago, either. Several properties on Patrick Street still aren't connected to the sewer.

A single roller-door at the rear of Sarah's property opens onto a concrete parking space in her back garden, but the lane is so narrow Sarah often finds it easier to park out front. She reaches up over the top of the wooden gate and unlatches it.

"Wait here. Crouch down behind the rubbish bin, and they won't be able to see you from the house. I'll go around to the front and get rid of them."

Careful not to let the gate bang as she shuts and latches it, Sarah retraces her steps, walking down Patrick Street toward her front gate and trying to look like a woman who's just returning from a quick trip to the shops. The police car is still there and her front gate is ajar, swinging in the wind. Sarah hears voices even before she enters the courtyard.

"Mrs. Andrews? Sarah Andrews?" Even from here she can hear their bare knuckles against the wood of her front door. Why don't they just ring the doorbell? Maybe they already did. "Anybody home in there?"

Suppose it isn't about Jennyfer Blanchard after all? Suppose something's happened to Sean or Felicity? Sarah enters her courtyard with swift firm steps and confronts them.

"What is it? What's happened?"

"Mrs. Andrews?"

"What are you doing here? What's wrong?"

"Are you Mrs. Andrews?" Sarah nods. "That's fine, then. Nothing's happened, Mrs. Andrews. Nothing's wrong, there's nothing for you to worry about. We'd just like a word, that's all."

Sarah feels her lips trembling but tells herself there's nothing wrong with that. Any normal person would panic, coming home and finding the police on their doorstep.

"A word about what?"

"There's no need to get yourself all worked up. We just need to ask you a few questions about that incident the other night."

Sarah looks at them for a moment. She doesn't want to talk to them, she doesn't want them inside her house. "All right, then." She fumbles in her purse for her keys. If she says she can't find them, they'll have to talk out here. But it's no use. She doesn't really have a choice. "I suppose you'd better come in."

They follow her into the living room, wiping their wet boots on the doormat but sitting down side by side on the couch without waiting for an invitation. Bantryd's blanket is still lying in a heap on the floor, but they don't seem to notice.

"I'll just put these things in the kitchen."

"Take your time, ma'am."

Sarah doesn't want to leave them alone in her sitting room for a moment more than necessary. "What do you want to ask me, then?"

"You've heard about the Blanchard girl?"

"I read about it in the paper. Awful, isn't it? A young girl like that." They nod solemnly and nobody says anything for several seconds. The older of the two officers tugs at the zip of the black vinyl folder he's carrying and extracts a large glossy black and white photograph which he places on the coffee table in front of Sarah. She sits down opposite them, pretending to study the photograph.

"That's Jennyfer Blanchard."

Sarah continues to gaze at Jennyfer Blanchard's confident smiling face for a moment longer, hoping to give the impression of thoughtfulness.

"She's very pretty, isn't she?"

"Have you seen her?"

"No."

"I mean, since the other night."

Sarah looks down at the photograph again, frowning. "What are you saying? Was that girl on the beach Jennyfer Blanchard?"

"What do you think? You saw her yourself, didn't you? And this here, this is Jennyfer Blanchard. Looks like the same girl, I reckon. Two peas in a pod."

She forces herself to hesitate, to take her time and seem to be seriously considering the possibility. "I don't know. The hair, maybe. But it was so dark. I never really got much of a look at her face."

"Be understandable, especially if you were a bloke." They both snicker. "Seriously, but. Wouldn't you say there's a likeness?"

"A likeness, yes." Sarah waits for whatever is coming next, but neither of them says anything. "But what's it got to do with me?" she asks at last.

"You said she told you she was going to stay with friends. What friends? Did she mention any names? Addresses?"

"No, nothing like that. I'm sorry." They're investigating, they're simply doing their job. She was on the beach in the middle of the night with a girl who has turned out to look like Jennyfer Blanchard. If Bantryd wasn't Bantryd, this whole thing could be cleared up in five minutes. "I've already told you everything I know."

The younger officer shuffles his feet and Sarah wonders if she dare suggest they leave. No, better not. Most people would offer them a cuppa, but Bantryd is outside by herself, in the rain. The older officer stands up and takes a step across the room to gaze at the Klimt print hanging over the fireplace. He turns back toward Sarah and hands her a card.

"If she does contact you, I'd appreciate it if you'd ring this number. It's a direct line."

"Of course." Sarah feels that something more is needed but hesitates, reluctant to strike a false note that might ruin everything. "I can't imagine that she'll contact me, though. I don't even think she knows my name."

This seems to satisfy them. They move slowly toward the front door, seeming very large in their uniforms. It feels as if they've been here for hours, as if they've somehow used up all the air.

Sarah locks the front gate behind them and stands in the doorway, listening for the sound of the motor as the patrol car starts up, watching as it moves away. Then she goes back through the house and out through her tiny back garden to where Bantryd is still crouched behind the rubbish bin.

The wind has picked up, gusting sheets of rain across the yard beneath the corrugated iron roof. Bantryd is shivering, her long, dark hair wet and flattened against her skull. She looks younger and thinner, almost fragile.

"It's all right. They're gone." Bantryd's shirt and jeans are soaked, clinging to her body and dripping puddles on the wood floors. "Come on upstairs and I'll find you some dry clothes." Most of Sarah's clothes are too big, even for Sarah; she lost a lot of weight after Charles died. She finds a blue track-suit that shrunk in the wash and a pair of silly pink slippers that Charles bought for a joke one Valentine's Day. "Dry yourself off and put these on. I'll be downstairs."

Sarah's own legs are trembling. Alone, she sinks down on the couch and puts both hands over her face, just for a moment. But the police are gone, it's all right. Nothing happened. Bantryd is safe.

The card the police left is still lying on the coffee table. Sarah picks it up, turns it over and over.

Bantryd is working her way slowly down the stairs, clinging to the banister and looking unwell, the track-suit hanging on her body like a hand-me-down. She's put the slippers on the wrong feet.

"They were looking for me, weren't they?"

"They were looking for that other girl, Jennyfer Blanchard. The one whose picture was in the newspaper."

Bantryd's hair, still damp, hangs limply on her shoulders and down her back. Sarah feels guilty for having left her out in the rain like that.

"Are you okay?"

"I don't know what's wrong with me. I've never felt like this before."

She sits down next to Sarah, lifts her hands slowly and places them palms upward upon her knees. She stares at them for a moment, then slowly raises them, still staring. Her head moves slightly as she scrutinizes first one palm and then the other. Sarah looks but can't see anything out of the ordinary. A whole minute passes. Bantryd remains absorbed, oblivious. At last she gives a tremulous little sigh and places her hands carefully back in her lap.

"I think I'm going to die."

"Don't be ridiculous." Sarah is alarmed, nonetheless. "You're coming down with something, that's all. Maybe you've caught a cold."

Bantryd shakes her head.

"You're not going to die. Not for a long while, anyway. People your age don't die."

They do, though. Papa's brother died when he was seven. His appendix burst and by the time they got him to the hospital, it was too late. Whenever Sarah had a stomach ache, Papa used to make her lie down on the floor and draw her knees up to her chest. If you can do that, Papa said, you don't have appendicitis. Stop it. Bantryd does not have appendicitis. Bantryd probably doesn't even have an appendix.

But her skin does look sallow, almost as if it's been stained. And in this light Bantryd's face seems long and pinched, hinting at what she'll look like when she's older. She's sitting quietly and she certainly doesn't seem to be in any pain. She's overtired, that's all. Or she's allergic to something. Or Sarah was right the first time, and she's caught a cold.

"Why don't you lie down for a while? Just for a few minutes, just to see if it helps." Bantryd lets Sarah help her stretch out on the couch, rolling over onto her side, drawing up her legs, closing her eyes. Sarah retrieves the blanket and places it lightly over Bantryd's shoulders. "Is that better?"

"I don't know. A little, maybe."

"You're tired, that's all. Try to sleep for a bit."

It's stopped raining. Sarah goes out into the courtyard and checks the sky toward the south, where the weather comes from. It *is* a little lighter, although still quite overcast. Damn the weather. Bantryd could have been home by now.

Back indoors, Sarah lights a lamp and picks up Tacitus but puts the book down again after a moment or two. You have to be in the mood for Tacitus. It's raining again. Just a drizzle, but a steady, determined drizzle that could continue until morning.

Bantryd must go back where she belongs, back to her own world and her own kind. That's what has to happen. Rain or no rain. Let her get some rest and later this afternoon when she's feeling better, I'll take her to the beach.

In the kitchen, Sarah takes the scotch bottle out of the cupboard and pours a generous amount into a water tumbler, not bothering with ice. Even though it's close to noon, the kitchen window is dark. Sarah sips the scotch, scowling back at her disapproving reflection.

It would all be a lot easier if they found Jennyfer Blanchard. Maybe Felicity has heard something. Upstairs, Sarah punches in Felicity's number.

"Hi, Mum. What did you think of my story?"

"Very good. Very thorough. Although I have to say, I wish you hadn't used my name."

"Couldn't help it, Mum. The facts are the facts, and the public has a right to know."

They were disappointed when Felicity decided to be a journalist. Charles in particular had hoped she'd choose what he called a proper profession. God knows, they'd given her every opportunity.

"Felicity, the police were just here. They wanted to know if I'd heard from that girl on the beach."

"I told you, Mum. That girl was Jennyfer Blanchard. So of course they want to ask you questions. They're questioning everybody who came into contact with her, even the shrinks."

"Then they haven't found her yet."

"Found her? They don't even know where to start looking. Wait, here's something coming in. It says the Blanchards just taped a press conference. They're offering a five hundred thousand dollar reward."

"My God."

"Five hundred thousand dollars." Felicity's voice is subdued, even reverent. "Mum, do you know what a person could do with that much money? You could buy a car. You could buy a house. You could take ten years off and live on the Left Bank."

"But what else is happening? Are there any leads?"

"Since when do you care?"

Sarah hesitates. "Well, if you're right and that girl really was Jennyfer Blanchard, I suppose I'm involved."

"It's Jennyfer Blanchard, Mum. Trust me. And I'll tell you something else." Felicity lowers her voice. "I don't think she ran away. I mean, why would she run away? She's Jennyfer Blanchard, for Christ's sake. She's going to inherit a zillion dollars."

Sarah wants to say that money isn't everything, but doesn't. "Where is she, then? Do you think someone kidnapped her?"

"It's a possibility, yeah. But if she's been kidnapped, like for ransom, I personally think there would have been a note or something by now. On the other hand, somebody did abduct her from the hospital. Although they don't even know that for certain. It might have just been one of her girlfriends helping her."

"Or one of her boyfriends."

"No, it wasn't a guy. It was a woman. There was a witness. They've even got a description." Sarah hears the rustle of papers. "Here it is. Caucasian female, medium height, medium weight, light brown hair, sun glasses. Driving a white car."

"It's not as though it was a crime," Sarah says thoughtfully.

"Abducting a patient from a mental hospital? Of course it's a crime, Mum!"

"I wasn't talking about whoever helped her. I meant Jennyfer Blanchard isn't a criminal. She didn't kill anyone or rob a bank. She's just missing, and that's not a crime, is it?" It wouldn't be a crime in the United States, although Sarah knows better than to say anything positive about America to Felicity. "So why is it a crime if someone helped her? She was a patient, not a prisoner."

"Mum, you don't understand. This isn't some kid gone missing. This is Jennyfer Blanchard. And if you're Jennyfer Blanchard, you don't just piss off."

You might.

"And even if she did, all she'd have to do is ring up the police from a pay phone or a mobile and say, I'm Jennyfer Blanchard and I'm fine, so get off my case."

"But how would they know it was really her?"

"They'd ask her a question, like they do when you forget your PIN number. Her mother's maiden name, something like that." A telephone rings. "Mum, my other phone's ringing. Catch you later, okay?"

Mothers' maiden names are a matter of public record, accessible to anyone. Sarah sits down in front of Charles's computer. It takes less than ten minutes to confirm that Jennyfer Blanchard's mother's maiden name was Dawkins.

If they believe Jennyfer is safe, they'll stop looking for her. They'll leave me alone, and they'll leave Bantryd alone, too. It'll just take one little telephone call. But suppose Jennyfer Blanchard really has been kidnapped? Impeding a police investigation is a crime, almost as bad as kidnapping. But they're not looking for Jennyfer Blanchard, they're looking for Bantryd. And they're looking in the wrong place, because Jennyfer Blanchard was never even on the beach that night.

Bantryd murmurs in her sleep and stirs slightly. Bending over her, Sarah touches her lips lightly to Bantryd's forehead, checking to make sure she isn't running a fever.

She'll drive to King's Cross and make the call from there. That way, they can't trace it. It won't take long, there's hardly any traffic at noon. Everyone's doing lunch.

It's me, Jennyfer. I just called to tell you to stop looking for me. I'm all right, but I don't want to go home. And just so you know it's really me, my mother's maiden name is Dawkins.

There's a bank of pay phones just outside the King's Cross station. Sarah parks a couple of blocks away on a meter and walks the rest of the way. All the kiosks are occupied, and she has to wait nearly ten minutes for an empty one. But in the end, she doesn't make the call. Jennyfer Blanchard really is missing, and it would be wrong to mislead the police.

BANTRYD SLEEPS THROUGH most of the afternoon. Loath to wake her, Sarah reads a novel and sips scotch. Nobody else calls and nobody comes to the door. It's like this most days. It might be nice to have a little dog, for company. She and Charles had a wonderful dog when the children were young, Penny. She grew up with them, ended up living nearly fifteen years and dying peacefully in Charles's arms. Good innings for a Dalmatian, people said. It seems so long ago, another person living another life.

You have to move on, Kahn says. Life without Charles is different, but it's still life. It can still be wonderful. It can be whatever you make it.

Sarah rubs her eyes, which have begun to itch. Her eyes always itch when it rains. Charles would have known what to do. For better or for worse, till death do us part. She always thought she and Charles would grow old together, die together. Or that she'd die first.

It's almost dark. The sun must be setting and even if it wasn't raining, it's now too late to go to the beach.

"Behind the clouds," Kahn once said, "the stars still shine."

"But that's not true. The stars died millions of years ago and what we call starlight is that final explosion of light, travelling soundlessly through the universe. Charles knew all about it. The stars themselves no longer exist."

"Perhaps," Kahn said. "But I still think the night sky is beautiful."

This awful, interminable day is almost over. Time goes faster now. Sarah remembers an afternoon when she was six, helping Papa plant beans, and afterward, squatting there and waiting for them to come up. She was devastated when Papa told her it would take days, maybe a whole week. A week seemed such a long time when she was six.

She switches on the lights in the kitchen and living room and is drawing the curtains when she hears Bantryd cough.

"Are you okay? Are you hungry?"

Bantryd shakes her head, again scrutinizing the palms of her hands. "I don't know what's wrong with me. Nothing like this ever happened before. I don't know what to do."

Sarah takes one of Bantryd's hands and looks at it, but Bantryd's skin still looks smooth and young.

"I don't want to die."

She's genuinely frightened. Sarah can smell her fear. "You're not going to die, Bantryd. You've caught cold, that's all. Let's see what's on the news."

The leader of the opposition party is demanding the immediate resignation of the minister for health following the disappearance of missing Queensland heiress Jennyfer Blanchard, and police are seeking a woman as yet unnamed for further questioning. Police are also interviewing owners of late-model white Nissan sedans. Meanwhile, search teams combing the beach have recovered items that may be significant.

They have it wrong. It wasn't Jennyfer Balanchard, not on the beach and not in the hospital, either. Jennyfer Blanchard could be anywhere in Australia, she could be anywhere in the world. They think they're looking for her, but they're not. They're looking for the girl on the beach. They're looking for Bantryd.

Sarah and Bantryd sit side by side for some minutes, until Sarah turns off the television. "I don't know about you, but I'm hungry. I'm going to fix soup. Do you want some?"

Bantryd shakes her head but Sarah heats enough for two anyway, in case she changes her mind. Feed a cold, starve a fever—or is it starve a cold, feed a fever? Whatever, Bantryd needs to keep her strength up. First thing tomorrow morning they'll go to the beach, even if it's still raining. The avocado is tempting, but Sarah doesn't dare cut into it while Bantryd is here. Waiting for the soup to warm, she pours herself a glass of red wine. Charles always said that cheap Australian reds left French vin ordinaire for dead. Sarah divides the hot soup between two bowls and calls Bantryd.

"At least come and sit with me, keep me company." Bantryd settles herself obediently across from Sarah. "I wish you'd try to eat some of this. We didn't have any lunch, you know." Maybe that's all that's wrong with Bantryd. She's young, she needs nourishment, and she's hardly eaten a thing.

Listlessly, Bantryd sips the soup a spoonful at a time. "You're in trouble now, aren't you? And it's all because of me. I'm sorry. I didn't mean for any of this to happen."

"It's all right. It's not your fault. And I'm not in trouble, not really. Everything's going to be fine."

"And I'm scared." Bantryd puts down her spoon. "I don't want to die."

"Stop talking like that! You're not going to die. You're going home. Tomorrow morning, first thing. After you've had a good night's sleep."

"No! You said we'd talk about it!"

"Bantryd, look at yourself! Something's making you sick. Something here, in this world. You don't belong here. If you stay, you'll just get worse. Something is wrong, and I don't know what it is and I don't know what to do about it. And neither do you." Bantryd bites her lip but doesn't say anything. "You've got to go home. Unless you've got a better idea?"

After a long moment Bantryd shakes her head. There are tears in her eyes. There are tears in Sarah's eyes too.

"I don't want you to go. But it's for the best, you know that, don't you?"

Bantryd seems about to say something, but doesn't.

"I'd never forgive myself if anything happened to you," Sarah says.

Another silence.

"I know," Bantryd says at last. Her voice is low, barely audible. "And you're right. I'll go. I'll do whatever you say."

Sarah pours herself another glass of wine. Again she has the impression that Bantryd is quietly fading away before her eyes, becoming younger and smaller. She remembers a story she once read about a beautiful, aging woman who discovered a potion that made her younger and younger, until she finally died at birth. But it was just a story.

"I never thought it would be like this. Nobody did." Bantryd is staring at her palms again. "What will you tell Xaxanader?"

"I won't tell him anything, because there's nothing to tell. You're going home, and you'll be fine." It's time for the Blanchard's press conference. Sarah leaves the dirty bowls and spoons in the sink, goes to the sitting room, and turns on the television.

There's a montage of photographs onscreen; Jennyfer at a party, Jennyfer laughing with friends, Jennyfer emerging from a swimming pool. Happy, rich Jennyfer Blanchard. The camera cuts to Stanley Blanchard, balding and perspiring through his makeup, seated next to his wife Therese in front of a table. Stanley speaks, obviously reading from a prompt. "If you can hear this, Jennyfer, Mum and I want you to know that we love you. Don't be afraid. Everything's going to be all right." Here Stanley lifts his chin, suddenly pugnacious. "My wife and I are offering a cash reward of five hundred thousand dollars to anyone who has information that will help us bring our daughter home. Five hundred thousand and no questions asked." His small, dark eyes brim with a baleful intelligence. "Five hundred thousand dollars," Stanley says again, slowly and thoughtfully this time, as if he doesn't quite believe it himself.

Alongside him, Therese sniffles and dabs at her eyes with a tissue.

"That's a lot of money, folks," anchorman Paul Parsons says. "Five hundred thousand dollars. Half a million, just for helping Stanley and Therese find their little girl."

Bantryd is back on the couch, curled up with the blanket pulled over her shoulders. Sarah turns off the television, and the lights.

"Get some rest," she tells Bantryd. "We'll leave as soon as the sun is up."

SARAH USUALLY READS IN BED, but unable to concentrate tonight she lies on her back, staring at the ceiling.

Maybe something like this happened to Bantryd's mother and the others. Maybe it was nothing sinister, after all. Maybe they just got sick and died.

She must have dozed off, because when she looks at the clock again it's past ten. Is Bantryd all right? Should she go downstairs and check?

Bantryd is fine. It's a cold, nothing more. People catch cold all the time. Sarah sighs and closes her eyes.

Chapter Seven

The sun is already up, climbing steadily higher in the cloudless sky, drawing moisture from the saturated earth and transforming it into a diaphanous mist. It's going to be a scorcher. Sarah stretches. She feels strong and rested.

Downstairs, Bantryd lies motionless on the couch. It doesn't look as if she's moved since last night. Uneasily, Sarah lifts the blanket just long enough to see that she's still breathing. It may still be all right. They say sleep is the best medicine.

Sarah makes coffee and toast, brings a tray back into the sitting room so she can catch the morning news. No new developments, although there's a long segment about Jennyfer Blanchard cobbled together from last night's footage, stills of Jennyfer intercut with excerpts from Stanley Blanchard's press conference.

Despite the noise, Bantryd doesn't stir.

Outside, it's bright and sunny. Sarah finishes the crossword puzzle, always a good omen. Then she sits quietly, looking at the glorious blue sky. Australians hate having to go to work on a day like this, and many of them won't. They'll phone in sick and head for the beach. Taking a sickie, it's called.

So we'd better get going. It's too far for Bantryd to walk, and in a few hours there won't be any parking spaces left.

"Hey, Bantryd. Time to rise and shine." When there's no response, Sarah leans close and raises her voice. "Wake up, sleepyhead!"

There's no response. Sean used to do this too. When he was little, he slept so deeply that if you didn't know better you'd think he was dead. Sarah yanks the blanket away.

Bantryd is awake. Her eyes stare up at Sarah, wide and terrified. She doesn't seem to be able to move or to speak, although her lips quiver slightly. What happened? She was fine last night. Well, not fine. But not like this. Bending down, Sarah touches Bantryd's forehead with her lips and recoils. Bantryd is burning with fever.

"Bantryd, talk to me! Tell me what's wrong."

Tears well in Bantryd's eyes and run down her wan cheeks. Sarah shakes her head as if to clear it. This isn't happening. It can't be happening. "Bantryd! For the love of God, say something!"

She should call an ambulance. But the paramedics will ask, What's her name? Bantryd who? Where does she live? What's her Medicare number? They won't touch you without a Medicare number.

Besides, Bantryd may be different. The same organs, Xaxanader said. The same processes. But how would he know? He's not even a vestigant. And suppose he's wrong?

She can't call an ambulance. She doesn't dare.

Bantryd's lips are moving again. She's trying to say something. Sarah leans close.

" . . . the sea."

"Yes, all right." Sarah forces herself to take a deep breath, to remain calm. "You need to go home, you need to be in the sea. I'll take you there, I promise. It's all right. But Bantryd, I need you to help me. Can you move your legs? Can you sit up?"

Bantryd continues to weep, silently. Sarah strokes her hair, which now feels coarse and dry. She should have come downstairs during the night and checked. She tucks the blanket gently around Bantryd's shoulders.

"Don't worry," Sarah says, as much for her own benefit as Bantryd's. "Don't be frightened. It's going to be all right."

Her heart thuds against her ribcage, the way it did that day she came home from a session with Kahn and found her front door gaping open. She hadn't closed it properly. That's what she thinks happened, because nothing was missing. That was a false alarm. But this isn't.

If Charles was here, he'd know what to do. Charles was good in emergencies. He kept his head. He never shouted at people, he never even raised his voice. I got used to it, she told Kahn. Charles took such good care of me that I forgot how to take care of myself. Kahn stared and nodded and said he could hear the little child speaking, the lost, abandoned child within.

Bantryd's bare arm has fallen from beneath the blanket, her veins showing greenish blue beneath the translucent flesh. Bantryd has blood in her veins, the same as anyone else. Blood is salty, like the sea. The chemical composition of blood resembles sea water, Sarah remembers reading this. And that the human body is mostly composed of water. Might Bantryd be dehydrated? Could it be as simple as that?

Filling a tumbler, Sarah brings it into the sitting room and holds it to Bantryd's lips. But she can't swallow, and the water dribbles uselessly down her chin. At a loss, Sarah sits on the floor and stares into Bantryd's pale, frightened face.

"Talk to me, Bantryd. Tell me what to do."

Bantryd shuts her eyes. Something else is happening, she's having some kind of spasm. Her limbs twitch and jerk, and then her eyes fly open.

"I have to . . . go back . . . to . . . the sea."

If she was a child, Sarah could simply pick her up and carry her. But that might not help. She's already so sick. And I can't carry her anyway. She's too heavy, I'm not strong enough.

What would Charles do? He'd analyze the situation, then list the possible options. The situation is that Bantryd needs to be in the ocean. There are two options: I've either got take her there or bring the ocean here.

But I can do that. Not the whole ocean, of course. I don't need the whole ocean. All I need is enough of it to fill the bathtub, enough so Bantryd can be submerged in salt water. At least it's a plan.

Sarah scrambles to her feet. First she'll need to find things that will hold water. The plastic bucket, the watering can. The pot she uses to cook spaghetti. What else? Wastepaper baskets. The plastic garbage bin under the sink. Pots and pans. The bowl from the electric mixer.

Sarah carries it all out to the car, then comes back for towels and cushions to wedge between the containers, so they won't fall over when they're full of water.

The closest beach is Maroubra, a family beach with swings and slides and a parking lot conveniently adjacent to the water. At this hour, it's all but deserted. The tide is out, leaving a vast expanse of sand between the edge of the parking lot and the breaking waves.

Selecting the two largest containers, Sarah trots into the surf and fills them, but they're too heavy to carry. She has to tip half the water out, and even then it's a struggle. Water is incredibly heavy. Only part of the way up the beach, her arms feel as if they've being pulled from their sockets.

A better method is to use bowls to fetch water, decanting them into the larger containers. But this involves dozens of trips back and forth, and by the time she's managed to fill the bucket, the wastebaskets, and the watering can, Sarah is drenched with perspiration.

Collecting the water has taken nearly two hours, and now there are cars parked all around her and more arriving every minute. Women and small, shrieking children are everywhere, arranging towels and blankets and deck chairs on the sand, hoisting bright umbrellas, shouting gleefully to one another.

Sarah backs out carefully, mindful of the water sloshing back and forth in the back seat. If anyone stops and asks what she's doing, she'll say she's collecting sea water for salt water body wraps.

No matter how slowly she drives, the water continues to slosh out onto the upholstery. All she can do is hope that when she does get home, there'll be enough left to fill the tub.

Bantryd is still lying on the couch, still breathing, thank God. She stirs slightly when she hears Sarah come in and opens her eyes.

Who would have thought it would take so much water to fill a bathtub? Chagrined, Sarah sits back upon her heels. After all that effort, she's ended up with barely enough water to bathe a child. It won't even cover Bantryd's legs, assuming she can get Bantryd into the tub.

Back in the sitting room, Sarah positions herself on the edge of the couch and puts her aching arms around Bantryd's shoulders, slowly maneuvering her into a sitting position. But Bantryd can't even support her own weight, and when Sarah slackens her grip, she sags like a rag doll. With a sigh, Sarah eases Bantryd back onto the couch.

If it wasn't for the Jennyfer Blanchard complication, she might risk calling an ambulance. But maybe she'll get lucky, maybe they've already found Jennyfer Blanchard. There are news updates on the hour, and it's almost noon.

Sarah turns on the television, idly watching the closing minutes of a documentary about fishermen as she waits for the news. The fishermen are sluicing water over their catch to keep it fresh.

Ah. Sarah returns to the bathroom, saturates a wash-cloth with sea water and drapes it, dripping and smelling of salt, across Bantryd's forehead. At first, watching the water run down Bantryd's neck, shoulders and chest, she thinks all she's done is make a mess. But when she starts to take the cloth away, Bantryd whispers, "No, leave it there. It feels good."

Sarah turns the television off when the announcer says there are no new developments in the search for Jennyfer Blanchard. She goes back into the bathroom and tosses bath towels into the tub, letting them soak before carrying them into the sitting room and wrapping them around Bantryd's bare arms and legs. Bantryd moans softly and tries to smile.

The couch is awash, and pools of water are forming on the floor. Bantryd is lying still with her eyes shut, but Sarah thinks she looks a little bit better.

Bantryd moves, she's trying to reposition the washcloth on her forehead. Sarah helps her. "Is this what you want? Is it working?"

"Yes. But I need more."

With a small saucepan, Sarah dips water from the tub and trickles it carefully over the towels. She doesn't know what's happening or why, but it seems to be helping and that's all that matters. The couch will probably have to be recovered but Sarah never liked the green upholstery anyway. She tries to sponge up some of the water from the floor, thinking to recycle it, but it's too dirty.

Her back aches rather badly. She's too old for this. With a sigh, Sarah pushes the damp hair back off her forehead and thinks she sees a flash of blue light. She blinks and looks again, but it's gone. She closes both her eyes tightly for a moment, then opens them wide.

She sees another flash of blue light. It's real, she didn't imagine it. It's coming from the street, on the other side of the iron grating in her courtyard wall. Hastily, she draws the blinds. A moment later, there's a peremptory knock on the front door.

"Mrs Andrews? Sarah Andrews? Anybody home?"

They must not find Bantryd. Sarah stands perfectly still, scarcely breathing. No matter what happens, no matter what she has to do, they must not find Bantryd. Seconds pass, perhaps a minute. Sarah tiptoes into the kitchen and picks up a bread knife. She will not let them take Bantryd, not without a fight.

She hears the sound of her front gate being opened and then shut again but can't be sure and doesn't dare look. There's another flash of blue light, and from this angle she sees that it's the revolving light on the roof of a patrol car, moving slowly out of her line of vision.

When she's sure they're gone, Sarah opens the front door, and a bit of cardboard wedged between the door and the jamb flutters to her feet. It's another of Detective Sergeant McGraw's business cards, the same as the one he gave her yesterday. There's a message scrawled in pencil on the back: Call me, ASAP.

Placing the card on the table next to the telephone, Sarah considers her options. She should call him, right away. That's what she'd do if she had nothing to hide. But she does have something to hide. And he'll want to know why she didn't answer the door.

I'll say I was in the shower. Sarah dials the number and asks the operator to please put her through to Detective Sergeant McGraw.

"We're expecting Detective Sergeant McGraw back any minute now," the operator says. "Give me your name and number, and he'll get back to you."

He does, almost immediately. He needs to ask her some more questions, but not over the telephone. He'll come back and see her at home, or if she'd rather, she can talk to him at the station.

"I'll come there. Shall I make an appointment?"

"Not necessary." The tone of his voice changes, ever so slightly. "But we need to see you right away. Well, within the hour. We want to get this cleared up."

"I'm in the middle of something right now." Sarah glances at Bantryd. "How about later this afternoon?"

"Look, you just go on with whatever you're doing, and I'll come there. As I say, we really need to get this cleared up as soon as possible. I can be there in five minutes."

"No need, I'll be right over."

"Good. Just ask for me at the front desk." Detective Sergeant McGraw thanks her for her cooperation and rings off.

She doesn't want to go to the police station, she doesn't want to talk to Detective Sergeant McGraw, not until Bantryd is gone. She aches all over. What she'd really like is a scotch and a hot bath.

She's about to go upstairs when she realizes that Bantryd is standing up, swaying but on her feet. Sarah feels a momentary wave of exultation, but then Bantryd topples back onto the soaked cushions of the couch, breathing hard.

"More water." It comes out as a hoarse whisper.

Sarah gathers up the towels and carries them back to the tub. It seems to be working like a transfusion or an intravenous drip, Bantryd absorbing what her body needs through the pores of her skin. Even so, most of the water is going to waste, dripping away onto the cushions or the floor.

Suppose she fills four bowls with water and arranges them so that Bantryd's hands and feet are completely submerged? That should work as well as the towels and not waste so much of the water.

Bantryd snatches at the towels, and Sarah says, "It's going to be better this way. And I'll bring the towels back, I promise." She positions the bowls, shows Bantryd where to put her hands and feet. "You're already feeling better, I can tell. It's going to be all right, Bantryd. You're going to be fine. I've just got to go out for a few minutes, so I need you to stay right where you are until I come back."

Hopefully, whatever Detective Sergeant McGraw wants to say to her won't take long. At dusk they'll go to the beach, and Bantryd will be safe, on her way back to where she belongs.

(((◎_

AT THE POLICE STATION, she follows Detective Sergeant McGraw into the same small room where she was interviewed last time. Sarah and the detective sit facing one another across the table. He thanks her for her time and turns on a tape recorder. Then he opens a nondescript briefcase and takes out two plastic bags, placing them carefully on the table in front of her. One of them contains her sunglasses, the expensive ones, the ones she lost on the beach. The other bag holds an assortment of keys and key rings.

"You've found my sunglasses! I thought somebody walked off with them, I thought I'd never see them again."

"They're yours? Are you sure?"

"Of course I'm sure. There's not another pair like them in Australia. And they're prescription, my prescription. You don't have to take my word for it, you can check with my optometrist."

"So how did you lose them?"

"It was a couple of weeks ago, at the beach. I left them on my towel when I went swimming and when I got back, they were gone."

"But you didn't report it."

"Well, no. I didn't think there was any point. Like I said, I thought someone took them."

Detective Sergeant McGraw nods and upends the bag of keys and key rings, which clatter noisily onto the desk. "What about this lot? Any of these look familiar?"

Sarah shakes her head, still pleased about the glasses. "I really love those glasses. My husband bought them for me, in Hong Kong. What a coincidence that you'd find them, after all this time."

Detective Sergeant McGraw's silence is odd. This isn't just about returning her lost property. Sitting there opposite him, Sarah wonders what's next.

"A coincidence. But that's it, you see." Detective Sergeant McGraw has become meditative, speaking so quietly that he might be talking to himself. "That's what's worrying me. All these coincidences, if you follow my meaning."

"I don't think I do."

"You were there with that crazy kid down on the beach, the other night. Coincidence number one. Then you turned up at the hospital, wanting to know what happened to her. Meanwhile, the kid turned out to be Jennyfer Blanchard. That's coincidence number two."

"I wouldn't exactly call that a coincidence. I didn't know who she was. I was worried about her, that's all." Lest this seem argumentative, Sarah attempts a deprecatory smile. "I have children of my own, I was concerned. Any mother would be, don't you think?"

Detective Sergeant McGraw purses his lips, keeping whatever thoughts he has to himself. "Your car was spotted in the parking garage at Western Sydney, the same day Jennyfer Blanchard walks out of the place and disappears into thin air." He consults the open file. "A woman, who could have been you, and Jennyfer Blanchard were seen getting into a white Nissan hatchback. Coincidence number three."

Sarah looks directly at him, forcing him to meet her gaze. "It wasn't me, and it wasn't my car. There must be hundreds of white Nissan hatchbacks in Sydney."

"Now, we find your glasses at what might be the crime scene. Coincidence number four."

"What are you talking about? Crime scene? What crime scene?"

Detective Sergeant McGraw lowers his head and thumbs through the pages of the file before him, as if seeking a fifth coincidence. Then he closes the file and stares at her.

"I think you need to be aware that we're treating Jennyfer Blanchard's disappearance as a possible homicide."

Sarah's mouth opens slightly but she manages to say nothing.

"You see, the time frame here is all wrong." Detective Sergeant McGraw shakes his head irritably. "Kids run away every day of the week. Poor kids, not-so-poor kids, rich kids, doesn't matter. There's a pattern, you know what I'm saying? If Jennyfer Blanchard was a runaway, she'd have turned up by now. Or phoned, or sent a note, or something. And if it was about the old man's money, we'd know that by now, too. But there's nobody out there writing letters or making phone calls or demanding ransom. There's nobody out there, period." Sarah's mind is racing, but she remains silent, letting him talk. "So if she didn't run away and she hasn't been kidnapped, what's left? Misadventure," Detective Sergeant McGraw says. "That's what's left. And that's what we've got at the moment. Matter of fact, that's all we've got."

"You said homicide."

"Homicide is a kind of misadventure. Probably the worst kind."

"You think I *killed* her?"

"I didn't say that. But it's a possibility."

At a loss, Sarah gapes at him. "You can't be serious."

"Oh, I'm very serious, Sarah. Make no mistake. Homicide is a serious business."

He isn't calling her Mrs. Andrews any more. He's using her first name. That's not good.

"But it doesn't make sense. Why would I want to kill a girl I don't even know? Why would I want to kill anyone? People like me don't kill people."

"As a matter of fact they do, Sarah. The jails are full of people like you."

"Look, I've never so much as met Jennyfer Blanchard. I don't know her, and I don't know her parents, and I don't know anything about her except what I read in the papers. I've never even been to Brisbane."

Detective Sergeant McGraw doesn't dispute any of this. Instead, he begins to nod to himself, the way Kahn does. When she sees Kahn tomorrow, she'll tell him about this meeting with Detective Sergeant McGraw. The man actually thinks I've killed Jennyfer Blanchard, she'll tell Kahn.

Detective Sergeant McGraw heaves himself abruptly to his feet and after a moment, Sarah stands up as well. "Thanks for coming in. We might want to talk to you again, further down the track." He turns, opens the door. "You're not planning to leave town, are you?"

"Of course not."

"That's all right, then. So like I said, thanks for coming in. And we'll be in touch."

Her sunglasses are still there on the table, sealed in the plastic bag. Sarah reaches for it, but Detective Sergeant McGraw stops her with a gesture. "Sorry, but they're evidence."

"I can't have them back?"

"Not till this is over."

"But they're mine."

"That's why they're evidence."

Wordlessly, Sarah follows him down the hall and through the reception area. The bottom line is they can't prove anything, because there's nothing to prove. Whatever else she's done, she has not harmed Jennyfer Blanchard.

SARAH HURRIES HOME, only to find Felicity waiting for her inside the front courtyard. "You ought to get in the habit of locking the gate, Mum. It was wide open. Anybody could just walk right in."

"You certainly did." Sarah feels suddenly uneasy. Felicity doesn't do impromptu visits, Felicity is up to something. She pretends to search for the front door keys. How is she going to get rid of Felicity? "What are you doing here at this time of day anyway? Shouldn't you be at work?"

"I *am* working. I have an interview with the police in Bondi Junction, but I'm early, so I was thinking we could have a sandwich or something." Felicity consults her watch, a cheap watch on a cheap black band. Sarah and Charles gave her a lovely little gold watch for her eighteenth birthday. *To Felicity with love, from Mum and Dad.* Felicity never wears it.

"All right." Anything to get her away from the house. "Where shall we go? There's that new place on Oxford Street, near the station."

"Why not here?"

"Here?" Sarah glances involuntarily toward the window, making sure the blinds are still drawn. "No, bad idea. The place is a mess."

"It's always a mess. You're a messy person, Mum. You never clean. So what's the big deal?"

"I'm out of bread. Actually, I'm out of everything. I was just going to the shops."

"I thought you were just coming back."

"When I got to the bank, I couldn't find my ATM card. I mean, I thought I forgot it. But look. Here it is. I don't know what's wrong with me today. What are you staring at, Felicity? Come on, if you're coming."

Pushing open the gate, Sarah goes out again and after a moment's hesitation, Felicity follows. They sit opposite one

another in a cluster of small wrought-iron tables, eating sand-
wiches they've selected from the case inside. There's a dead
pigeon lying on the pavement about ten feet away. Felicity
mentions that her appointment is with Detective Sergeant
McGraw and Sarah acknowledges this with a nod. They sit
in silence for a minute or so.

"Five hundred thousand dollars," Felicity says then,
looking up at the fringed umbrella rather than directly at
Sarah. "That's such a lot of money. Half a million, just for
telling them where she is."

"So where do you think she is?"

Felicity looks away. "I wish I knew. But I do have a
theory." Sarah sips her coffee, waits. "I think she's hiding,"
Felicity says, and now she's staring intently at Sarah. Or
is she imagining it? "And I think somebody's helping her.
Maybe it's someone she met on the street, someone who
doesn't even know who she is. You know, someone who's
just trying to be kind."

Sarah thinks this is unlikely, especially in view of the
media coverage. "Unless this hypothetical, kind person of
yours never reads the newspaper or watches television."

"Maybe she didn't know, at first. Maybe she thought she
was doing a good deed, rescuing an abused kid, something
like that. But now she does know, and maybe she's scared.
Maybe she doesn't know what to do." Felicity places her cup

carefully upon the table. "Like, suppose it was you, Mum? Suppose you'd taken Jennyfer Blanchard in, not knowing who she really was. But now you know. So what would you do?"

"I don't know," Sarah says, truthfully. She hasn't really considered Jennyfer Blanchard at all, except as a complication. But Felicity's hypothesis is interesting. "It would depend, I suppose."

"On what?"

"The circumstances, for a start. I'd want to know why she ran away in the first place."

"But what about the reward? Wouldn't you want the five hundred thousand dollars?"

"Of course I'd want it. Who wouldn't? But I think I'd also want to be sure I was doing the right thing."

Felicity rolls her eyes. "You'd give up half a million dollars?"

"Felicity, I honestly don't know what I'd do. What would you do?"

"Me? I'd go straight to the police and I'd tell them the truth. I might not get the whole five hundred thousand. But they'd have to give me something." Felicity's voice has become hard, as if she's arguing her case. "I mean, the guy was on national television. Everyone in Australia heard him. Five hundred thousand dollars, and no questions asked. I could probably sue him for it, if it came to that. But it wouldn't. It would cost him more than that just to pay his solicitors."

Vaguely alarmed by Felicity's vehemence, Sarah takes a ten-dollar bill from her change purse and puts it on the table. "Here, I'll get it. Sorry to rush off, but I've got stuff to do. Good luck with your interview."

When she arrives home, Sarah makes sure to lock the gate before she goes inside. Felicity is right, anybody could have walked in.

Bantryd seems slightly improved, lying back against the cushions, both hands and feet immersed. The water in the bowls is opaque and muddy, but Bantryd's eyes are bright. "I think your daughter was here."

"Yes, she was waiting for me outside. We went for a quick bite to eat."

"She wanted to know who I was, and why I was here in your house. I did try to explain, but I don't think she believed me." Bantryd pauses, takes a breath. "She was very nice. She said everything was all right, and that none of it was my fault, so I shouldn't worry. She's going to take care of it. That's what she said. She doesn't look much like you, does she?"

Felicity still has the spare set of keys. Felicity knows, she knew all along. This changes everything. Bantryd can't stay here, not if Felicity knows.

"Bantryd, can you stand up? Can you walk?" Bantryd gives a helpless grimace. "Let's try. Here. I'll help you." Grasping Bantryd firmly under the arms, Sarah manages to haul her to her feet. "Put your feet flat on the floor. That's right." She's doing it, she's taking most of her weight. "That's good. Now, try to walk. Lift your right foot. Don't worry, I've got you, I won't let you fall. Good. Now, put that foot down and lift the left one. Take a step. That's right, that's great. Okay, that's enough for now. Come on, sit back down."

It's too soon. Bantryd needs to rest, to regain more of her strength. If only they'd been able to wait a few more hours until dusk, the beach wouldn't be as crowded and it would all be so much easier.

"Listen to me, Bantryd. You have to go home, and you have to go now."

Sarah carries the bowls into the bathroom and throws the dirty water in the sink. Back in the sitting room, she gathers up the damp blanket and the towels, puts them in the washing machine, pours in detergent and turns it on. So much for the evidence.

I'd go straight to the police and I'd tell them the truth. I might not get the whole five hundred thousand. But they'd have to give me something.

The trouble with the truth is that nobody believes it. There are moments when Sarah doesn't even believe it. She returns to the sitting room. "Okay, Bantryd. Here we go. Put your arm around my waist. Hang onto me. Ready?"

It's only a dozen steps from the house to the car and Sarah is taking most of Bantryd's weight, but even so, the effort exhausts her. Once she's in the car, Bantryd slumps sideways against the door, head hanging and eyes shut. Sarah straps her in, drawing the seat belt tight to hold her upright. If Bantryd isn't even strong enough to sit up, she probably won't be able to swim, either. They needed more time. Damn Felicity.

They have to leave before the police get here. But where can they go? Sarah slides in behind the steering wheel and sits there, trying to think. It's no good just driving around, and besides, the police will be looking for a white Nissan. They need some kind of plan.

Her gaze falls on a flyer someone left on the windshield, advertising a newly open, automated car wash. Nobody would think to look for them in a car wash. And it'll give her a few minutes' respite, time to think things through.

A lackadaisical attendant swipes Sarah's credit card, and they roll up the windows and move slowly into a whirl of stiff black brushes and cascading water. Bantryd moans.

"It's all right. It's just a car wash."

Her hands resting lightly on the steering wheel, Sarah watches as the successive waves of soapy water and swirling brushes engulf them. Even Bantryd seems to relax, putting her head back against the seat and closing her eyes. Bantryd looks better. There's even some color in her cheeks. But it won't last, not unless Sarah gets her back into the ocean.

They emerge from the car wash, and Sarah heads east. School is out, and they have to stop at every second crosswalk for jostling, chattering groups of children. Bantryd hasn't spoken, not even to ask where they're going. The sun is still high in the western sky, shining through the rear window of the hatchback. Sarah turns on the air conditioning.

Although the chances of finding a parking space near the beach this late in the afternoon are remote, Sarah tries anyway. But there's nothing, even the illegal spaces are taken. It's risky to continue driving around like this, but she's concerned about Bantryd, unsure how far she can walk without collapsing. Following the curve of the road past the beach for the third time, Sarah notices that the chain barrier of the Surf Lifesaving Club's parking lot is lying on the ground. There's a blue and silver bus parked in the lot, and Sarah pulls up alongside it, her car close to the bluff. It's a tour bus decorated with flowing oriental calligraphy and black lettering that says, Xi Feng Gong Che.

A flight of concrete steps leads from the parking area up to the club house, but there's no one around, not even the bus driver. Sarah can just catch the faint beat of music, far above. Off to the right, a sandy track winds down through the rocks to the surf.

"We're here, Bantryd." She opens her eyes. "Look, there's the sea."

"All the way down there?"

"It's not so far. See, there's a path. It'll be easy, it's all downhill."

"I can't."

"Yes, you can. You have to, Bantryd. I'll help you. If you walked to the car, you can walk to the beach." But they manage only a dozen steps before Bantryd's legs buckle beneath her.

"I can't go any farther. I've got to rest."

If Bantryd sits down she might not be able to get up again. But it's too late. Bantryd is already sitting on a flat rock, panting.

"All right," Sarah says, sitting down beside her. "But just for a minute, just until you get your breath back."

They sit side by side, facing the sea. A slight breeze ruffles Bantryd's hair and Sarah lifts her face to its coolness. There's no hurry, not really. Nobody will think to look for them halfway down the Surf Lifesaving Club track.

Bantryd smiles, for the first time. "It's nice here, isn't it? Nobody's angry, and nothing's dead. This is how it must have been in the beginning, before it all got spoiled."

"It'll be even nicer in the water."

They set off again, Sarah holding Bantryd firmly around the waist, supporting her. She's seen men walking like this, drunken pairs of men staggering out of the pubs on Oxford Street. Suddenly her foot slips and they fall heavily against one of the boulders, almost losing their footing. Bantryd yelps, but Sarah manages to hold her and they lean wearily back against the sun-warmed rock. Sarah's leg hurts and when she touches it, her fingers come away sticky with blood.

"You're bleeding!"

"It's nothing, only a scrape. Come on, we've got to keep going."

"I can't."

"Yes, you can. We're so close. You can see the waves breaking against the rocks."

But Bantryd's legs will take her no farther. Maybe I can drag her the rest of the way. It's not that far, and this part of the track is all sand. Bracing herself, Sarah grabs Bantryd beneath the armpits and pulls.

The track drops off abruptly into the sea. There's no beach here, just rocks. At low tide, you can wade around the base of the cliffs to the sandy beach beyond the point, but now the tide is coming in, splashing over the line of large flat rocks favored by the fishermen who frequent this part of the beach.

Sarah positions Bantryd so that her legs are dangling in the water and they remain here, gazing at the horizon. The incoming tide surges against the base of the cliff, the waves rattling the scatter of shale and shiny black pebbles as they recede.

Sarah can feel Bantryd's strength returning, flowing into her body with the rising tide.

Above them, sporadic snatches of music waft down from the Surf Lifesaving Club. Someone shouts, and there's a burst of laughter. You can't actually see the Surf Lifesaving Club from down here, but that means nobody from the Surf Lifesaving Club can see them, either. It's still too early for fishermen and too dangerous for swimmers. She couldn't have picked a better spot if she'd tried.

Bantryd stirs. Sarah knows what she's going to do but isn't quick enough to stop her as she slips deftly into the water.

"Bantryd, wait! I don't think you're strong enough yet."

"But I am. You said it yourself, I need to be here. I need to be in the sea."

"At least hold my hand."

Up to her waist in water, Bantryd holds out her hand. "You come too."

"Oh, Bantryd. I don't know."

"Just part of the way."

Sarah eases herself off the boulder. The water isn't deep, but the salt stings her scraped shin. Submerged rocks shift treacherously underfoot. The tide is almost full, although there's hardly any swell and no current. There won't be any current until the tide turns. It's a good time.

"We've got to get into deeper water," she tells Bantryd. "Away from these rocks."

Still holding Bantryd's hand, Sarah reaches out and grabs the jagged edge of a boulder. "Okay, here's the plan. The tide is about to turn and that should make it easier for us. But we don't want to get caught in the current, so what we'll do is work our way around the point. Then we'll be back at the north end of the beach, and all we'll have to do is swim south. I'll hold onto the rocks and you hold onto me."

They begin to wade slowly through the swell along the base of the cliff. It isn't as easy as Sarah hoped. Halfway along, the tide begins to tug at them and the currents become more unpredictable as they near the point. Even surfers stay away from the point.

Several times, they're pushed hard against the cliff. Sarah keeps one hand on the rock face, concentrating on each step, trying to read the changing directions of the moving water.

Bantryd is mostly supporting herself, but Sarah's arm aches with the effort of pulling them along. Her leg continues to sting and the right side of her body is bruised and sore.

"How much farther?"

"Just to the end of the point," Sarah gasps. "A hundred meters, maybe less. But the current's strongest here, so don't let go of my hand."

Somewhere to the west, the sun is sinking slowly toward the horizon, turning the lengthening shadows from blue to dark purple. Sarah wonders how long they've been in the water. She glances down at her watch, but the crystal is smashed. It doesn't matter, it won't be dark for a long time yet. Beyond the shadow of the cliff, sunlight still shimmers gaily upon the waves.

When they reach the point they pause to rest, standing still, making sure to keep hold of the rocky outcrop, catching their breath. Sarah glances at Bantryd. She looks healthy, even pretty. It's actually going to be all right.

"Why are you looking at me like that?"

"Because you look good. I was so scared, Bantryd. What happened, do you think? What made you so sick?"

"I don't know. But it must have something to do with the sea, because the sea made me better. Thanks to you. Oh, Sarah, if it hadn't been for you, I would have died."

Sarah gazes out at the expanse of open ocean before them. "We can wait, as long you like. You want to be sure you're strong enough."

"I'm strong enough now."

They've come so far, it would be awful if something went wrong right at the end. Still, Bantryd seems confident. But Bantryd nearly always seems confident.

"I'll swim along with you for a bit," Sarah says. "Just to be sure everything's okay."

Together they push off from the rocks, swimming perpendicular to the current, the way they tell you to swim if you get caught in a rip. The turning tide is helping them. It's working, it's perfect. Looking back over her shoulder, Sarah can see the Surf Lifesaving Club on top of the cliff, tiny, gesticulating figures gathered on its patio. The tide and the current continue to carry them along, and now even the swimming beach looks very far away.

Bantryd pauses. "This feels like the right place. I guess I'd better go now."

They embrace, and Sarah tastes salt on Bantryd's cheek. Her own eyes, she realizes, have filled with tears.

"I love you, Sarah."

"I love you too."

"I tried, you know. I did my best."

"You did, your very best. Xaxanader should be proud of you. Tell him I said so."

"You won't forget me, will you? Promise you won't forget me."

"I'll never forget you, Bantryd. I promise. Cross my heart."

Sarah closes her stinging eyes for a moment and when she opens them, Bantryd is gone. It's almost as if Bantryd never existed in the first place, and none of it really happened. But it did.

Now Sarah must swim all the way back to the beach by herself and she's tired, more tired than she realized. And it's harder swimming against the tide. Her arms and shoulders ache and her legs feel like dead weights. She swims on doggedly, but it's like swimming in one of those exercise pools where you never get anywhere. The beach looks as far away as ever.

Is she in a rip? You don't necessarily know it when you're caught in a rip, you don't feel anything different, at first. You get out of a rip by swimming sideways, parallel to the shore.

Sarah hangs suspended in the water for a moment, her head back, almost floating. She's so incredibly tired. She doesn't want to swim parallel to the shore, she doesn't want to swim at all. She'll close her eyes for a little while. Rest. There's a dull roaring in her ears, like surf pounding a shore, and Sarah thinks she hears a man's voice.

The roaring in her ears becomes louder, drowning out the splash and gurgle of the water. Eyes still closed, Sarah allows herself to be caught up in the sound, whirled round and round in its vortex, knowing that this is dangerous but unable to resist. It feels so good, so comfortable, going lazily round and round and gently down, peacefully to sleep.

A man's muscular arm grabs her tightly around the waist, drawing her body close to his own. Charles? Xaxanader?

"Hang on, luv. You'll be right, now."

Other arms drag her from the water, into a surf-lifesaving boat. When she opens her eyes, three very young men are staring down at her. Sarah stares back at them, astonished.

"Where's your friend?"

She's lying on her back in the bottom of the boat, facing west into the setting sun. The brilliance of it hurts her eyes, so she closes them.

A motor roars to life and they speed off, hitting the waves hard. The ribs of the heaving boat press painfully against her own ribs and just for a moment, Sarah wishes they'd let her drown.

The three young men aren't paying any attention to her at all. They're talking earnestly among themselves, and Sarah hears one of them say, "No sign of anyone else. Not a trace."

"Fucking nip said he saw two people."

"He was wrong, then, wasn't he?"

"Ma'am." He's talking to her, now. Who else could he be talking to? She's the only woman in the boat. "Ma'am, can you hear me?"

Sarah squints at him against the slanting red rays of the sun and tries to speak but can't. Her back aches horribly. The young man at the tiller turns the boat into the blaze and glory of the sunset and opens the throttle wide, and they skim across the tops of the waves toward shore.

"Ma'am. Can you tell me what happened here?"

Sarah wets her lips with her tongue, tries to breathe deeply. "I don't know."

"Were you in a boat? Did you capsize?"

Sarah shakes her head. "Not a boat. I slipped on the rocks and fell in."

"Was there anyone with you?" Sarah simply looks at him. "One of the Japs thought it looked like there were two of you."

They don't know, then. They're only guessing. "No. I'm alone."

Nobody questions this, not even after they've pulled the boat up on the sand, helped her scramble out, and wrapped her in a rough woollen blanket. They want more details, though. Sarah makes it as simple as she can.

"I was walking on the rocks, and I slipped. I thought if I could just get around the point, I could swim back to the beach. But I wasn't strong enough." She's wearing jeans and a shirt. Surely, she must look like someone who fell into the water. "Then I got caught in the rip. I thought I was going to drown."

"D'you want the paramedics?"

"No," Sarah says quickly. "I'm all right. I'm fine. I just want to go home."

In the parking lot, the Japanese tourists are lining up to board their bus. Sarah hears their incomprehensible, excited jabber, as if all of them are talking at once. It's a difficult language, Japanese. They say you can't learn to speak it, not really, unless you're born Japanese.

The surf lifesavers follow her gaze. "They're on a tour," one of them says. "They reckoned they wanted to visit a real Surf Lifesaving Club. So Masters says, Fine, just so long as they can come up with the do, re, mi."

"Masters is the president," adds his mate. "Bonzer when it comes to raising money."

"Turns out they wanted lunch, too. So Masters says, Fine. Twenty five dollars a head. You wouldn't credit it. Twenty five dollars for a few snags and a bread roll and some salad and a couple of pitchers of Aussie beer."

"They don't drink much, the Japs. Can't hold their liquor."

"Old Foster reckons it's a damn shame."

"Fuck Foster. The war ended fifty years ago. And Christ knows, this poor fucking club can use the money."

They fall suddenly silent, looking at Sarah, who looks away. "I really want to go home."

"You got transportation?"

"My car, yes. It's here, in the lot."

"Parking lot's private, but."

"I'm sorry. I didn't know."

"Didn't you see the sign?"

"I didn't, actually. I just saw the bus. I thought it would be all right." She pauses. "I'm really sorry. My purse is in the car. I can pay, if you like."

"What the hell. Forget it."

The sun is very low on the horizon and the evening breeze off the water is drying Sarah's wet clothes against her body. Mercifully, her car keys are still where she put them, in the back pocket of her jeans. She thanks them as they climb from the beach back up the path to the parking lot. She thanks them again as she opens the car door. Rolling the window down as she prepares to reverse out of the parking lot, she sees they're all still standing there, so she thanks them a third time, grinning broadly.

She's still grinning, driving down Oxford Street. She's done it. She's outwitted them all, including Felicity. She feels good, she feels wonderful. Chuffed, that's what they say here. When you've done something perfectly, when you've beat all the odds and got away with it.

God knows, it wasn't easy. There aren't many people who could have done what I've just done, actually pulled it off. She's proud of herself. Charles would have been proud, too. Until this moment, Sarah would not have said she was a strong person. But I am strong. I've always been strong.

The thought astonishes her, and she shakes her head. How could she have lived half her life and not known such an important thing about herself?

Tonight, she'll celebrate. She'll go to the David Jones Food Hall and buy herself a crayfish and a bottle of champagne. She'll drink a toast to Bantryd. She'll miss Bantryd. The house is going to seem empty, but it was fun while it lasted. And Bantryd is safe now, that's the important thing.

She slows for an amber light, thinking about what she'll do tomorrow. Her appointment with Kahn isn't until Friday. She doesn't need Kahn. She doesn't need Felicity, either. Maybe she should go back to school, and become a lawyer. Maybe she should go back to Xaxanader. She contemplates this, feeling that anything is possible.

She's still thinking about Xaxanader as she makes the left turn onto her street, and it's only then that she notices the patrol car parked outside her house. Detective Sergeant McGraw is behind the wheel and Constable Wysincki is sitting next to him. Sarah parks behind them and gets out of her car.

"Were you guys looking for me?"

"We were, indeed. Thing is, we'd like to have a bit of a look around," Detective Sergeant McGraw says. "I mean, inside."

"No problem."

If her jauntiness surprises him, he doesn't show it. Sarah unlocks the front door, preceding them into the little sitting room. Everything is as she left it. The cushions on the sofa look damp, but there's no sign that Bantryd, or anybody else, has been here. Sarah feels oddly light-headed. She waits in the sitting room as they move through the rest of the house. When they come back downstairs, Sarah is sitting on the sofa paging through a travel magazine.

"Everything okay?"

They exchange a look. "Sorry for the inconvenience." Nothing personal, Detective Sergeant McGraw's gaze seems to be saying. "A call comes in, we have to check it out. Mostly, it's cranks. But you never know."

"No, it's perfectly all right." Sarah puts the magazine back on the coffee table. "I do understand. And I feel sorry for the girl's parents. The Blanchards. It must be awful for them."

They thank her for her time and leave.

Sarah knows who called them but isn't angry. It's no good being angry about things you can't change, and Sarah knows she can't change Felicity. I used to wonder what I did wrong, she told Kahn. But I don't any more. Felicity is what she is, and always has been, and I don't think anything I did or didn't do made a bit of difference.

Kahn thinks it's good that she doesn't blame herself. But he wonders if it was always like this, between Sarah and Felicity. He wonders if there was ever a time when they were close.

Sarah doesn't think so. Even as a baby, Felicity was . . . Felicity. Few things pleased her, and nothing delighted her. She was never like Bantryd, not at all. Thinking about Bantryd is comforting, makes her smile. Bantryd was a delight. I miss her. I do.

Still barefoot, Sarah walks slowly through the rooms of her house, feeling as if she's actually seeing them for the first time since she's lived here. It's not such a bad house. It doesn't matter that Charles wouldn't have liked it.

It's getting dark. But instead of turning on the lights as she usually does, Sarah impulsively lights a candle and sits in front of it, soothed by the softness of the flame. She feels peaceful, and serene. She imagines Xaxanader here, beside her.

She's suddenly, ravenously hungry. And David Jones will be closed by now, she's left it too late. Never mind. There's a Chinese takeaway next to the supermarket.

Charles liked Chinese food, but it had to be authentic, and served in a proper restaurant. He would have called this ersatz Chinese, fabricated for unsophisticated Australian palettes. Sarah doesn't mind. Walking home along the darkened street, carrying her carton of sweet and sour pork, she's still pondering the extraordinary events of the past few days.

A damp blanket and towels in the washing machine, that's all that's left of Bantryd. It all happened, though. The towels in the washing machine prove it. So does Xaxanader's pebble, upstairs on the glass shelf next to her toothbrush. It's quite amazing that such incredible things could happen to her.

She eats straight out of the carton, using the plastic fork and watching an episode of "The Golden Girls" on television. Charles would be appalled. He despised American sitcoms. But Charles isn't here.

I can do whatever I like, Sarah thinks. And that's what I will do, from now on.

Afterward, she runs a hot bath, as hot as she can get it, using up all the water in the water heater. It's supposed to provide continuous hot water, but it doesn't, not really. You only get enough to fill up the tub once a day.

Lying back in the hot water, Sarah closes her eyes and relaxes. There's nothing like a hot bath. The bruises on her hip and upper arms are already starting to turn purple. They don't hurt, though. And they're just bruises, they'll heal.

It's good to be home, good to be in her own bed. She kept her promise to Xaxanader, and she feels good about that, too. She took care of Bantryd, and kept her safe. It's over now, but nothing bad happened and nobody got hurt. Although, Sarah thinks, it's a shame about Jennyfer Blanchard.

Chapter Eight

Now, Sarah wants to talk about it. She wants to tell someone, the way you want to tell someone about your first date or your first kiss. For once, she's looking forward to her session with Kahn.

She no longer has to put any energy into thinking about whether or not it actually happened—which seems to Sarah beside the point, anyway. She experienced it, that's what matters. She felt it, she lived through it. and she remembers it. It has become part of her, the way Charles's death is part of her. It belongs to her.

And she isn't crazy, any more than someone who writes novels is crazy. A parallel world is a parallel world, whether you describe it in a book or remember it.

The question isn't, Are you sane? but rather, Are you functional? If you're living in the real world with real people, brushing your teeth and paying your bills, you're okay. Functional is what matters.

For the first time, Sarah is aware of being alone in the house. That's odd, because she's always been alone in this house and never really noticed. She misses Charles, of course, but she doesn't mind being on her own, she rather likes it. Or has, up until now.

If she'd had more children, one of them might be Bantryd's age, still in school and living at home. Sarah thinks she might like that, which strikes her as strange. She certainly doesn't want to live with Felicity.

It might not have been Felicity who called the police. You don't know it for a fact, Kahn would say. And that's true. But who else could it have been? And someone called them. Otherwise, why would they suddenly turn up wanting to search the house?

There's nothing about Jennyfer Blanchard in the paper this morning. Maybe they've found her, or maybe the Blanchards have decided they've had enough publicity. Or maybe it's just old news. Or the wrong paper.

The couch is no worse for wear. That's the thing about cheap furniture, it lasts forever. The cushions are still damp, but they'll dry out, they'll be good as new. She wishes she knew what made Bantryd so desperately ill. It might have been anything, or more likely, a combination of things. Perhaps she shouldn't have forced Bantryd to eat. It doesn't matter. In the end, it all worked out.

Sarah is early for her appointment with Kahn, but she doesn't want to wait in Reception. Instead, she walks around the block a couple of times, trying to see her surroundings through Bantryd's eyes. Brick buildings, power lines, pavements, chain-link fences, asphalt. Why is it all dead? Bantryd kept asking. Sarah didn't know, doesn't know. Someday, the earth will rid itself of man and all his works with a single, chthonic shudder and everything will begin anew.

It would be a relief to know that Bantryd got home safely. Of course she did. There's no reason to think otherwise.

That's Kahn's car, moving silently past her. Sarah gives a little wave, but Kahn pretends he doesn't see her. Or maybe he's not pretending. Sarah suspects she doesn't exist for Kahn until she walks through the door of his room and sits in the black vinyl chair.

She watches him back deftly into a tight parking space directly in front of the Centre. She couldn't squeeze into a space that small and wouldn't even try, though her car is smaller than his. Kahn gets out, locks the car, and hastens along the concrete path, his back slightly bent as if it were windy, which it isn't. Many Australian men walk like this, as if readying themselves for an unexpected blow from behind.

The session starts as it always does, with Kahn gazing silently at her and giving her the opportunity to say whatever comes to mind. But where to begin?

"We were talking about a dream you've been having," he says at last. "I wonder, is it always exactly the same dream?"

If he insists upon calling it a dream, she'll go along. She's told the truth. It's not her fault if he refuses to believe it.

"No," Sarah says. "It's different each time. It's like a story, but it's about the same people. For instance, a few nights ago, I dreamed that Bantryd was here, with me. She was staying in my house. But then she got sick. It was awful. I didn't know what was wrong with her, I didn't have a clue. But I was afraid she was going to die, and I didn't know what to do, how to help her. And she just kept getting worse and worse."

Kahn says nothing.

"Then I suddenly had this idea that whatever was wrong with her had something to do with being away from the sea. I mean, she lives in the ocean. Water is her element. I thought, If I can just get her back to the beach and into the water, she'll get better, she'll be okay. So basically, that's what I did. I brought sea water to her, then I took her back to the sea, half carrying her, and she got better. Like, instantly. And then she went home, to her world." Kahn is listening intently. "It was scary, though. I really thought she was going to die. I still feel a little bit frightened. You know, the way you feel when someone steps in front of your car and you almost hit them. It's not your fault, but you still feel awful."

"Sometimes our dreams can be extremely vivid," Kahn says thoughtfully. "Especially when they're important dreams."

He doesn't elaborate, and Sarah can't think of anything further to add. For several minutes they sit there silently in the morning sunlight.

"Why did you think she got sick?"

"I don't know. At first I thought maybe she was allergic to something. People don't eat in her world, not the way we do. She thought the idea of putting something in your mouth and chewing it and swallowing it was disgusting. But she was starving, so she had to eat. I made eggs for her. And pancakes, with maple syrup."

"So you think the food you gave her made her sick?"

"No, I don't think that at all. I actually think it had something to do with her being out of the sea. I think she needs to be in water, just the way we need to be in air. But it was awful. I was so scared. I thought she was going to die."

"And how did that make you feel?"

"I told you, I was terrified. She just kept getting worse and worse and I didn't know what to do."

Kahn nods. "You were trying to take care of her, though. You cooked for her. You've told me how much you used to enjoy preparing meals for Charles. Cooking is a kind of loving, for you. But then Charles died, and there was nothing you could do about it. You couldn't save him. But you were able to save Bantryd. Who do you suppose Bantryd really is?"

"You mean, who does she remind me of? Nobody," Sarah says. "Although she looks something like Jennyfer Blanchard. You know, the girl who's gone missing. The one whose picture was in the paper."

"That's not what I meant. You've described a creature from another world. She lives in water, not air. She doesn't have to eat. She comes and goes as she pleases. She resembles a human being, but she's not human. She's incorporeal, ethereal. Perhaps she even has wings."

"Bantryd doesn't have wings."

"I mean, metaphorically. Dreams are symbols and the language of dreams is symbolic. Has it ever occurred to you that Bantryd is an angel?"

Sarah is astonished. "You think an angel came to me in a dream?"

"Not a real angel. A symbolic angel." He's leaning forward, intent upon what he's saying. "Angels are messengers, you know. They come from another realm, to tell us things we need to know. And that's what Bantryd did. She came to you because she had something to tell you. But where did she come from?" Sarah is too confounded to say anything at all. "She didn't come from heaven. She came from you. She's part of you, part of your psyche. She was sick, she was about to die. But you took care of her. You saved her. And in doing so, you saved yourself. You healed yourself. Do you see what a wonderful dream it really is?"

Kahn is more pleased than she's ever seen him. He wants them to talk about this, about her angel and about the part of her that needs to be healed. The only thing wrong with his interpretation of her dream is that it wasn't a dream. But she knows how futile it is to tell him that, so she changes the subject.

"Afterward, the police came."

"The police?"

"Detective Sergeant McGraw. He thinks I've got something to do with this Jennyfer Blanchard business."

"I'm not following you, Mrs. Andrews. Are we still talking about your dream?"

"No. I'm telling you what really happened. Yesterday, Detective Sergeant McGraw came to my house. And then I had to go to the police station and he asked me a lot of questions about Jennyfer Blanchard."

"I wouldn't worry about it. After all, you did see her on the beach that night. I expect they're just doing their job, following up every possible lead."

"But I didn't see her. I mean, I saw a girl on the beach that night, but it wasn't her. It wasn't Jennyfer Blanchard."

"You don't know that. You told me you didn't even know her name."

"I didn't. I don't know her name. But now that I've seen photographs of the real Jennyfer Blanchard, I know it wasn't her."

"We are talking about the same girl we talked about on Tuesday, aren't we? The one you said had been transferred to Western Sydney?" Sarah nods. "Then I'm afraid you're mistaken, Mrs. Andrews. I happen to know for a fact that the girl in that hospital was Jennyfer Blanchard."

Kahn believes what everyone else believes. Sarah would believe it too, if she didn't know better.

"Even if it was, why do they think she's dead? And why would anyone think I wanted to kill her?"

"I'm sure nobody thinks that."

"Detective Sergeant McGraw does. He told me I was a suspect. If I'm a suspect, that means they think I might have killed her, doesn't it?"

"But why would you be a suspect?"

"Because I telephoned the next day and asked what had happened to her. And because someone saw a white car the day she disappeared, and I happen to have a white car." Saying it aloud, Sarah sees it from Detective Sergeant McGraw's point of view; a case can be made against her. A case *is* being made against her. "And I lost my prescription sunglasses on the beach, a while ago. And now the police have them."

Kahn's face is grave. "You need to see a solicitor, Mrs. Andrews."

"Why? I didn't do anything."

"It doesn't matter. As you say, you're a suspect. They've told you so. And you did drive out to Western Sydney that day, didn't you?"

"It was your idea."

"But what did you do? You must have done something to make them suspicious. What happened at Western Sydney?" His face is unreadable. "You can tell me, you know. Nothing you say will leave this room. They can't even subpoena my notes."

She didn't know he made notes of their sessions. But of course he does. "Why would anyone want your notes?"

"What happened at Western Sydney?"

"Nothing happened. There was a lot of traffic, and by the time I got there visiting hours were over. So I drove home."

Kahn looks relieved. "All the same, you still need to talk to a solicitor. And you should do it right away, before this goes any further. You have to protect yourself."

"Protect myself against what? I haven't done anything."

"Once you've been accused of committing a crime, it doesn't actually matter whether you did it or not. It's what they can prove, what the jury believes. The police tell their side of the story, and then you tell yours. That's why you need a solicitor. And a barrister too, if the matter goes to court. You need legal professionals to tell your side of the story, and you have to hire them and pay for them yourself."

"What happens if I don't? What if I can't afford a solicitor?"

"You'll probably be found guilty. This isn't the United States, you know. We don't have public defenders. What we have are solicitors, barristers, and judges. And you're not automatically entitled to representation. If you can't afford it, you don't get it. But you can afford it, Mrs. Andrews. And with all due respect, you need a solicitor."

"But it doesn't make sense. Here's this girl who's gone missing. Okay, so she's rich. And maybe you're right, maybe she is the girl I met on the beach. Why would I want to kill her?"

"If the police are saying you're a suspect, it doesn't matter. I don't know why, Mrs. Andrews. What I do know is that you need a solicitor."

His earnest concern is making her more and more uneasy. "But why do they think I'd kill someone I don't even know?"

"You're asking the wrong person. You should be asking a solicitor. And the solicitor should be asking the police. But first you need a solicitor." Jumping up, Kahn walks rapidly to his desk and rummages in a drawer. "I can give you the name of someone. Tell him you're one of my clients and I told you to call him." He scribbles something on the back of one of his business cards and hands it to her.

Sarah stares at the unfamiliar name. "It's just so bizarre. Do you honestly believe I'm capable of murder?"

"What I believe isn't important. It's what the police and the prosecutor and the judge and the jury believe that matters." Kahn sits down again, heavily. "Why didn't you tell me you were in trouble?"

"Because I wasn't in trouble, until yesterday."

His telephone rings, startling them both. Kahn returns to his desk, snatching the receiver from its cradle and turning his back to Sarah. He mumbles something, then hangs up and returns to his chair, looking distracted. "I really do have to stop, now. My next client is here. But you need to call that solicitor, Mrs. Andrews. Promise me you'll do it today."

HOME AGAIN, SARAH SITS on the couch, thinking. It's difficult to take any of this seriously. Sunlight streams through the windows, burnishing the bricks of the fireplace to a rosy, pinkish gold; in this light they look elegant rather than merely old. Taking the card Kahn gave her out of her handbag, Sarah places it beside the telephone.

It's all so extraordinary. Here she is, an ordinary, middle-aged woman, a widow. She's not a murderer, anyone can see that. She doesn't need a solicitor. Now that Bantryd is gone, everything will be fine. It was a case of mistaken identity, that's all.

She wishes she'd gone with Bantryd. If she wasn't here, they couldn't arrest her, and she wouldn't have to hire a solicitor. They don't have solicitors in Bantryd's world, or psychotherapists, either. Sarah glances at the solicitor's card, next to the telephone. It's too bad they don't have telephones in Bantryd's world. It would be nice to be able to ring up Xaxanader and ask him if Bantryd got home safely. The thought makes her smile, and the smile makes her feel better.

The telephone rings.

"Mum, it's me. Felicity."

"Hello, Felicity."

"Mum, we have to talk."

"We are talking."

"Listen, Mum. I've told Max everything, the whole story. He thinks you need to see a solicitor, right away. And I agree with him. I know you've been upset, but it's still no excuse. I mean, you can't plead insanity."

"I don't intend to."

"Mum, will you just listen? Max knows a really good solicitor, and he's already made an appointment for you to see him, this afternoon. I'll go with you, if you like. His chambers are on Macquarie Street."

Sarah holds the phone at arm's length and gazes at it for a moment. Felicity is still talking.

"Tell Max I appreciate his concern," Sarah says, interrupting Felicity in mid-sentence. "But I don't need a solicitor."

"Mum, this is no time to play games. I saw her, Mum. I saw Jennyfer Blanchard right there in your house."

"No, you didn't."

"I did."

"The girl you saw wasn't Jennyfer Blanchard. It was Bantryd."

"Mum, it was Jennyfer bloody Blanchard, and you know it as well as I do. What happened to her? What was wrong with her? Why were you keeping her locked up in your house?"

"Nobody is locked up in my house, Felicity. There isn't anyone here, except me."

"Oh, God. Where is she, then? What did you do with her?"

"She went home."

"She did not go home, Mum. Jennyfer Blanchard is still missing."

"I'm not talking about Jennyfer Blanchard, Felicity. I'm talking about Bantryd."

"There's no such person as Bantryd! I keep telling you, it's Jennyfer Blanchard!"

"And I keep telling you, it isn't. Felicity, stop yelling and listen to me. They're two different girls. They both have long hair, but that's all. I don't know where Jennyfer Blanchard is, but I do know that Bantryd went home. That's the story. That's it."

"You did something to her, didn't you? Or she did it to herself. I was there, Mum. I talked to her. You know what she said? She looked me straight in the eye and said, I live at the bottom of the ocean. Those were her exact words." Felicity pauses, breathing hard. "Mum, she's crazy. She needs help. And so do you."

"She might have been speaking metaphorically. Maybe it was just an expression. You know, like saying you live back of beyond."

"It wasn't a metaphor. Mum, where is she?"

"I told you, she went home."

"To the bottom of the ocean?"

"I suppose."

For a moment, Sarah thinks Felicity has hung up. "This isn't funny, Mum."

"I'm not trying to be funny."

"All right, then." The tone of Felicity's voice has flattened and deepened. "Here's the thing. I think they've found her body."

"Oh, my God." But wait. Felicity doesn't know, she's only a journalist. She's guessing. "What makes you think that?"

"The chief of police is going to call a press conference in a couple of hours. He wouldn't be calling a press conference if they'd found her and she was all right. He'd be shouting it from the roof tops. And he certainly wouldn't be calling a press conference just to say there are no new developments. So something's happened. Something big. I think Jennyfer Blanchard is dead, and they've found her body."

Sarah imagines the lovely, long, dark, wet curls lying still upon the bare back; the dark wet lashes motionless upon pale cheeks. It isn't Jennyfer Blanchard's body they've found. It's Bantryd's. But where is she now? Where would they have taken her?

"Mum, are you there?"

"No." Sarah hangs up.

She mustn't jump to conclusions. There might not even be a body. Felicity isn't infallible. Or it might be Jennyfer Blanchard's body after all. It's possible. Anything is possible.

And there could be all sorts of other reasons why the chief of police has called a press conference. Perhaps they found jewelry that belongs to Jennyfer Blanchard, or some of her clothing. Or even a ransom note. Sarah bites her lip. None of those things would warrant a press conference.

Felicity probably is right. They've found a body.

Bantryd's illness came on quickly but it abated quickly, too. That happens with children, sometimes. One minute you're ready to head for the emergency room and the next minute they're out playing on the swings. She'd thought Bantryd was better. Even so, I shouldn't have let her go alone. I should have gone with her, made sure she got back safely. If they've found a body, it's probably Bantryd's body.

They won't know that, though. They'll think they've found Jennyfer Blanchard. Sarah remembers that she had to formally identify Charles's body, to stand there with the doctor and a police officer while a nurse lifted the white sheet. They told her it was the law, that someone had to identify a body before it could be released for burial. The Blanchards will have to do the same for Jennyfer because the law is the law, even if you're Stanley Blanchard. And then Stanley Blanchard will turn to his wife, eyes wide with wonder and relief. It isn't her. It isn't our little girl.

Sarah sinks down onto the bottom step of the stairs, her face in her hands. Charles, and now Bantryd. "It's as if I'm a curse to everyone I love," she once told Kahn when he asked, How does it feel?

"Survivors often blame themselves."

"I'm not a survivor."

"I think you are," Kahn said.

She's let Bantryd down, horribly. But there's nothing more she can do for Bantryd. It's over. Bantryd is gone. Now she must tell Xaxanader, because if nobody tells him, he won't know what happened, and he needs to know.

Just the thought of it makes Sarah feel sick. Do I have to? Does he really need to know? Wouldn't he be better off, not knowing? She often thinks that if Charles had simply disappeared, she could at least hope that someday he'd come back. Dead people don't come back. Not in this world and not in Xaxanader's world, either.

The telephone rings again. Sarah remains motionless and after five rings, the machine picks up. "Mum, this is crazy. Whatever happened, you've got to go to the police and tell them the truth, before it's too late. I'm not saying you did anything wrong. But she was there, at your house. I saw her. You've got to cooperate with the police. It's the law, Mum."

Even when she was a child, Felicity always sided against Sarah. No matter what, Sarah was always the one who was in the wrong, the one who had to defend herself. Mama was like that too.

"Mum, are you there? Can you hear me? Mum, if you're there, pick up."

Sarah goes upstairs and changes into her bathing suit. She ties a sarong under her armpits and slips on her sandals. She always knew she'd go back, although not like this.

The green light on the answering machine continues to blink angrily. It mightn't even be true. Felicity is capable of making up anything, if it will get her what she wants. But Felicity was here, she saw Bantryd. What would Sarah do, if she were Felicity? She doesn't know. She can't imagine being Felicity.

Outside, the street is deserted.

It would be faster to drive, but the beach will probably be as crowded as it was yesterday, with no place to park. And she'd rather walk. She needs to think about what she's going to say to Xaxanader.

Maybe it's someone else who drowned. Not Jennyfer Blanchard and not Bantryd, either. People do drown. Sarah almost drowned yesterday. She shakes her head, dismissing this bit of wishful thinking with a grimace.

Everybody who didn't take a sickie yesterday appears to have done so today, and the gourmet sandwich shop on the esplanade is doing a brisk business. Charles once took a sickie, but it was no good. He spent the whole day sitting around the house feeling guilty. The kids wanted him to take them to the beach and couldn't understand why he wouldn't.

Sarah heads for her usual spot beneath the cliffs, following the curve of the esplanade past the Surf Lifesaving
Club driveway to where the paving ends and the sand begins.
People are already here, sprawled motionless on towels or sitting up with their backs resting against the rock. One woman
has placed a silver reflector around her face, like a collar.
Sarah steps down onto the hot sand and slips off her sandals.

The tide is coming in, hungry little waves flinging themselves on the wet sand, chasing one another up the beach
like children playing a game. Threading her way carefully
between the beach towels and the still, oiled bodies, Sarah
continues on around the point of the promontory into the
area of tumbled rocks and splashing water on the other side.

The water is already up to her knees but it's warm, and
despite the incoming tide, there's hardly any current or swell.
It's like wading in a vast, peaceful lake. Sarah continues to
follow the line of the cliff until she reaches the spot where
she and Bantryd rested yesterday. She remembers seeing a
little ledge here just above the high-water mark and thinking
what a good place it would be to leave things, directly beneath
the Surf Lifesaving Club and therefore easy to find again.

Standing here in the water and looking up at the face
of the cliff, Sarah suddenly notices it's pocked with small
crumbling caves. She never knew there were caves here. But
she never really looked, either. Some of the caves are little

more than indentations in the rock, but others seem larger and show signs of human habitation. Squinting slightly, Sarah can make out a patch of black ash residue about halfway up, and farther along, a pair of dun-colored trousers strung up to dry on a length of rope. People live here, and good luck to them. It's better than living on a park bench or in a bus shelter or beneath a railway overpass, which is where most of the city's homeless people live.

There's also a network of branching little pathways, scribbled down the cliff on either side of the main track. She hadn't noticed them yesterday, but she does now. And one cave in particular catches her eye, near the top of the cliff, tucked away beneath a large triangular outcrop of rock. You'd feel as if you were king of the world living in a place like that, with the rocks, the ocean, and the other beaches up and down the coast all spread out before you in a glorious panorama of sky and sea.

Untying her sarong, Sarah takes it off and wraps it firmly around her keys, glasses and sandals. Then, shoving the bundle as far back onto the ledge as possible, she secures it with a rock.

She doesn't know what she'll say to Xaxanader. They say you shouldn't tell people bad news, straight off. You're meant to build up to it, to prepare them. But it's hard to think how to build up to this. Bantryd got sick. Then she got better. I thought she'd be all right. I should have brought her all the way home. I'm sorry, Xaxanader. I'm so sorry.

He trusted her. That's the worst of it, the idea that she's betrayed his trust. And it's so unfair, because she did try, she did her best. But Xaxanader won't see it that way. Bantryd was all he had.

Blinking in the noonday glare, Sarah wades out and starts to swim. She knows it's dangerous to swim so close to the rocks, but she doesn't want to be seen, she doesn't want to be the target of another rescue. Sometimes there's a rip along here, but not today. There's no current at all, and hardly any swell.

Sarah tells herself she doesn't have to do this. It's still not too late to change her mind and simply go home. Nothing has happened, yet. Schrodinger's box is still shut, Xaxanader still trusts her, Bantryd is still alive. Maybe nothing did happen. Kahn says Bantryd is a repressed part of my psyche. If that's true and Bantryd only exists in my imagination, then she can't be dead. But it's not true. Bantryd is real.

Sarah is swimming briskly and the physical effort soothes her, so that her thoughts begin to drift. Why couldn't she have had a daughter like Bantryd? An eager, laughing, loving daughter, like other people's daughters. All those years ago she so looked forward to having a daughter, she was so excited when she was pregnant with Felicity.

She's so far out she can barely see the beach. Now, she must think of Xaxanader, then dive. But she can't, it doesn't work. All she can see is Bantryd's face, shining and happy and alive. Sarah comes up spluttering and treads water. Closing her eyes, she concentrates on Xaxanader, recreating his eyes, his smile. She imagines the touch of his hand, and dives.

It's no good. Xaxanader has become Bantryd again. But Sarah keeps going, pushing herself deeper and deeper. Maybe it's better this way.

And it *is* Bantryd, kneeling in the midst of what looks like an alcove made of air. For a moment, Sarah is too dazed to do more than stare. Bantryd's hands are cupped around something small that's growing out of the ground in front of her. She's murmuring to it, whatever it is, but as soon as she sees Sarah, she looks up with a radiant smile of sheer delight.

"You're here! I brought you! I knew I could do it!" She sits back on her heels. "Now everything's perfect. I so wanted you to be here. Sarah, look! It's my Telling. Isn't it beautiful?"

"You're alive."

"You saved my life. Xaxanader thinks you're wonderful. Everybody thinks you're wonderful. You *are* wonderful. I love you, Sarah!"

"You're really alive. I love you too!"

"I'm going to be famous. I'm going to be even more famous than Xaxanader."

"Let's just take things one Telling at a time, shall we?" Xaxanader is coming eagerly toward her, arms outstretched. "Sarah! How can I even begin to thank you?" For a tremulous moment she thinks he's going to take her into his arms again, but he doesn't, and she feels a pang of disappointment. "And you're just in time. But how did you know?"

"I didn't. I thought Bantryd was dead. I wanted to explain. I wanted you to know how it happened."

"Bantryd dead? Why would you think that? You're the one who saved her."

"They found a body, a corpse. I thought it was Bantryd."

"But why?"

"She was so sick. And I didn't bring her home, not all the way. I brought her back to the sea, and I swam with her for a while, but then I let her go on by herself. I know I shouldn't have, but she seemed okay. I never would have let her go alone if I hadn't thought she'd be all right."

"She *is* all right."

"And then when Felicity told me they found a body, naturally I thought it was Bantryd. I don't know for certain that it's a body, but they found something. They're having a press conference. Felicity thinks it's a body and she's a journalist, it's her job to know things like that." She pauses. "Felicity is my daughter. I'm not making much sense, am I?"

"Sarah, for the love of Commons, calm down. Bantryd is fine."

"Maybe it was that other girl," Bantryd says. "You know, the one you thought looked like me." Some of the pleasure has faded from her eyes. "Is that the only reason you came back? Because you thought I was dead?"

Sarah turns to Xaxanader. "You don't know how I felt! I wanted to tell you in person. I didn't want you to wait, and wonder, the way you've been waiting all these years for your sister. I wanted you to know. And I wanted to apologize, because it was my fault."

"But it wasn't your fault, because nothing happened. And it wouldn't have been your fault, in any case. It was dangerous. We all knew that."

"It was awful. Did she tell you about it? She almost died, Xaxanader. Do you know what it was like, watching her get worse and worse and not knowing what to do?"

"But you did know. You worked it out somehow."

An awful thought crosses her mind. "Did you know she'd get sick?"

"Of course I didn't know. None of us knew. How could we? But there were so many things we didn't know. We certainly didn't know you had to feed."

"What's that got to do with it?" He does blame her, then. He thinks she poisoned Bantryd, with food. "In my world, people have to eat. If they don't, they starve. And we don't call it feeding."

"But you do it, that's the point. Instead of absorbing nourishment normally, you feed. We didn't know that. We had no idea. How could we?"

"You knew we weren't like you."

"But you *are* like us. You can absorb nourishment, you're doing it right now. You're a vestigant."

"Okay, so it works here. But it doesn't work in my world."

Xaxanader nods, then ponders something. "But how do you know what to eat?" he asks. "And when, and how much? Is your sixth sense so finely developed?"

"We only have five senses."

"No, you have eight. Symmetry—the innate knowledge of what your body requires, or lacks—is your sixth sense. Symmetry is balance, the state of being in rhythm with the world. And after symmetry come synthesis and transcendence, the seventh and eighth senses. Symmetry, synthesis and transcendence are what differentiate us from other life forms."

Eight senses. But why not? Symmetry is balance and we talk about balanced diets, don't we?

"So what you're saying is Bantryd needed some other kind of food."

Xaxanader nods. "Something was missing, something vital. You knew that, you sensed the asymmetry. And you knew where to look for it, too. You knew you'd find what Bantryd required in the sea."

"So what you call symmetry is a kind of physiological balance," Sarah says. "Being in balance and knowing you're in balance." Xaxanader nods. "I never thought of it as a sense. How does it feel?"

"Basically, it's a feeling of wellness. We absorb what we need, no more and no less. So do you, while you're here."

A feeling of wellness. Sarah nods, understanding.

"And synthesis? What's that?"

"This is synthesis. What we're doing."

"Talking?"

"In your world, yes. But not here. You don't hear me, because there's no sound. It's our sense of synthesis that makes it possible for us to communicate. Synthesis lets us understand one another. Synthesis lets us move through our world. Synthesis allows us to create and share our Tellings."

"Like a sixth sense." Actually, a seventh sense. Sarah doesn't really understand, but she doesn't have to. Bantryd is alive. And she's here, with Xaxanader. You don't have to understand everything.

"And transcendence?"

"That's more complicated. We all have the potential for transcendence, for becoming one with the entirety of existence. But only a few of us achieve it."

Sarah is thinking about Bantryd's mother. "I wonder if that's what happened to her. I wonder if she got sick, the way Bantryd did, because she needed to be in the sea." She looks questioningly at Xaxanader. "But Bantryd knew what was wrong. So she'd have known too. Wouldn't she?"

"Knowing might not have been enough. Bantryd knew, but how could she get back to the sea without help? It came on quickly, you said." Sarah nods, remembering. "By the time Thasqia realized what was happening, it was probably too late."

"I wonder what they were like—my ancestors, I mean." Sarah is gazing at Xaxanader, looking at the image of her own face floating in his eyes. "The ones who left the sea."

"We can find out. There are Tellings of Exile, although they're not often consulted these days. But I can find them, I know my way around the archives. It might be interesting."

Like Australians, looking up their convict predecessors and never knowing quite what they'll find.

What might her life have been? Mama wouldn't be Mama, and she wouldn't have met Charles. Sean and Felicity wouldn't exist. Sarah herself wouldn't exist. She'd be somebody else.

"I can't even imagine it, living here."

"Nor can I imagine what it would be like to live in your world. Feeding morning, noon, and night. Finding nutrition, preparing nutrition, ingesting nutrition. No time for higher thoughts, no time for any of the things that make life wonderful. No wonder you're angry all the time!"

"It's not like that. And we do think higher thoughts. We write books. We paint pictures. We don't spend all our time feeding. Lots of us enjoy our lives, the same as you."

He doesn't believe her. And most people don't enjoy their lives. People starve. People die of horrible diseases. And mostly, people aren't nice to one another. It was even worse a hundred years ago. No wonder all those vestigants stayed. They probably thought they'd died and gone to heaven. Sarah thinks about what Xaxanader's grandfather's life must have been like, back then. Who in their right mind would have wanted to return to a world like that?

Xaxanader is watching her as if he's following her thoughts, and perhaps he is. Maybe she wants him to know what she's thinking, to know she's trying to decide. Am I trying to decide? Decide what?

"Stay here," Xaxanader says. "Stay here with us. With me."

"I can't."

"Why?"

"Lots of reasons."

What would they all think, if I suddenly disappeared? Do I even care what they think? I cared about what Charles thought, but Charles is dead. But what would he say if he was here? Go for it, Charles would say.

"And what do you say?"

"I don't know."

"You can't go on like this, living in two worlds."

Especially when one of them doesn't exist.

"I can't just disappear, either. It wouldn't be fair. They'd never know what happened to me. My children, I mean. Sean and Felicity."

"Your children. You never speak of them."

"Well, they're grown up. Sean, that's my son, works on an oil rig, and I hardly ever see him. But he's a good boy. He turned out well."

"And Felicity?"

"She doesn't like me very much. She never has. But she's still my daughter." Sarah pauses. "Children don't always turn out to be what you expected. It's nobody's fault. It just happens."

"But as you say, they're grown up. Children usually outlive their parents, in this world. I assume it's the same in yours." Sarah nods. "So they'll have to manage without you one day. No matter what you decide."

"Yes, but when your parents get old, you know what's happening, you're prepared. And when they die, there's a funeral, there's closure. They don't just vanish off the face of the earth. I can't do that to my children."

What do you want? Kahn once asked her.

I want my life back, she told him. I want everything to be the way it used to be.

Kahn said that wasn't possible.

Neither is this.

"You don't still think you're dreaming, do you?"

"Don't make fun of me."

"I'm not. Sarah, come here."

She walks right into his arms. Well, why not? In dreams, you let all sorts of things happen, because nobody can blame you for anything you do in a dream. Sarah feels his warmth, the beating of his heart. She's been lucky. Papa didn't love Mama, how could he? And nobody will ever love Felicity.

Xaxanader releases her. Reluctantly.

Sarah remembers that time passes differently here, and she looks up at Xaxanader. "I have to go. I have to get back before it gets dark."

He puts his arm around her again, guiding her along.

"Will I see you again?"

"I don't know."

But he's right. She can't keep doing this.

His arm is still around her waist.

"I don't want you to go."

"I know. I don't want to go either. But I can't just vanish. It wouldn't be fair. It would be like Thasqia. Nobody would ever know for sure." Felicity probably wouldn't care. But Sean would be like Bantryd, he'd keep looking for her, he'd want to know what happened. Sarah sighs. "I can't do that."

They walk on together, and when they finally stop, Xaxanader raises her hand solemnly to his lips.

You only get one life. She might decide to stay, it's not impossible. Other people have stayed, other vestigants. This is where she belongs. This is where we all belong. If not, why are we made of water? Why do our tears and blood and perspiration taste of salt?

But if she stays—if she disappears—everyone will think she really did kill Jennyfer Blanchard. Mama will read about it in the newspaper, smoking one of her cigarettes. (Mama, whose lungs are perfect. Mama, who will live forever) It doesn't surprise me, Mama will say. I always knew there was something wrong with that girl.

Felicity will be embarrassed and change her name. Or maybe she'll write a book about being a murderess' daughter.

"It's no good. I have to go."

Deliberately, she doesn't look back.

THE HORIZON IS OBSCURED by striated layers of magenta cloud, translucent against the mauve sky. Sunset or sunrise? Sarah can't be certain so she treads water, watching the colors fade and deepen.

She starts swimming toward shore, the swell periodically lifting her high enough to see waves breaking on the beach. When she reaches shallow water she stands up and squints into the gathering dusk. The sand is dark and furrowed with elongated purple shadows. A gust of wind swirls off the water, and she hugs herself and shivers.

Behind her the sea has darkened to the color of red wine—it could as easily be the Mediterranean as the Pacific. The wine-dark sea and the rosy-fingered dawn; she's always remembered that line but nothing else, except that it's from an ancient Greek poem.

Night is falling quickly. Sarah can no longer see the waves, only the scallops of phosphorescence they leave on the wet sand.

She had to come back, she had no choice. She has children, she has obligations.

On the beach, the sand is still warm from the sun. Sarah picks her way carefully toward the cliff and the rocks, wary of broken glass and anything else people may have left lying around.

At the other end of the beach she sees figures silhouetted against a fire in a metal barrel, the early stages of a beach party.

Despite the dark, she knows exactly where she is. But the water is deeper than she thought it would be and when she reaches the first tumble of boulders, Sarah realizes that she'll have to wade back out in order to reach the rock ledge. The tide should be falling, not rising. Maybe she's got her times wrong. She proceeds slowly around the point, testing each submerged rock before she trusts her weight to it.

It might have been smarter to simply wait for the moon to rise. She's already caught glimpses of it, riding the horizon behind the clouds. And there are stars, thousands and thousands of them.

Although it's dark in the lee of the cliff, she's able to feel her way, the water sloshing busily around her legs. Suddenly, a translucent wash of moonlight throws everything into vivid relief, and there's the ledge, almost close enough to touch, and the rock, exactly as she left it.

Then stealthy clouds extinguish the moon again, leaving an inky void of water and sound. Sarah stands quite still, the swell of the tide insistent against the backs of her legs, giving her eyes time to readjust themselves to the darkness. She mustn't slip, or fall.

Again she moves carefully forward, a step at a time, hands extended in front of her. She doesn't have to do this. She can come back tomorrow, when it's light. But that will mean walking home barefoot, and without her keys and glasses.

Her fingertips touch the cliff face and she begins to feel her way, moving her hands a couple of inches to the left and back again, to the right. The rock is here, she saw it. She just needs to be patient until she finds it. All around her, the waves whisper and hiss against the boulders.

At last, Sarah's fingers locate the wedged rock and she withdraws her bundled sarong from the crevice, hugging it close against her body. Glasses, sandals, keys, she can feel everything through the thin layers of cloth. The moon reappears just in time to guide her back past the rocks and around the point to the deserted beach.

Sitting on a boulder, Sarah unwraps the sarong, trying to be careful, not wanting to lose anything in the dark. A mosquito bites her shoulder and she slaps it and drops her keys. But she plants her glasses firmly on the bridge of her nose and methodically pats the sand around the boulder until she finds them.

Now she can see all those thousands and thousands of stars clearly. If they're really dead suns, their light travelling through space, why are they always in the same place? Charles would have known.

She slips on her sandals, and holding her keys in her teeth, wraps the sarong around her wet bathing suit and knots it.

Once upon a time there was a princess who didn't kiss the frog, so she didn't live happily ever after and nobody bothered to write a story about her. Sarah's fingers linger on the knot in the sarong. Untie it, kick off the sandals, wade back into the sea. It's not too late.

Raucous laughter from the beach party shatters the silence and orange flames soar skyward, gradually sub-siding into a cloud of swirling sparks. There's applause, more laughter, and the abrupt throb of music, so loud that it obliterates the sound of the waves.

The moon is still struggling with the clouds. Sarah shivers slightly and sets off toward the esplanade. At the foot of the concrete steps she pauses and looks up at the sky, where God is supposed to be.

The beach suburbs look fragile tonight. In the wan glow of the streetlights, the rows of cars parked along either side of the road resemble a painted backdrop. Even the lamps glowing behind the curtained windows seem contrived.

Sarah walks wearily home, wondering why fish move so effortlessly; birds, too, riding the thermals. Xaxanader would say it's because fish and birds are where they're meant to be, at ease in their intended world.

Sagging power lines and the stumps of brutally pruned trees trace tortured silhouettes against the sky. It all looks the same as always and yet it also looks different, like a room when someone has moved the furniture.

Behind her, a car slows. A middle-aged balding man sticks his head out and spits. Farther along on the far side of the road, another man is walking two large dogs. Closer to Oxford Street, the reflected glow of the city lights stains the sky red, and the stars vanish.

Sarah feels goose pimples rising from the exposed flesh of her arms and shoulders. Goose pimples, goose skin, the flesh of freshly plucked geese. There's a word for it, Charles told her. Horripilation, from the Latin word *horrere*, to bristle.

She misses Charles, misses the contagious joy he took in the vagaries of the world, misses his unquenchable, eclectic curiosity. Everything interested Charles and he made everything interesting.

She's walking more briskly, almost jogging in an effort to keep warm. Music from Oxford Street pubs pulses beneath the crimson sky. The moon wins its battle with the clouds and soars above the cassia trees that line the footpath. It's a full moon, the color of ripe brie.

There's more traffic than you'd expect on a Friday night, more noise. Beyond the shuttered shop at the corner, cars are double-parked and people carrying bottles of wine in brown paper sacks move toward a house where all the lights are on and all the doors and windows appear to be open.

From the next intersection Sarah can see her own house, its courtyard walls illuminated by the streetlight in front of it. The streetlight is a liability, one of the reasons the house remained on the market for so long. Most people don't want a light shining into their bedroom window. But the light discourages drunks from the pubs.

As she walks toward her front gate, she sees yellow ribbon on it—which makes no sense. When she gets closer she sees that it's not ribbon, it's tape. Someone has strung tape across the front of her house and out over the footpath and the nature strip.

She continues to walk until she's directly across from her front gate. Cars are parked all along both sides of the street, and lights are on in most of the houses, although her own house is dark and silent. From here, Sarah sees lettering on the tape, but she can't read it.

A man and woman walk down the other side of the street, carrying brown paper bags from the Chinese takeaway. When they're abreast of her house, they detour into the road so as not to disturb the tape.

"You wouldn't credit it," the man says. "That quiet little old lady."

"She's not old, she just looks old. And that's how it always is, but. It's always the quiet ones." The woman looks back over her shoulder. "You never know, do you?"

Sarah presses back against the wall. She doesn't know their names, but she recognizes them. They live in a terrace at the end of the street and they both go out to work. They let their pit bull run loose mornings and evenings. Although they don't call them pit bulls here. They call them Staffordshire terriers.

Sarah remains where she is, in the shadows. She looks at the tape, clearly visible beneath the streetlight. It's the tape police use to cordon off a crime scene.

Chapter Nine

In one of the parked cars a match flares, illuminating epaulets. From the shadows Sarah watches two police officers light their cigarettes. When the match is extinguished the tips of the cigarettes glow orange in the darkness.

They've been here twice, they've searched the house. They've seen for themselves there's nothing to see. Something else has obviously happened, but even so. Crime scene tape and surveillance is going too far. She needs to put an end to it. She'll walk across the street to their car, knock on the window, and explain what they're doing is absurd, that there's no earthly reason why she should harm Jennyfer Blanchard. That's what an innocent person would do. Although she isn't exactly innocent.

They don't think she's innocent either. They wouldn't be sitting there if they thought she was innocent. They're here to arrest her. And Kahn was right, this isn't the United States. Australians don't have the right to remain silent or the right to legal counsel, or any rights at all. They don't have a Bill of Rights in Australia. They don't even have a Constitution.

She can't stand here forever. It's not safe, not even in the shadows. All they'd need to do is shine a torch this way. Or a neighbor might see her from an upstairs window.

Sarah backs away, staying close to the wall and retracing her steps, slowly and carefully. It seems to take hours, just to get back to the end of the street where she can slip around the corner.

She keeps walking. If she stops, someone might think she's loitering and call the police. She walks on toward Oxford Street, pausing to read the banner on a newspaper dispenser; "HORROR VIDEOTAPE." She peers into the plastic bin but there are no papers left, and in any case, she has no money. Her handbag is in the house.

The news agency is still open. Beneath fluorescent lights a queue of men and women wait their turn to buy tickets in the weekly lottery. That's odd too. Most people buy their lottery tickets at the last minute, just before the Saturday night draw.

Maybe it is Saturday night. That would explain the traffic and the parties.

The horror videotape mightn't have anything to do with Jennyfer Blanchard. It could be about a car accident or pedophiles or even a football game. But she needs to find out. She needs to find a newspaper.

There's probably one in her courtyard, unless the police took it. Perhaps she could sneak in from the back, open the front door and grab it. It's the last thing they'd expect, that she'd return to the scene of the crime. Or maybe not. What if someone is waiting inside?

People leave newspapers everywhere when they're done with them. And some cafés provide newspapers for their customers. The one down the street, for instance. If I had some money, I could order a coffee and read the newspaper while I wait. But I can do that anyway. Order a coffee and leave before they bring it.

But the café is closed.

There are newspapers in the rubbish bins, and there are rubbish bins on every corner. If she was a bag lady, she could rummage through them and nobody would notice. But she's not a bag lady and she doesn't want to attract attention.

Where else? They have newspapers at the public library, attached to long wooden poles so people can't steal them. Old men in dirty jumpers sit there all day, reading them.

Bondi Junction Library shares a building with the struggling community theatre and some professional office suites. It's closed on Sunday, Sarah knows that. But it might be open on Saturday night. The theatre is dark, yet there are lights on in all the upstairs windows of the library. But when

Sarah makes her way to the main entrance and peers into the deserted vestibule, she sees a sign propped on an easel, Private Function.

Properly dressed she might attempt it, might even persuade someone she'd been invited. But not like this, not in sandals and a sarong.

There's a newspaper lying on a bench and Sarah pounces on it. But it's just the weekly rag, mostly advertising. There are no pubs on this street and no pedestrians. All the little shops and cafes are shut. Sarah pauses in front of an electronics shop, gazing at the flood-lit display of appliances and DVD players and television sets, their screens blank and silent.

If it's a videotape, it'll be on the news. All she needs to do is find a television set. Department stores sell televisions, and if it's Saturday night they're open for late night shopping.

Grace Brothers' electronics section is on the lower ground floor, toward the back. Sarah walks briskly past racks of skirts and tables stacked with books and boxes of imported chocolates. Television sets are displayed in an alcove beyond a pair of stucco arches.

A few dozen people are already watching, their plastic shopping bags dangling as they stare up at the monitors. Behind them, Sarah only sees endless footage depicting open water. There's no audio.

She goes farther, pretending to be interested in the more expensive plasma sets, but all these are airing a football game. Odd that nobody is watching football. She turns back. The people watching the other television sets are sighing and murmuring quietly to one another.

Sarah sees a single, fleeting image of an open boat bobbing in the sea, followed by a commercial break. It's as if a spell has been broken and the shoppers start to drift away. Shocking, a woman says to her husband. Sarah follows several steps behind them, past the books and boxes of chocolates, trying to overhear something further.

There are four pubs at the main intersection and they're already crowded, their patrons shouting to make themselves heard over the blasts of music and shrieking, preening women.

There are television sets in pubs, too.

A man in shorts and work boots comes staggering out of The Irish Pig, grabs hold of a signpost, and vomits into the gutter. Shaking his head, he wipes his nose and mouth on his sleeve and goes back inside.

Sarah crosses the street to Horseman's Rest, a former bookies' pub transmogrified into a launching pad for local musicians. It's too early for the first gig, although amplifiers pump out a throbbing promise of things to come. The main bar and the lounge are packed and the place reeks of spilled beer and burned meat.

The big attraction at Pat O'Leary's on the northwest corner is an immense television screen propped over the main bar, which continually broadcasts football games from all over the world. Sarah enters the lounge area, which isn't quite so crowded, and hesitates. A lone woman in an Australian pub on Saturday night is on the make, and fair game.

Two men and a woman leave, abandoning half empty wine glasses. Sarah sits down at the vacated table and picks up one of the glasses. The wine is red and cheap but she doesn't have to drink it. She just needs to sit here and wait for the news. She crosses her legs, self-conscious, seeing herself as the rest of them must see her, an older woman in a sarong. Mutton dressed up like lamb, Australians would say.

There are two television sets in the lounge area, mounted high above the bar at opposite ends of the room. The one closest to Sarah is tuned to the football, but there's something else on the other one, too far away for her to see what. But there's an empty table and chair right underneath it.

Holding her glass of wine, she stands up again and works her way carefully past the men sitting at the bar. Nobody even looks at her. Sarah sits down at the empty table and pretends to sip her wine. The television above her head is showing a game show, but there'll be a news bulletin on the hour.

"Well, fancy meeting you here! One of my new ladies. Sandra, isn't it?"

Sarah's hand jerks involuntarily and some of the wine slops onto the table. It's him, she recognizes him although she can't recall his name. Bennett? Brett? Brian, that's it. He grabs an unoccupied chair from another table, drags it across the floor and straddles it.

"Mind if I join you." It isn't a question. "So, Sandra. You here on your own?"

Sarah nods, not saying anything, hoping he'll go away.

"So what are we drinking, then? A bit of the house burgundy, is it? Looks to me like you're ready for a refill." He waves imperiously and a barmaid appears out of nowhere and bustles toward them, smiling and carrying a tray. "Two more of the same, luv."

Above her head Sarah recognizes the signature music that precedes news bulletins but doesn't look up. People don't watch television in pubs, unless it's the football. "Sydney police still have no information regarding the whereabouts of the woman thought to be responsible for the drowning death of Queensland heiress Jennyfer Blanchard."

Now she does look up, too surprised to be cautious. "That's what happened to her? She drowned?"

"Where the fuck have you been, in outer space? Yeah, she drowned. At least, that's what they reckon. They haven't found the body yet. Probably never will. It's a big ocean." He's staring up at the flickering screen and Sarah realizes the room has become quiet, that everyone is watching. "It's been the same thing, all day. They keep playing this same bit of tape, over and over again. Ask me, they should give it a rest. I mean, how do you think it makes her folks feel, watching this? Bloody fucking journalists. No sense of decency."

There's that shot of open water again. "A Japanese tourist attending a private function at a Surf Lifesaving Club thought he was filming rescuers responding to swimmers in distress. Instead, he found himself filming a murder."

The camera zooms shakily in on two women, impressionistic smudges of color in the green water. The women are treading water and appear to be discussing something. Then, there's just one woman. The other one has vanished beneath the surface of the sea.

"Did you see that? Did you see what that bitch did? Can you believe it?" Brian shakes his head. "Murder, that's what it is. Cold-blooded murder. And look at her, swimming away, cool as a cucumber. Butter wouldn't melt."

A Surf Lifesaving Rescue boat moves into the frame and Sarah watches herself flop headfirst over its gunnels, buttocks wide, the backs of her legs slack and dimpled with cellulite.

Whoever is holding the camera tries to focus on her face, but the image is grainy, unrecognizable.

"One chance in a million. You wouldn't credit it, would you? Wasn't for that Jap, she'd have got away with it. Home and hosed, no questions asked."

The camera cuts to the newsreader, sitting serious and solemn behind his fake desk in front of a fake window. "Surf lifesavers say the woman they rescued told them she'd fallen into the water and was alone. After viewing the tourist's video, officials realized a second woman was involved. Efforts to find this second woman's body have been unsuccessful, but digitally enhanced frames from the taped sequence indicate that she was Jennyfer Blanchard, the Brisbane heiress missing since last Friday."

"I don't believe it." Sarah shakes her head. "It's totally insane. That wasn't Jennyfer Blanchard."

"So who was it, then? And how the fuck would you know?" His eyes narrow. "What do you know about anything?"

"Nothing." The last thing, the very last thing she needs at this point is to get into a public argument with this awful man. "Look, maybe it was Jennyfer Blanchard. All I meant was that it didn't look like her."

"Yeah, and how do you know what she looks like? She's a fucking millionaire. It's not like the two of you do lunch."

"No, but I met her, once."

"You met Jennyfer Blanchard. Yeah, sure you did. Go on, pull the other one."

"No, really. I did." She has to get away from him, she has to get out of here. "It was years ago, when my husband was still alive. We were at a reception at the university. Her father had donated a lot of money, to build a new laboratory or something. So they gave him an honorary doctorate and she was there, with him. She was lovely. She shook hands with everyone." Sarah hesitates. "It's awful, isn't it? If it was really her, I mean."

The waitress returns with their drinks, two glasses of red wine on a wet wooden tray. She puts one glass down in front of Brian, the other in front of Sarah.

"She's just a kid," Sarah says. "Why would anyone want to hurt a kid? She's too young to have enemies. Who'd want to kill her?"

Brian picks up his glass. "Maybe it started off being a kidnapping. Who knows? Cheers."

Above their heads, the journalist continues to read the news. "The Prime Minister has announced he'll establish a Royal Commission to report on alleged irregularities in the Electoral Rolls of New South Wales, Victoria, and Tasmania. And ladies and gentlemen, I've just been handed a bulletin, it's just come in, just this minute." He looks at a piece of paper in his hand and draws a breath. "What you're about to see on your screen is a digital enhancement of the face of the woman believed to have killed Jennyfer Blanchard."

Sarah stares at her own face for a single, awful moment before she leaps to her feet, bumping the flimsy table with her knees and upsetting the wine. One of the glasses tips into Brian's lap, splashing across the front of his shirt and into his lap. "What the fuck? What's wrong with you?"

"Excuse me. I'm sorry, I feel sick. I've got to go to the loo."

"Just a fucking minute!"

Racing through the pub, Sarah places one hand over her mouth and people hastily get out of her way. Once she's safely through the swinging doors and outside on the pavement, she pauses to catch her breath.

"I said, just a fucking minute!" Sarah whirls to face Brian. "You owe me for that glass of wine. And for the dry cleaning, thank you very much. You know what this suit cost? It's a fucking Armani." He grabs her arm.

"Let go! You're hurting me!"

"Oh, I'm hurting you. Am I hurting you fifty bucks' worth? That's what it's going to cost, to get this cleaned up. Not to mention the shirt. I mean what the fuck do you think you're doing?"

He's strong, and he's not going to let go of her, she knows that. But he didn't see it, he couldn't have seen it. There wasn't time. All he cares about is his suit, and how much it's going to cost to clean it.

"All right," Sarah says. "Look, I'm sorry. Just let go of me, okay?" She pulls clear of him and takes a couple of steps backward. "I'll send you a check, how's that? Just give me your card, or write down your name and address, and I'll send you a check."

His tie is ruined too. A little knot of onlookers has gathered and he turns to them, arms spread in supplication. "Look at me. Look at what she did to me. This is a new suit, I just bought this suit." An unshaven man in cut-off jeans and thongs nods sympathetically.

"Hang on—that's her! The one we just saw on the telly. The one what drowned that girl." The woman points. "It's her, all right."

Sarah plunges into the dark alley that runs along the side of the pub, all the way through, she hopes, to the next street. It's hard to see where she's going or what's beneath her feet but she keeps running, bumps into the side of a building, grazes her elbow on a brick wall, runs on. Then she collides with a rubbish bin and something smashes into her shin and she drops to her knees on the cold cobblestones, in agony.

The pain paralyzes her and she can't breathe, can't inhale. Rocking back and forth, she's racked with silent sobs, can feel hot tears pouring from her eyes. Moaning softly, she crouches against the brick wall. If they're chasing her they'll catch her, and she no longer cares.

Nothing happens. It's very quiet, although she can hear the distant, muted roar of the traffic on Oxford Street. Gingerly, Sarah touches the broken skin on her leg with her forefinger and gasps. It's bleeding, there's blood everywhere. She wipes her finger on the sarong, then carefully straightens her leg. The pain is already easing, it's not broken.

They're probably not chasing her, those people from the pub. It's Saturday night, they have better things to do. Somebody will call the police and that will be the end of it, except for Brian and his ruined suit. In spite of the pain, Sarah grins. She's glad she spilled the wine, glad she ruined his suit.

She moves carefully to a more comfortable position, braced against the wall with her knees drawn up. She can't stay here. The police will come after her, down the alley. She has to keep going.

Pushing herself up with her hands and using the wall for balance, Sarah struggles back to her feet. Her knees are trembling. She touches the wall for support when she needs it and limps on through the darkness.

This is crazy and wrong, and totally unfair. I'm not a criminal. I obey the laws, I vote, I pay taxes. I'm the one who pays for the courts and the police and all the rest of it. I'm one of the good guys.

Moreover, nobody was murdered. It wasn't Jennyfer Blanchard, it was Bantryd. And I didn't drown her. I didn't drown anyone. Bantryd isn't dead.

But suppose I *am* crazy? Suppose I thought it was Bantryd when all along it really was Jennyfer Blanchard? Even so, I didn't kill her. And I'm not crazy and it wasn't Jennyfer Blanchard. It was Bantryd.

It's like one of those films. You didn't do it, but you're the suspect and the only way you can prove you're innocent is to find the real murderer. But there isn't a real murderer because there wasn't a murder.

Her leg aches abominably. You stub your toe or bang your shin or elbow against something, and it hurts as much as a childbirth contraction. Charles used to joke about it. Why do they call it a funny bone? Because it's humerus.

Taking small, shuffling steps she finally emerges onto a broad suburban street. Streetlights that look like old-fashioned gas lamps cast warm, inviting pools of light but Sarah skirts them, squinting into the darkness and trying to figure out where she is.

The gabled houses look familiar and so do the trees, their leafy branches forming a canopy over the road. She's been here before, she's walked here. She knows this place.

In the months after Charles's death, Sarah spent entire days walking to fill the empty hours. Somehow, walking deadened the pain. Some days she walked from Bondi Junction and King's Cross all the way to George Street and then back again along Edgecliff Road to Bondi Beach. She wore out her favorite sandals, and having them resoled cost more than buying new ones.

In her mind's eye, Sarah positions herself on a map of Bondi Junction. She's north of Oxford Street near Edgecliff Road, in the cheap part of Woollahra where houses cost less than a million dollars. She recognizes the street, although she can't remember what it's called. There's a bus shed up ahead and a pay telephone in front of a café, then Edgecliff Road.

Where is Jennyfer Blanchard, anyway? Sarah doesn't think she's dead, or even kidnapped. Most likely, she ran away. Maybe she had a fight with her parents. Kids are kids, rich or not. Jennyfer Blanchard ran away, and they haven't found her because she doesn't want to be found.

The trouble is, they're looking for the girl on the beach, and the girl on the beach was Bantryd. So it's all worked out perfectly for Jennyfer Blanchard, hasn't it? She could be anywhere in Australia by now. She could be anywhere in the world.

Edgecliff Road winds silently beneath the street lights. There's no traffic. This is Woollahra proper, elegant even in the dark. Flowering shrubs in terra cotta pots bloom within spacious courtyards secured by elaborate wrought-iron gates. Behind walls, chained dogs bark as she passes.

Her leg is hurting so much, Sarah again wonders if she's broken a bone. They say you go into shock after a severe injury, so for a while you don't feel any pain. She pauses, leaning heavily against a wall. She needs to rest. She's passing the little park, and moonlight falling through the branches illuminates the white gravel path that leads past the bench to the sunken garden.

Sarah sinks down on the bench, closes her eyes. She should have listened to Kahn. She should have called the solicitor. But what would she have said to him?

None of this would be happening, if not for bloody Jennyfer Blanchard. People go missing all the time and nobody notices or even cares, because they're not heiresses to millions of dollars.

She's thirsty. Is there a bubbler in this park? Sarah doesn't know, can't remember. Besides, she doesn't want to get up again. She doesn't want to move.

It's cooling off and all she has is the sarong. Huddling against the bench, Sarah hugs herself. The wooden slats are hard and uncomfortable. Where else is there to go? Not home, and not to Felicity. If Sean was here, she could go to him. But Sean is on an oil rig somewhere in the North Sea.

Above her head the moon sails its course, high and proud, casting an ethereal light upon the grass and pebbles and burnishing the leaves of the trees.

If she had a friend, she could go there. But she doesn't have that kind of friend. She did once, when she was a little girl, but that friend lives in Michigan and Sarah hasn't seen her in thirty years, although they still exchange Christmas cards.

Kahn will have seen the videotape by now. Perhaps he's trying to reach her. Sarah envisions the answering machine's angry green light, blinking impotently in the dark house. Does Kahn think she did it? He couldn't possibly, he knows her better than that.

Kahn knows she didn't do it, knows she couldn't possibly kill anyone. He's a psychotherapist. If Kahn testifies on her behalf, they'll believe him. He'll make a good witness, well spoken and sure of himself but also deferential to the judge's authority.

Mrs. Andrews has been a client for nearly two years, Kahn will testify. I see her regularly, twice a week. Mrs. Andrews is very good about keeping her appointments, but she's been depressed over the loss of her husband.

Is Mrs. Andrews capable of murder? asks the prosecutor. Kahn hesitates. The prosecutor repeats the question. Mr. Kahn, is she capable of murder?

It would depend on the circumstances, Kahn says reluctantly. Under certain circumstances, I suppose everyone is capable of murder.

Not such a good witness, after all. But he might be willing to help. What if I call him and say I'm in trouble and need a place to stay? He won't just hang up. Maybe he'll lend me some money. If I had money, I could check into a motel.

Kahn lives somewhere nearby. He once said it was quicker for him to walk to work than to drive, because he can never find a place to park.

Of course she doesn't know his telephone number, but there's a directory in the telephone booth. Paging through it, Sarah realizes she doesn't know Kahn's first name, either. But there are only three Kahns listed, one on Watts Street, one on Pelham Avenue, and one on Edgecliff Road. Watts Street is mostly boarding houses, and he couldn't afford Pelham Avenue.

But she can't call him. She has no money. She'll go to his house and ask him in person. It's only a few blocks, and he's at home. His car is parked at the curb. Kahn won't like it that she looked him up in the telephone directory, he won't like her coming to his house. Still, it's an emergency. That's what she'll say. I'm sorry to bother you at home, but this is an emergency.

The house is an older cottage, unrenovated and set well back behind a low iron fence. A brick path leads to the veranda steps and the outside lights are on, as if Kahn is expecting company. There's a bronze plaque mounted alongside the door.

It's strange she doesn't know his first name. She should have asked. But he might not have told her. He might have just sat there and stared. He does that when he doesn't want to answer a question. His name is probably engraved on the plaque, but she can't make it out.

The lights are on inside and Sarah can hear music—classical music, piano and violin. Behind sheer curtains, people are moving back and forth, at least two people, one a woman. Kahn might not want to introduce her to his wife. He might not even want her in his house. Perhaps he'll come out and close the door, and talk to her on the veranda. She realizes she was hoping he'd invite her inside, even offer her something cold to drink.

The moon is still high, giving off enough light to cast shadows. Her hand upon the latch, Sarah sighs. She mustn't be seen hanging around in front of someone's home, especially in Woollahra. One of Kahn's neighbors might call the police.

Open the gate, then. Go up the steps. Ring the doorbell.

Kahn will want to know who was in the water with her. Why didn't you try to save her, Mrs. Andrews? If she tells him, he won't believe her. He'll believe what he saw on television, like everybody else.

Slowly, Sarah backs away from the gate. She gazes for a moment longer at the yellow warmth of the lamplight and shakes her head. It was a dumb idea.

Unwilling to return to the park, Sarah limps aimlessly through the quiet streets, through puddles of light alternating with patches of darkness. Her leg burns and throbs.

It would be better if she really had killed someone. At least she'd have had a plan, and an alibi, and an escape route. Charles always said any intelligent person can rob a bank and get away with it, so long as they only do it once.

The dignified quiet and the spacious homes set behind their walls and surrounded with shrubbery somehow reassure her. This is the kind of neighborhood she and Charles would have chosen. If it wasn't for her leg, she could spend the night walking back and forth along the footpaths beneath the trees.

But she can't do that. She's tired and she needs to sleep. Tired people make mistakes. It was a mistake not to have listened to Kahn and called a solicitor. It was a mistake to run away from the pub. Sarah can't afford to make any more mistakes. She needs to be rested and alert.

Homeless people sleep among the headstones in the little graveyard, against the cold concrete walls of the highway overpasses. They sleep curled in nests of plastic bags in the lantana thickets at Queens Park, they even sprawl in storefronts on Oxford Street. Sleeping rough, they call it. So there are places you can go. But Sarah doesn't know them, because she's never had to know, she's never been homeless.

The police are watching her house and they're probably watching Felicity's house too. They know she ran away from the pub. Where will they look for her next? If she had money, she'd get on a train or check into a motel. That's what they'll expect her to do. What they won't expect her to do is return to the beach. Even homeless people avoid the beaches at night. They're too dark, too exposed, too windy.

But what about all those caves?

Sarah retraces her steps, walking faster and barely noticing her leg. The way is downhill, and east. I'm strong, she reminds herself. Tomorrow I'll sort this out. Meanwhile, at least I have a plan.

What would Xaxanader say? He'd say, You should have stayed here with us. He'd say, Come back to me. And I will, I promise. But it has to be because I want to, not because I have to. After this mess is straightened out.

She can smell the sea, briny and cold. It's not much farther. And it will feel so good to just sit down and close her eyes. She recognizes the curve of the esplanade, and staying in the shadows on the darker side of the street, she continues south until she hears the distant throb of the Saturday night party at the Surf Lifesaving Club.

She's on the high side of the promontory, which falls away to the southern beach. Sarah crosses the street and walks along the gravel footpath that runs along the top of the cliffs. The path is usually crowded with power walkers and their dogs, but not at night. Plantings of pig face, its succulent leaves black in the moonlight, separate the path from the precipitous drop to the sea below. The Surf Lifesaving Club is just ahead, perched like a beacon at the top of the hill.

She wishes Bantryd had seen this, the magical full moon stitching its silvery light across the undulating surface of the sea. It isn't a perfect world. But occasionally, it can stop your breath with its beauty.

She starts down the sandy track that leads to the sea. The silhouettes of a few beach fisherman are outlined against the water, far below to her left. Nobody will take any notice of her. For all anyone knows, she's a fisherman's wife, come to fetch her man home. Ahead, a triangular rock juts upward into the night sky.

The path is more precipitous than she remembers, and the crashing waves at the base of the cliffs remind Sarah of how dangerous it would be to slip and fall. But the moonlight helps. She picks her way cautiously, watching her footing and reaching for a handhold before each step, keeping an eye out for an empty cave.

The larger ones are occupied. As she passes, Sarah glimpses the occasional flicker of flame and smells food cooking. At one cave, an angry shout stops her in her tracks but nobody comes out to accost her, nothing else happens. The whole thing is like a dream or one of those surrealist paintings; a woman in a sarong, climbing down the face of a cliff in the middle of the night.

A space opens in front of her, dark and silent. Sarah stands still and listens carefully for several minutes. There's no sound but the crash of the surf against the base of the cliffs below.

"Hello? Is anyone in there?"

Her whisper seems loud as a shout but elicits no response. Very carefully, Sarah takes a step into the darkness, then another—and bangs her forehead sharply against a rock overhang. The shock of it is worse than the pain, startling her so that for several moments she can't move. Gradually, she extends her arms until her fingertips touch cold stone. It's not a proper cave but a shallow, triangular wedge of space impressed into the face of the cliff. But it's sheltered from the wind, it'll do.

Inside, Sarah eases herself into a sitting position, her back braced against the sloping wall with her legs slightly drawn up in front of her. She's looking out across the Pacific Ocean, an endless expanse of rippling black and silver that stretches all the way to the hidden horizon. As her eyes become accustomed to the darkness, she can make out the shapes of a couple of tankers, darker forms against the dark sea. The cave reminds her of the troglodyte caves she and Charles visited in the Dordogne. She unties the sarong, slips it off, and wraps it tightly around her shoulders like a shawl.

This isn't so bad, not really. The rock is hard and cold, but Sarah lies down anyway, pillowing her head on her hands. Her leg doesn't hurt quite so much, or perhaps she's just getting used to it. Cautiously, she explores her wounds. There's a big lump on her shin and another on her forehead, over her eye.

The moon continues across the sky, allowing Sarah to measure the minutes and hours of the night. She closes her eyes but she's uncomfortable, and her thoughts race and jump like monkeys in a cage. She can't sleep, but she mustn't waste these precious hours. At least think about what you're going to do in the morning, she tells herself. Make another plan.

But it's difficult to concentrate. And tomorrow seems remote, almost theoretical. It's all so implausible, like a dream. Maybe it is a dream. Maybe she's about to wake up and find herself in her own house, in her own bed.

Why shouldn't there be two worlds? Why shouldn't there be a world on every planet, on every star in every solar system in every galaxy? Why shouldn't there be worlds within worlds?

Her thoughts drift, riding the waves and the moonlight. She's sitting in the black vinyl chair, talking to Kahn. My life ended when Charles died, she tells him. My life is over now. And yet I'm still alive. How can that be?

It can't be, says Kahn. You're right. Your life is over. You died with Charles. But he was good and you were bad, and this is your punishment. You're in hell, Mrs. Andrews.

Her eyes fly open. Her legs are stiff and her toes are numb, although she still feels the pain in her shin. Sarah wriggles awkwardly, trying to find a more comfortable position, but the rock beneath her is unyielding.

It's even darker now than it was before and although she can still hear the sea, she can no longer distinguish it from the sky. Clouds must have drifted across the face of the moon, or perhaps the moon has already set.

She moves restlessly against the rock and finally sits up. She must decide what she's going to do tomorrow. But it's too late and too dark, and Sarah is too cold. She can't focus, except on the inexorable present, the obduracy of the stone against her buttocks and back and the invisible, hungry sea. She pulls the sarong more tightly about her, closing her eyes against the darkness.

Again she dozes but is almost immediately startled awake by dogs barking. Big dogs, salvering hounds out of a nightmare. Staring into the darkness, Sarah listens intently but hears nothing. She was dreaming. Or maybe someone is out late, walking his dogs along the rim of the cliff.

This is all so unfair. Things like this aren't supposed to happen to people like me. I've always told the truth, always admitted it when I was wrong. I did it. I broke it. I'm sorry. But I didn't do this. I didn't do anything to anyone, but nobody believes me. Not even Felicity, my own daughter. Sarah closes her eyes, too baffled to weep. Again, she dozes.

She's standing alongside Xaxanader, tending a newly born Telling, her own Telling. He puts his arm around her shoulders and she when looks up at him, his smile is like a benediction. But this isn't really happening, she tells him sadly. This is just a dream. No, he says, you're wrong. The other was a dream, but this is real. You're here, you're safe, you're with me. Reassured, she allows herself to relax, her head against his chest.

Something digs into the small of her back and it hurts so much that she cries out and opens her eyes. Xaxanader is gone. She's alone, lying on a spur of rock. When she tries to sit up, she almost tumbles out of the cave and down the side of the cliff, only just catching herself in time. Breathing hard, she lies still, her cheek pressed against the cold stone.

A salty breeze gusts into her face. It feels good at first, bracing. Her mind is clear now, and she lies curled on the rock platform, the gravel path just beyond and the surf pounding invisibly far below, gazing idly at the fading stars. One of them seems to be moving very slowly. Perhaps it's a satellite. The sky is full of rubbish, Charles used to say.

The wind grows stronger. She can hear it whistling faintly around the rock faces. It's cold, and she tries to move away from it, farther back into the cave, but there's no place to go.

This is awful. If they'd caught her and put her in jail, she'd have a bed, with blankets and a pillow. She'll probably be arrested, anyway. Sarah has never been inside a jail, can't even imagine it. How big is a prison cell? Big enough for a bed set against the wall, and a toilet and a sink. She knows that much from films. There are usually two beds, one above the other. She won't be alone. She'll have a cellmate.

Sitting with her back to the wall and her arms wrapped around her knees, Sarah can see her cellmate's mocking smile, hear her harsh laughter. Think you're better than the rest of us, don't you?

Sarah closes her eyes. She feels sick. She can taste the bile at the back of her throat. She can't go to jail. She won't. She'd rather be dead.

The sky has taken on a new translucence, and Sarah realizes that she can distinguish the horizon, a different shade of gray. She doesn't want to go to jail. But she doesn't want to die, either.

It's getting lighter. Sarah sees birds, riding the thermals. She's not a criminal. She didn't do anything wrong. Jail might not be as bad as she thinks. Although somehow, she knows it is.

A pale light seeps up from below the horizon, limning the underbellies of the clouds. There are more birds, swooping and calling to one another. Sarah sits quietly, watching the sky. The night was endless, but now it's almost morning, and she still doesn't have a plan.

Suddenly, she hears the crunch of boots upon the gravel path. There's nothing she can do, no place to run. Inanely, she counts the steps coming closer and watches in breathless silence as a figure moves slowly past the gaping entrance of the cave. It's a fisherman, wearing rubber hip boots and some kind of hooded cape and carrying two rods and a tackle box. If he turns his head, he'll see her. But he doesn't.

There'll be other fishermen. That's why there's a path in the first place, because people use it. It's no longer dark but it's not light, either. Sarah decides to remain here a little while longer, until the sun rises.

The eastern sky turns from pale apricot to pink and then to gold as the sun begins to push its way up toward the lightening sky. The waves murmur. The tide must be about to turn.

Nobody else comes along the path. It's Sunday, after all. Even fishermen sleep in on Sunday mornings. Slowly Sarah gets to her feet, moves to the front of the cave, and stretches, realizing that she needs to pee. There are public toilets down on the beach, in a green shed at the bottom of the cliff.

Emerging from the cave, Sarah decides it will be easier to go back up to the top of the cliff and then follow the road down to the swimming beach than to scramble the rest of the way down the track. Besides, the tide is in and if she climbs down to the base of the cliffs, she might have to swim for it.

Her back aches and she's exhausted, even though she slept a little. Slowly she makes her way back along the path, which is steeper than she remembers, working her way toward the top. She feels better, now that there's light. Things aren't as bad as they look. The whole thing is crazy. But it can be sorted.

There are sinks in the public toilets, and running water. She wishes she had soap and a toothbrush, but at least she'll be able to rinse her mouth. Sarah remembers how she'd wake up next to Charles when they were still dating and tiptoe into his bathroom to brush her teeth before slipping back into bed.

A cup of coffee would be good too. And why not? She'll walk into a café, sit down and order coffee and a croissant. Afterward, she'll say she forgot her purse, that she'll come back and pay later. She even knows of a café that opens early. It's not as if she's really a criminal. She didn't drown anyone.

It's warming up, although the sun's rays aren't strong enough to cast shadows. Sarah pauses for a moment to look back down at the lone fisherman, standing on a rock and casting his line into the surf. The track is steep and narrow, and directly below her an angry froth of spume marks an ancient rock spill. She might easily have missed her footing in the dark last night.

She pictures it, her body lying broken on the rocks, the waves breaking over her. And if she'd survived? She might have spent the rest of her life in a wheelchair, in jail. No, that wouldn't have happened. That's not going to happen. Nobody was murdered. Nobody is dead. Nobody is going to jail. She rubs her eyes, takes a deep breath. It's going to be okay.

The climb leaves her breathless and perspiring. When she finally emerges onto the gravel path atop the cliffs, Sarah stops for a moment to wipe her face with a corner of the sarong.

She's on the ocean side of the road that runs along the top of the cliff, parallel to the path—which, thanks to its wonderful vistas overlooking the sea, is popular with joggers. But there's nobody out this morning, no walkers, no dogs, not even any traffic. Everything on this side of the road is public domain, although on the other side of the road, it's different. You can't own the beachfront in Australia, but a couple of million dollars will buy you a more or less unobstructed view of it. That's what any one of the row of brick cottages facing her across the strip of asphalt would cost. None of them are large houses, not by American standards. But they all have fabulous views from their second story windows, which now reflect the early morning sunshine back into Sarah's eyes.

It's as if the world ended last night while she slept, and she's the only human being left on the face of the earth.

Suddenly there's an explosion of incandescent light, white and a thousand times brighter than the sun. It envelops her, blinds her. For a moment she thinks maybe she did fall off the cliff, and this really is the white light.

Someone is saying her name. "Sarah Andrews!" Dazed, she doesn't respond but continues to stare into the light. "Sarah Andrews," the voice says again. It's not the kind of voice you'd associate with an angel, or with God. It's a stern, unforgiving voice. "Sarah Andrews."

The light is growing smaller and Sarah finds she can look away from it. There are spots swimming before her eyes, but they fade and she sees people pouring out of the houses across the street, dozens of people carrying searchlights and bullhorns. They all look the same, like an army. They're wearing uniforms and they form a semi-circular cordon on the other side of the street. The cordon begins to move toward her, very slowly. Sarah shakes her head. Can she possibly be worth all this trouble? "Sarah Andrews," the voice says again.

A dog barks. Sarah sees it, a big dog, chocolate-colored and wearing a sort of harness. It knows she's looking at it and barks furiously, again and again, until its handler bends over and silences it. That must be the dog she heard last night. The police used it to track her, the way they use dogs to track runaway aboriginals.

"Police," says the voice. "Raise your hands above your head."

She does raise her hands, but only as high as her shoulders, turning her palms inward and looking sadly at them. The skin is dirty, her fingers torn and bleeding from the rocks.

"Don't move."

She drops her eyes and then raises them carefully, avoiding the glaring orbs of the searchlights. I'm strong, she reminds herself. Black shoes, blue trouser legs, coming toward her. "Stop! Don't come near me, or I'll jump!"

To her mild amazement, they do stop. The dog barks, just once. Nobody says anything.

"Turn off those lights! I can't see."

"Nobody's going to hurt you, Mrs. Andrews."

"Turn off the lights or I'll jump!" She turns, as if to take a step backward.

"All right." The voice is conciliatory, almost supplicating. "We're turning them off, see?" The lights fade away. "There's nothing to be afraid of, ma'am. Nobody's going to get hurt here."

The sky above the red tiled roofs is the color of pale rose velvet. At the edge of her vision something moves and she turns her head to see half a dozen patrol cars, lights twinkling like jewels, coming down the esplanade. Behind the patrol cars are white vans topped with miniature satellite dishes and emblazoned with the icons of the three television networks.

Without thinking, Sarah takes another step backward. This, she observes with interest and some satisfaction, seems to alarm them. They don't want her to jump, or fall. She begins to plan.

"Ma'am, you want to come away from there."

It might still be possible to make a run for it, down the track. But there are so many of them, and for all she knows there are others, waiting for her down on the beach. It obviously makes them nervous when she moves but she doesn't want to take another step back, she's already too close to the edge.

She needs time, she needs to think this through.

The officer holding the loud hailer is now deep in conversation with a shorter man who's wearing ordinary clothes instead of a uniform. The officer finally gives this man the loud hailer and steps away.

"Mrs. Andrews." It's Kahn. "I'm right here, Mrs. Andrews. Don't be frightened. I'm going to help you. We're all going to help you. We're going to sort this thing out."

Kahn takes a step forward, then another. He crosses the footpath and the nature strip, then begins to cross the road. He's close enough for Sarah to recognize the pattern of blue and red stripes on his shirt. He's fond of that shirt, maybe his wife gave it to him. Kahn is looking at her impassively, the way he usually looks at her.

"Stop! That's far enough. I mean it!"

He stops in the middle of the road, and his lips part as if he's about to say something. But he's still holding the loud hailer, and now he looks down at it as if he's not sure what he's meant to do with such a thing. Kahn is out of his element.

"Do you think I killed that girl?" she asks him.

"I'm sorry," Kahn says. "I can't really hear you. I need to get a little bit closer."

"No!" She raises her voice. "I asked you a question. Do you think I killed that girl?"

"Mrs. Andrews, we need to talk."

"Just answer me."

"You're tired. You're upset. Let's go somewhere and have a cup of coffee."

Sarah stares at him. "My God. You actually think I did it."

Kahn smiles uneasily and shakes his head. He glances toward the figures standing behind him but turns quickly back to Sarah when she moves to the left, taking a couple of tiny steps.

"Mrs. Andrews, stop! It's only me. Nobody is going to hurt you."

It seems an odd thing to say, under the circumstances. Of course they're going to hurt her. They're going to arrest her and put her on trial for murder. And then they're going to put her in jail for the rest of her life. But maybe not. It's her choice. They don't realize that, yet.

"Mrs. Andrews?"

She looks at him.

"Mrs. Andrews, you and I both know that this is all a mistake. Charles's death was a terrible shock for you. You've been distraught. You've been depressed. You've been through so much, Mrs. Andrews. And you've handled it all so well, there's a lot to be said in your behalf. You've tried to get a grip, I can vouch for that. You've acted responsibly, you've sought professional help. That's why I'm here, Mrs. Andrews. I'm here for you. I'm here to help you get through this."

He isn't, though. He's here for himself, because he wants to see himself on the six o'clock news. Or maybe he wants a share of the reward. He'll have to fight Felicity for it, and good luck to him. Again, Sarah turns away and looks at the crimson horizon, remembering how magnificently the sun bursts forth to turn the rosy sky to azure.

"Mrs. Andrews!"

They're afraid she's going to jump. They don't want her to jump, because if she does they won't be able to arrest her, they won't get justice.

"Mrs. Andrews! I have Felicity here. She wants to talk to you, Mrs. Andrews. Your daughter, Felicity."

As if she's crazy, as if she doesn't know Felicity is her daughter.

"Mrs. Andrews! Here she is. Here's Felicity."

Pretending she either doesn't hear them or doesn't care, Sarah doesn't look up. Let them think she's going to jump. She's only a step or two from the edge of the cliff, she can see the white water roiling across the rocks directly below. If she jumps here, she'll be killed. But just to the north, the swell is washing quietly against the sheer face of the cliff, because the water is deep there. If she's going to jump, that's where she has to do it. She moves closer to the edge of the cliff but sideways, toward the deep water. But she hasn't decided, not yet. She's simply keeping her options open.

"Mum! Don't do it!"

Sarah takes another step.

"Mum! Oh, Mum, oh God!"

Is the tide in or out? Sarah can't tell from here. But there are no rocks visible above the surface of the water. She wishes they'd all leave her alone for a few minutes, give her time to think. If they arrest her, she'll never see Xaxanader again. But if she jumps, she can come back. She's done it three times. If she jumps, her options stay open. Unless she imagined the whole thing. No, she didn't imagine it. If she's sure of anything, she's sure of that. All right, then. Ten more steps.

"Mum, talk to me!"

Sarah turns to face Felicity. "All right, I'm talking to you. And I'm asking you the same question. Do you think I killed her?"

Felicity doesn't reply and Sarah continues to edge crab-wise along the edge of the cliff. Her foot dislodges a small stone and she watches it roll down and down and down until it vanishes.

"Mum, stop!"

"You're my daughter," Sarah says. "You should be on my side, you should be trying to help me. What kind of daughter are you?"

"I *am* on your side." Felicity moves away from Kahn, closer to Sarah. She mustn't let anyone get close enough to grab her before she jumps. If she jumps. She realizes she still hasn't decided. "And you're right, Mum. You do need help. That's why I'm here, that's why we're all here. We want to help you." Felicity is close enough so that in the brightening light Sarah can see she's wearing makeup. Eyeliner, lipstick, even mascara. Felicity hardly ever wears makeup. And at this hour? "Mum, come on. Here, take my hand."

"Get back! Get away from me!"

Felicity hesitates and Sarah takes two more small steps. Almost there.

When she looks back toward Felicity, Sarah sees two people wearing brogues and jeans and carrying camcorders on their shoulders coming toward her from either side. They also stop but continue filming.

"Mum. This is so silly. I mean, you're not going to jump. You don't really want to die, do you?"

"I won't die."

Felicity looks back at Kahn, who also moves forward, still holding the loud hailer. "Mrs. Andrews. You know who I am, don't you?"

"Of course I know who you are."

"You know you can trust me."

Sarah says nothing. In the scrub that grows patchily along the edge of the cliff, birds have begun to call out to one another, and far away a siren wails. People are waking up. Soon there will be other, more interesting disasters to film.

"Mrs. Andrews."

"Why do you keep calling me that?"

His eyes widen slightly. "Because it's your name."

"No. My name is Sarah."

He begins to nod slowly, just as he does when he's sitting opposite her in his black vinyl chair. "We obviously need to talk about that," Kahn says at last. "We need to talk about lots of things. And we will, I promise. But first I need you to come away from there. It's not safe. You might fall and hurt yourself."

This seems as good a time as any to take another couple of steps sideways, as if she's about to do what he asked and come away. It's time to decide. In the end, it all comes down to what she believes. And she believes in her perceptions, in herself. She believes in Xaxanader. She trusts him. She trusts herself. So that's settled.

They're all watching her, waiting to see what she's going to do. Sarah glances quickly over her shoulder. She's here, she's positioned herself well. Once again, she's outsmarted them. Below her, the water is deep. That's important. Vestigant or no vestigant, if she hits a rock, she'll die.

She must somehow get a running start. The farther away from the cliff she can project herself, the better her chances. What she needs to do is back off and then run to the very edge of the cliff before she dives, the way you'd dive into a river, or a water hole. But if she does that, they might shoot her.

Kahn and Felicity are standing side by side. To Sarah's right and left the cameramen are filming; they don't care what happens, as long as they can film it. The patrol cars are parked in a row along the esplanade and Sarah sees there's also an ambulance.

Even now, she's amazed they think she's a murderer. The police are merely doing their job, but you'd think Felicity and Kahn would know better.

"I want you to tell me something," Sarah says. Both Kahn and Felicity stare at her and nod vigorously, smiling wide, fake smiles of encouragement. "It's important. I want to know what I've ever done or said to either of you to make you think I'm capable of killing another human being."

They look at one another, then back at Sarah. Kahn's eyes are wide. He's not going to commit himself one way or the other. He never does.

"Mum, it doesn't matter what we believe."

"It matters to me." Sarah turns away from Felicity, toward Kahn. "What do you think? Do you honestly believe I could do such a thing?"

"I don't think . . ." Kahn begins carefully, choosing his words. He pauses and swallows. "I don't think you really want a simple answer."

"But I do. That is exactly what I want, a simple answer." Sarah looks back at Felicity. "What about you? Do you believe I killed Jennyfer Blanchard?"

"Mum, they've got it all on videotape!"

Sarah stares at Kahn. "I asked you the same question. Are you going to answer it or not?"

Kahn opens his mouth and closes it again. "I think that what happened probably isn't as important as why it happened."

The police have taken advantage of all this to move into a flanking semicircle. They're all in uniform, but now Sarah notices another man accompanying them. He's wearing ordinary clothes rather than a uniform, but he's carrying something that looks like a rifle.

They won't shoot her. They wouldn't dare. Stanley Blanchard wants his pound of flesh. In her attempt to give herself a running start, Sarah has moved back away from the edge of the cliff. The rifle might be one of those stun gun things. Or something that shoots tranquillizer darts, like they use to stop wild animals.

"Listen to me!" Sarah whirls to face them. "Listen to what I'm going to tell you, because I'm only going to say it once. I didn't do it. I didn't kill Jennyfer Blanchard. I didn't kill anybody."

Nobody moves or speaks. They seem to be waiting, listening. What else do they think she's going to say? What else can she say?

Sarah breaks and runs to the edge of the cliff, wind-milling her arms, gaining momentum. Her bare toes grip the edge of the rock. She mustn't look back, mustn't hesitate. She flexes her knees, swings both her arms up over her head, the tips of her fingers touching, and flings herself forward.

A shot rings out, too late.

Now there is only the sound of air rushing past her, and the sea. Sarah isn't afraid, but briefly wonders if the cameramen got their shot and what the rest of them are doing. Felicity is probably mad as hell. Kahn will wonder how it feels.

It feels like flying, in your dreams.

Beneath her, the blue and silver sea stretches in every direction, shimmering and glittering in the sun. A bird soars past. No, she isn't afraid. She isn't sorry, either. In a moment she'll be with Xaxanader.

Anything is possible.

Epilogue

Happy Ending for Heiress

By Felicity Andrews

Missing teenage heiress, Jennyfer Blanchard, was reunited with her parents last night in a tearful reunion at the Blanchard's ocean-front residence in the exclusive Brisbane suburb of Cuttlefish Bay.

Jennyfer went missing nearly three weeks ago. She was thought to have fled from a mental health unit in Parramatta, only to become the victim of an inexplicable drowning off Sydney's Tamarama Beach. The apparent drowning was filmed by a Japanese tourist who was visiting the Tamarama Surf Lifesaving Club.

Police say Jennyfer walked into a Brisbane police station early yesterday morning, identified herself and asked to be taken home. An unidentified Brisbane man was subsequently apprehended, taken into custody, and charged with endangerment of a minor.

The Blanchards remain in seclusion. A spokesperson for the family said, "Jennyfer realizes that she has acted foolishly and irresponsibly, and is very, very sorry for the anguish she has caused. She is grateful to be safe, and back home with her family. All she wants to do now is to put this unfortunate episode behind her, go back to school and get on with her life."

Police say they have no further leads regarding the identity of the young woman whose apparent drowning was captured on videotape and viewed by thousands of Australians.

The other woman who appeared in the taped sequence has been identified as Sarah Andrews of Bondi Junction. Ms. Andrews fell from a cliff at Tamarama Beach last week, and is presumed dead. Her body has not been recovered.

Acknowledgements

I would like to thank Renni Browne and the wonderful people at The Editorial Department for their ongoing assistance, encouragement and support.

And Carolyn, Jamie, Michele, Ronda, Amy, Jennifer, Lori and Jane for everything they did to make it all come true.